PRECIOUS HEART

Diamond returned Steven's kisses with a hunger that was released from the depths of her soul. Unleashed was the passion she had bridled so long ago. Hidden only until it could be given unashamedly to the one she truly loved. And she knew that she was in the arms of that man.

"Diamond, can I love you?" Steven whispered against her mouth.

"Yes, God, yes," Diamond breathed. Her body and her mind seemed to suddenly dance in such a fit of rejoicing that she had to suppress a giddy giggle.

"Diamond," he muttered, stealing one more kiss from her swollen lips. "Not here," he said huskily. He fixed her bra and pulled her blouse closed, buttoning it slowly, all the time, nuzzling her neck and pecking her face with tiny kisses. When his lips touched her eyes, he was surprised. Her lashes were wet with tears. Frowning he said, "What's wrong?" How had he hurt her? he wondered. Surely, she could understand that anyone could burst in on them. "Diamond, what's wrong?" he repeated softly.

Catching her breath, and smoothing her clothes, Diamond sat and pulled Steven down with her. She held his hand tightly as she sought to regain her composure. He had been right to stop them because she had been perfectly willing to have him take her right here on the sofa. Her body ached to release the love that was still pent up inside her. Her tongue darted out to taste him on her swollen lips. Feeling his worried gaze, Diamond brushed a hand to his cheek.

Steven watched her inner struggle. He caught her hand and kissed the slender fingers, then waited.

"Steven. I do want to make love with you, but it . . . it wouldn't be right."

"Right?" Steven frowned. "It certainly feels right to me," he said huskily, wondering what was coming.

"To me too," Diamond w   you would hate me and I'd b   between us and then, just l   glad you stopped us." Her

"Leave?" Steven looked

D0816144

BOOK YOUR PLACE ON OUR WEBSITE AND MAKE THE ARABESQUE ROMANCE CONNECTION!

We've created a customized website just for our very special Arabesque readers, where you can get the inside scoop on everything that's going on with Arabesque romance novels.

When you come online, you'll have the exciting opportunity to:

- View covers of upcoming books

- Learn about our future publishing schedule (listed by publication month and author)

- Find out when your favorite authors will be visiting a city near you

- Search for and order backlist books

- Check out author bios and background information

- Send e-mail to your favorite authors

- Join us in weekly chats with authors, readers and other guests

- Get writing guidelines

- AND MUCH MORE!

Visit our website at
http://www.arabesquebooks.com

PRECIOUS HEART

DORIS JOHNSON

ARABESQUE
★BET.
BOOKS

BET Publications, LLC
www.msbet.com
www.arabesquebooks.com

ARABESQUE BOOKS are published by

BET Publications, LLC
C/o BET BOOKS
1900 W Place NE
Washington, D.C. 20018-1211

First Printing: March, 2000
10 9 8 7 6 5 4 3 2 1

Printed in the United States of America

Dedicated to our granddaughter . . .
Our own precious heart,

Brittany Simone Johnson

Special thanks to:

The friendly Charlestonians I met one Sunday afternoon. You all know who you are. The tidbits you shared about Mount Pleasant were great.

All the staff at the Avery Research Center for African-American History and Culture. You were wonderful.

Claudette Smith, for opening your home and also touring with us. The Rumford house on Mount Pleasant was only imaginary until you drove onto a street and I saw the very home I had envisioned.

Evelyn Carter, my friend and traveling buddy. Get the Benz ready for the Wild Wild West?

PROLOGUE

September 1, 1998

Dear Ms. Yarborough,

It is with mixed emotions that I write to you. Please believe me when I say that it is with deep sorrow that I sympathize with your loss. Yet in my next breath, I am deeply grateful that your mother chose to carry an organ donor card. If not for her caring, my mother would be dead, as would others who were beneficiaries of her life-giving organs.

Please don't be alarmed. I do not know your given name nor where you and your family reside, except that it is in New York State. Because I am part of the medical community, certain information comes my way. Rest assured that the medical professionals in no way compromised themselves in identifying the donor family. The information came to me in a completely informal manner and I am personally taking it upon myself to contact you. Again, I've no knowledge of your address. Once out of my hands, this letter will be addressed and mailed by someone else.

When news of your continued grief reached me, I felt compelled to act. I've learned that you were distraught at the untimeliness of your mother's death and that you strongly opposed her support of organ dona-

tion. Even as your mother's wish was carried out, you resented that her body was violated. I want to put your mind at rest and hope that you can find some small solace in the fact that your mother's heart has not been rejected and is still giving life to my mother. These past three months have been a test of love and strength for all of us. But with hope, the skill of the doctors and their ever-increasing knowledge, and with God's will, my mother has another chance.

I can only hope that as time passes you can find it in your heart to accept your mother's decision. Although a stranger to me, I'm certain that she was a kind and selfless woman and I will always be in her debt for caring enough to give life to a total stranger.

There will be no further contact from me, or members of my family, to you and yours. But, should you want to write me, I have no objections. I only ask that you respond to the P.O. box that I've enclosed in the event that your negative reply may be a setback to my mother. She is unaware of this letter and I'm not all that certain that she would approve. This is my way of expressing my gratitude to the donor family. I hope that my words have helped in any small way to ease the pain of your loss. And, to say again, that organ donors do give the gift of life. For that, we are profoundly thankful to your mother.

Sincerely,
Steven Rumford

ONE

Three months later,
Brooklyn, NY

Diamond Drew was sitting on the windowsill peering up at the inky blackness, looking for the first stars to appear on the clear December night. For the past fifteen minutes, she'd tried to drown out the sounds behind her. The sounds of sorting and packing. The sounds of moving. A sigh escaped and a no-nonsense voice penetrated her ears.

"Stop that now. I heard you. Come here and help me with this last bag. I think I may have stuffed it just a bit much." Peaches Ferguson eyed her goddaughter, and as Diamond left the window, Peaches quickly ducked her head, hiding her glistening brown eyes. Head still bent, she sniffed and cleared her throat. "That's it. Hold down that end while I pull this zipper." Peaches closed the bag with exaggerated grunts and groans, more to keep from speaking than from feeling an excess surge of energy. After snapping closed the small, for-show-only lock, she swung the large Pullman-size bag to the floor, pulled up the handle, and rolled the bag to the bedroom door. She pushed it next to an overnight bag that had a matching garment bag folded over it. The tall, thin woman surveyed her luggage; then with a sigh, she turned to face the young woman who sat on the bed staring at her with sad eyes.

Peaches walked across the room and joined the quiet, younger woman. She draped a slender arm around her shoulders and pulled her head onto her shoulder.

"Florida's not another world, you know. It's not like I'm deserting you, honey." Peaches raked her fingers through Diamond's short, naturally styled hair.

"I know," Diamond mumbled against the soft, sweatshirt-clad chest. Sighing, she shifted out of Peaches's mothering embrace, scooted up to the headboard, and drew her knees up to her chin. "I know," she repeated, hugging her knees.

Peaches settled herself beside Diamond, imitating the position, one that they'd assumed together many times over the years. Her eyes roamed the room where she'd made her bed for the last twenty-four years. She could hardly remember ever living anyplace else. Was Diamond really a pretty, twenty-seven-year-old career woman? It seemed only months ago that Peaches had rented this top-floor apartment from a young widow with a three-year-old adopted daughter. Now that woman, Phyllis Yarborough, was dead. And Peaches was getting married and moving to Florida. No wonder Diamond had the look of a forlorn waif. Peaches sat up straight and looked over at her god-daughter.

"You okay, honey?"

Diamond sat up and stretched out her legs. Meeting her friend's eyes—that is what they were to each other—she said, "I'm going to miss you like you wouldn't believe. You're my big sister, second mother, and best friend. Did I leave anything out?" Diamond managed to squeeze out a small smile.

Peaches laughed. It was always disconcerting to strangers when they heard the deep rumble coming from the belly of the slender, wiry woman. Her laugh was infectious and yet so different from the quiet but assertive way she had of speaking. "Well," she answered, "I can think of one thing that I definitely will never be." Her eyes sparkled with mischief, and the grin that parted her generous mouth showed fine, even white teeth. Her deep-tan face was lit with a smile. She jumped at the hit on her thigh. "Ouch!" But her wide grin remained.

"Boyfriend, lover, whatever," Diamond said huffily. Then in a mock hurt tone she said, "Well, it seems like it's the year for the older woman. Us under thirty-somethings don't have a chance with fifty-six-year-old foxes snaring the eligibles."

Peaches's smile broadened. "And my fifty-year-old Jimmy is considered an eligible? Hmm, I must be cooking with gas." Her laughter filled the room.

Diamond's own melodious laughter mingled with her godmother's. "You know you are," she said. "There are a lot of women out there who wouldn't mind snuggling up to a good-looking fifty-year-old like Jimmy Johnson. Retired, going back to Miami to run the family business . . . what's not to like? He's just a plain, eligible black man, take it or leave it."

"Oh, I'm taking it, honey," Peaches said, in a voice implying that she wasn't crazy.

Diamond smiled, thinking about the longtime courtship between the two people, now the closest in her life. The sixteen-year relationship had had its ups and downs, Diamond knew, but she'd always felt that they were right for each other. In the beginning, Peaches, who had been widowed when Diamond was six years old, had scoffed at the relationship, thinking that nothing would come of a forty-year-old woman falling for a thirty-four-year-old man. Many times, Diamond overheard Peaches trying to give a convincing argument to her best friend, Phyllis, about the heartbreak that was almost certain to come. Phyllis, with her practical common sense, dismissed the flimsy excuses, telling Peaches to stop putting the bad mouth on herself and get on with life and live it to the fullest. As she thought of her mother, Diamond's eyes watered and she closed them, hoping that her sudden melancholia went un-noticed, but she was not a good enough actress. The squeeze on her shoulder brought her eyes open, and she looked at her friend.

"Honey, I know it still hurts," Peaches said. "After all, it's only been six months since your mother died. You won't forget her, not ever. But you're not being fair to yourself in not allowing natural healing to begin. You're still so bitter over something that was not your decision. Phyllis did what she knew was right in her heart. She believed in organ donation passionately."

"I know," Diamond replied as she slid off the bed. "It's still something that I have to deal with." She shuddered. "Parts of her are alive in other bodies . . ." Walking to the bedroom door, she turned to Peaches. "Come on downstairs. It's your last chance to partake of my home cooking. I made all your favorites." Peaches's gentle voice stopped her.

"You're not evading the issue are you?"

"No," answered Diamond, resignation filling her voice. "You've been wanting this talk forever, so let's have it in Mama's kitchen." She walked through the apartment to the front door and slowly went down the stairs to the first-floor rooms that she'd grown up in. She didn't remember moving into the house when she was a three-year-old toddler. Her adoptive father, Bill Yarborough, a New York City Transit worker, was killed in an accident on the job. Months later, her mother purchased the two-family house for herself and her daughter. Keeping the five rooms, she rented out the second-floor four rooms to a childless couple.

Diamond began turning on stove burners, heating up the pots of food. She'd cooked dinner earlier, but Peaches was in the middle of packing and didn't want to stop, claiming she'd never get done before the night was through. She said that the Amtrak train would leave her running down the platform at seven-forty-five in the morning as sure as there was a day called Tuesday.

"Mm," said Peaches when she entered the medium-size kitchen. "Me and your mama always said that you got both of us beat around these pots, honey."

"Oh, I knew the deal. Y'all just wanted a month of Sundays off from burning. I just went along with the program." Diamond smiled and winked at her godmother as she began to spoon food onto the plates and then set them onto the table. But Diamond was pleased at the compliment. She was a good cook and loved cooking for others.

Peaches poured apple cider into tall glasses, put the butter dish on the table, and then sat down. "Oh?" she said, her glance brushing Diamond's left arm. "And what about our tribal marks there?" One thin brow arched upward as she buttered and bit into a soft yeast roll.

Diamond looked down at her arm. Her skin was a deep tan. The back of her hand was marred. The skin was crinkled into a small, dark brown circle. Her inner arm, between her elbow and her wrist, sported two long dark lines the same size. She laughed at the memory of how she used to be teased that she had burned ancient African tribal markings into her skin. "I'd forgotten all about these," she said. "Can't even remember what in the world could have made such a perfect circle, but I certainly remember pulling that oven rack onto my arm." She winced.

"Then you should very well remember sticking your hand in that oven, holding nothing but a dish rag, and the back of your hand brushing the knob on that Pyrex dish cover."

"Ooh, stop. I remember," Diamond said. "That's when I called myself helping Mama because she was so tired."

Peaches smiled. "And she was happy for your concern, honey, but she sure tanned your hide for fooling around that stove when she wasn't there." Her voice softened. "But it didn't take you long to learn your way around."

She savored the spicy pork loin chops and then the fried corn. "Not long at all, my dear."

"Thank you, ma'am, for those kind words."

The two women ate in silence, each having similar thoughts about the absence of the woman whose presence was still felt at the table.

"She was proud of you. But I think you already know that," Peaches said. Suddenly her eyes twinkled.

"What?" Diamond was curious.

"Did you ever know her secret name for you when you were growing up?"

"These walls are solid but not enough to drown out *every* private conversation." Diamond grinned at the surprised look on her friend's face. "Rough Cut," she said.

"Well, I'll be . . ." Peaches said, then laughed. "You mean to say you knew that all these years? Phyllis said that you were so sensitive that your feelings would be hurt for years if she ever called you that."

"I know. But I *was* a tomboy. That is, until I discovered what a boy was."

"And when they discovered you!" Peaches studied the pretty, oval face that was smooth and flawless. The dark brown, doe-shaped eyes that were framed by silky black brows were her best feature. Peaches had never seen such expressive eyes that talked at you, beneath long, fluttery eyelashes. Since Diamond was in high school, she'd worn her hair short, sometimes natural, other times chemically straightened. Most of the time it was cut close in the back, with a little left on top to part and curl, wave, or spike into short tufts that went helter-skelter. As pretty as she was on the outside, the beauty wasn't only skin deep. Diamond's sense of humor and impish jokes kept Phyllis laughing on many a weekend. The only time that there was dissension in the house was when mother and daughter bumped heads on the donor issue. Peaches cleared her throat and looked at her watch. It was after nine o'clock.

"I think we'd better talk now or I'll never say what I want to once I leave in the morning." She cleared the table while Diamond poured coffee and sliced two pieces of sweet potato pie.

Diamond sipped the hot beverage and tasted the pie. Her shoulders lifted in a useless gesture. "I can't help the way I feel, Peaches. I could never get Mama to understand, or you either, for that matter. It's just that the body is being invaded by foreign tissue that used to belong to another human being. No wonder rejection occurs so frequently." She waved her fork in the air. "Who knows whether my mother's heart was cut out of her body for nothing? That woman could be dead by now. Whoever received her liver, her kidneys, they could be dead for all I know. Then what was Mama's body violated for?"

"As a health professional, I think you know the answer to that," Phyllis chided. "Why are you so closed-minded to a miracle technology that saves lives? As a physical therapist, don't you feel joy when your patients improve under your care? You're helping them back to normal lives. In your mother's case, she gave the ultimate gift of life."

"You're absolutely right," Diamond replied. "I guess this weird idiosyncrasy of mine makes me a flawed person." She lifted a shoulder in a helpless gesture. "I've always had this crazy, superstitious notion that bad things happen to known card carriers. It probably started when I was a kid. I'll never forget the day one of my teachers read an old newspaper clipping to us about the first heart transplant and what a miracle it was. She was overjoyed and talked excitedly about this advanced medical procedure. What it would mean in saving lives. I remember clutching myself. I felt as though someone was clawing at my chest to try to take my heart." Diamond unconsciously touched her breast.

"But that shouldn't have put such fear into you. It was just a lesson."

Diamond shook her head. "It was what happened a month later. That teacher was mugged and killed. They say it was an attempted purse-snatching but she died from a hit on the head and the guy ran, leaving the bag."

"Don't you think that it was all coincidence?"

"Could be. But the seed was already planted in my mind. Who's to stop someone from killing me to get my heart, once they knew I was a donor?" She raised a skeptical brow. "Well, as far as donating my organs, I believe in free choice just as you do. But, on the back of my drivers license, unlike Mama, I left all the organ donation information boxes blank. Upon my death I'm not making an anatomical gift of my organs or body parts. That's my choice."

Peaches sighed. "You're free to believe what you want, Diamond. But sometimes I wish that there were more community education programs that speak to the lack of life-giving organs, especially the heart." She grimaced. "It might be that someday the government can demand to take your heart whether it's your choice or not."

Diamond rolled her eyes. "Yes, I heard something about a few states getting organs for research or transplantation. Supposed to be legal under what they call presumed consent."

Peache nodded. "Yes, but consent only to remove such parts as corneas and kidneys, not hearts. And it's done without prior permission of the deceased."

"Or from the family." Diamond sniffed. "There ought to be a law," she said sarcastically.

"Well, if a person knew to make the request beforehand, it would be against the law to go ahead and remove anything from that body."

Diamond sniffed. "Whoopee. So much for the law." She gave Peaches a firm look. "Well, I haven't changed my mind. I'm taking everything with me."

Peaches frowned. Many times the three women had argued and reasoned about organs being removed for transplantation without the prior consent of the deceased or even the consent of the family. But in the case of presumed consent, provided one knew about the law in some states, a person can prevent the taking of tissues and organs, namely corneas and kidneys, by making the request before death. As in the case of conscription, organs are removed without seeking prior consent. In every discussion, Diamond had never been convinced to change her mind and had developed a strong aversion to even thinking about donating her organs.

"Diamond," Peaches said, suddenly exasperated, "you're all grown up now and work at healing people. It's time for you to let go of those archaic, unhealthy thoughts. Just put yourself in the deathbed. Then, what? Haven't you ever thought of that?" Peaches inclined her head toward the recesses of the apartment. "That letter you received from that man was thrown in your desk drawer, never to be thought about again. He was only trying to ease your pain, yet you never gave a second thought to responding to him. You disregard every attempt by sympathetic friends to help you forget and move forward." Peaches poured another cup of coffee and sighed heavily after sipping. "It's just that I hate leaving you in this big house by yourself," she said, "moping and feeling low. It's just not healthy."

"I'll be fine," Diamond answered. "And I don't want to forget."

"Who knows what kind of tenants you'll wind up with," Peaches continued as if she hadn't heard her goddaughter's response. "Nonpaying freeloaders who're looking for a free ride in life. Then it'll take months of headaches before you're rid of 'em."

"I don't want to forget," Diamond repeated softly. How could she erase memories of her mother?

"Oh honey, you know what I mean. None of us can ever forget her." Peaches smiled and looked around the room, then glanced at the half-empty pie plate on the table. "With every bite we took she was enjoying it right along with us. After all, it is her recipe."

Diamond smiled. "Always will be, even though it belongs to the new owners now. I often wondered if she was sitting right here when I decided to sell the bakery. So many years . . . from this small kitchen to that tiny storefront. Yarborough's Homemade Pies and Cakes."

"You did the best thing, Diamond. That bakery gave you and your mother a good life. Phyllis would not fault you for selling and going back to the profession you were trained for." Peaches looked pointedly across the table. "Are you going back? It's been a long time since you left. Don't want to lose your skills."

Diamond shook her head. "No fear of that. You know I've been volunteering downtown at the University Center. I'm okay."

Peaches detected a restlessness. "I do wish that you would take my advice and sell the house . . . move away . . . start anew . . . different faces, personalities. Sometimes that helps, Diamond. All you have to remember is that home is wherever you are. Your mama's gone but you'll take her spirit wherever you go. And you know I'll be a phone call away no matter what time you want to talk."

"I don't know if Jimmy agrees with this 'call anytime' business."

"You call me anytime," Peaches said with emphasis.

"Oh, where would I go, Peaches? You know that I'm not a wanderer. Just a plain old homebody. Never hankered to see what was over the next hill."

"That's because you had your mama. Best buddies is what y'all were. And a homebody you're not, so don't kid yourself into thinking that you're the shrinking violet type. Never was and never will be, so lose that thought, Ms. Rough Cut."

"Lost." Diamond grinned. She stood up and began clearing the table. Peaches joined her and soon the leftovers were stored away, the pots washed, and the dishwasher humming.

Before the light was turned out, Peaches, her hand on the wall switch, whispered, "I'm going to miss this place. Lotta memories."

It was after eleven o'clock. Diamond was walking Peaches back upstairs. "Now are you sure you're okay about me not taking you to Penn Station? You know it wouldn't be a hassle." Both women knew the reason Peaches had hired a car service to arrive at five forty-five in the morning, but during their long conversation, neither wanted to discuss the impending departure.

"I'll be fine, honey," Peaches answered. "I'm going to take this daylong ride to be alone with my thoughts." She chuckled. "I think Jimmy got a little attitudinal when I arranged to take the sleeper. Said nobody in her right mind traveled that many hours alone. Seems downright spooky." Peaches turned and hugged her goddaughter. "I'm going to miss you, girl." She cleared her throat. "And if you don't show up in Florida for my wedding in January . . ."

"I know. You're in my face." Diamond laughed, remembering and tasting the soap bubbles in her mouth when she first used the expression with her mother. And she'd been a grown-up twelve!

Peaches chuckled, then said, "You're right about that. Now go on downstairs and get some sleep." Without another word, she turned and went into her apartment and softly closed the door.

Diamond couldn't believe how fast the weeks had flown by since the wedding. Jimmy and Peaches had made a beautiful couple, and their love was evident for all to see and bestow blessings. On the flight home, Diamond had grown a little melancholy, wondering if she would ever be so lucky in love. But she threw those dark thoughts away, especially since she would be living alone with no one around with whom she could voice her feelings.

Today was February eighteenth. Her twenty-eighth birthday! "My God, I'm getting old!" Now those dark thoughts came back, hitting her in the face with the force of a steel glove. She was nearing thirty and she was alone: no parents, no lover, and her closest friend lived miles away in another state, embarking on a new life. And here she was, soon to be homeless, with not a thought of where she was going to live once the house was sold.

When Peaches had moved early in December, Diamond was left alone in the big house, wondering to whom she would rent the upstairs apartment. The family would include children, she figured, to take advantage of the four rooms. Should she limit the number of children? Allow only adults? Would she develop a long-lasting relationship like her mother did with Peaches and her husband? Diamond was plagued with doubts and sorrow, missing her mother more than ever before. Every room was filled with the presence of Phyllis Yarborough. Especially the kitchen where years before Phyllis had started what was to become a booming business. To make ends meet she would bake pies and cakes for her friends and neighbors. Soon she was taking orders that consumed all her free time after work and weekends. It wasn't long before she found it necessary to open a small shop where she would do nothing but bake. Her specialties were sweet potato pie and coconut cake with pineapple filling. Customers came from the other New York boroughs to stand on long lines to take home the sweets. The holidays, without homemade Yarborough pies on the table, were unthinkable. For years Peaches worked beside Phyllis in the bakery, as did Diamond, working summers and around her classes.

Diamond had taken over for her mother when Phyllis

developed cramping in her hands so badly she'd found it hard to roll dough for her pies. Diamond took a leave of absence from her job at the rehabilitation center. She had been working in the shop for six months when Phyllis was struck and killed by a speeding car on Empire Boulevard, in Brooklyn, only blocks away from the bakery. She'd been standing on the corner, waiting to cross. Later, Diamond read in the newspapers that witnesses said the woman never knew what hit her. The driver had jumped a red light, and to avoid colliding with another vehicle, swerved and lost control, hitting Phyllis from behind. She had been thrown clear across the street. By the time Diamond got the news and arrived at Downstate Hospital, her mother was dead and the removal of her organs had begun. Dazed and heartbroken, Diamond had sat in a waiting room, grieving in the arms of Peaches. She couldn't harbor thoughts and visions of her mother lying cold and unmoving while strangers hovered over her body, examining, cutting, lifting parts of her and putting the pieces in Igloo carryalls. *To be transported to unknown places.* That was the rule; no one was to divulge who received what or where her mother's organs would wind up. The stark vision Diamond had of what was taking place behind the walls immobilized her until all she could do was allow herself to be rocked in the comforting embrace of her godmother. It was there that she unwittingly learned where her mother's heart was going. She saw and overheard two female residents, dressed in the wrinkled pale green baggy garments, talking as they helped themselves to the bottled water just outside the waiting room.

"Looks like the heart's traveling to Charleston . . . Some Queen Bee socialite is getting a second chance."

"Yeah. A few more years of partying it up. Wonder how long it will take her to wear out this heart? Guess when you got money, life's made pretty darn easy."

Diamond was too broken up to give the words much

thought. But as the weeks and months passed, she recalled the rashly spoken words. How ironic that a God-fearing, caring, and tenderhearted person such as her mother would give life to a party-going socialite. Probably a selfish and uncaring individual who never knew what it was like to feel the soft squish of sticky dough melding to her hands.

Every hushed moment in the silent house forced Diamond to think about her mother, the circumstances of her death, and that day in the hospital. Then finally, weeks after Peaches left in December, on the last day of the month and on the brink of a new year, Diamond had called a realtor to put the house up for sale. When she'd returned from Florida, she had a buyer. Now in two weeks she would have the closing and the next day she would spend her first night in a strange bed. She'd sold most of her mother's and her own furniture. Old clothing had been donated and the few precious memorabilia had been boxed and stored until she made a permanent home somewhere.

Diamond was in the kitchen drinking herb tea and sorting through some old bills and letters that she'd thrown in a carton when she had sold her desk and file cabinet.

"Some way to celebrate a birthday." She shrugged, and picked up another envelope. The unfamiliar handwriting stayed her hand, and she sat down the mug as she remembered.

The son's letter. Diamond pulled the single sheet from the envelope, glancing briefly at the five-month-old date. Had he expected a reply? Surely he knew by now that she had no intention of answering. Slowly she read the words. When she finished, the letter dropped to the table and Diamond sat back, thoughtfully pondering the heartfelt words of a son who obviously loved his mother. She smoothed the hard-faceted amethyst stones of the bracelet Peaches had sent her. It was an exact match to the single cabochon amethyst pendant, given to Diamond by her mother the year before. She wore the stone on a gold chain and was almost never without it. Just as she habitually smoothed the stone resting at her throat, she now fingered the bracelet as she thought about the writer of the letter. The tone was that of a caring man. Not only was he grateful that his mother was given a chance to live, but he was concerned about the grief of a stranger. He sought to ease her fear that her mother's generous gift had been to no avail, but that the heart transplant was a success.

Diamond wondered if there were many caring sons like that left in the world. It had not been her joy to encounter any when she was "out there" looking for a companion. She had long ago given up bringing that suitable male home to meet the folks. Her eyes clouded. The two times that she thought she had been in love had soured her against the male population. It had been three years since her last romantic encounter, and as far as she was concerned, she could breeze through three more without so much as a flutter in her stomach when sly, come-hither glances came her way.

Diamond dropped the assorted documents back in the carton and closed the flaps. Tomorrow was another day to deal with saving and discarding. She was going to spend the rest of her natal day indulging herself. She'd bought a fine bottle of champagne and never opened it, thinking it silly to toast herself. "But, why not? If not me, then who will?" She left the carton on the table and then spied the letter beside it. Frowning, she wondered how that had gotten left out. Diamond put the paper inside the envelope and it slipped out of her hand and sailed to the floor. "Clumsy," she muttered as she bent to pick it up. "Now aren't you the recalcitrant one . . ." She paused mid-sentence, then sat back down.

Diamond was superstitious but she was not occult-minded. But she did believe that sometimes you just don't question some things. Like now. Was her mother trying to tell her something? Is Steven Rumford patiently waiting for a reply? Or is that odd desire she'd buried deep within finally coming to the fore. For months, since that night in the waiting room, when she'd overheard some rash remarks, she'd wondered about the sort of person who had claimed the heart of the unselfish Phyllis Yarborough. Diamond had yearned to eavesdrop, to observe the woman. Was she deserving of a longer life? Could someone else have better benefited? Is she selfish or caring? Did she warrant the love of such a son? Or was she back to being a social butterfly? Was she a loving grandmother? Did she love to bake for her family? Did she even know how to cook?

All these questions had filtered through Diamond's mind over the last eight months. Questions she'd never shared with Peaches or anyone else. But now they were clogging her brain. It was as if the letter was the catalyst to unleashing all the pent-up curiosity and anger toward a perfect stranger. A person who lived only because Phyllis Yarborough had died.

Diamond remembered the salutation. *Dear Ms. Yarborough* . . . "He doesn't know my name is Drew." She thought for a moment and then stood. Seconds later, she popped the champagne cork and poured the golden liquid. Picking up the envelope, she carried it and the glass to the bedroom, where she sat them down on the nightstand and began to undress. Once in flannel pajamas and in bed, she picked up the glass and lifted it to the ceiling. "Happy birthday to me." She sipped the cool liquid, then smiled, and a feeling of contentment settled over her as she glanced at the letter. The plan was already formulating in her mind. She wouldn't have to worry any longer about where she was going to make her new home. At least for the next few months.

Diamond was going to Charleston, South Carolina.

The next day Diamond spent hours in the main branch of the Brooklyn Public Library on Grand Army Plaza, por-

ing through filmstrip of backdated Charleston newspapers.
Later, at home, she searched the Internet for additional information until late into the night. It was nearly midnight
when, bleary-eyed, she shut down the computer and rubbed
her tired eyes. Her limbs were stiff but Diamond didn't
care. She'd been on a mission once she'd decided to put
her plan into action, and her diligent information gathering
had paid off. Practically all she needed to get started on
her bold adventure was stacked in a tidy pile on the
kitchen table. She gathered some of the papers, carried
them to the bedroom, and dumped them on the bed with
the materials she'd copied from the library. She folded herself into her favorite position on the bed and began to pe-
ruse the items. "So much for being a socialite," Diamond
muttered as she picked up a copy of a Charleston newspaper article. It was from the African-American weekly
The Chronicle, and it was dated the week after her mother's
death. It wasn't hard to spot the story of a heart transplant
that had occurred the week before at Roper Hospital in
downtown Charleston. It was a lengthy article that, after
reporting on the life-giving surgery, went on to explain
what the thankful recipient, Cecelia Rumford, meant to the
community. A press conference had been held. The reporter wrote that the widow of the town's beloved surgeon,
Cyril Rumford, was "doing just fine," in the words of the
head doctor of the transplantation team. The patient's son,
Dr. Steven Rumford, and his sister, Jacqui Craven, also expressed their gratitude to the medical staff. They had special words of thanks for the donor's family.

Diamond finished the article, and then went over the
notes she'd made on her itinerary starting in two weeks.
Satisfied with her travel arrangements and accommodations, she gathered the papers and put them on the nightstand. Twenty minutes later she was ready for bed.

Exhausted, she turned out the light, but instead of allowing sleep to claim her, she stared into the dark, disturbed by her thoughts. Was she right in pursuing what
might become the biggest mistake of her life? Was she

going for all the wrong reasons? Embarking on a dark mission that might disrupt the lives of others? But more than doing what was right, would her fears ever dissipate, leaving behind an inner peace? Finally, Diamond slept, but fitfully. There were no answers to her questions.

On the Friday after Easter Sunday, Diamond was enjoying a leisurely late lunch at one of her favorite Low-Country restaurants. The sun was bright and she basked in it at the outdoor café. A smile parted her lips as she people-watched—a spectator sport that had become one of her favorite pastimes. She glanced at her watch. There was plenty of time before she kept her four o'clock appointment. Two hours to laze away. As she ate, she mused over her reflection in the sparkling glass window. Was she the calm, chic individual dressed in the coral two-piece linen sheath? What a difference a day makes, she thought.

Five weeks had passed since the day Diamond's plane landed at Charleston International Airport. Almost from the moment she stepped on the ground and almost certainly once she was in a taxi, riding on International Boulevard, she had felt something. She'd never visited South Carolina, but she felt that she'd been here before, that the place welcomed her! Before the night ended and she'd awakened the next morning in a strange bed . . . that really wasn't . . . she knew that somehow she was where she should have been all her life.

Diamond's waitress brought her back to the present by clearing away the salad plate and replacing it with grilled chicken cutlets. Diamond quenched her thirst with cool limeade. She'd loved to have had a fine wine with her meal but nixed the idea.

As she sipped, she comforted herself with the fact that no matter how her interview went this afternoon, she was going to remain a permanent resident of Charleston. She was home.

TWO

Steven Rumford made an effort not to slam his bedroom door as he closed it. Anger from last night's dinner discussion had not dissipated, and he swore softly because he anticipated that breakfast would be a repeat affair. It was barely eight o'clock and not a sound came from behind the closed doors of the other second-floor bedrooms. His quick, firm stride on the wool carpet slowed as he passed his sister Jacqui's door. He knew that she wouldn't stir until at least ten this morning, probably not even caring whether her husband, Christopher, ever returned home from his late-night rambling. Steven's face twisted in disgust. He failed to understand the bizarre relationship between Jacqui and Christopher. He reached the wide staircase and paused on the landing, standing in the sunlight that streamed through the steel-beveled glass window. He grimaced and continued down the stairs. *No sense in avoiding the inevitable*. Invisibly steeling himself, he strode into the dining room.

"Good morning, Mother." He passed by the older, late fiftyish woman with the perfect oval face. Before seating himself across from a skinny young girl, he gave his niece a peck on the cheek. "Morning, Riss," he said.

The solemn young girl's face glowed. "Good morning, Unc," she answered.

"Good morning, Steven. And how many times must I tell you to stop calling her that awful name? Nerissa is an acceptable name, though heaven only knows its derivation. However, I can't see what the trouble is in adding two more syllables." Cecelia Rumford turned her sharp gaze on her granddaughter. Her acerbic voice was penetrating. "The same goes for you, young lady. *Uncle* is the proper word."

"It's just a pet name, Mother." Steven prepared a bowl of corn flakes with milk and sugar and added sliced banana. "And I'll answer to 'Unc' anytime from my favorite niece." He winked at Nerissa, who'd slunk down in her chair at the rebuke from her grandmother. Steven frowned. *Not already!* Would he ever get through one peaceful meal in this house?

"She's not a dog, Steven, she's a child."

" 'She' is your granddaughter and is sitting in front of you so stop talking about her as though she were in the hinterlands."

Nerissa Craven kept her head bowed and continued to eat in silence. The hand that was in her lap was pressed tightly against her stomach.

Cecelia eyed her thirty-eight-year-old son with alert light brown eyes that suddenly grew dark. "Don't chastise me in front of the child, Steven. How many times must you be told? I will not have her using street slang under this roof, and she *will* respect my wishes."

"Slang? Just listen to yourself. You sound as if you're living in the Victorian Age. When are you going to wake up? If Nerissa ever let half the dirty words out of her mouth as those of her peers, you'd probably want to pack her off to a boot camp for wayward teens. So quit picking at her." Steven glanced toward his niece, who suddenly excused herself and rushed from the table. He did not miss her clutching at her stomach. His keen physician's eye observed the fleeting look of pain on her face.

"Oh, let her go," Cecelia huffed. "Just theatrics. Looking for attention again."

Anger filling his eyes, Steven threw his napkin down and pushed away from the table. "And just what is so bad about her wanting attention from her only grandmother? She gets little enough of it from anyone else in this house. What is so wrong with her that you can't show her any affection? Don't answer that. I think we all already know why," he said in disgust. As his mother started to reply, he stopped her with a hand. He had no time to listen to her weak arguments, the same he'd heard far too many times. Instead, he filled his cup with coffee, added milk and sugar, and drank to still his tongue.

Cecelia watched her only son warily, sensing his disgust and shortness of patience with her. He was wearing that look that said "Enough!" She waited, clasping her hands tightly in her lap, playing the part of the willing listener, but the shadow of a smile on her lips belied the look of innocence.

Steven knew his mother all too well to be cajoled into a false sense of calm, only for her to pounce like a provoked tigress. "Nerissa is not whom I want to discuss this morning, Mother," Steven said calmly. "I want to continue the unfinished business of last night."

Cecelia lifted a slight shoulder, then a manicured hand to the coil of light brown braids. "What more is there to discuss? You did agree to cancel some appointments today so that you could be home early for the interview. Has anything happened to change your mind?" The brightness of her glinting eyes competed with the sun, which drenched the large dining room.

Steven ignored her question. Instead, he answered, "I want it clear that if you can't make the decision to hire this woman today, then the matter will be taken out of your hands. I'll take responsibility for hiring your personal assistant or secretary or whatever she'll be to you. And unless this person today is absolutely intolerable with the personality of a boor, with intelligence to match, she's hired on the spot!" He waited for a response, and when he was met with silence, he continued. "I'm sick and tired of these agencies bothering me weekly for the past two months asking just what kind of person will suit your needs. They don't understand what you're looking for and neither do I. So since this is the last agency we will be dealing with, I will be sitting in on this, and if necessary, any other interview from now on." He paused. "And no, I haven't changed my mind. I will be back here at four o'clock." He finished his coffee and stood. "It's getting late. I'd better get Riss to school on time before she gets another detention through no fault of her own." Passing by his mother, who remained seated, he said, "You *are* all right with this." He was surprised at her lack of response throughout his diatribe.

"I'll see you at four, Steven. Do be on time." Cecelia watched her son leave without changing her expression, dismissing every word he'd said. *She* knew that no one was coming to live in her house, unless *she* said so. No, she amended, his house but *her* home until the day she died. Cecelia poured another glass of milk, filled her plate with another helping of grits, and bit into a second buttermilk biscuit, savoring the golden brown, flaky treat. She'd purposely waited until Steven left before taking a second helping, especially of the heavily buttered bread. Since her surgery, she was still awed by the fact that she could eat practically anything she wanted. No cautious diet to protect her old, sick heart. But sometimes, she couldn't help herself, and she wondered if her new eating habits would put a strain on her new heart. She'd always been a picky eater and now her appetite was absolutely ravenous. Briefly pondering the result of her greediness on her figure over time, Cecelia shrugged away the possible consequences and happily enjoyed a third biscuit.

* * *

Steven found his niece waiting for him in the front seat of his late-model black Lexus. She was buckled in and staring glumly straight ahead, not turning to greet him as he started the engine and drove down the driveway. He glanced at her, remembering the look of pain on her face. Although in the past he had seen her experience mental anguish because of his mother's caustic tongue, he suspected that his fourteen-year-old niece was feeling some physical discomfort that might eventually become serious. He worried about her.

"Feeling better now?" Steven hoped that she would open up just a little today.

"I'm okay, Uncle Steven," Nerissa answered in a low voice. She didn't turn her head.

"Hey," Steven protested. "You're not going formal on me, are you?" He threw her an exaggerated look of shock.

Nerissa looked at her uncle, whose antics brought a smile to her full lips.

Steven grinned. *It worked.* With that slight movement, Nerissa's thin face was transformed from its nearly perpetual dourness to that of an almost happy teenager. Now if he could only get her to talk about what was bothering her . . . besides her grandmother, then he would be getting somewhere. He'd better hurry, because the fifteen-minute ride from Mount Pleasant to downtown Charleston to her school and his office would soon be over.

"Nerissa . . ."

"Now who's being so formal?" Nerissa asked, a soft giggle escaping.

Steven smiled at her rare attempt at humor but forced a serious tone into his voice. "I'm acting like Uncle Steven because I want you to give me an honest answer. Okay?"

Nerissa's smile faded, but she nodded. She stared out the window.

"How long have you been getting stomach pains when you eat?"

"About four weeks," Nerissa replied.

How could he have missed that for so long! But then, he'd been taking more and more of his meals out, preferring not to deal with his mother's constant nit-picking.

"Have you told your mother or grandmother?" Steven asked.

"You know Grandmother doesn't care about me, and my mother is too busy with trying to keep her husband, instead of holding my hand when I'm sick. Besides, she'd just tell me to take an aspirin and go to bed. So, that's what I do without even asking!"

Steven swore beneath his breath but ignored the reference to her parents' marriage. "What? For how long?"

"Since the pain started getting worse."

"As of now, you will not take another one, do you hear?" Steven shouted. He could almost feel her shudder, and he calmed his voice. "Couldn't you have come to me, Nerissa?" He added in a softer voice, "It's not true about your mother not caring. I know that she loves you very much." He didn't mention her grandmother.

Nerissa didn't answer but shook her head. She was aware that he didn't mention Grandmother.

Steven kept his attempted smile at bay. He knew the reason his niece couldn't come to him about her body. She was a young woman now. Was it already three years since she had told her mother that she wasn't a baby anymore, and that she was too embarrassed for Uncle Steven to continue to be her doctor?

"Riss," Steven said. "No matter what, I want you to let me know whenever something is making you feel bad. No more guessing about what's wrong and how it should be treated. Understand?" When she nodded, he said, "If everybody diagnosed and treated his own ailments, I'd be looking for another job!"

Steven pulled up to her school, and before Nerissa opened the door, he stopped her with a touch to her arm.

"I'm calling your mother today to tell her to make an appointment for you with your doctor. I don't want you to give her any arguments why you can't go. Okay?"

"Yes."

"All right, then. I'll see you at dinner." He released her. "Did your stomach stop hurting?"

"It's okay, now," Nerissa answered, as she opened the door.

"Good. You probably know what brings on the pain and what doesn't so watch what you eat until after you see your doctor. Okay?" Steven watched until she ran toward the doors and entered the building, and then he drove off, a shadow covering his already dark eyes.

Steven pulled into the parking space reserved for him on the side of the house that looked like someone's home rather than medical offices. Located in downtown Charleston on Ashley Avenue, it was only blocks away from Medical University of South Carolina Medical Center (MUSC) where he was staff surgeon.

Feeling a little drained, though he'd not yet started his day, Steven entered his first-floor office, glum-faced. The morning greeting to the receptionist and to his nurse assistant was a cheerless mumble as he passed them and closed the door to his office with a firm snap. The aroma of fresh-brewed coffee filled his nostrils and he headed straight for the pot and poured a cup. He sat down and drank deeply, grateful for his efficient assistant. Ginger Lafitte had been with him for five years and he swore that he didn't know how he existed before he hired her. The minute he walked through the door, she always detected his mood and acted accordingly. Like now, she knew he didn't want to be disturbed for at least twenty minutes until he had his head on straight and was ready to act civil toward his patients. When he had lost Elise, Ginger had been irreplaceable, knowing when to placate, and when to pull his coat, if he became too obnoxious.

Steven brushed a hand across his forehead and swiveled in his high-backed chair until he faced a long mahogany credenza behind his desk, the top laden with books and folders. On the corner sat a picture of Elise Cantwell, his former fiancée. She'd been dead for three years. He stared for a long time at the picture of the woman he'd loved enough to want to grow old with. He'd never met anyone like her before her death, and afterward there had been no desire to go looking. Steven couldn't imagine loving someone the way he'd loved Elise. As he stared at the cocoa-colored skin that matched his own, the wide-set dark-colored eyes, he almost imagined her here in his office, laughing that deep, sexy laugh and making him squirm as she kissed him senseless. Sweet promises of things to come would make him wish that they alone existed on the planet. Their exquisite love-making had defied description. Suddenly, Steven's eyes turned blacker than a midnight sky on a starless night, as he twisted back toward his desk. Fury so incensed him that his body stiffened. He'd thought that he had forgiven her . . . forgiven his mother . . . but the pain inside him was perpetually renewed. Almost as if the sadistic butcher inside his chest were torturing him daily by finding new pieces of him to slice away. *The two most important women in his life had betrayed him*. No, he could never forgive either of them!

It took several seconds before Steven had cleared his mind of the dark thoughts, surprised at where he'd allowed himself to drift. Why now? He'd thought that finally he was able to forget. Maybe it was his mother's coldness toward her granddaughter, or his sister's lack of mothering. Women! Too many selfish and trifling women in his life! He picked up the phone and readied himself for his sister's sarcasm.

Jacqui Craven sleepily picked up the phone, one eye on the digital clock. She sat up quickly after noting it was only nine-twenty and her brother Steven's office number was displayed on the Caller ID panel. Nerissa! Something's happened.

"Steven, what's wrong? Is Nerissa . . .?"

Unsympathetically, Steven answered, "Yes, something's wrong with Nerissa."

"What? Where is she? At school?" Jacqui was out of bed, stepping out of her silk pajama pants. "What happened to her?" She held back a sob as she tried to shrug out of her top.

"Nerissa's in school and she's fine, Jacqui. Right now."

Jacqui stared at the phone as if her brother had lost it. She sank down on the bed.

"What the hell is wrong with you? Are you going crazy?" she yelled. She ran her fingers through her hair, imagining that, finally, her brother was cracking.

"No," Steven answered in a solemn voice, "but you may if your daughter becomes ill." He heard his sister gasp and he continued before she caught her breath. "From what I see, she may be on the verge of developing an ulcer."

"Ulcer? She's just a baby. What are you saying?"

"I'm saying that if you spent more time observing your daughter than your husband's comings and goings, you might see what's happening to her. She's your only child and you can't even see that the girl is in pain in more ways than one."

"Pain?" Jacqui's eyes narrowed. "What pain?"

"Stomach pain for one and mental anguish for another. I've told you a thousand times if I've told you once to take charge of your daughter's life and stop letting Mother treat her as if she were a stranger, and not her own flesh and blood. I swear I don't know why Nerissa hasn't taken off long ago."

"Nerissa would never run away." Jacqui's eyes flashed indignantly.

"No, because she loves you and her father." Steven paused. "I think the only reason she stays around is that you keep giving her hope that she'll still have a father around."

"What I do about my marriage is none of your business. And the way I'm raising Nerissa is not your concern either, so stop giving me orders, Steven."

"All of you are my concern as long as you're living under my roof," Steven said calmly. "Jacqui, I didn't call you to have a family conference. I want you to call Nerissa's doctor and schedule an appointment as soon as you can get one. Yesterday would be fine." He hung up the phone and, elbow on the desk, cradled his head in his hand.

Ginger Lafitte eyed the digital clock on her desk. Exactly twenty minutes had passed since her boss had closed his door. She patted her stylishly cut, short, auburn silky hair and pushed back her chair. She knocked, and after a second, stepped inside, closing the door behind her.

"Good morning, Doctor," she said in a crisp voice. "Mr. Burrows is ready and waiting in Room One." She paused. "Is there anything else?"

Steven looked up. Ginger Lafitte waited expectantly, with not a trace of annoyance on her mocha-colored features, that she'd had to wait for him to start his day. He smiled as he pushed his chair back and stood, while gesturing at his appointment book. "No, Ms. Lafitte. I see you've already canceled all appointments after one o'clock. Efficient as always. Thank you." He walked toward the door that led to three examining rooms. He turned and said, "Oh, no need for you to stay after I leave. I'm sure you can find something to do with a few extra hours of personal time."

"Thank you, Doctor," Ginger answered, but she was talking to an empty room. Steven had already disappeared. She went back to her desk to prepare the next patient, trying not to think about the handsome man who hardly knew that she existed. "One day," she murmured softly. But then, she thought, after three years, would he ever be ready to look at her or anyone else? She held back a sigh. With a pleasant smile, she picked up a folder from her desk. "Ms. Cruz," she said, "you're next."

Nerissa watched from behind the glass doors as her uncle drove away. Before anyone noticed her standing there, she opened the door and ran down the steps. Quickly she walked down Rutledge Avenue, away from Ashley Hall, the private school that she'd attended all her school life. As she stepped on the bus, she prayed that the day would come when another bus would whisk her away from Charleston, forever!

Jacqui Craven hung up the phone after making an appointment with Doctor Hamilton. Tomorrow: at two o'clock. Saturday! No amount of pleading would make Ms. Shepherd, the nurse, change it to early morning, and next week was booked solid. Jacqui threw off the covers and swung her legs over the side of the bed. She sat there, fuming. Tomorrow, she'd planned to spend the day in Myrtle Beach with a realtor. Now her plans were ruined. "Thanks, big brother," she spat as she walked to her connecting bathroom. She opened the door on the other side that led to her husband Christopher's bedroom. The bed was unslept in and Jacqui slammed the door. She looked in the mirror and stared at her puffy face. Another sleepless night spent listening for the sounds of her husband coming—no, sneaking—into his room. A bitter smile parted her lips as she stepped into the shower. She was right in making her secret plans to get out of this house. If she didn't change her life, she would go crazy staying under the same roof with her domineering brother, and her cheating husband could go bark at the moon for all she cared. And if Jacqui didn't get Nerissa away from her mother's caustic tongue, the child's life would be ruined. Her eyes sparked. Ulcers! *Steven suspects my baby has an ulcer! And blames me for not loving or caring for my own daughter? How could he believe that?* Jacqui soaped her trim body and her eyes misted, not from the steam but with tears. All her life she'd allowed herself to shrink from her overbearing mother, giving in so as not to be the brunt of vindictive criticisms. It had been so much less hassle. But Nerissa sick? After all these years had her own timidity affected Nerissa? Jacqui was right in planning to get her daughter out of this house, and yesterday wouldn't be too soon.

Cecelia looked up as Jacqui entered the dining room. Deliberately checking the time of her slim gold watch, she raised an artfully thin eyebrow at her daughter's appearance for lunch. It was twelve-thirty and Cecelia had nearly finished her meal.

"You would think I lived alone in this house, as much company as I have at mealtimes. Seems I'm always alone," she huffed. "I had more attention than this when I was ill and at death's door." She tasted a forkful of chocolate cake. "Now that I've been transplanted with a strong new heart, I can be left to my own devices. Is that the plan that you and your brother have for me? To leave me rambling about in this big old house?"

"Mother, please," Jacqui said. "I've a headache." She sat down and surveyed the table. She was in no mood to listen to another account of a near-death experience. Everyone was thankful that her mother had been given a second chance at life, but her mother never let anyone forget how ill she'd been.

Finally opting for the chef's salad, Jacqui filled a plate and added a light dressing.

"Is it any wonder? Sleeping past noon?" Cecelia finished her cake and pushed the plate away. "Am I right, then? Are you planning to leave too, like Steven?" Cecelia's lips parted in a sly smile. "Oh, don't tell me that you didn't know that your big brother wants to move. Of course, he didn't come right out and tell me, but I hear the undercurrents and the innuendos. Not very much passes me by, dear."

Relieved that her mother didn't guess about her own plans, Jacqui hid her surprise about her brother. Steven leaving, too! She looked at her mother and said, "If he does leave, it would probably do him good. Since Elise died, it's almost as if he died too." Jacqui bit into the crunchy lettuce. "Who knows, maybe he'll find someone else to love and have a houseful of babies. That's all he and Elise ever talked about."

Cecelia's face flushed with excitement. "You would both leave me, alone?"

"Hardly alone, Mother," Jacqui answered. "Besides, you're healthy again and doing wonderfully." She gestured at the air. "You've been looking for a companion or a secretary or whatever, for months now. When you finally find this suitable person you'll have her and Tina, who will be here to cook your meals. Ferdie'll still do the housekeeping. Nurse Stanley looks in regularly. Never alone, Mother." Jacqui continued to eat, unperturbed by her mother's feigned distress.

Before emerging from her bedroom, Jacqui had sworn that her mother's penchant for picking arguments would not send her into a silent sulk, Jacqui's usual way of tuning her out. Since Steven had told her about Nerissa, as much as calling her an unfit mother, Jacqui had become furious with her own negligence regarding her daughter's welfare. What kind of mother was she not to have noticed Nerissa's pain? Did she wait too long to finally make the decision to move? Jacqui looked at Cecelia, who sounded annoyed.

"I'm sorry. What did you say, Mother?"

"For the second time, I'm asking you have you seen your husband, today?"

"No."

"No? That's it?" Cecelia's light brown eyes flashed angrily. "What kind of marriage do you have? You're certainly not setting a good example for your daughter. Sleeping with the man one night and not the next. How do you know that he's not bringing you some kind of disease? If you ask me, you'd be better off without him. You're only thirty-six, young, and still pretty enough to attract an eligible man. And one that's not old enough to be your father."

"Enough, Mother. I'm not asking you. What Christopher and I do about our marriage is our business." Her eyes narrowed. "And about my daughter, *I* will decide what's best for her. And it will be about time." She snapped her jaws shut. She'd already said too much.

Cecelia looked sharply at her daughter. What had gotten into her? Defending that gigolo man of hers, and Nerissa, all in the same breath!

Cecelia and Jacqui both looked toward the sound of the front door opening and closing and soon heard the dull thud of footsteps on the stairs. Cecelia looked at her daughter and Jacqui looked down at her plate as she slowly continued to eat. Christopher Craven had just come home.

"Well, are you just going to sit there?"

For a long moment, Jacqui sat, lost in thought, oblivious to the presence of her irate mother.

"Well?"

Slowly Jacqui answered. "Actually, no, Mother." She filled her glass with cold lemonade and eyed the impatient woman as she sipped. Jacqui stood. "It's so warm for

April, don't you think? I'm going to finish eating outside, by the pool." Without another word she picked up her plate and turned and walked out of the room.

"Well, I never!" In one of the rare moments of her life, Cecelia was rendered speechless.

"What do they say about some of the best laid plans? Don't sweat it, man. I'm sure your mother's handling everything just beautifully."

"That's what I'm afraid of," Steven answered, and then he swore. "Russ, I've got to get over there before that woman leaves or I'll be eating my words from now until." He raised his dark brown eyes to the ceiling. "As if I need *that* on my plate."

Dr. Russell Padget, pediatrician, was sitting on a stool in the emergency room at MUSC where he'd finished examining Steven's young patient. The nine-year-old boy's X rays showed that he had a fractured wrist, and the boy was now with an orthopedic resident.

"Look, man, everything's under control. Why don't you get out of here if it'll make you feel better; you can't change what happened. An emergency is just that, an emergency. You're a doctor and things happen. Surely your mother won't hold that against you." The good-looking man with the brown-berry skin with eyes to match saw the look on his friend's face. He showed large even white teeth when he grinned. "Okay, rescind that." In the next second he became serious. "Steven, you're wound up tighter than the strings on my guitar. How much longer before you come unstrung?"

Steven stood also and wearily rubbed his forehead. "You got me," he answered.

"Yeah, and MUSC will have you, as a patient if you don't get it together." He paused. "When's the last time you took yourself a real vacation? And I'm not talking about going down to the pier once in a while to hold a line and stare off into the wild blue yonder."

"Can't beat it for unwinding, man. Ought to try it sometimes."

"No, thanks," Russ replied dryly. "After a couple of hours of that *I'd* need a bed in this place. Seriously, when?"

"About three years ago," Steven said in a low voice.

"Three . . ." Russ stopped himself. "Sorry, man." He remembered that after Elise's funeral, Steven had refused to take any time off and had worked exhaustively until he nearly collapsed. He had been forced to take a break, spending a week in Myrtle Beach. "The time has come for you to take a real vacation, friend. I mean that," Russ said softly.

"You're probably right."

"I know I am." Russ hesitated, then spoke his mind, as he usually did with his friend. "You mentioned some time ago that you were thinking about relocating. Given any more thought to that? I'll miss you like hell, but that may be what you need, man. It doesn't have to be forever."

Steven nodded. "As a matter of fact, I have. Sent out some feelers. Connecticut looks interesting." He shrugged. "Nothing firm, yet."

Russ whistled. "That's getting away!"

"Like I said, nothing's been put into motion." He clapped his friend on the shoulder and then walked toward the door of the examining room. "Look, I'm outta here. Glad you were here and able to see that little guy. Look in on him for me, will you?"

Russ walked with him. "You know I will. And Steven, tomorrow's Saturday. Travel agencies open real early."

"You're like a dog with a raggedy old shirt who won't

give it up," Steven said grinning. He shook his head and waved as he walked down the corridor.

No sense in rushing now, Steven thought, as he tooled through the traffic on Ashley Avenue. It was nearly four-thirty and late was late. Not a thing in the world he could have done about it. He'd done what he had to. Earlier, he'd seen his last patient, finished the lunch that Ginger had ordered for him before she'd left for the day, and he was about to lock up when a distraught mother arrived with his young patient in tow. That had been the beginning of the end to getting home in time for a four o'clock interview.

As he drove, Steven mulled over his friend's words. It was long past due for some serious time off and he knew it. But now was not the time. Although he knew that his mother was doing well, he wanted her to get adjusted to a new household member, whenever the long sought after companion was to be hired. Then there was this new discovery about his niece. His dark eyes narrowed. He couldn't abandon the unhappy girl. Especially if she was seriously ill. No one championed her but him and he hated to think about Nerissa's being left with a grandmother and a mother who never defended her.

Sometimes when Steven thought of his mother and all she'd been through he wondered why Cecelia could not be thankful enough for her gift of life to begin to show affection toward her only granddaughter. The donor's heart that beat inside her surely had come from a caring individual. *So much for those rumors of personality transference after surgery!* His thoughts drifted to the letter he'd written months ago. Strange, how he'd never received a reply from the family. It was probably just as well, Steven thought. No good would ever come from a meeting between that grieving young woman and the recipient, who was the least caring person he'd ever known.

When Steven pulled into the driveway he frowned. The navy blue Camry was in the last available spot. He parked behind it. Suddenly the frown was replaced by a smile. Looks like he was going to have his say after all. Almost gleefully, and like a kid who'd snared the last Thanksgiving turkey drumstick, he walked toward the house.

Diamond Drew arrived at the Rumford home at exactly three fifty-five. She parked her leased Camry at the end of a row of cars in front of a large white garage door. "Hmm, wonder how many are *inside*," she muttered, getting out and appraising the surroundings.

In five weeks Diamond had driven around the greater Charleston area and had visited many neighborhoods. One was more unique than the next. Old Village in Mount Pleasant was one of the most appealing in the area. She had driven down the tree-lined streets with its village look and had passed many of the huge restored antebellum homes that sat on large lots. Diamond was impressed with the acreage that boasted pools and tennis courts. Some held guest cottages and huge garages. The Rumford home was a delight to look at. It was an old Victorian with two stories, and Diamond assessed the columned veranda on both floors to run at least seventy feet. "A real dream," she whispered and walked up the redbrick steps.

When the personnel agent had offered Diamond the opportunity to apply for the hard-to-fill position, she'd hoped that she would get it but didn't care that much if she too were turned down by the very particular woman. All she wanted was a chance to meet Cecelia Rumford. But now as Diamond stood on the steps, hesitating to ring the doorbell, all apprehension left her. The same eerie feeling that had swept through her at the airport enveloped her now. Somehow Diamond knew that when she left this house today she would return as the paid companion to Cecelia Rumford.

THREE

Diamond was led through a large bare-wood floor foyer that could be someone's small bedroom. On either side were doors, some solid wood and others French with shining glass panes. The pleasant-faced woman opened one of the wood doors.

"Mrs. Rumford, Ms. Diamond Drew." She left, closing the door softly behind her.

Cecelia eyed the young woman who stood calmly by the door looking at her with a pleasant smile and fearless eyes. Cecelia's recognition of the absence of trepidation in the stranger was instant, and her eyes sparkled. Oh ho, she thought, is this going to be a different interview. *A woman with spunk in her spine!*

"Come in, come in, you don't expect me to interview you with my neck craned up like a silly ostrich. How tall are you anyway?" She gestured to the long flower-print sofa. "Sit, sit."

"Actually, not that tall at all. I'm five-five." Diamond took the offered seat. "I appear taller than I am because of my carriage, I suppose." She lifted a shoulder. "And probably because I'm so slender."

"Almost skinny, you mean."

Diamond laughed. "I happen to like slender. It gives a different connotation."

Cecelia raised a brow. "Skinny is skinny," she harumphed. She ran an appraising eye over the outspoken young woman. This was the first person that walked through the door not wearing undertaker's black or nurse's blue. All the others looked as if they were ready to do their solemn duty in nursing an old invalid back to life and had yessed her to death. None of them had offered a single thought that was their own. This girl, dressed in her coral suit and black patent, sling-back pumps was a shock. But she was hardly a girl.

"How old are you?"

"Twenty-eight this past February eighteenth."

An Aquarian! Cecelia had given birth to one thirty-eight years ago and *he* never bit his tongue either. *Are they all like that?*

The door opened and a thirtyish woman entered, carrying a tray with sandwiches, little cakes, and a pitcher filled with a tangerine-colored beverage. She set the tray on a coffee table. "Shall I serve, Mrs. Rumford?"

"No, Tina, I think Ms. Drew and I can handle that. That'll be all." Cecelia waited until the door closed before she said, "I'm certain lunch was hours ago, Ms. Drew. Tina's a great cook and her sandwiches will tide you over until dinner. Please, help yourself." As she spoke, she filled a plate and poured a drink. After several moments, she said, "So, tell me, Ms. Drew. At twenty-eight do you really think that you're up to the job, and exactly what did they tell you at the agency?"

Diamond finished one of the finger sandwiches and swallowed half a glass of the cold punch. It was delicious and she couldn't identify the fruit flavors. She put her napkin down and finally looked over at Mrs. Rumford. Since she'd walked into the room her heart had started pumping wildly in her chest and she'd felt like turning around and running away. She was finally here and she couldn't believe it. The imperious-looking woman staring at her was alive because Diamond's mother's heart was beating in her chest! God, why was she in this house? Diamond implored.

What had she expected to see? The plump face of Phyllis Yarborough? Her sweet smile? A sign on the woman's chest heralding that she carried the heart of a stranger? The crazy thoughts caromed in her head until she thought she would go into a tailspin. Diamond was grateful that the woman had wanted to eat instead of talk. She, too, busied herself with eating, making a show of how famished she was. The woman obviously enjoyed her food and appeared pleased that her guest did too. Recovered, Diamond took a deep breath and answered her hostess. It was apparent that Mrs. Rumford was enjoying the repartee the two were having. Diamond was not going to disappoint her by not continuing giving tit for tat.

"At my age and as a trained physical therapist for several years, I think I'm perfectly capable of doing this job. Although the agent did not go specifically into details—she said that you would do that—she did say that I would act as the companion to one of Charleston's most prominent citizens. There may be secretarial duties involved, maybe some traveling on short notice, and sundry other duties." Diamond held the woman's gaze. "Maybe you can tell me what those other duties entail?"

"You don't bite your tongue, do you, child?" Cecelia's eyes brightened, enjoying this woman with every word that came from her mouth.

"Is there any reason I should?" Diamond asked. "I hardly think it's a silent secretary you're looking for."

Cecelia let out a raucous laugh that had not been heard in the house for years. Not since her husband, Cyril, had died and who had been the only one who could draw such an undignified reaction from her. She coughed, and in a serious voice, trying to recover her dignity, said, "You will be required to accompany me to several social functions a year. I also like to shop, and Ferdie, our housekeeper, whom you've already met, can't continue to let her other duties go to be with me. I would like to travel again.

There's no one in this house with the personality that would make vacations enjoyable. When I entertain, I expect you to assist in the planning and then be in attendance to see that the party is a success. Weekends are yours." Cecelia took another sweet cake, and bit into it. She eyed the young woman, who looked at her unblinkingly. "Well, anything to say?"

"Yes," Diamond answered with a casual air. "The duties sound pleasant enough and not insurmountable. If the salary is commensurate, then I would like to be considered for the job."

Cecelia's hand rose midway to her mouth and she nearly dropped the cake. As before, her deep laugh filled the room. When she recovered, she said, "When can you start?"

Steven's hand was stayed on the doorknob when he heard the laughter.

"Mam?" he whispered, shocked at his reverting to the childhood name for his mother. He hadn't used it since his father died and she had turned into "Mother" to him and his sister. But who in the world could make her laugh like that? He opened the door.

Both women looked up.

A triumphant gleam appeared in Cecelia's eyes and her lips parted in a fey smile. Without looking at her, Cecelia said, "Ms. Drew, meet my son, Dr. Steven Rumford. Steven this is Diamond Drew, my new companion."

Dumbfounded, Steven walked toward the woman who'd stood and waited with outstretched hand. Hired? Just like that? Dazedly, he took the woman's hand.

"Pleased to meet you, Dr. Rumford."

"My . . . my pleasure, Ms. Drew," Steven stammered, extracting his hand as if he'd been scorched. "Please, sit down." He walked to a chair next to his mother and sat. His head was spinning. What in God's name went on here? he wondered. His mother laughing? And she looks as if she's just won the county fair's blue ribbon for the best-told joke. Not a chance, he reasoned. No Rumford could ever lay claim to owning such a funny bone. To his mother he said, "Hired?"

"Yes, Steven," Cecelia answered. "I offered, and she's accepted."

Steven breathed deeply. "Forgive me for being late, Mother, but I thought that you might have entertained Ms. Drew until I arrived. It was my understanding that we'd interview together." Steven's hand still tingled where the visitor had grasped it. He wanted to rub it but instead held both hands palms down on his knees, his feet planted firmly on the floor.

"Oh, Steven, would you really have wanted me to waste this young woman's time for no need? After all, a doctor's emergency could last forever and she did arrive exactly on time." Cecelia smiled sweetly at her son. "Think about it, Steven. This is the end of it. No more agencies, no more appointments. Just look at her. I think Ms. Drew will fit into our household just beautifully. Isn't that what you wanted?"

That's exactly what he was afraid to do. Look into the eyes of Diamond Drew again. From the moment he'd started walking toward her until he'd snatched his hand from hers, he'd been consumed by fire. He willed the conflagration in his loins to subside as he faced his mother.

"Your satisfaction is what we all want, foremost," Steven said. "But is Ms. Drew qualified to attend to your needs sufficiently?" He still avoided looking at the woman whose presence mysteriously disturbed him. "You've hardly had time to cover that ground have you?"

"I'm sure I have, Steven," Cecelia answered. "But why not ask her yourself? I'm sure Ms. Drew won't mind repeating her vitae. After all, you are her ultimate employer." She looked at Diamond. "Would you, dear?"

Diamond was glad that Steven had taken the seat next

to his mother rather than sitting in the chair closest to her knee. She'd taken quiet deep breaths, hoping they went unnoticed by the Rumfords. She needn't have worried, because they were intent on sparring with each other and her little gasps were unheard. The first moment he appeared in the door and began his slow-motion walk toward her, a signal went off in her brain that she'd come to heed in recent years. *Dangerous!* Panic welled up in her throat when she knew he would clasp her outstretched hand. Nowhere to run, nowhere to hide. The silly chant screamed in her head until, when he finally reached her, she thought that she would faint like a Victorian maiden. After all these years, was she finally caught? *No,* she cried to no one who would hear, *don't let it happen again!* Without warning, the heat in her body gave way to little beads of perspiration popping out on her forehead, and her underarms felt damp. So much for being cool and casual. How dare she not choose the right deodorant for such an important moment, she thought giddily. From afar, she heard his baritone voice. Refraining from wiping her damp palms on her skirt, she clutched her Dooney & Bourke bag.

"Ms. Drew, are you all right?" Steven's dark brows were drawn into a frown. Her obvious sudden discomfort had caught him by surprise when he'd finally looked at her. Was she going to faint? He poured some punch into her glass. "Here, drink this." He held the glass out to her.

"N—No," Diamond stammered. "I'll be fine." She looked at his hand on the glass, fearful that their hands should touch. Then what would she do?

Cecelia said, "I think that a sip of the cold drink would do you good, dear. Sometimes an unseasonably warm April has the undesirable effect of a vicious heat wave." She gave Diamond an encouraging smile, knowing that the young woman was embarrassed. She wondered if Diamond was feeling intimidated by Steven's unfriendly welcome and was thinking twice about accepting the position. Her eyes narrowed. *He will not dismiss her.* But she remained silent.

"You're probably right," Diamond said and drank deeply of the soothing beverage. Feeling refreshed, she set the glass back down and looked at them both. "Guess I'll have to get used to the seasons."

"You're not a Charlestonian?" Steven was able to look into those beautiful dark eyes without fiery fingers attacking his innards.

"No. I haven't been here long enough to call myself that, though I intend to remain in Charleston," Diamond replied. She forced herself to look into those curious dark brown eyes. Her gaze fleetingly took in the rest of his face and body. But her daring treaded on thin ice and she swiftly brought her eyes back to his. She spoke directly to him. "Is that a requirement for the position?" she asked. Her voice implied that if it was, it was the silliest request of all.

Steven did not miss the implication. He bristled. "Not at all," he answered. "But seeing as you will be acting as my mother's social planner and the like, it would be a step ahead of the game to know of the Who's Who in the neighborhood and beyond."

"That's hardly a problem, Dr. Rumford." Diamond lifted a shoulder. "Are there no libraries? Is there no cyberspace?" Her smile did not mean that she was happy. He didn't want her here, Diamond realized. He'd prejudiced himself against his mother's choice. What had she walked into here? It didn't take a year of graduate study to see that mother and son played games of one-upmanship.

Cecelia smiled gleefully at the incredulous look spreading over her son's face as he stared at Diamond. A body in this house answering him back was unsettling to say the least.

"Of course, that has no bearing, Diamond," Cecelia answered for her son, who appeared at a loss for words.

"But, there's no need for any of that sort of research. I have all the information you need right in my head." She paused. "But Steven is as curious as I am. I neglected to ask you—especially seeing as I didn't request a formal résumé—where you are from."

"I was born and raised in New York City."

"New York?" Cecelia's elegantly shaped brows rose a half inch.

Steven echoed his mother. "New York?"

"Yes, Brooklyn, New York. It's one of the largest of the five boroughs and is known as the borough of churches," answered Diamond. She looked from one to the other, amused at their reaction. "Is there anything wrong?"

"No, Ms. Drew. We've visited the city and we're not totally ignorant of its makeup. It's just that we . . . you . . ."

" . . . don't speak in *dese, dems,* and *dose,* Dr. Rumford?"

Steven's nostrils flared angrily. "Now, see here, Ms. Drew, that was uncalled for. You know perfectly well I didn't mean that."

"Then what did you mean?" Diamond, though outwardly composed, was dying to end this interview and run out the front door as fast as she could. "That a physical therapist from South Carolina was more capable and suitable than one from New York?"

"A what?" Steven was taken aback.

"You never gave Diamond the chance to speak before you attacked her," Cecelia interrupted.

"Attacked?" Steven stared at his mother like she'd sprouted another perfectly coiffed head. This had gone far enough. He said, "Would you excuse us for a minute, Ms. Drew? I would like to speak to my mother alone." He stood and walked past the sofa. "I'm certain that you'll be comfortable here for a few minutes." He opened the French doors, which led to a piazza where there were cushioned chairs. "Please," he said, as Diamond joined him. When she stepped outside, he said, "Thank you," and closed the doors. He winced as he caught a whiff of her scent when she passed dangerously close to him. Her musk, mingling with her tantalizing perfume and something else. Fear! Like an animal that was cornered. Steven turned to face his mother.

"Exactly what is it about this woman that pleases you so much that she's hired in the blink of an eye?" He moved away from the doors and sat on the sofa in the spot evacuated by Diamond. Steven hurriedly moved over. "You know nothing about her. She's a stranger to Charleston, and to the south, for that matter. How in the world can she be of any help to you? You'll have to school her, for heaven's sake. And you're calling her Diamond? It was months before you warmed to using Tina's and Ferdie's Christian names."

Cecelia listened to her son patiently. She knew that Diamond Drew was going to be her companion no matter how much he expostulated. When he drew a breath, she said quietly, "I really can't see what you're complaining about, Steven."

"That's not it. I simply want to know why you're so intent on taking this woman into our home. You've no résumé. Do you even have a decent reference? She's a stranger from another state and could probably con you into believing her words were golden drops of nectar. Her only strong point is that she is a trained health professional." He paused. "Are you even certain of that?" Steven's heart thumped. *Diamond Drew can't live in this house!*

"Really. What's gotten into you?" Cecelia said. Her eyes flashed. "Of course, Ms. Crenshaw gave me a sketch of the person that she was sending. It was I who didn't want to bother with details unless the person was someone that I was interested in. I've learned that over the past few months. How dreary to waste my time with someone who wasn't suitable."

"And what makes this person so desirable to you? A stranger in town?"

"Because she has a brain and I don't have to mince my words."

"When have you ever?" Steven replied, dryly.

Cecelia ignored his remark, and with a pointed look, said, "Unless this person is absolutely intolerable with the personality of a boor, with intelligence to match, she's hired on the spot."

Steven winced.

"In your own words, Diamond Drew is none of the above. Would you agree? Steven, what is your problem with her? She suits me and I want her. I think you'd better decide and bring Ms. Drew inside before she decides that *she* doesn't want *us*. Our behavior is bordering on the uncouth. Really!"

No, definitely none of the above, Steven thought. Slowly, the feeling of defeat sidled over his body like an unwanted reptile and he resisted a shudder. His mother was right. He had no argument with which to defend his dismissing Ms. Drew. She was going to be living under his roof. Worse, the guest bedroom that she would occupy was right next to his. That knowledge seeped into his brain and started the warmth to roil in his stomach.

"Steven!" Cecelia's voice was sharp.

With slow strides, he walked to the doors and opened them. "Ms. Drew, please," he said, gesturing inside. He stepped away, bridging the distance between them. When she resumed her same seat on the sofa, he took the chair opposite her.

"It appears that you are my mother's choice of companion. Welcome to our household, Ms. Drew." He was drawn into those deep brown eyes but was helpless to turn away. *With my barbaric attitude toward her, why doesn't she re-*

fuse the position? he agonized. Everything about her was fuel. Her way of looking at him, welcoming him to bare his soul to her. That slender body with full breasts exuded a sensuality that was not to be ignored. Her hypnotizing voice sent him to a painful place in his past, one that would best be forgotten. This lovely stranger would open a world of hurt for him. There'd been no one for him since Elise. Since her death he'd never met a woman who stirred his inner self with the same passionate urgings. Not until he'd laid eyes on Diamond Drew. Now for the first time in years, other than gratuitous dalliances, his desire to know this woman was instant, sending vibrating messages to his loins. Was it possible to recapture the passion he'd once known? The passion that had been lost to him forever? Diamond Drew was temptation. How in God's name could he resist knowing whether she could bring him back to life? Steven wondered how easy it would be to avoid Diamond . . . with her sleeping quarters a stone's throw away from his. Aroused from his tortuous thoughts, he turned toward Diamond, who had spoken.

"I'm sorry?" Steven hoped he looked as composed as he tried to sound.

Wondering where he'd gone for a second, Diamond repeated her question. "Are your words of welcome sincere, Dr. Rumford? I'd hate to upset the routine of your household with my presence. I'm certain that I will be interacting with other family members, and I think you will agree that if I don't have your approval, performing my duties will become quite awkward. So I'd rather not begin . . ."

Steven's icy voice stopped her. "Ms. Drew. Whatever they may think, my employees refrain from questioning my word, at least not in front of my face. You will be required to do the same. Now as I've said, the position is yours if you want it. If not, feel free to leave." After pausing, he said, "My mother will be more than happy to acquaint you with the different personalities you'll encounter." Steven stood. "After that, you may not want to stay after all. Again, the choice is yours. If you'll excuse me ladies, I've work to do." With a stiff nod to his mother, he left the room without another glance at Diamond.

Cecelia took in the action and reaction between her son and the newest member of the household. Her eyes sparkled with a humor she hadn't felt in months. She hadn't realized how incensed her son could become at losing. He really hadn't expected her to make a choice and it had almost floored him, Cecelia thought gleefully.

"Well, Diamond . . . I won't be calling you Ms. Drew . . . has meeting my son changed your mind? He can be quite overbearing at times, but after a while you'll hardly notice."

Surely you jest. Who can help but notice six feet of dark chocolate, walking and talking and looking as fine as he wanna be? If Diamond had good sense, she would run, not walk, as fast as her legs could carry her, out that door.

"I haven't changed my mind, Mrs. Rumford," Diamond said. *So much for good sense,* she thought. "I believe that I'll do just fine." She cocked her head to one side. "Er . . . about the other personalities?"

"What?" Cecelia was taken aback for a moment until she realized. Her face flushed and she nearly choked on her laughter. Instead, she let out another laugh and held her chest as she shook with laughter. She took a swallow of punch and said, "I don't know how this new heart of mine can stand you making me laugh like this, Diamond. I believe that you will do just fine. When can you start?"

Diamond shuttered her eyes with her long lashes. It wouldn't do to have her dislike for this woman showing. Cecelia's heart could stand anything that a healthy, fifty year-old woman's could, she thought bitterly. *Laugh. Laugh. It shouldn't be so foreign to you now. It never was to the woman whose heart is now yours!*

Cecelia stood and gestured for Diamond to follow her to the door. "Come with me. I'll get Ferdie so that she can show you your room. If it's to your liking and there are no changes to be made then you can move in a week from today and officially start work the following Monday. Is that satisfactory?" Without waiting for an answer, Cecelia left Diamond standing in the foyer. She soon returned with Ferdie, and after the introductions Cecelia breezed off into another part of the house. Diamond had been dismissed.

Ferdie Black, who never used her given name, Frederica, was sitting in the only comfortable chair in the room watching Diamond. Her hazel eyes held a smile that was as bright as the one on her full, rouged lips. Her ivory-colored skin was carefully made up and her dark brown hair was styled with one long fish tail that stretched past her shoulders. Her deep mellow voice interrupted Diamond's investigation of the room.

"It's pretty, isn't it? Like it?"

Diamond turned from the sheer-curtained window and sat on the bed again. "It's fantabulous! What's not to like?" She smoothed her hand over the ecru-colored scalloped coverlet with matching tailored petticoat. The elegant matelassé fabric was heavily textured with a swirling scroll motif. Mounds of pillows nearly hid the tall brass headboard. A Victorian bench with rounded arms and tailored skirt was at the foot of the bed. Diamond looked at the other woman in disbelief. "And she would change this if it were not to my liking?"

Ferdie's eyes crinkled with mirth. "That's what she tells all her guests. Of course, no one finds a thing wrong."

"I'm sure they wouldn't," Diamond exclaimed. She kicked off her shoes and lay against the soft mountain. "I think I'll be quite comfortable here." She sat up, put on her shoes, and walked to the connecting bath.

"Most of the bedrooms have small baths, but this one is the largest and more modern," Ferdie said.

"Really?" Diamond said, sitting down on the armless bench. It was obvious that the housekeeper loved to talk although she wasn't acting gossipy. She smiled pleasantly and appeared to let Diamond take all the time she needed to inspect her living quarters. Diamond liked her. Ferdie's figure was far from youthful, and Diamond assessed her to be near the fiftyish age bracket although her face had not a wrinkle in it.

"Yes," Ferdie answered. "This room was occupied by Ms. Cecelia's mother, and the bathroom was done over to her specifications when she moved in eleven years ago."

Diamond frowned. Mrs. Rumford had made no mention of her mother when she was filling Diamond in on the household. "Oh, where is she now?"

"She died nine years ago, one year after Mrs. Rumford's husband."

"Oh." Diamond had no words. Her own loss was still so tender. She stood and picked up her bag. "Well, I thank you for showing me around, Ferdie." Then she smiled. "I hope using first names is okay. Do we have to pretend and say 'Ms.' in front of everyone else?" She and Ferdie walked to the door, and the housekeeper laughed as she pushed her fish tail braid off her shoulder.

"Nah," Ferdie answered, her light eyes appearing to change color with her moods. "Everyone in the house are just regular folks, except for Mrs. . . . well, you met her . . . but everybody else is just fine. The doctor wants to be called plain old Steven. Says this is his home, not his examining room. You'll like him a lot."

That's what I'm afraid of. Diamond only nodded her head.

The two women were walking down the wide staircase

when they heard the front door slam and footsteps racing over the foyer's hardwood floor. The screeching voice could be heard all over the big house. Soon a woman pushed past them on the steps.

"Steven!" Jacqui paused momentarily to stare at Ferdie and the strange woman. Then dismissing them, she ran down the hall, yelling her brother's name again. "Steven!"

The door next to Diamond's bedroom opened, and Dr. Steven Rumford came running out.

Oh, God. Right next door to me? Diamond felt her throat go dry. *Oh, no!*

"What in God's name is wrong with you, Jacqui? What's happened?" Steven was walking toward his sister.

Diamond could only stare at the shirtless, shoeless man, clad only in his suit pants. His bare chest heaved rhythmically, moving in and out from the excitement his sister's voice had brought on. The dark buds of his nipples rose and fell on his broad, hairy chest. The taut stomach was tensed into muscles that disappeared beneath the belt-free pants, and Diamond's tongue darted out and wet her lips. His barefooted stance tensed his thigh muscles until they rippled underneath the soft fabric. Briefly his eyes locked on hers as she stared, and Diamond blushed to the roots of her hair. She was mesmerized and felt relieved when he turned his attention to his sister.

He grabbed Jacqui by the shoulders and shook her. "Calm down," he shouted. "What happened to you?"

"Nerissa." Jacqui gulped air, as she clung to her brother. "Nerissa is missing."

"Missing?" Steven was incredulous. "What in God's name are you talking about?"

"I waited outside of her dance school to pick her up and she never came out. When I went inside to get her, the teacher said she'd never arrived."

Steven let go of her and said, "Pick her up? Your car

is sitting outside." His eyes darkened suspiciously. "How'd you get there?"

"What difference does that make?" Jacqui shouted, flinging back from him in anger. "Your niece is missing. She wasn't even in school today. I thought you dropped her off this morning. You told me you did!"

"I dropped her at the door. What, do you mean she wasn't there and how do you know? Did you speak to the principal?"

"I didn't have to, and besides, the school was closed by that time. Nerissa's friend Candy said she waited for Nerissa after school but she finally had to leave or else she'd have been late for dance class. Nerissa wasn't in any of the classes that they have together." Jacqui's shoulders started to shake.

"Damn." Steven drew a hand across his forehead. "What else can go wrong . . .?" He stopped at the appearance of his mother, who'd gotten out of the small elevator at the end of the hall, then he looked at a man who'd come out of one of the bedrooms.

"Steven. What are you doing standing out here half naked? And Jacqui, you sounded like a madwoman. What's going on here?" To the handsome man who looked like he was sleepwalking, Cecelia said in disgust, "Christopher. Just like you to be starting the day at five-thirty in the afternoon." She looked at Ferdie and Diamond, who were speechless. "Diamond, I thought you had gone. I take it the room is satisfactory?" With a dismissive air she said, "Then we'll see you next Friday." She turned away and walked toward her son.

Ferdie rushed down the stairs, taking Diamond's hand as she went. At the front door, she opened it and said, "Things are popping. If anything's happened to that little girl, the doctor will be on everybody's case." She waved at Diamond. "I'd better get back there. See you on Friday,

Diamond, and I'm glad you're joining the household. 'Bye," she said, and closed the door.

Diamond's thoughts were moving as slowly as the so-called rush-hour traffic, as she drove home. *Mama, where has your heart gone?* Diamond's inner dialogue with her mother continued. *See what you've gone and done,* she thought. *Given your life-saving gift to an arrogant, ungrateful, selfish termagant whose words spew from her mouth like acid-tipped darts! Certainly there were more deserving people on earth than that horrible woman. What luck for Ms. Socialite that you and she matched perfectly. If not for you she would have put her family out of their misery months ago. Whatever possessed Steven Rumford to write such a beautiful letter about such a horrid woman? Does he really love her?*

Diamond Drew: bite your tongue. Why have you become so hard?

Almost as though her mother were sitting beside her, Diamond heard those words so clearly that she snapped her head, only to find the passenger seat empty. She drew a deep breath and prayed for an end to this day. She also prayed for the strength to return to that house next Friday. She was tempted to pack up and move far away from Charleston . . . and that dangerous man. But Diamond knew she couldn't do that, even if she became defenseless against the powerful sensuousness of Steven Rumford. She had been drawn to him instantly . . . *and he to her*. She'd seen the desire that he'd tried so hard to mask with abrasive behavior.

But in order to save herself from becoming a bitter old woman and to rid her mind of the archaic, selfish, attitude toward life-saving transplants, she had to follow through with her plan. She had to see that there was some sense in the hand of fate or destiny, that a caring woman should have given life to such a beast. There had to be some good in Cecelia Rumford if she had been destined to live, but Diamond failed to see the reasoning in His choice.

FOUR

They were sitting in various places in Steven's bedroom. Cecelia sat in a tan leather grandfather chair. Steven, who'd put on his rumpled dress shirt, sat with one hip resting on his dresser. Jacqui and Christopher were on the bed.

"Before we get excited and call the authorities, think about where the child may have gone. She could be doing this to scare everyone. Looking for attention as usual." Cecelia looked at her family as if no one would dare to make another suggestion. Her eyes flew wide open at the vehement blasts of protests that met her words.

"How dare you say that, mother," Jacqui cried. "If anything, you're the one she's running away from!"

Christopher Craven's dark brown eyes burned with fury. "You've got one hell of a nerve, saying that. God only knows what you've got against my daughter, but you've hated her since the day she was born. She'd be better off living far away from you!"

Steven clenched his fists against his taut thighs. "You were your usual kind self to her this morning, Mother, and you know it. She was nearly in tears when she ran from the table. So don't give us any of that 'wanting attention' stuff." His eyes blazed with anger. He turned to his sister and her husband, ignoring Cecelia's sound of injured protest. His voice calm, he said to Jacqui, "Who else does she hang with besides Candy? What about that kid Letty, who comes by here sometimes with that boy B. J.? Can you reach them?"

Jacqui nodded. "Yes, I know their parents. I can call them. But . . ." she raised fearful eyes to her brother. "What if . . . her stomach. Suppose she's someplace . . ."

"Stop it. Her stomach is not that bad, yet. So don't even go there with what you're thinking," Steven said.

"But you said that the ulcer . . ."

"Ulcer?" Christopher blurted. "What are you two talking about?" he demanded.

Steven ignored his brother-in-law, after throwing him a look of disgust, and spoke to Jacqui. "I told you that it may be an ulcer to make you act immediately on getting her to Hamilton. I don't believe it's an ulcer but she does have stomach distress and should be examined without delay."

Cecelia raised a brow. "What's this about an ulcer?"

"You . . . you did that to me?" Jacqui sputtered. "What right had you to scare the hell out of me like that?"

"Because it's time someone else besides me in this house cared about what's going on in her life."

"Just what the hell do you mean by that, man?" Christopher demanded. He eyed his brother-in-law.

"Exactly what I said." Steven dared the man to dispute him, and he stared without blinking an eye.

Christopher's jaws tightened but he backed down.

"All of this is not taking care of finding Nerissa," Cecelia said.

"As if you care," Jacqui spat as she got up from the bed. "I'll make the calls from my room and I'll let you all know as soon as I find out anything." She hurried from the room.

Steven looked at his watch. "It's nearly six now. If we don't have anything concrete by six-thirty, we'll start looking. We'll each take a different section of town, but it would help to know if Nerissa cut school with a buddy."

He moved off the dresser and started to unbutton the rest of his shirt. "If you'll excuse me, I'd like to change."

Cecelia was at the door before Steven shrugged off his shirt. "I still think that all of you are making too much of this." She left the room quickly, escaping her son's barbed look.

Christopher glared at Steven and followed his mother-in-law, leaving the door wide open.

Steven slammed the door behind them and stepped out of his pants. "Riss," he muttered, "what are you doing?" But his voice matched the troubled look in his eye.

Seven days later, on Friday morning, Diamond carried her last bag outside to the car and then went back inside to her two-room suite, her home for the past six weeks. "Where did the days go?" she said to the empty room. Looking around, checking drawers and closets and satisfied that she was not leaving anything behind, she sat on the bed. She would miss the quiet of this place, she thought. It was a boardinghouse that she'd found on the Internet before she'd left New York. When she'd arrived it was all that they'd said it would be, and she'd made arrangements to stay and pay monthly until she found her land legs in a strange place. Immediately she had felt at home as she traveled about the city, exploring potential permanent quarters. Finding employment was not her immediate goal, as she was quite comfortable. The sale of the house and the business plus her mother's estate afforded her the luxury to seek employment in a leisurely fashion.

Diamond didn't believe in fate, but she told herself she should, especially after what happened the week before she met the Rumfords. She'd taken to eating breakfast in the same café every morning and became friendly with one of the personable waitresses. Diamond found that practically everyone in Charleston was pleasant and she thought it quite refreshing, experiencing firsthand the legendary southern hospitality. Junie Washington had been particularly talkative as she took a "feet break," as she called it, joining Diamond at a table.

"Diamond, I sure envy you, girl." She blew a blue-black strand from her wig out of her mouth. "Taking your time before you start hitting the employment agencies! Life is sure sweet for some of us folks."

Diamond hid the sorrow in her eyes behind her coffee cup. Junie didn't know the reason behind Diamond's arrival in Charleston. She looked at the younger woman, who had a different wig for every day of the week and had explained that she was a fan of Star Jones, the TV personality. "Life is what we're handed, Junie, and we try to make it work. At times it's good and other times . . . well, it's not." She shrugged.

"Well, I still say you're lucky. Bet my sister would look at you with eyes like that old green-eyed monster, if she could see how you spend your time. Sightseeing!"

"Jealous?" Diamond was surprised. "Why?"

"Because she just got turned down for the umpteenth time for a job. She's having a devil of a time getting work. I tried to get her on here, but there's just no openings right now."

"Ah, that's awful," Diamond exclaimed. "What does she do?"

"Anything right now," Junie answered. "She's only twenty-one and not really skilled at anything, so she's limited. No college. No trade school. Like me, until I wised up. I'm in my last year of college and I'll be getting my sheepskin next May," Junie said proudly.

"Congratulations. I know it's not easy. Well, it seems like your sister should be following in your footsteps, right?"

"She wants to. But she has to find work first to pay her way."

"So what was the job she tried for and didn't get that required skills?" Diamond asked curiously.

"A companion."

"Companion?"

"Yeah, you know," Junie answered. "Fetch and carry for the rich and famous? She begged the woman at the personnel agency to let her take a shot at the job. It's been going begging for months, because old lady Rumford is so damn particular. Nobody knows what type of person she has in her mind to hire. But the agency people are desperate to fill the job."

"What . . . did you say?" Diamond choked on her coffee.

"Careful, girl. You all right?" Junie asked. She went on talking. "Yeah, like I was saying, she's sickly, because she had a heart transplant last year, saved her life. Was in all the papers. Could've been in papers up north too. The family is well known. Old Doc Rumford, the father, Cyril, was a big shot surgeon down here. His son's following right in his footsteps. Well, anyway, my sister didn't get the job. Said she was in that house barely ten minutes before the old lady looked down her nose and those weird light brown eyes of hers rolled to the sky. Just dismissed her in the blink of an eye." Junie stood. "My break's up. See you same time tomorrow?"

Diamond found her voice. "Sure thing." She hesitated, then said, "But, ah, Junie, what qualifications are they looking for?"

Junie quirked a brow. "You interested? Well, now, that kind of work might suit someone who's just marking time. Might do you just fine while you're still trying to settle in. I don't rightly know what they want but the people at the agency can fill you in. Why don't you take a shot at it?"

Diamond couldn't believe her ears. This can't be happening, she thought. "Well, I don't know . . ."

"Look, what've you got to lose but time? If you get it and you don't like it, just get your hat. I'll get the name of the agency from my sister and give it to you in the morning. How's that?" She walked away after giving Diamond a broad smile and a wink.

Just fate, Diamond now thought, as she left her perch on the bed. An impromptu conversation about a job had changed the course of Diamond's life. She was now employed as the companion-slash-whatever-person to the quirky grande dame Cecelia Rumford.

Giving one last look around, Diamond sighed heavily, locked the door, and walked downstairs. When she handed over her key she felt a moment of fear, almost wanting to snatch it back. The next key she held—would it only unlock the door to brick and mortar? Or would it also be the key to unlocking the secrets she held close in her heart?

It was twelve-thirty when Diamond neared the Rumford home. She'd planned it so that she'd arrive, hopefully, when the house would be near empty. The doctor would *have* to be at work, she prayed. Nerissa would be in school and maybe Jacqui and Christopher had important irons in the fire elsewhere that needed tending. She needed time to get her bearings. The last time she'd seen this family, holy bedlam was breaking loose. She'd been embarrassed and she was sure that they had felt awkward at her being privy to a private family matter. Diamond just wanted to catch her breath and let them all come home and find her there, instead of her being met and gawked at like an oddity from a curiosity shop. When she drove up the driveway, there was not one car parked in front of the wide garage door.

"Thank you," she whispered, as she parked. She rested her head on the steering wheel for a moment, waiting for the thumping in her chest subside. *Well, girlie, you're here. No backing out now!*

Diamond got out of the car and carried one bag to the

front door. With a deep breath she rang the bell. For the first time in her life, Diamond felt afraid of the unknown. *No fearless "Rough Cut" this time, Mama.* She smiled when the door opened, expecting to be greeted by Ferdie. The smile died on her lips. What was *he* doing home?

"Dr. Rumford," Diamond managed to say.

Steven looked at the woman who appeared calm on the outside, but he saw the slow rise of her chest that was a dead giveaway to her nervousness. She was startled to see him. Vaguely wondering why, Steven stepped back. "Ms. Drew," he said. "I guess you expected Ferdie, but she's out with my mother. As a matter of fact, I'm your welcoming committee. Solo. Come in." He looked at her one piece of luggage. "Is that it?" He looked past her for other bags and not seeing any, said, as he glanced at the green paisley oversize duffel, "I hope that doesn't mean you're not planning on staying. I believe the position is long-term."

Diamond thought she heard a note of hope in his voice. "Is that wishful thinking, Dr. Rumford?" Her dark eyes flashed.

Steven nearly smiled. *You couldn't be closer to the truth!* But keeping a straight face as he lied, he said, "Not at all, Ms. Drew. You do have a way of jumping to conclusions. I merely meant that all one's worldly possessions might require more than one bag. No harm meant." His mouth twitched, causing the thick brush of mustache to move slightly. "But I hope what's in there is not more of the same." His bold look encompassed her body from her neck down and up again, resting briefly on her breasts. He met her eyes. "I don't think those will be the accepted uniform of the day." Diamond was wearing baggy jeans and a T-shirt, and thinking about his mother, Steven chuckled to himself. No, not hardly, he thought. He bent to lift the bag. "Come, I'll help you upstairs with this." He looked curiously at Diamond, who held out her car keys.

"Thank you. I can use another pair of hands." Diamond smiled sweetly and lifted the duffel. "I can handle this and since I know where my room is, if you'll be so kind as to get the others . . ." She held the smile while he took the keys, and then said, "I hardly think your mother would approve of one wearing Albert Nipon on moving day." She walked across the foyer to the staircase, and without a backward glance, carried her bag upstairs.

Steven stared at her until she disappeared, warmth spreading through his body as he watched the slow undulation of her small hips. There wasn't much meat on her but what she did with what she had was torture to a man's mind. She couldn't be more than five-five, he thought, but she carried herself like she was a Nubian queen moving with the grace and stealth of a sleek feline—one that was ever on the watch for prey.

Steven turned and walked outside to her car. If his mother didn't, he would have to protest about Diamond's choice of tops. He had no intention of jumping into a cold shower every time she walked past him with one of those shirts molded to her body. Where the rest of her was lacking in an abundance of flesh, there was no hiding the ampleness of her breasts. They invited him to nestle his head in the deep crevice just like he used to do with . . . Steven caught himself and uttered a curse, angry at his thoughts. He lifted three large pieces of luggage from the trunk of the car. After making two trips, he finally had them on the small elevator, and he rode upstairs.

The door to Diamond's room was open and she was unpacking, separating colorful lingerie on the bed. At the sound of heavy footsteps, she looked up to see Steven standing outside with one of the large, wheeled suitcases. She peered past him and raised an eyebrow. "Oh, I'm sorry," she said, dropping a bra on the bed. "Do you need some help?" She started to walk toward him but stopped when he glared at her and disappeared. He soon returned with the other two smaller-size bags and rolled them inside. Leaving them standing in the middle of the large room, he walked back to the door. Before he left, he said, "That can be left until later. Tina's expecting you for lunch. If you've already eaten pretend you haven't; otherwise she'll be upset." He paused. "It wouldn't do to have your cook getting mad at you. Since it's just the two of us, I asked her to set us up in the kitchen. I hope you don't mind. It'll probably be the first and last time you'll take a meal there. My mother hardly thinks it appropriate." He started to close the door and stopped. "Meet me at the foot of the stairs in ten minutes. I'll show you the way." He closed the door firmly.

Diamond heard the solid closing of his door. Listening for sounds coming from his room, and surprised when there were none filtering through the walls of the very old house, she felt relieved. Diamond would be horrified if she thought he knew when she got in and out of bed. Further mortified at the thought of hearing her snores, she breathed, "Thank heaven for small things." Suddenly it penetrated that they'd be eating alone. She'd have to sit across from him, look into those mysterious eyes, and make intelligent conversation without squirming in her chair. So much for her careful planning. Of all the people to be alone with, her first hour in this house. Diamond sighed. *You asked for this girl, so back up your bold move!* Quickly walking to the bathroom to wash up, she decided that she wasn't going to be late. The master of the house said ten minutes and she'd make it in nine. But Diamond still wondered: what was he doing home at midday?

Steven made it in eight. He was standing at the bottom of the staircase, one black-boot-clad foot resting on the bottom step as he leaned against the newel. He was dressed in black jeans and a short-sleeve red turtleneck T-shirt. He straightened up as Diamond came down the stairs. His eyes met hers and then he checked his watch. "Punctual. You'll fall in fine with the house routine, Ms. Drew." Ignoring Diamond's cutting look, he said, "The kitchen's this way." Steven walked behind the staircase to a short hallway and opened a wide, dark-wood door.

"Tina, we're here."

Diamond smiled at the young woman she'd only seen for a hot minute last Friday. She held out her hand. "Hi, I'm Diamond Drew. We weren't introduced last week, but I wanted to tell you the sandwiches were delicious and the punch, out of this world."

Tina White beamed. "Actually, it is," she said, and then laughed at Diamond's quizzical look. "The punch. It's my own concoction and no one can guess the ingredients except for the orange juice. But they keep trying." She winked at Steven. "Have a seat. I like to see people sitting in my kitchen eating. Happens all too rare though." She looked at Steven and smiled as if they shared a private joke. "Except for Steven. With those odd hours, I'm liable to find him raiding the fridge anytime."

For the first time, Diamond saw Steven grin. She'd never noticed the small chipped tooth on the bottom right side of his mouth, and it made him appear rakish. Gone was the stuffed shirt, lord of the manor persona, and Diamond was startled by the transformation—which made him all the more dangerous. It would be easier for her if he never grinned.

Tina had set their plates before them and filled tall glasses with cold lemonade. The aroma made Diamond think about how hungry she really was, since all she'd had for breakfast was coffee and juice. She was starving and wasted no time in tasting the food.

"Umm," she said after the first forkful. "Jambalaya!"

"Right," Tina answered. "Like it?"

"How can I not," exclaimed Diamond. "This is fantastic. The best I've had since I arrived."

"You shouldn't have told her that," Steven said as he

ate with relish. "Now we'll drown in the dish for the next few months."

Diamond looked up in surprise. Had he actually spoken to her without scowling? Must be the food, she thought. Tina interrupted before Diamond could answer him.

"You two'll be just fine for a while. I'm going to Ferdie's room to watch the soaps before I finish dinner," she said. "Just help yourself to whatever you need."

Surprised, Diamond said, after Tina left, "She doesn't live in?"

"No. You would think so, though. She's here every day but Saturday and Sunday. She prepares lunch and dinner."

"And breakfast?"

"Ferdie takes care of that except for her days off which are Sundays and Mondays."

"Oh," Diamond said. They ate in silence for a moment; then Diamond frowned.

"Something wrong with the food, Ms. Drew?"

"What? Oh, of course not. Nothing's wrong."

Steven looked at her in irritation. *Why do women do that? Frowns make wrinkles, and since there isn't a one in sight on her beautiful face, she's definitely not used to making them. So why is she trying to hide behind that inane response?*

Diamond saw his growing annoyance and decided to speak her mind as she was used to doing. After all, she was now part of this household, employee though she might be. That didn't mean she should walk on eggshells and wear a snood over her mouth. She took a deep breath. "Dr. Rumford . . ."

He held up his hand. "Steven."

"What?"

"At home everyone calls me by my first name. Since you're living here now, please do the same." He took a drink. "Now let's hear what's wrong."

Inwardly Diamond smiled at his doctor's tone, certain

he was unaware of the change in his voice. "Nothing's wrong. All week, I've been thinking about your niece. I—I didn't call because it was a family matter and I didn't want to appear nosy, but I was concerned. Is she all right?"

"Was that so hard?"

"I'm sorry?" Diamond looked puzzled.

Impatience covered Steven's face. "To say that nothing was wrong was hardly necessary, if that was what was weighing on your mind so heavily. You will be living here as a member of the family, Diamond, so it's only natural that you should feel some concern."

Does he realize he used my first name? Diamond mused. She hardly thought so, since in the next breath, he said, "That says a lot, Ms. Drew . . ." He stopped when he saw her smile. "Do I amuse you?"

"Sometimes," Diamond answered. Then, noticing his deepening scowl, she hastily added, "Especially when I'm 'Ms. Drew' one second and in the next I'm 'Diamond.' I won't mind it a bit if you want to use my first name all the time."

Steven looked at her in surprise. *Had he called her Diamond?* "Yes, yes, that's not a problem," he answered gruffly, and then returned to the reason for her concern. "Nerissa is fine. She cut school and hung out all day with some friends. She was afraid of what was in store for her so she just stayed away. A few minutes before seven, she walked in, looking like a frightened kitten."

Diamond listened carefully, attuned to the softening voice and concern in his eyes as he spoke about his niece. Recalling the worried look she'd seen on his face last week, she realized that Steven loved his niece a great deal.

"I'm sure she was," Diamond replied. "From what you said, she doesn't do that often. Did she explain what was bothering her?"

"No," Steven answered tersely. How could he tell this woman the real reason for Nerissa's behavior? A shadow crossed his face. She'd find out soon enough. He looked closely at Diamond. *Does she really care or is that look a show for my benefit?* Maybe Nerissa will . . . No, with all the females in the house, he was almost certain that his niece has never confided in any of them, so what would make Diamond her confidante? Steven wondered just how often his sister had made herself available for mother and daughter conversations.

"Steven?"

Startled, he looked at Diamond. His name on her lips sounded so strange . . . and seductive.

Where had he gone? Diamond repeated his name, then said, "I couldn't help hearing—is Nerissa a dancer?"

Steven smiled. "She's a fine dancer. So graceful she moves like she's having a love affair with the wind when she's on the stage."

"Ballerina?"

"Interpretive. Sways like a gazelle in flight. Has the body shape for dance; slender, strong like yours." *Did he really say that?* Steven pushed away from the table. Taking their dishes and carrying them to the sink, he shook his head. *Foolish to apologize now. What's true is true.*

"I danced too when I was her age," Diamond said. She was standing beside him, scraping the dishes and putting them in the dishwasher. She'd flushed at his description of her and sensed that he was embarrassed, so she followed his lead and ignored the remark. Almost by mutual agreement, they cleaned the kitchen, leaving it spotless for Tina. When they finished, Diamond realized that she'd held her breath for a good part of the time. The closeness to Steven had set her blood boiling, and to prevent another "overheating" episode, every chance she got, she dug her fingernails into the palms of her hands. Diamond was determined to find a way to interact with this man without going into a swoon. Her *reaction* to him would hardly get her through one day.

"Finished," Diamond said, lamely.

"Looks like it." Steven was leaning against the sink, watching her.

"Well, I guess I'll go upstairs and finish unpacking."

"Do you really want to do that, right this minute?" His voice was noncommittal as he stared into her eyes. Steven hadn't felt this relaxed in his own home in years and he didn't want to lose the feeling. If she left, he knew he would, and he was not willing to let it go, not yet. He waited.

Diamond stared back. "No."

Pushing off the sink, Steven asked, "Have you seen the rest of the grounds?"

"No."

"How about now?"

"I'd like that," Diamond said and followed him as he left the kitchen through the back door.

The back of the house was enclosed with white wood fencing. In the center of the yard was a square-shaped pool, surrounded by a brick patio. Diamond had seen the swimming pool from her bedroom window on her first visit and had envisioned herself taking laps. She'd hoped that her employer was a sun person because Diamond wouldn't mind spending a good deal of her time in these peaceful surroundings. But after meeting Cecelia Rumford, she quickly doused that thought.

"What are you thinking?" Steven said, wondering why she'd grown so quiet.

"Why you're at home today," Diamond answered. She looked at his attire. "You appear dressed for going out. Were you the one elected to stay and greet me?"

"I'm taking an R and R day, for one," Steven answered. "And yes, I was asked to make you feel at home."

"And then you would be on your way." Diamond started to get up. They'd taken seats by the side of the pool. "Please, don't change your plans on my account. I've probably ruined them already; it's so late in the day. I appreciate the welcome and really enjoyed lunch but my bags do need emptying."

"I haven't changed my plans," Steven answered. "Just delayed my ride. I'll make it a short one."

"Ride?" Diamond looked at his leather boots. She smiled. "I should have guessed. Those are for riding, not walking. What kind do you have? Harley or Ducati?"

Steven's brows went up. "Ducati. You ride?"

Diamond shook her head. "Not anymore. Got spooked after a spill."

Steven frowned. "That was wrong." But his eyes shone at her admission. "What did you ride?" Over the years at various meets, he'd met several women bike enthusiasts. He loved the fast sport bikes and wished he had the time to indulge himself much more than he did.

"I owned a Kawasaki Ninja 600. It was a sweet-handling sport bike," Diamond answered. "What's yours?"

"The Ducati 996."

Diamond frowned. "I'm not familiar with that one," she said.

"The model name changed. It used to be the old 916. New and improved, more power, but the same handling."

Diamond was impressed. "Oh, excu-u-u-se me, sir. Only the *premier* of the Italian bikes." A smile was in her voice.

Steven grinned. "That's the one," he said, then asked, "How do you know so much about them?"

"I don't really," Diamond replied. "My godmother's boyfriend, now her husband, got me interested when I was still in college. It was the thing to be into at the time and when I graduated, he, my godmother, and my mom bought me my first, and what was to be my last, bike." Diamond gave him a rueful smile.

"The accident?" Steven asked.

"Yep. But I enjoyed riding for two years. That is, whenever I got the chance."

Steven sensed that she'd loved the sport before her accident. She was wrong to have given it up just like that.

"You were still wrong to just walk away."

"I know. Like the hair of the dog that bit me, I should
have jumped right back on." She laughed. "Call me
chicken."

"Anytime you'd like to get rid of your fear, you're welcome to give it a try with me." Steven was serious as he
stared at her. "Fear is immobilizing. You never know when
the very thing that you're afraid of will become so life
threatening that you almost regret not conquering it when
you had the chance."

"I've thought about it," Diamond answered. "But no,
thanks. I'll pass."

"Must have traumatized you." Steven's frown deepened.
"I'm sorry."

"Thanks, but I've dealt with it." She stood up. "Well,
I don't want to keep you any longer. It'll be dinner time
before you get back."

Steven walked by her side, all his senses totally wired
to the max. He thought he'd kept monumental control, sitting and talking normally like any sane man pretending
that he was oblivious to her charms. And did he offer to
take her riding? He suppressed the groan in his throat that
struggled for release. He nearly winced, as if he could feel
her slender arms grasping his middle and her breasts pressing into his back. Yes, he was going nuts. Steven quickened
his steps.

Once inside the kitchen, Diamond stopped. Her arms
were folded across her chest only to keep her fingernails
from damaging the skin of her palms. She wouldn't go
upstairs with him because that meant walking side by side.
Her senses were already on overload and she wished that
he would hustle out of the house as fast as he could move.
Otherwise, even a baby would figure out the inevitable.
They were both aware of the strong attraction between

them, and Diamond wondered who was going to be the first to admit it. And this was only the first day of the rest of—what?

"Steven." She stopped him from leaving the kitchen. "I think I'll have another cold drink before I go up. Thanks again for being here. It was the nicest welcome I've received anywhere."

Steven turned and looked at her with surprise. But all he said was, "It wasn't a problem. I'll see you at dinner." He left, closing the door behind him.

Diamond sat down with a heavy sigh. Her legs were weak and she crossed one over the other to keep them from shaking. "I hope dinner is served European style— late," she said aloud. "Maybe by eight or nine, I'll be back on earth." She helped herself to more cold lemonade and sat back down. Finally relaxing, she surveyed her surroundings.

When she had first followed Steven into the kitchen, all the trepidation that Diamond had felt beforehand had faded away like a will-o'-the-wisp, leaving behind peaceful feelings. She felt at home. Not only because of Tina's welcome but because the *room* welcomed her. She'd never been in a kitchen of this size before. It was a cook's dream. Even the tiny bakery that her mother had owned never boasted this much space.

The walls and cabinetry were light beige pine and all of the appliances had matching covering. She wouldn't have known the fridge if Tina hadn't opened the door. The only telltale signs that a dishwasher existed were the stainless steel knobs. The wall behind the sink was lined with square-pane windows with matching wood. The range was built in to a long cooking island that also housed a mini–wine cellar. The room was a place that invited one to stay awhile. It was no wonder that Steven appeared relaxed in here. Diamond walked over to the huge wall ovens. There were two of them, side by side. She opened the door and grinned, imagining the racks to be filled with her mother's specialty pies. "Mama, you'd love this," she whispered. A shadow crossed her face and her eyes misted. "I sure do miss you." Diamond heard the door open and she turned.

Christopher Craven stared at Diamond with the same brooding dark look she'd seen on his face a week ago. Like his wife, he'd glanced distastefully at the stranger who had watched the Rumfords perform at less than their company best.

"Hello. I'm Diamond Drew, Mrs. Rumford's companion. I moved in today."

Christopher appeared taller than his five-ten height. He had boyish good looks, was clean-shaven, and wore his hair natural but cut not too close. If he hadn't worn a perpetual look of doom and gloom, his good looks would have been evident much sooner. He didn't crack a smile when Diamond greeted him. Instead, he walked to the fridge and got a beer, opened it, and took a long swallow.

"Is that so? My bet is that you'll be moving out sooner than you think. So there's really no need for us to make small talk under the guise of getting acquainted. Is there?" Without waiting for an answer, he sauntered out the back door.

Diamond's jaw dropped as she glared after the obnoxious man. *What is wrong with the people who live in this house?* A shudder shook her body and she rubbed her arms.

I was right, Mama, she thought. *Your heart is in the wrong place and will never survive amid this anger and hate. Your gift was a waste!*

FIVE

Diamond was aroused by a soft tapping on her door. She lifted her head from the pillow and peered at the clock. "Oh, no," she said and jumped up from the bed. She'd only meant to close her eyes for a minute. That was two hours ago and it was now after five o' clock. The knock sounded again and she said, "Come in."

"Hi."

"Hi. You must be Nerissa." Diamond stared at the young girl who stood unsmiling in the doorway. "Come on in. I know, I'm late for dinner, right?"

"Almost," Nerissa replied, looking at Diamond's rumpled clothes. "Ferdie asked me to remind you that dinner is at six-thirty in the dining room." She stepped back. "Do you want me to come back to show you where it is?"

"No, that's all right. I passed it this afternoon. I'm sure I'll find it okay." What a solemn girl, Diamond thought. What a *pretty*, sad child! She wanted to reach out and give her a hug. Just like Peaches used to do when Diamond got mad at her mother for some childish reason. But she was sure that Nerissa's hurts went deeper than a simple foolish want.

"No, don't go," Diamond said softly. "Can you stay and talk a little bit?"

Nerissa stepped farther into the room and sat in the big chair. "Sure." She looked around with curiosity.

Diamond noticed and said, "It is a nice room isn't it?" She began hanging up the remainder of her clothes.

Nerissa nodded. "I remember visiting Granny in here."

Diamond was surprised. "Your grandmother?"

"No, Great-granny. But now that it's used for guests, there's no reason for me to be in here." She thought for a moment. "Except sometimes when I visited Elise. She liked when I stopped by."

"Elise?" The name was unfamiliar to Diamond.

"Uncle Steven's fiancée."

Diamond became still. She could feel her heart sinking and wondered why. Shouldn't this be good news? Now she wouldn't have to worry about staying away from the man. This automatically made him off-limits. But why wasn't she relieved?

Nerissa's knowing, bright eyes followed the pretty young woman. "You've met my uncle."

Diamond nodded as she hung the last garment and then chose one and laid it on the bed.

"You like him. I know. Everyone does. Elise loved him, passionately."

"And just how do you know that?" Diamond looked curiously at the young girl, who'd yet to smile. Passionately? How could the woman help herself? And why "loved"?

"She told me." Nerissa looked impatiently at Diamond. "How else would I know something like that?"

"I guess you wouldn't," Diamond replied with a shrug of her shoulders. "They broke up?" Did her voice sound casual enough?

"Elise died." Nerissa unfolded herself out of the chair gracefully. "I'd better go so you can shower up. I'll see you later." She disappeared before Diamond could say a word.

"Fiancée? Died?" Diamond said, as she stripped on the way to her bath. What other turn of events had she yet to discover about the strange Rumford household? As the water pelted her, she couldn't help feeling that she was playing the role of a lonely damsel in a modern gothic whose duty it was to resolve the myriad problems of the troubled family. But who would play her inevitable rescuer? she wondered.

"No, not him," Diamond told her alter ego, who whispered his name in her ear. As she smoothed lotion over her moist skin, she said, "Definitely not him." She'd decided that although they would be living together, she and Dr. Steven Rumford would not be playing together. As long as Diamond lived under this roof with him, she was not going to open herself up to a world where she'd be hurt and made to feel worthless. She would never let another man get that close again—as she'd almost fallen under the spell of this man who held heated desire in his eyes for her.

Visions of him and Elise making passionate love in the big bed chilled her insides. She wondered if she would be the ghost between them tonight when she slid beneath the cool sheets. And would he be lying awake on the other side of the wall, remembering? Diamond's body reacted to the thought, suddenly making a mockery of her strong convictions of a few moments ago. As she dressed, Diamond prayed for the strength to resist temptation. Her self-respect depended upon it.

Cecelia was seated at one end of the table, frowning and drumming her freshly manicured nails on the white linen tablecloth. Finally, she waved her hand in frustration and picked up a tiny crystal bell and shook it. When the door opened, Cecelia said, "We may as well begin, Tina. I've had a long day and I want to eat on time. I intend to go to bed early tonight." Tina disappeared and Cecelia looked at the empty chairs.

"I'm sorry about my family's rude behavior, Diamond.

After all, this is your first day and the perfect opportunity for you to meet everyone. Really!" She looked at her granddaughter. "Nerissa is hardly what I'd call a welcoming committee."

Diamond's eyes widened in disbelief. How crude and hurtful, she thought. The slight cringe of Nerissa's shoulders as she stared at the table was not hard to miss. Couldn't the woman see the young girl's discomfort?

"I wouldn't say that, Mrs. Rumford," Diamond answered, giving her employer a direct stare.

"Is that so?" Cecelia lifted an imperial brow. "I prefer the use of my first name. Didn't I make myself clear last week?"

"Yes, you did. I'm sorry if I forgot," Diamond answered. "But your granddaughter's presence is a fine introduction to the family." She smiled at the teenager who was sitting to Diamond's left. "Nice to see you again, Nerissa. Maybe we can talk a little bit longer tonight."

"You've already met?" Cecelia eyed Nerissa with suspicion. "When did you have time to go gallivanting around the house? I thought your mother confined you to your room after school for a week." She was interrupted by Tina's arrival with a rolling cart filled with chafing dishes. When plates were filled and the cart pushed against the wall, Cecelia resumed her interrogation.

"Well? Have you completed your assignments?"

Diamond held her tongue as she watched the slow disintegration of Nerissa's self-esteem. The sharp voice from the doorway turned everyone's head.

"I've told you before, Mother, that that is my concern." Jacqui took an empty plate and filled it before sitting down next to her daughter.

Diamond looked at her in surprise. She'd have thought the other end seat would be reserved for the master. Curious. She waited expectantly for the others to arrive.

"Welcome to the Rumford home." Jacqui looked at Dia-

mond. "Nerissa's told me that you two've already met."
She looked at her mother and back to the newcomer.
"Hope you'll decide to stay a while. My daughter thinks
you're okay."

"Ma!" Nerissa ducked her head.

"What's wrong with telling the truth, Nerissa? And how
many times have I told you to look people in the eye?"

Cecelia interrupted. "Just what do you mean by that remark?" she asked her daughter. "Diamond is not temporary. Of course she's going to stay."

"Who else thinks she's temporary?" Christopher walked
in and kissed Nerissa on the cheek. "Hi, kitten," he said.
"Hello, Cecelia." He nodded at Diamond. "So far, so
good?" Grinning, he helped himself, then took the chair
closest to Cecelia and facing Diamond.

With only one chair left, that meant Steven would sit
next to his sister and across from his niece. Interesting,
Diamond thought. Christopher sits far from his wife and
daughter and Steven prefers not to face his mother directly.
Diamond ate the delicious roast chicken in silence, waiting
for more family dynamics.

Jacqui looked from her husband to Diamond. "You've
met."

"Sort of," Diamond answered, dryly, as she and Christopher eyed each other.

A wary look settled over Jacqui's face as she eyed the
pretty young woman, her gaze assessing the whole package. *Don't tell me. Another potential conquest and right
under my nose? It'll never happen.* She cut a disgusted
look at her husband. Then, in a sugary voice, said to Diamond, "And can you define 'sort of,' to me, dear?" A false
smile lay on her lips. "Is that a New York expression and
exactly what does it mean? Here in Charleston, we expect
that either it is or it isn't." She lifted a delicate shoulder.
"Very simple."

All eyes turned to Diamond, including Nerissa's.

Diamond was taken aback by the uncalled for sarcasm. She stared into the eyes of the woman who had the same color eyes as her mother. The light hit them, and instantly Diamond was reminded of a cornered cat. Surely this woman didn't think that Diamond wanted her husband! Stifling a laugh, she answered. "Yes, I believe you are."

Cecelia's eyes sparkled with unmasked glee. She was right. *This girl has spunk,* she thought.

Jacqui's mouth twisted into a surprised smile, but before she shot back, her brother chuckled as he walked into the room.

"Evening, folks." To Jacqui, he winked and said, "Diamond's giving you as good as she gets, huh, sister?" He sat after filling his plate and began to eat, ignoring his sister's glaring stare. After a moment, he asked Diamond, "Finished everything okay?" His voice and look were casual, with not a hint of anything but genuine concern over a guest's comfort.

For the second time in almost as many minutes, Diamond was startled. Gone was the deep smoldering desire he'd unmasked to her earlier. His whole manner was that of a man welcoming a stranger into his home. Nothing more. She was further surprised by the genuine smile he gave her. Diamond could read nothing in that either except a natural politeness.

"Yes, thanks. Finally." She smiled and could feel her body untwine. Now she wouldn't have to invent a thousand ways of avoiding him in his own house, or averting her eyes from his to prevent losing herself in them.

Jacqui looked at them both. "It appears you've met all the Rumfords and the Cravens, Diamond. All in one afternoon. Fast," she said with a devious smile.

"It was my request that Steven delay his pleasure to stay and meet Diamond today," Cecelia told her daughter. "After all, no telling when you would return from wherever. And Christopher," she flicked a look at him. "Well, we won't bother with *that*, right now. Thank you, Steven. I was glad you stayed. You know how dreadfully long it takes to undo and then rebraid this hair. Hours! I really don't know how long I can continue with this style, but I love the look." She patted the brown braids that were pulled back from her face and done in an intricate upsweep.

"It's a great look," Diamond offered. She had to admit the style suited the woman's angular face, although Diamond would have preferred a softer look.

"Thank you, dear." Turning to Steven, Cecelia said, "Did you enjoy your ride? Now I don't feel so bad asking you to stay today. After all, you did take the day to clear your head. Really, I don't know why you don't take more time for yourself. You'd think the house would burn down before you reached the airport."

"It's not the house I would worry about, Mother," Steven answered. "It's about who would be left alive in it."

"As if you cared about what happens to any of us," Jacqui said.

"And you do?" Christopher said to his wife.

"Of course he cares, Jacqui." Cecelia turned her bright eyes on her son. "He's doing exactly what he was charged to do by his father. I think he's playing his role rather well."

"Stop it!" Steven roared, slamming his fist down on the table. "Why in God's name can't this family sit down to one meal a day without baiting and spewing garbage like jungle animals?"

Nerissa jumped and her eyes clouded. *Now he'll really find excuses not to join them at dinner,* she thought. She hated it when her family made her uncle mad. She hated them.

Diamond saw Nerissa's face and her heart went out to

the unhappy girl. Can't these adults see what they're doing to her? What's wrong with these people?

"Riss, are you okay?" Steven's voice softened as he eyed his niece. God, this time *he* had put that sad look in her eyes. He studied her carefully. At least she wasn't clutching her stomach. He knew there was no possibility of an ulcer and it was confirmed when he'd spoken to his colleague, Hamilton, but she did have stomach distress.

"What's wrong, Nerissa?" Christopher asked.

"Oh, now, you're interested?" Jacqui said. "After she's developed a condition, you want to know what's wrong?"

"I'm fine, Uncle Steven." Nerissa pushed away from the table. "May I be excused? I want to do some research."

"But it's Friday, honey." Jacqui's eyes were worried. "Why don't you take the night off from studying? You can do that tomorrow or Sunday, can't you? You know what Dr. Hamilton said."

"Oh, excuse the child," Cecelia said impatiently. "Why spend so much time with her? She does the opposite of what you want, anyway."

Nerissa cut her eyes at her grandmother, then turned and left the room.

Steven glared at his mother, threw his napkin down, and followed his niece.

"Oh, how dramatic we all are tonight." She tinkled her little bell. "I'd like dessert now," she said, when Tina appeared.

"Coming up," Tina said, as she cleared the table. "For four?"

"Yes, Tina. Steven and Nerissa are apparently too full for one of your exotic creations."

Christopher stood up. "Make it three, Tina. No harm intended. I'll probably raid the fridge later on, so don't freeze anything." To Diamond he said, "Light stuff, tonight." He left without a word to his wife or his mother-in-law.

Diamond almost pinched herself to assure that she was awake. She felt as if she were walking through someone else's nightmare. Although she was an only child, she did have playmates and later, a friend or two whom she'd visited on occasion. Mealtimes were never like this, and in comparison to her own home life, with her mother and Peaches, this was a bona fide scene from a TV soap opera. Diamond found it hard to swallow the apple and raisin deep-dish pie.

"Diamond," Cecelia said. "You really must be tired. Are you sleeping with your eyes open?"

"I'm sorry?" Diamond blinked her eyes.

"I'm just reminding you that your time is your own tomorrow and Sunday. Monday will begin your official employment."

"Yes, I remember, Cecelia," she answered. "What time do you expect me and where shall I look for you?"

"After breakfast is fine. Around nine-thirty in the sitting room." Cecelia stood up and sighed. "It's been a long day and I'm going to my room now." She looked at Jacqui. "I do hope you can do something with that daughter of yours. I'll not have her displaying temper around here." She left the room in an indignant huff.

"Still want to stick it out?" Jacqui asked. "You heard my husband. You ain't seen a thing, yet." She sat back in her chair, crossed her legs, and smiled. "Jobs pretty hard to come by in New York? It's tough all over, but I suggest you go back and try a little harder. What you're obviously looking for isn't in this house and that's for certain."

"I don't remember telling you a thing about what I'm after," Diamond answered. "For someone who *obviously* has no idea what work is, I wonder why she thinks she's such an expert on the job market, anywhere." Diamond's eyes flashed. "And what I was looking for, I've already found in this very house."

Jacqui's eyes narrowed.

Diamond laughed. "No, you can lose that thought. Not my kind of stuff. But to ease your suspicious mind, what I've found is your mother. She is exactly the reason why I'm here, and she's offered me the perfect job . . . and until neither of us can stand the sight of the other, I intend to stay awhile." She pushed her chair back. "And with that, I'll say good night. Thanks for the warm welcome, Jacqui." Diamond turned and walked from the room.

Jacqui sat alone at the table for a long time, moving only when Tina and Ferdie came in to clean up. When she reached her room, a genuine smile was on her lips, as she wondered if Cecelia hadn't finally met her match. "Welcome, for real, Diamond Drew," she whispered.

An hour after she left the dining room, Diamond was still sitting in the big chair in her room. She felt miserable, and for the first time since she arrived in Charleston, she wanted to leave. But where would she go now? She couldn't barge in on Peaches and her new husband. Besides, she thought, Charleston was where she wanted to be. She just didn't want to be in this house. Maybe she'd made a mistake after all coming here and trying to question His will. Every time Diamond looked at the selfish Cecelia Rumford, knowing that the heart of a good woman kept her alive, she wanted to cry and reveal her identity. She wanted the woman to know that she didn't deserve to have the heart of a gentle woman beating inside her.

Restless, Diamond stirred from the chair. She listened. The house was so quiet. Did they all retreat to their rooms at nine o'clock? Did they really hate each other so much? She sighed and opened her door. The hall was empty. She could hear the faint sounds of TV chatter coming from the room next to hers. It must be Nerissa's room, she decided, because last week she'd seen Christopher come from a room on the opposite side of the hall. Diamond assumed that it was Jacqui's room also. Quietly she slipped past the closed doors and walked down the wide staircase. Such a beautiful house with ugly people inside it, she thought. Making her way to the kitchen she immediately felt that at-home feeling envelop her as it had earlier. She put the teakettle on and helped herself to some more of the delicious apple dessert. Moments later she was sitting in the same chair she'd sat in when she'd lunched with Steven. She ate her snack wondering what had caused the change in his behavior. She welcomed it because now she could look upon him as a friend and not someone who would put the move on her in a neon second. She wished that he would appear, because suddenly she needed someone to talk to. With all Diamond's desire to hold her emotions in check around him, she believed that he would become her one friend in this loveless house.

Diamond ended her wishful thinking, washed her dishes, and looked about. Not ready to end the night aimlessly channel surfing, she took a sweater from the tree stand by the back door and went outside. It was a bit chilly, but the night breeze might bring on sleep a little faster, she hoped. Maybe she'd find the answer to how to handle this family in the rippling aquamarine waters of the pool. And just maybe she could come to terms with what she now realized had been a bad decision.

Steven was standing in his dark bedroom, staring outside, watching the reflection of the night lamps dancing in the pool. Ever since trying to console his niece he'd been trying to settle his temper. He'd been shocked at Nerissa's plea to be sent away to a boarding school. She hated living in this house and wanted to leave it any way she could.

Steven felt renewed anger toward his family. All of them. More than ever, he thought about the résumés he had floating about in various cities. Right now, Connecticut looked mighty good. Startled at the slight figure moving about the yard, he recognized Diamond. She walked around the perimeter of the pool, stopping and staring every once in a while; then, finally, she sat down in the same chair she'd used earlier in the day. His heart quickened as he observed her slumped shoulders. Although he couldn't see her face clearly, he didn't doubt that she was feeling a little bit lonely and sad. Surprised, because she was so frank and matter-of-fact, he didn't think she let too many things get to her. Then, bitterly, he thought, how many families suffer a case of indigestion night after night after what is supposed to be a pleasant coming together?

Steven watched Diamond as she stood up and walked toward the house. Suddenly he had the urge to talk to her, to be with her even though it meant treading into dangerous territory. But recklessly he didn't care. About to leave the window to meet her as she entered the kitchen, he frowned when he saw her again. She was looking up at the windows and throwing her hands up to the sky. Steven could see her mouth moving and guessed that she wasn't saying her prayers. Instantly, he realized what her dilemma was. She was locked out. The back door had a slam lock that required a key for entry. She disappeared from view again and reappeared almost immediately. Amused, Steven left his room. Talk about opportunity and wishful thinking, he thought. He took the stairs two at a time.

Diamond had her hands on her hips, staring at the windows of the house. Not a light to be seen, she thought. She'd tried the front door, which was bolted tight. "Damn!" she said. "Now I have to wake up the whole house?" *Won't the master think this an intelligent move! And Miss Jacqui will chortle to beat the band at Miss New York Smart,* she fumed. *Might as well get it over with.* Diamond walked to the back door and started to ring the bell when the door opened. Startled to see the man who remained a constant in her subconscious, all she could say was "Oh!"

"Forget your keys?" Steven asked, stepping back, inviting her inside with a gesture.

"I think that's . . ." Diamond bit back the sarcastic remark she'd been about to toss at him when she saw his eyes begin to cloud. *The man's put up with enough smart mouths for one night,* she thought. Starting over, she said, "Thanks; you came to my rescue." As he closed the door she tilted her head up at him. "You weren't laughing at me from your window, were you?" Her eyes twinkled.

Steven saw the about-face she did and matched her change of attitude. Neither of them welcomed harsh words. "Not really," he said with a hint of a smile. "That's happened to one or all of us at one point." Very solemn, he added, "One day, I'll show you how to get in without waking the house."

Equally as solemn, Diamond said, "Sounds like that was something you needed to know."

"You're right. Came in downright handy, especially when my dad was at home. Almost always, that was the case and I had to be extra quiet."

"Don't tell me that you were a handful?" Diamond said with mock incredulity.

Steven looked thoughtful. "I guess you could say that. But that was a long time ago." His eyes saddened. "Almost ancient history."

Diamond saw and wondered what he was thinking. "You've lived here long, then," she stated.

"For thirty-eight years. I was born here." He paused. "My father was a young man here."

"Hmm, I guess you can say that you have roots," Diamond said. "Grandparents, great-grandparents?"

"Don't we all?" Steven asked. He saw the wistful look in her eyes.

"We're all not that lucky."

"Sorry. It's hard for me to imagine a kid not having grandparents around to spoil them rotten. I don't remember my great-grandparents." Was she an orphan, then? Steven wondered.

Diamond shrugged off his apology. "That's okay. If you're loved, you don't miss it."

Steven frowned. "I'm not so sure about that," he said dryly. "Do you have siblings?" Steven somehow guessed her answer.

Diamond knew that he was thinking about his niece. "No. An only child, and unspoiled, thank you," she said, lightly.

"No, I can see that," Steven said slowly, watching her closely.

"You can?" She twisted her head over each shoulder and patted her body. "You mean it shows?"

Steven half smiled but was serious when he said, "I saw the play of emotions on your face at the dinner table. Nerissa has a friend in you." He didn't miss the reluctance to talk about her past.

Diamond remembered the anger she'd felt and the willpower it had taken not to butt in to the family business. She hadn't realized she'd been watched.

"We spoke for a bit when she visited me earlier. I like her."

Steven was surprised. "Visited?" He looked away briefly.

"Yes, Ferdie sent her." Diamond knew that he was thinking of other times when his niece went into that room. But why concern herself with his grief?

Steven shook away thoughts of his family. He wanted to know more about Diamond and what it was about her that calmed him to the point of feeling hypnotic. After their first two explosive encounters, he could see beyond her quick tongue. Granted, that was a requirement in order to work for his mother, but he could see that she was warm and caring and, uncannily, spread healing balm over one's mind.

"We really have to find another place." Steven impaled her with a stare.

"I'm sorry?" Diamond looked puzzled.

"To get acquainted. Tina's kitchen. It really is very popular and no telling when someone'll come barging in." He looked at the wall clock. It was ten minutes to ten. "I'm surprised the raid hasn't started yet."

"I'm afraid it has," Diamond admitted. At his inquisitive look, she added, "I cleared away the evidence before I went wandering."

Steven hesitated for a second. "Then if it's not too late would you care to join me in the library for a nightcap?"

Diamond warmed all over. "Love to," she said. As she stood up, she followed his look toward the door as it opened, and Steven and Diamond exchanged amused looks.

Christopher stopped as he spied his brother-in-law with Diamond. He looked from one to the other. Then, with a crooked grin, he said, "I see I'm not the only one with a taste for late night sweets." He walked past them to the fridge, barely missing Steven's shoulder.

Neither Steven nor Diamond missed the implication, or the challenge, and Diamond flinched inwardly at the cold, hard look the man beside her gave Christopher. She could see the tenseness enveloping Steven's body like a steel web. Why couldn't the man end just one night in this house on a peaceful note? she asked herself. She found herself feeling very annoyed with the object of Steven's discomfort and tried hard not to glare at the man.

"This way, Diamond," Steven said, leading her out of the room. He never gave Christopher another look.

"What's your pleasure?" Steven asked, as he stood by a tall piece of dark cherry wood furniture. He opened the double doors to reveal a lighted interior. It was a well-stocked liquor cabinet with a pull-down leaf, beneath which was a tiny refrigerator.

You! Diamond blushed as if she'd answered his question aloud. "Apricot brandy, thanks." *Get control, Diamond,* she told herself. You were doing just fine a while ago!

Steven fixed her drink, poured a Johnny Walker Black with water for himself, and joined her on the long, black leather sofa. He raised his glass to Diamond. "To you and Charleston. Hope you find the experience to your liking." He took a long swallow.

"I'm not letting anything ruin it for me," Diamond answered firmly. They drank in silence. After a moment, she said in a quiet voice, "I'm curious about your family."

Steven nearly choked on a sip of scotch. With a raised brow, he said, with a sardonic grin, "Not surprising. What is it that you want to know?"

"Is Dr. Steven Rumford the only employed member of the family?"

This time, Steven did smile. "You do speak your mind, don't you?"

Diamond shrugged. "It eliminates misunderstandings, don't you think?"

"Sometimes it does," he answered. "But to answer your question, no."

Diamond looked askance.

"I know, it appears that that's not the truth, but it is." Steven was amused by her look of skepticism. "Jacqui is an accomplished cosmetologist and wigmaker and is quite successful." He gestured toward a wall with ceiling-high bookcases.

Diamond looked at some of the shelves, which held various plaques and framed certificates. "Jacqui's?"

"Most of them. Are you familiar with the name Black Unicorn?"

"Hers?" Diamond looked at her polished fingernails. "I've worn their polish for years."

Steven nodded. "She started that line of cosmetics while she was still in college. She sold it about nine years ago because she was bored with it. So she started another company, Lady Jacqui."

"The wigmaker."

"That's her. So you see how she can make her own hours and appear not to work at all."

Diamond whistled. "I do see." She finished her drink and set the glass on the table. "And her husband?"

"Would you care for another?" Steven asked, getting up.

"No, thanks," Diamond said. He nodded, and after refreshing his own drink, sat beside her again.

Steven erased the dark scowl from his face. "Christopher is a skilled auto mechanic." He paused, then said, "Where he's employed at the moment I haven't got a clue."

"Thanks for satisfying my curiosity," Diamond said.

"Not a problem," Steven shrugged. "You'd have discovered all of that yourself, before long." He stood up. "You've had a long day and must be exhausted."

"Yes, I am a little sleepy, but the day has been very . . ." Diamond faltered, and flushed for lack of a suitable adjective. "Interesting" was much too inadequate, she thought.

Steven smiled at her embarrassment. "You're forgiven. My family does have its own unique description." At the door, he hesitated and stopped her from leaving the room.

"Diamond, I know you're on your own for the next two days and you must have a million things to take care of before you begin dealing with my . . . well, when you start working." Steven stared into her curious eyes.

Diamond could only nod her head as she returned his stare. He was standing so close she could feel the heat of his body, and the faint scent of sandalwood drifting to her nostrils made her light-headed. She waited.

"You've probably seen quite a lot and been on numerous tours, but would you mind doing Charleston again with a personal guide?" Steven almost recalled his words. *What am I doing?*

"You?" Diamond whispered.

"Yes," Steven's voice was just as low.

"Tomorrow?" So far away, Diamond thought.

"Tomorrow," Steven answered.

"What time?"

"Early, before breakfast."

"I have to eat," Diamond said a little breathless.

"So do I." Steven swallowed deeply.

Diamond took a deep breath and started walking toward the staircase. She heard him turn out the light and soon felt his nearness. They walked side by side up the stairs.

At her door, Diamond stopped. "How early?" she whispered. The hall was so quiet, and she felt that the whole house was listening, but not a sound was heard behind the closed bedroom doors.

"Seven o'clock," Steven said in a low voice. "Meet you out front. Sleep well." He turned to go, then paused before saying, "Diamond . . ."

"Yes?"

Steven lifted his hand as if to touch her cheek, but then, stepping back, said, "Thanks for today . . . and . . . to-night." He turned and walked the few steps to his room.

Diamond closed her door softly and stood in the dark for a long moment before finally unbuttoning her blouse. She couldn't help but wonder what state of undress the man next door was in. Her visions chased her into the bath where soon the stinging shower spray cooled her burning skin. Wondering if a similar remedy would be available to her tomorrow, Diamond slipped into a cool satin chemise, hoping that sleep would claim her soon. Otherwise . . .

Diamond's eyes flew open. Was that sandalwood she smelled?

SIX

The next morning at seven o'clock, Steven was sitting on the top porch step, still second-guessing himself. He had to be crazy to go through with his impromptu suggestion of last night. After he'd done all he could to discourage her from taking the job, here he was, putting himself right on the path that might turn into one of self-destruction. Would it be possible to be so near her and not touch her just once? Even, accidentally? A quick brush of the hand, as they reached for the same condiment? Or a whisper-soft touch as she accepted a glass of wine? Last night, when she'd rolled the brandy around her tongue, tasting it so sensuously, he could almost feel the tiny pink tip of her tongue playing tag with his. The image had made him heady and he'd abruptly refreshed his drink. It was a long time before he'd fallen asleep, because memories of that room had taunted him. He turned at the sound of the opening door. One look at her brought back self-recriminations. He stood up.

"Mornin'," Steven said. She was really beautiful, he thought.

"Mornin' to you, too," Diamond answered as she kept her composure. The tall chocolate hunk looked delectable, and what she was thinking made her blush. She coughed to hide her embarrassment, then said, "I had an idea it might be a jeans kind of day." Her admiring glance covered him from head to toe.

Steven looked her over. They were both wearing jeans, but she did a hell of a lot more for hers. These were not baggy but straight-legged and hip-hugging, showing her womanly contours. The light blue shirt was open at the neck, and his bold look traveled down the valley of fine-textured skin until his exploration was abruptly, and annoyingly, halted by buttoned cotton and the arms of a navy sweater that was tied around her shoulders, effectively cloaking her full breasts. Steven, without apology, met her curious stare and nodded. "Albert Nipon has his place," he said. "Shall we go?"

Diamond followed him down the short flight of steps, nearly choking on a deep intake of air. *No fair, Steven Rumford,* she cried inwardly. *You've taken off the gloves!* Diamond buckled herself in the shiny black Lexus, and as they pulled out of the winding driveway, wondered what had happened overnight. All the desire that she'd seen in his eyes at their first meeting was back and nearly knocked her out of her old-fashioned penny loafers!

Neither Diamond nor Steven was aware of the eyes on them as they drove off. Even if they had, Steven wouldn't have cared and Diamond would have been amused.

Cecelia, whose bedroom was moved to the first floor when she became ill, heard the soft purr of the powerful Lexus engine. She'd just finished her bike exercises, which she'd been doing every day since three days after her heart surgery. Always a sedentary person, she now knew the benefits of daily exercise. Her strong new heart would serve her well if she followed her doctor's orders, and she intended to do just that. Sometimes she would swim but never this early, because her son used the pool almost every morning before he went to work. Knowing her presence would be unwelcome, she always delayed her swim until late morning or afternoon. But because it was Saturday, she was surprised to hear him going out so early instead of taking his laps. Cecelia's side window afforded her a view of the garage, and when she peered through the sheer mauve curtains, she was taken aback by seeing Diamond sitting in the passenger seat.

At a loss as to what to think, Cecelia became puzzled as she watched her son drive off. She couldn't see his face but the very fact that he was with a woman was astounding. Except for family, Cecelia doubted that there'd been a woman in that car since Elise. Suddenly an overwhelming feeling of sorrow enveloped her at the thought of Steven's dead fiancée. Annoyed, Cecelia sat down in the big rocking chair near the window. For the past few months, whenever Elise's name was mentioned, that same irritable feeling would wash over Cecelia like someone emptying a pail of water over her head. She felt drenched with emotion and became increasingly irritated with her feelings. Cecelia couldn't understand it, because she had never liked her son's choice for a wife. Elise didn't have the right family background, and was deliriously happy in her job as a head buyer of women's fashions at a department store! That wasn't the kind of person Cecelia wanted to converse with at dinnertime night after night. Besides, the woman was weak, and like everyone else in the house except Steven, yessed her to death, always willing to please.

Cecelia frowned. She wiggled in her seat, as if the movement would erase the uncomfortable warmth that once again enveloped her. How was she to know that Elise would seek out an incompetent abortionist? Sneaking off to some backwoods doctor, as if it was forty years ago, only because she didn't want to embarrass the Rumfords. *Well, it certainly wasn't* my *fault she died at the hands of that butcher,* Cecelia thought. Although it had been her suggestion, and Elise had agreed, she'd at least have thought that Elise would come to her when she decided to have the abortion. Cecelia could have discreetly arranged everything! Steven would never have been the wiser. But Elise ruined the plan by dying. Blaming Cecelia, Steven hated her more than he ever had since his father's death. Cecelia rocked herself, remembering that time. She believed that if she hadn't gotten so sick soon after Elise's death, her son would have left this house.

Relegating those bitter memories to the secret place in her mind, Cecelia wondered why she felt such strong emotion over someone she'd never cared for in the past. The voices of her support group resounded in her ears, but Cecelia scoffed at them as she always did. She wasn't living in the caveman era so she knew all about what happens to people—or so they think when they have a heart transplant. She never believed in that transference stuff and never attributed any of it to her case. At her last meeting she had proudly announced that in two months it would be a year since her surgery, and never once had she felt the slightest difference in her personality. Cravings and odd wishes? Unheard of! *She* was the same as ever!

Cecelia stopped rocking. But why now after all these years did she actually care that Elise was dead?

Jacqui was awake, listening for sounds indicating that her husband had spent the night in his room, when she heard the garage door open. Her bedroom windows faced the front of the house, and when she heard her brother's low voice, she got up and went to the window. She couldn't see to whom he was talking, but a moment later, when she saw Diamond walking beside Steven to the Lexus, she cocked a brow. Jacqui observed her brother's face and her eyes brightened in surprise. Gone was the ever-present scowl, and he actually looked glad that he was alive. *What goes here?* she wondered. The last time she'd seen him he was wearing the belligerent, Big Brother, master-of-the-mansion attitude.

Jacqui had been so engrossed, she didn't hear Christopher enter the room and stand beside her. He was staring out the window at the scene below.

"Don't tell me Mr. Cool has gotten bit. Little Miss worked her show right off, didn't she? Damn, she's good."

"You would know all about that," Jacqui said dryly as she turned from the window.

"Ah, Jacqui, don't start with me so early in the morning."

"Well it's as good a time as any, seeing that this is a rare opportunity for me." She scanned his pajama-clad body and bare feet. Deep down, she was glad that he was here but she couldn't bring herself to tell him. Not after all the hurt he'd put her through. She said, "What's the matter? None of your little girlies could come out to play last night?"

Christopher's jaw tightened. He stared down at the beautiful woman who was his wife. God, she was gorgeous, even first thing in the morning. Her skin was wrinkle-free, smooth, and soft as a new persimmon. Her deep auburn hair fell down to her shoulders in a cascade of waves. Why she liked to wear those wigs she created baffled him.

Jacqui watched him staring at her and she guessed what he was thinking. Those first years of their marriage, he used to look at her in that same desirable way. But that was a long time ago.

"Jacqui," Christopher said wearily. "I don't want to fight with you." He sat down on the bed, and hesitantly, Jacqui joined him.

"But you always leave yourself open to it. What do you expect me to do, look the other way? Why do you think we have separate bedrooms? Thank God, Mother had to move down to the first floor; otherwise, there would be no extra room so that we could pretend there's still a marriage happening here."

"Pretending has hurt us even more, Jacqui." He rubbed his forehead. "Maybe we should have broken up long ago, when I first screwed up. Staying together because of Nerissa wasn't the smartest thing, was it?" He felt bad for his little girl.

Jacqui's eyes saddened and she shook her head. "No."

"Did Dr. Hamilton say that her abdominal pain was due only to stress?"

"He took tests, and there is no infection or inflammation. He's pretty certain the last test she's scheduled to take will rule out any blockage." Jacqui shrugged. "He's pretty certain that it's stress-related."

Christopher's eyes grew dark at his wife's distressed tone. He took her hand. "I'm sorry, baby," he said softly.

Jacqui was surprised. He hadn't called her that in years. She wound her fingers through his, like she used to, and her eyes softened. When did they fall out of love?

"It's all my fault, baby," Christopher said. "If I hadn't given in to you to move back here after your father died, maybe things would have been better for us. Maybe Nerissa would have been a happier little girl. She used to laugh and giggle all the time. Remember?"

Jacqui smiled. "Yes, she was the happiest and sweetest little cutie pie."

They were quiet for a moment, remembering happier times.

"Jacqui?" Christopher's thick, dark eyebrows were knitted together. He drew his hand from hers and stood up, walking over to the window.

"What is it Chris?" When was the last time she had called him that?

Turning from the window, he smiled. "Chris" was used when things were fine and mellow. But he knew they really weren't so he grew serious again.

"I know we've asked each other the same question over and over for years, but never came up with anything that made any sense, but"—he paused—"have you ever given any more thought to why your mother hates our daughter?"

Jacqui took a breath before she spoke. This was a topic that always ended in a heated argument. "Yes," she said softly, "but as always, I just don't know."

"One thing we never did was to out-and-out confront her." Christopher stared at his wife's changed expression. "You did? And didn't tell me?"

Jacqui nodded.

"Well," Christopher said tersely. "What did she say?"

"Only that we were crazy for thinking such a thing. Said we ought to be ashamed of ourselves; that how could one hate one's own flesh and blood? Said she's not one for spoiling, and her manner of disciplining would teach the child to become a sought-after member of society."

"Whose society?" Christopher asked. "God, how in the world you and your brother made it to adulthood without being scarred is a miracle. Your mother thinks she's living in a world long gone. You'd think when she was at death's door she would have woken up a changed woman." Christopher shook his head. "Well, I've decided that I can't stay here any longer, Jacqui, watching what she's doing to my daughter. I didn't think it had gotten to this point."

"Just what are you saying, Christopher?" Jacqui's heart skipped a beat.

"That I've been too cowardly all these years . . . and yes, you too, not to take control of my life and my family. For not getting you both out of here, years ago!" He stared down at her. "I want my daughter out of this house. Either she comes to live with me or she stays with you . . . only if you move." His eyes never wavered.

Jacqui was silent. Finally, the words she dreaded to hear. *He's leaving us.*

"When did you decide?" she asked. Her eyes flashed. "You have an address already?"

Christopher flung both hands up in the air. "Why are you always so suspicious?" he raised his voice. "Can't you just accept what I've said without playing detective?" Exasperated, he said, "I've been thinking about it for some time and Nerissa's illness made it the deciding factor. And no, I haven't found a place yet." His eyes narrowed. "But after last night, I'll start looking immediately."

"What happened last night?" Jacqui's thoughts went to Diamond.

Christopher shook his head and gave her a hopeless smile. "No, I didn't try to seduce our guest, nor she me, Jacqui."

Jacqui flushed. "Then what happened last night?"

"Your brother." Christopher grew angry. "One day we're going to come to blows." He rested one hip on the windowsill and gave his wife a sad look. "At one time, we were friends, but now he hardly speaks unless he's forced to. I can see he's lost respect for me. He thinks I'm living off you and have no love for Nerissa."

"But that's not true," Jacqui said indignantly.

"I know it isn't but he doesn't care enough to come to me like a man would. I'm damn not going to him to explain myself." Christopher stood up.

"Christopher," Jacqui said, standing up and following him to the door that connected their rooms. "Would you wait? I mean, with Nerissa being sick . . . would you wait until after her next test? That's all she needs right now, is to have to deal with you leaving on top of everything else."

Christopher paused. "When's the test?"

"This Monday. The results will be back in a few days."

Christopher thought for a long moment. Once he'd made the decision to get out, he didn't want to delay. No telling how much longer he could continue living in his brother-in-law's house. Resignedly, he said, "Okay. But I'll start looking at places, anyway. Might be some time before something suitable turns up. I want a place big enough so that Nerissa can have privacy when she visits." Christopher's voice was firm. "You okay with that?"

Jacqui let out a deep breath. "I'm okay with that," she breathed.

Christopher nodded. "See ya later," he said and closed the door. Once in his room, Christopher sank down on the bed. He had to get away from her before he grabbed her in his arms and made wild love to her, the way he used to. Sometimes, they'd giggle like two kids wondering if their passionate sounds had Cecelia squirming in her bed. But he had no right and he knew it. Not since Jacqui had followed him five years ago to a hotel and waited long enough until he and the woman were in bed. He'd never forget the hurt look in her eyes and the tears that welled up in them. Jacqui was a strong woman and not a crier. The sight of her that night still haunted him. Afterward, he'd tried to make it up and show how much he loved her. Their lovemaking after that had only been lukewarm. Her desire for him had gone. Soon afterward, he'd moved to his own bedroom and the farce of a marriage had continued for their daughter's benefit. But only hers. The rest of the household was not fooled, especially Steven.

Christopher began to undress. Another surge of anger hit him in the gut. He and Steven had enjoyed a pleasant relationship and it hurt that they could no longer talk man-to-man. He walked resolutely to the bathroom. In less than two weeks, he would be out of here, and his only regret was that he would be leaving his daughter behind.

Nerissa was in the living room when she heard her uncle open the front door. Peering through the white lacy curtains, she saw him get his car and then return to sit on the steps. Soon after, Diamond appeared and Nerissa, unseen, watched the two adults. She could hear their brief conversation and when they left, she sat down on the sofa, drawing her slim legs beneath her. Nerissa liked Diamond and knew instantly that her uncle liked her too. She could tell by the way he looked at her. He used to look at Elise the same way when he thought no one was watching him. Nerissa frowned. There was something different about him though, she thought. The way he acted around Diamond. With Elise, he smiled and always wanted to touch her. But he never smiled with Diamond and he stayed so far away from her.

Nerissa unwound herself and stood up, wondering why grownups liked to pretend with each other. Just like her parents did. She knew they were headed for a divorce and they pretended like nothing was wrong. She wished that they would go ahead and get it over with. If they didn't, she didn't know how long she could stand living in this house. Her uncle refused to send her away to school like she'd asked, telling her that he'd miss her too much. "You'd be the only one," she'd told him, and he'd gotten angry.

Walking upstairs to shower and get ready for breakfast, Nerissa heard her father's angry voice. They were arguing again. Hurrying past their door, Nerissa clutched her stomach as the cramping pain burned her insides. With tears in her eyes, she closed her bedroom door and instead of preparing to wash up, she lay on her bed, doubled up in pain and sobbing softly.

"Hungry?" Steven eyed Diamond over the glass of cranapple juice.

"Famished." It was after eight o'clock and they'd just been served breakfast. Diamond rolled her eyes at Steven. "A jet would have been faster than your scenic route." She dug into the steaming hot flapjacks before they cooled off, then sipped the heavenly smelling fresh-brewed coffee.

"Sorry, couldn't accommodate today." Steven said seriously.

Diamond's eyes widened. "You have one?"

"Not a jet. A friend has a small plane," Steven answered, this time a smile touching his lips. "He gives flying lessons on weekends." He cocked his head. "But I'll hold that thought in case you want to take a class one day."

"Best lose it," Diamond said, getting back to the delicious food. "I fly with a mouth full of prayers and a pocketful of rabbit foots."

"There's actually something that Diamond Drew is afraid of?" Steven looked with renewed curiosity at the young woman.

"Just respectful of things out of my control."

"Are you always in control?"

"Always."

Diamond was warm and not because of the hot brew. His deliberately sexy voice and smoky eyes were doing a number on her libido. And the day was just starting.

"Hmm. Does that make life interesting for you?"

"What do you mean?"

"I think you know," Steven answered in a low voice. "To have absolute control over every nuance of your life leaves nothing to the imagination. The joy of discovery soon disappears."

Diamond gulped down her second cup of coffee. His voice purred like the sexy hum of a drone of pollinating bees, and her secret places grew warm. "You're so sure about that?" she managed, willing her thighs still.

"I am," Steven answered firmly. He finished his second cup of coffee while quietly watching her. "I've made you uncomfortable. Why?"

"Because your subliminal messages are working, just like you intended," Diamond answered, staring at him frankly. "Why do you want to do this?" Her eyes pleaded with him to stop seducing her. Painful memories pushed themselves into her brain, making her head throb. She closed her eyes briefly. "Please don't," she whispered.

Steven, ignoring Diamond's plea for help, deliberately leaned forward, spearing her with a dark look. "It's too late," he murmured. "I thought I could handle this with aplomb and so much nonchalance but"—he shrugged— "I'm not as strong as I thought." He leaned back again but his eyes never wavered. "We both know what happened to us last Friday when I walked into that room." His nostrils flared at the memory. "There's no denying that you felt what I did, is there?"

Diamond shook her head. "No." Her voice was a bare whisper.

Steven expelled a breath. His voice was raw when he said, "I thought so." He continued to hold her with a riveting look. "I wanted you then and later, on the stairs, when I saw you watching me . . . when your tongue darted out of your mouth, it was all I could do to maintain my cool." He took a deep breath. "Last night in the kitchen, and out by the pool, I tricked myself into believing that I could live under the same roof with you, not touching you. Ha! Was I cut down to size when I was in bed and knew that you were right next door! I wanted you in my arms, in my bed." As though relieved of a great pressure, he heaved a great sigh. "So, this morning, I vowed there would be no more pretense between us. Just lay it open." Steven raised a brow. "Only, I don't really have to ask you, do I?"

"Why?" Diamond asked in an awed voice. She was enthralled by all he'd said.

"Because you have the most expressive eyes and they've already told me what I know to be true."

"And that is?"

"That you feel the same as I do. You want me too."

Diamond didn't answer; she just stared at the man who'd

so skillfully read her soul. And her heart? How could she know for certain that her body wasn't misleading her heart again? No, she couldn't let it happen. Not again!

"Diamond?"

Lifting her eyes to his, she could only stare and force herself not to give in to her lust. Surely that was all it was, she told herself.

"So what are we going to do about us?" Steven asked, husky voiced.

"Nothing."

Steven gave her a smoldering look. "You can't be serious."

"We can't." Her voice was barely audible.

"Why?"

"Why? Because . . . because." Suddenly, Diamond shivered. She couldn't make love to this man. She'd promised herself . . .

Steven studied her, watching her nervous shaking. Puzzled, he didn't understand. She was a beautiful, sensuous woman. Surely she realized that, and men coming on to her would definitely not be foreign to her. Finally it hit him! She was scared!

"Are you afraid of me, Diamond?"

Yes! She screamed inwardly. *And of myself!* Aloud, she said, "No."

"Then what is it?" Steven softened his voice. "Am I coming on too strong for you? Would you prefer I wait for a decent interval to pass before I approach you?"

Diamond looked away from the searing heat in his eyes.

Abruptly, Steven stood up. "Let's get out of here," he said.

Diamond excused herself, hurrying off to the ladies' room, where she doused her face with cold water. How easy it would be, she told herself. The inn that he'd driven to was out of the way, quaint, and absolutely gorgeous. How easy to take a room and spend all day making love!

Is that why he chose this place, she wondered. Did he really see that she would be willing to climb into bed with him just because of their mutually strong attraction? Which was nothing more than lust and sex! Her head pounded with questions that had no answers. But she was adamant, resolving not to weaken. She'd promised herself that the next man she made love to would be the man she'd fallen in love with. But how was she to know? she agonized. Her heart had given her false signals twice before.

Steven was standing against the white wooden railing, feet crossed at the ankles. His back was to the door and when it opened, he turned, knowing he'd see her. She'd been upset when she hurried away and he'd waited patiently. Steven studied her closely.

"Are you all right?"

"Fine," Diamond answered in a strong voice.

"Good. Shall we go?"

Diamond nodded. "Back to the house?" She walked beside him to the car.

"No. I promised you a daylong tour." He hesitated before starting the engine. "That is, unless you want to." When she shook her head, he turned the key. Steven drove for a few minutes in silence. Then with a brief look at Diamond, he said, "I never asked. Is there someone waiting in New York? Or have you met someone here?"

Diamond laughed. "In just over six weeks? That is a femme fatale at work!"

Steven was annoyed. "I don't find that laughable. You're a beautiful woman."

Diamond's laughter died. "There's no one." After a slight hesitation, she said, "And you?" Her breathing faltered.

Steven's hands tightened on the steering wheel. "I had a fiancée. She died three years ago. There's no one in my life." After busying himself with getting on the road he wanted, he said calmly, "You're certain to hear all the details."

Recognizing the absence of sadness in his tone, Diamond was curious, and for the first time, wondered how Elise had died.

"I'm sorry," Diamond murmured.

"You are?" Steven said brusquely. "I don't see why. You never knew her."

Shocked, Diamond said, "I thought that expression was to relieve the sorrow and pain of the people left behind," she retorted. "You're cold!"

"Can we drop this, please?" His voice had grown weary and he threw her an odd look.

Wondering where the writer of that sensitive letter had gone, Diamond found it hard to believe that he was sitting beside her. Sensing his sudden rigidity, she could see his thigh muscles tense up beneath his jeans-clad legs, reminding her of his anger a week ago. *This is turning out to be a day of horror instead of a pleasure jaunt,* she thought, suddenly determined to reverse the trend.

Diamond looked with interest at her surroundings. Although she'd done a lot of tours and driving on her own, there was no way she'd covered everything. So she was delighted when she saw the signs leading to McClellanville, a place she'd intended to visit.

"Oh," she exclaimed.

Steven turned to her in surprise. "Back burner?" He felt strangely satisfied that he was responsible for her excitement.

"Yes, kept putting it off," Diamond replied. "The tour brochures are pretty vivid in describing the wrath of Hurricane Hugo and the safe haven hundreds of people found in McClellanville, back in 1989. I want to see the high school that became their refuge. Is it still standing?"

"It is. People are still calling it a miracle," Steven answered. "While the center of the storm was over Charleston thirty-five miles away, the tidal surge rushed on to McClellanville with the speed and force of demons." He paused and shook his head. "You can imagine the terror of the people inside when they heard a new rush of water over the already fierce storm."

"It's amazing no one drowned. I read where the water hit the building with such force and eventually rose up to six feet! Where'd they all run to?" Diamond said in awe.

"Anyplace up high: the stage in the auditorium, the bleachers in the gymnasium. When the water rose to their chests, people held children up over their heads. Mercifully, the waters receded, and miraculously, no one drowned," Steven said.

"Incredible!"

"The will of God," Steven murmured. "The destruction was not to be believed but people are survivors and they rebuild." Gesturing to a structure on Pinckney Street, he said, "Like that."

Diamond looked at the Wappetaw Presbyterian Church building. It looked brand new. When Steven reached Lincoln High School, Diamond got out of the car and walked to the building.

Steven's gaze was on her. From afar she looked so delicate but he knew better. The first time he'd seen her there was no overlooking the shapely, powerful calves, and he could only imagine the smoothness of her firm thighs. The morning had grown warm and sunny, and Diamond had discarded her sweater. Steven observed her movement, assured but graceful, and the craziest thought crossed his mind; he wondered if she could dance. Then he realized that she said she'd danced, but that was then, when she was a kid. He wanted to feel her in his arms as a woman, snuggled close, with her head on his chest, swaying to the smooth crooning of Luther Vandross.

Steven realized that Diamond was walking back to him, a curious look on her face. He wondered if the vision he'd just had was plastered all over his mug and the reason for the twinkle in her eyes.

"Are you all right?" Diamond asked, tilting her head to one side.

"Why wouldn't I be?" Steven answered in a gruff tone.

"Oh, nothing." Turning and gesturing around her, Diamond said, "Thanks for this. No telling when I would have made the trip." She glanced at her watch. "Is there time for more?" she asked hopefully.

"The day is yours," Steven answered, as he opened the door and she slid inside. Relieved that she'd suspected nothing, he moved to the driver's seat with the barest hint of a smile on his lips.

Diamond settled back, amused that she'd caught him in an uncharacteristic daydream. She knew she was the star of it because Steven's eyes never wavered from her body. She'd actually surprised him when she started walking back to him. This man made her so conscious of being a woman, Diamond thought, and she wondered if she was fighting a battle in a war that couldn't be won.

Over the next several hours, the black Lexus covered ground that took them from the Rice Museum in Georgetown to Summerville's Old Town section, with its mid-nineteenth-century charming homes and well-kept gardens. They enjoyed lunch at another beautiful inn and visited some of Steven's fishing haunts.

Once again, almost as if by their previous nonverbal mutual agreement, Steven and Diamond pretended that they were two ordinary people enjoying a gorgeous spring day. They found that they could talk easily on nontaboo subjects. Shared stories about their education, travel, and hobbies were safe and nonthreatening. Finally exhausted, but exhilarated, they rested their tired bones in a quiet restaurant on the Isle of Palms.

"God, this is beautiful," Diamond whispered. They'd chosen to sit at an outside table and they were rewarded with the beautiful red-gold colors of sunset. She looked at Steven. "Thanks for a fabulous day," she said. "Seeing Charleston through the eyes of a native is the way to tour." The fabulous spring day was fast turning into evening, and Diamond's eyes sparkled in the fading light. "Ever wondered what to do with your spare time?"

Steven nodded and said, solemn voiced. "Done that." But his eyes held a teasing smile.

Diamond's brow rose. "You? I don't believe it! Where?"

"Right in Low Country. Me and a buddy, soon as we were able to drive, started our own little business." Steven grinned at the memory. "Was going good for all of two weeks until Russ scratched up his father's prize-winning Ford. The customers sure loved riding in that antique." Steven liked that he'd caused the delightful sound coming from Diamond's throat. Her laugh was refreshing, like shimmering cool water on a summer's day.

"And while Russell was grounded, did the enterprising Steven find a new partner?" Diamond had learned earlier about the friendship between the two young men who'd gone to Meharry Medical College together.

Steven shook his head. "That was the end of my entrepreneurial pursuits," he said. "Especially after my dad got a call from Mr. Padget."

"I think it's great that your friendship lasted through the years."

Steven shrugged. "Yeah, it's been a long time. Since the little red tricycle days."

Diamond watched as Steven glanced down at his beeper. She'd seen him look at it at least twice during the day, when he apparently felt it vibrating against his waist. Both times he ignored the interruption. But now he lifted his portable phone from his shirt pocket.

"Excuse me," Steven said to Diamond as he dialed a number. After a moment, he said brusquely, "Yes? What is it?"

Diamond could see Steven's whole demeanor change. It didn't take a handful of guesses to know that he was talking to a family member.

"She did what?" Steven's eyes narrowed in disbelief as he listened. "How bad is it? Was the fire department necessary?" After a brief look of disgust at Diamond, he stared out into the darkened dunes, while listening to his sister, Jacqui. "Who helped Ferdie put out the fire?" he finally asked, then snorted. "Finally, made himself useful, huh?" After listening to her smart retort, Steven said, "Since everything is under control, there's no reason for me to rush home, is there?" He ended the call and returned the phone to his pocket.

"What happened, Steven?" Diamond asked. Her soft voice brought his angry eyes to hers and she stifled an annoyed sigh. *Is there never any peace?*

"There was a small fire in the kitchen. Nothing major, and Ferdie and Christopher handled it. No need to panic." Regret edged his voice when he added, "I was rude to Jacqui and there was no need."

"How did it start?"

Steven's look was remote. "My mother. For some strange reason she got the urge to cook. She wasn't attentive to what she was doing and the icing she was making burned. How the pot caught on fire is still a mystery to Ferdie. But luckily she and Christopher discovered it when the smoke alarm sounded. My mother just panicked and ran from the kitchen."

"Icing?" Diamond could only stare at Steven as she held her breath.

"Yes." Wrinkles creased Steven's forehead. "It's the strangest thing," he said as if to himself. "Mam hasn't baked a cake since my father died ten years ago. It was his favorite and she hated it."

Diamond fingered the amethyst at her neck. "What kind?" she whispered.

"Coconut," Steven answered. Then, concern filling his eyes, he said, "Diamond, are you all right?"

SEVEN

Steven rushed to Diamond's side, fearful that she would slide out of the chair. He felt her pulse and was amazed at the rapidity. Her palms were clammy and beads of perspiration covered her forehead. She looked faint, and he held her head down and rubbed an ice cube across the back of her neck. After a few seconds he felt her relax, and she sat back. Steven pulled up a chair and sat down next to her. He still held her hand, while staring at her curiously.

"Thanks," Diamond said. Her voice was strong and she drank some cold water.

"Feeling better?" Steven was highly aware of her slender fingers lying limply in his big hand. The tender but innocent touch was almost anathema to his body, because he was suddenly consumed by a fire that had to be the work of demons. His resolve was shattered when her head dipped onto his shoulder and she shuddered. Putting an arm around her shoulders, Steven held her close. He shut his eyes against the demons continuing to run amok.

Diamond lifted her head. Moving away from Steven, she pulled her hand from his. "I'm fine," she managed to say. "I think maybe we should leave, now."

Steven continued to regard Diamond closely. In the manner of his profession, he took her pulse again, this time relegating his emotions to the hinterlands of his mind. Satisfied that she was okay, he nodded and stood up.

"Yes, it's been a long day." Picking her navy sweater up from the back of her chair, he said, "Put this on." In silence, he watched her comply. Minutes after settling the bill, they were walking to his car.

"What happened back there, Diamond?" Steven asked. He stopped in his tracks, a sudden thought hitting him in the gut. "You're not ill, are you?"

The worry in his voice overwhelmed Diamond to the point of her touching his arm. "Oh, no, Steven, I'm in excellent health. I'm sorry if I scared you." She gazed up at him with an apologetic smile.

It was too dark to look into her eyes, so Steven accepted what she said with resignation. But something had scared her breathless and he wasn't about to let it slide.

Diamond's wanting to put Steven at ease seemed the most natural thing in the world, so she thought nothing of sliding her hand down his arm, slipping her hand in his.

Startled at first, Steven's reaction to her touch was spontaneous. He stopped, and grasping her by the shoulders, bent his head. Steven's mouth covered Diamond's hungrily as days of yearning turned into reality. Her full, pouty lips were as soft as he'd imagined, and he tasted them like a starving man, when she responded in kind, wrapping her arms around his waist. His kiss deepened as a soft sigh escaped between her parted lips. God, how he'd longed for this.

Diamond sighed as she pressed into Steven's hardened body, his kisses searing her lips and her senses. His back was a mass of hard muscle, and Diamond craved to feel his bare skin beneath her hands. She wanted to taste him, and the tip of her tongue darted out to fleck his lips and his chin. The bristly hairs of his mustache tickled her, heightening the sensation that heated her body. She was overcome with passion for this man. Suddenly, Diamond came to her senses. She couldn't let this go on. This was how it had started in the past. What would he think? No, she had come too far, schooled herself too well to be fooled again.

"Steven," Diamond said. She stepped away from him.

Dazed, Steven stared at the changed woman. Seconds ago she was a ball of fiery passion and now she stood before him as if they'd never touched, as if she'd willed an invisible sheet of ice to cover her body. Steven could sense the heated passion drying up inside of her.

"I know," he said, tersely. "We can't. Let's go home, Diamond."

When Steven pulled into the driveway, he knew that their relationship had reverted back to one of polite distance. And when they entered the house, no one would think that the day had been anything more than a pleasant excursion around the city. An employer with his employee.

Ferdie met them at the door, her long fish tail braid resting on her chest. She smiled at them both but said to Steven, "No need to have rushed home. Your mother's okay."

Brushing past her, Steven said brusquely, "It was well past time. Where is she?" He snatched his medical bag off the foyer table.

"Bedroom," Ferdie answered, raising a brow. She looked at Diamond, then at Steven's retreating back.

"Good night," Diamond said, rushing up the staircase.

Ferdie looked at her watch. It was not even eight o'clock. "Good night?" she said to the empty foyer and walked to her room, her eyes glimmering with curiosity.

Hoping she wouldn't see a soul, Diamond rushed into her room and closed the door. Her heart was beating faster than it should and she hurried to the bathroom and doused her face with cold water. Her head started to pound and the ringing in her ears wouldn't stop. With shaking hands she poured a glass of water and downed two aspirin.

Fifteen minutes later, Diamond was calm enough to sit up in the big bed and try to think clearly. Why had she reacted so violently to that one word? Coconut cake was the favorite dessert for thousands of people, and they all didn't live in Crown Heights in Brooklyn, New York. She grinned at the thought. Her mother and Peaches wouldn't have sworn to that on a holiday weekend!

Diamond had removed her shirt and jeans, and she hugged her bare knees, resting her chin on them as she wrestled with her thoughts. *You're smart, educated, and don't believe in ghosts or reincarnation,* she argued sensibly. *And Phyllis Yarborough is not living downstairs in the body of that horrible person, so lose that thought!* Diamond searched the recesses of her brain to recall everything she'd ever heard about the transference of personalities to heart recipients. The frank conversations she'd had with her mother and Peaches caused a jumble of confusion and she impatiently sorted them, trying to ferret out important words or phrases.

"*Mechanical pump!* That's all the human heart is," said Peaches.

"You're wrong," answered Phyllis. "It's part of the spirit."

Diamond argued, "It is not. It's just another organ that when it's broke you fix it. You don't *replace* it like you would a car engine!"

Phyllis looked kindly at her daughter. "One day you'll understand, sweetie."

Diamond shifted in the bed, shaking away the image of her mother's kind face and the memory of her soft voice. "But I don't understand, Mama," she said aloud, suddenly feeling lonely and frightened. "What if you and all those others are right?" she whispered. *What if genes and energy from her mother's body were transferred?* A shiver went down her spine, and Diamond reached for the phone.

"Diamond," Peaches said, when she heard her god-daughter's voice. "What's wrong?"

Just the sound of the familiar voice was enough to settle Diamond and she almost regretted making the panic call. "I'm okay, Peaches. Just acting stupid in my old age. Wanted to hear your voice, I guess."

Peaches frowned as she motioned to her worried-looking husband that Diamond was okay. But Peaches didn't believe it for a minute. Quietly, she said, "When you called me three days ago you sounded fine about taking that job, thinking that it was what you needed." Fearful, she asked, "What happened to upset you only one day after moving in?"

"Can't fool you, Godmother," Diamond replied.

"Do you want to?"

"No."

"Then tell me what happened." Peaches softened her tone. "You knew that it wouldn't be easy, Diamond. As close as you and your mother were, what you're doing could only bring you more pain instead of closure." After hesitating, she said, "Promise me, that you won't tough it out if things go badly?"

"I'm stubborn, not masochistic," Diamond responded lightly, finally beginning to feel her old self. She settled back against the pillows and began relating all—except one private moment—that had happened to her since her arrival at the Rumford house.

"Bet you can't top any of that," Diamond teased. "Hello? Hello? Are you there?"

Peaches, was slow in answering. What in heaven's name had that girl gone and gotten herself into, she wondered? She couldn't imagine such a good-natured person surviving among such a family of misfits. "I'm here."

"So, who's right? You, me, or Mama?" Diamond sighed.

"It's really not that cut-and-dried after all, is it?" Peaches said. Frustration put a frown on her face. "I'm afraid I can't help you on this one, Diamond. I have to do a lot of soul-searching. Much as I loved and miss my friend, I had to let her go. I've accepted that and I can't imagine telling myself that her spirit followed her heart to Charleston."

Diamond heard the doubt and pain in her friend's voice. "I know that I have to do this on my own, Peaches," she said in a soft voice. "We both know that. It's just that I became unglued for a minute. It was the first time that I was actually confronted with anything that was even remotely smacking of the possibility of transference."

After a few minutes, Diamond said good-bye, promising to call again soon and swore that the next time she would have brighter stories to tell.

The next morning, Diamond awakened to find she'd slept in her bra and panties. Stretching and yawning, she felt good, rested to the point of laziness after her event-filled day. It was Sunday and she intended to do absolutely nothing. Vaguely wondering if the Rumfords were church-goers she listened for sounds of movement but heard none. If they were, she reasoned, surely at seven-thirty in the morning someone would be stirring. Diamond was an occasional attendee, the denomination notwithstanding. But today she elected to remain quiet, probably sort through her wardrobe again, and maybe find a chat on the Net. Definitely nothing as strenuous or as emotional as yesterday.

The bright sun beckoned to her, making her think it would also be the perfect day to christen that fabulous pool. Hoping the sun was as warm as it looked, Diamond went to the window and, drawing aside the drapes and curtains, pushed it up. She looked down in surprise. Poised to dive, his back to her, was Steven. In a second he sprang high off the board and dived gracefully, slicing the water with little splash. He surfaced and swam the length of the pool twice before he climbed out. Without warning, he looked up and stared at her. Startled, Diamond stepped back. She was still in her underwear. Backing up out of view, Diamond licked her lips. Was that what she was clinging to last night? The strong body she'd melted into and fantasized about met all her expectations at first sight. The man's abs were tight, and she wondered if he lifted. The brief red swimsuit made a dramatic picture against his deep brown skin. Dying for another secret look, Diamond peered out the window but was surprised. He'd gone.

"It's a crime to look that good," Diamond muttered. She had to work out to keep herself fit in order to do her job as a therapist. Her clients hardly needed someone putting them through their paces who was huffing and puffing every grueling inch. Surprised at the knock on her door, she hastily put on a robe. "Just a minute," she called. She opened it to find Steven standing there in rubber thongs and belted white terry robe.

"Good . . . morning," she managed.

Steven looked her over as though surprised. "Good morning," he said. "I saw you standing at the window and wondered if you were feeling too shy to come down because I was there." He saw she didn't understand. Gesturing at her attire, he said, "From down there, it looked like you were in a suit." He turned to go. "Sorry."

"I—was thinking about it; that's why I went to the window."

"Then would you come do some laps and afterward join me for breakfast?" Steven said.

"I'd like that," Diamond answered, feeling relaxed in his presence. Nothing in his voice or attitude indicated his anger, from last night. "What time is breakfast?"

"Anytime. Apparently everyone is skipping church today. We usually attend service at the Friendship A.M.E. church on Royal Avenue, but my mother informed me she'll be resting all day," Steven replied, keeping his eyes on her face. "On Sundays, things're usually informal. Fer-

die, even though it's her day off, helps with the cooking.
Says it keeps her hand in, besides the fact that she likes
to eat, so she fixes a batch of stuff and leaves it warming.
Lunch is on your own and Jacqui prepares an early dinner
about four. Says she loves to cook and never gets the
chance. The one stipulation she has is that everyone show
up to eat."

"Sounds like the perfect Sunday to me," Diamond answered. "Give me a few seconds and I'll be right down."

Steven's lashes flickered. "See you outside," he said.

Diamond showered and was in a one-piece tangerine
maillot and walking to the pool in less than fifteen minutes. The morning was warmer than she expected and she
hoped the water was just as inviting.

Steven saw her shudder as she pulled an obvious favorite—a New York University sweatshirt—over her head and
stepped out of a pair of clear-colored clogs.

"It's heated," he said, amused at her hopping-around antics while dreading the first splash of cold water. He
couldn't help grinning when she ran to the board and without preamble dived in, cutting a wide swath with her noisy
dive.

Steven watched her cut the surface and begin her laps.
He grew thoughtful as he saw the unpretentiousness of the
woman. Another type of person would have thought twice
about wearing a worn school sweat and unglamorous clogs
the first time swimming with a strange man. Well, not exactly a stranger, after all. He remembered vividly the taste
of her delicious lips. Steven stood up and threw off the
robe. "Wrong thoughts, my man," he muttered, as he dived
in without using the diving board.

They swam neck and neck for three laps before Diamond called it quits. While she dried off, Steven took two
more and then climbed out of the pool, joining her at the
table.

"Were we racing?" he asked, a smile parting his lips.

"I could lie and say no," Diamond said, returning the smile. She poured the hot coffee for them both and pushed his cup toward him. She didn't know how the pot had gotten there, but she was grateful. The outdoor temperature was barely sixty degrees.

"Then you lost," Steven said smugly, his eyes laughing with her.

"I thought I was pretty swift, but you're good." She tilted her cup.

"Thanks. I try to jump in most mornings; otherwise, good intentions." He was interrupted by Ferdie arriving and setting a tray down on the table.

"Don't know what's wrong with you two," she said. "I don't care if the pool is heated. Hurry up and eat this while it's hot and then bring yourselves inside before you'll both be needing a doctor." She turned and walked back inside.

"Thanks, Ferdie," Diamond called after the woman. With the look the housekeeper threw her way, Diamond wasn't all that certain of the reason Ferdie'd given for her gesture. She caught Steven's look and realized he had the same thought. Ferdie had wanted them to eat alone.

"The rest of the house must be up." A humorless smile touched his lips before Steven started to eat. "She's right, though," he said. "Better eat fast, because there's nothing worse than cold lumpy grits and greasy ham."

Diamond finished her second cup of coffee and then started to stack their dishes on the tray. Steven helped, and their hands touched. Neither of them said a word as they continued to clear.

"What a great way to start a lazy day. Thanks for coming to get me, Steven."

"My pleasure," he answered, balancing the laden tray.

Diamond walked beside him carrying the coffeepot. She became thoughtful. After being in his presence only three times, one of them for at least twelve hours, she could sense his change of moods. The hour that had just passed showed a different man from the one that was walking beside her. Diamond could feel him tense up as they approached the back door to the kitchen. *He hates his home!* Steven reminded her of a man on a solitary walk on a lonely road knowing that despair waited for him at the end of it. She was so touched that she wanted to console him, but common sense told her that there wasn't a thing in the world she could do to help him.

Ferdie watched the doctor and Diamond from the kitchen window and she hummed and cleaned off the counter, trying hard not to take her eyes off the relaxed looking couple. Before, she'd known exactly what would happen when the two people outside came in from their swim and found the rest of the family in the kitchen looking for breakfast. Caustic remarks from Cecelia and sly looks from Christopher would make Steven disappear with a scowl and Diamond would be embarrassed. To prevent that, she'd decided to give them more time to themselves by serving them breakfast by the pool. This was the first time in months that the doctor had spent the entire weekend in his own bed and she suspected that Diamond was the reason why. Ferdie was pleased with herself that she'd given Steven a few peaceful minutes. Now she watched them approach the house and she was there to open the door.

"Thanks, Ferdie," Steven said as he put the tray on the counter. He looked surprised to see that she was in the room alone. "Where's everybody?"

"Gone. Off doing their thing, I suppose. Christopher fixed a tray for himself and Jacqui and took it upstairs. Cecelia preferred to eat in her room. Nerissa never did come down. At least not while I was around." She smiled at Diamond. "So how'd you like the swimming pool? You'll be out there a lot, especially in the summer. Cecelia loves to swim and sun."

"It's great, Ferdie, and thanks a lot for breakfast. It was a treat."

"No, it was my treat," she said, a mysterious smile parting her lips. "Now, I think both of you better go and get out of those wet suits."

"Is Cecelia feeling all right?" Diamond inquired. Steven hadn't mentioned his mother at all, this morning.

"Sure. She's fine. Go on now. I'm just getting the kitchen ready for Jacqui to do her thing."

Diamond and Steven were walking upstairs when she glanced at his face. "What's wrong, Steven?"

"I don't like it that Nerissa skipped breakfast." Anger filled his eyes. *Her mother has breakfast in bed and doesn't know that her daughter may be sick in her room, too ill to eat?*

"Maybe she didn't. Ferdie could have missed seeing her."

"Possible." He stopped at Nerissa's door, hesitant to knock. *She's entitled to her privacy, after all,* he thought. Turning away, Steven said, "I'll check in on her later. She probably wants a lazy day too." He was rewarded with a tiny smile.

They stopped at Diamond's bedroom door. Steven's gaze traveled from her feet to her neck, then captured her dark eyes. "This suit has nothing over the one I *thought* you had on, though I like this one too." His smile hinted of mysteries. "Don't be late for dinner." He slipped easily into his room and closed the door softly.

Diamond was very effectively unclothed, and her jaw dropped at the sensation of nakedness she felt. She looked down the hall. If anyone else had seen, she wondered if they had also noticed her pleasure. Surely they couldn't have missed the quiver that had passed over her.

But Diamond didn't really care who saw. She knew only that she liked his feathery glance tickling her body. It was like a silken whisper, promising unspeakable delights.

By late afternoon, Diamond had finished inventorying her wardrobe and found that she could use some new dresses. A little irked, she wished that Cecelia would've taken the time to mention her itinerary for the week so that Diamond could have a mental picture of what to lay out. "I guess that would make life too easy," Diamond muttered.

Bored and still feeling full from a sandwich she'd eaten only an hour ago, Diamond flopped down in the big chair ready to watch some television until dinner, which was only an hour and a half away. Except for music and sounds of voices every now and then, the house was quiet. She knew that Steven was out because soon after she'd showered and was drying her hair, Diamond had heard the roar of his Ducati and then the fading sound as he drove away. She never heard him return. Happy that he'd gotten away, she went about her day, feeling more contented then she had in the past few days.

Diamond clicked the mute button on the TV remote and listened. Was that crying? Frowning, she got up and went to her door and listened before opening it. Silence. Closing the door she sat down again but left the mute button depressed. She heard the soft sound again, coming from her—bathroom? Her feet were muffled over the carpet as she opened the door and listened. Nothing. Knowing she wasn't hearing things, Diamond tried the old glass trick—holding a tumbler to the wall and pressing her ear against it. Still nothing. She frowned, putting down the glass.

"Now, I know I'm surrounded by some strange folk," she murmured, "but crazy I'm not. I haven't been here long enough!" Always determined to prove herself right, Diamond stepped out into the hall, and walking to Nerissa's door, she knocked softly. There was no answer and no sound of sobbing. Puzzled, about to return to her room, she heard a noise. There was a door next to Nerissa's that Diamond had assumed was a closet of some sort since it wasn't on the tour that Ferdie had given her. Opening it, she was surprised to see that it led to a short flight of stairs. Curious, she closed the door and walked up the steps to find a huge room that covered half that side of the house. It was used as an attic-type storage room. There was a little light that filtered in through the pulled-down shade.

Standing still until her eyes could make out images, Diamond looked around and spotted Nerissa. She was hunched up in an ancient-looking grandfather chair that must have been grandiose in its time.

"Nerissa? Are you okay?" Uninvited, Diamond walked closer to the young girl, who simply stared with a wary expression. Pulling up another tattered relic of a chair, Diamond sat down. "Want to talk about it?" She saw the wadded tissue in Nerissa's lap that couldn't possibly handle another teardrop. Digging into her slacks pocket, Diamond handed the girl some crumpled tissues.

"Clean and dry." Diamond waited until Nerissa blew her nose and appeared to accept her presence before speaking. "I know a simple tissue isn't the cure-all you need, but at least you're good to go for another session if you want." Diamond smiled and winked at the surprised girl.

"Thanks," Nerissa said, staring at Diamond. No grown person, not even Elise, had acted so down to earth. Maybe because Diamond was younger? "How old are you?" she asked.

Surprised, Diamond cocked her head at Nerissa and scrunched up her face. "Well, before I was born, way back in the sixties, there used to be a saying by young folks: 'Don't trust anyone over thirty.' Ever hear that before?" When Nerissa shook her head, Diamond answered, "I'm twenty-eight." Sighing theatrically, she asked, "*Now*, do you want to talk about it?"

Nerissa laughed suddenly, and Diamond could see the sparkle in her luminous eyes, even in the sparse light. *Success at last,* she thought. *So much for the over-thirty crowd!*

"I think so," Nerissa answered.

"Great." Diamond peered around. "Is there any light up here?"

"Sure." Nerissa unfolded herself from the chair and walked to the wall by the door and flipped a switch. A small-wattage bulb added a dim light to the room.

Diamond reached down to pick up the tissues that had fallen out of Nerissa's lap and her hand folded around something hard. She didn't have to look down to know what she was holding. She'd carried enough of them when she thought she'd been in love. Unsure of what to say, it was too late. Nerissa was staring at the two condom packets, with widened eyes. Diamond could see the doubt spreading over her face and the decision to renege on her promise to talk. *That ain't gonna happen,* Diamond determined. Standing up and walking around, she peered into shadowy corners, peeking under dusty cloths and nosing into covered chests. Feeling Nerissa's eyes on her, Diamond could almost hear the young girl relax.

"This is some room you have, to think in private," Diamond said in an envious tone. "When I wanted to get away, I used to go upstairs to my godmother's apartment." Diamond had resumed her same seat and Nerissa followed suit, once again folding her legs beneath her in the oversize chair.

"How was that getting away to someplace private?" Nerissa was skeptical.

"She had a mad room and she let me use it whenever I needed to," Diamond answered. "Whenever Mama and me didn't see eye to eye on a lot of things, to keep from eating the soap she fed me when I smart-mouthed her, I went up to Peaches's. I stayed as long as I wanted, trying to sort out why my mother was being so unreasonable."

Rolling her eyes to the ceiling, Nerissa let out another laugh. "*She* was unreasonable?"

"And parents can't be sometimes?" Diamond said in a huff.

Subdued once again, Nerissa said in a low voice, "They can. A lot."

Diamond didn't want to go there, at least not yet. Holding out the condoms to her, she said, "Do you want these back?"

Hesitant, Nerissa nodded and took them, pushing them inside her jeans pocket.

"Is that the reason for your tears?" Diamond asked softly.

Nerissa said, "Sort of."

"Tears because he didn't use one and it's too late or tears because you're not sure you want to use 'em?" Diamond's eyes saddened as she remembered stories told to her about another fourteen-year old girl in this same predicament. But that young girl didn't have a caring mom or a godmother with a mad room. But she did have an older woman as a friend. Phyllis Yarborough.

"I'm not pregnant."

Diamond suppressed the relieved sigh. "How do you know?"

"I'm just not."

"Because he protected you?" Diamond was softly persistent.

"No."

Diamond frowned. "I don't understand, Nerissa. If he didn't use protection, how can you be so sure?"

"Because . . . we . . . I . . . we never did it." Her eyes welled up. "Not . . .yet," she whispered.

"Not . . ." Diamond wasn't ready for that. She shifted in her chair. "With him, you mean?"

"Him . . . or anybody," Nerissa answered. She lowered her head in shame.

Diamond saw, and anger flared up inside her, but her voice was calm when she said, "You're still a virgin."

Nerissa nodded, refusing to meet Diamond's eyes. A tear fell.

"And you're ashamed of that." Diamond's fingers pressed deeply into her palms. "Nerissa, look at me."

When the young girl raised her head, Diamond said, "Why do you feel ashamed?"

"Because I'm the only one left. Me and Letty."

"Left? Don't tell me. You and Letty are the only teenage virgins left in the neighborhood."

"So we're told by our friends," Nerissa said indignantly.

"So that makes you outcasts until you give it up."

Nerissa stared at Diamond. "Sounds like you know all about it."

Diamond shrugged. "I'm almost thirty. I know things."

That brought a small giggle.

"Look, Nerissa, if you feel so ashamed, then why do you cry about it? Why not just go ahead and do it if it will get you liked and accepted?"

"I . . . I tried to. Last week," she said miserably.

Last Friday, Diamond thought. When Nerissa had the house in an uproar over her absence.

"You cut school to . . . to lose your virginity?"

"Yeah," Nerissa sighed. "We were supposed to meet in the Battery Park in Low Country and then go somewhere. To whoever's parents were out."

"We? You and Letty?" Diamond's stomach knotted.

Nerissa grew angry. "Letty copped out. Had me waiting in the park and she never showed up. I figured I didn't need her anyway, so I went with them."

"Them? How many?"

"Two. Just B. J. and his friend Ki."

"So what happened when you went with them?"

"We drove to Ki's house on America Street, because B. J.'s sister was home sick."

"Drove? B. J. has a car?"

"No, B. J. is fifteen. It's Ki's car. He's eighteen," Nerissa answered.

The more she heard, the more Diamond became furious. "What did you do, Nerissa?" she asked softly.

"I left them standing in front of Ki's house and took the bus back to town."

"Why did you do that?"

"Because I didn't want to do it with Ki around. B. J. knew how I felt about that. So I just left."

Diamond looked at Nerissa, knowing there was more that the girl wanted to say. Otherwise why would she still be crying about it a week later? And holding condoms.

"All week, B. J.'s been after me, coming around to the school. Said any girl he took to his year-end school party had to be really his or . . ."

"Or he'd take someone else unless you have sex with him," Diamond said. She looked at the pocket where the condoms were. "You still don't want to, do you? That's why the tears?"

Nerissa nodded. "I don't want to. Not with him or anybody." Her voice dropped. "I just don't feel that way, and I wonder why everybody else does and not me. So I agreed to meet him tonight to just get it over with. Then I'll be just like everybody else and he'll leave me alone." Her eyes grew wide with fright. "But now I've changed my mind again and if I don't go, no telling what he'll do."

"Tonight? You were planning to sneak out tonight?" Diamond sounded worried.

"No. After dinner I'm supposed to meet with Letty to make plans for the party."

"Instead, you were going to meet B. J." Diamond looked thoughtful. "Who's driving you to Letty's?"

"No one. I walk there."

"Well, not tonight," Diamond said, suddenly smiling at the look on Nerissa's face. "Dry those beautiful eyes and come give me a tour around this grand old stuff. Nothing I like better than snooping in old trunks. Never know what you'll find."

Nerissa stared at Diamond with amazement.

"Well, come on now," insisted Diamond. "Don't think about B. J. After dinner's plenty of time to do that."

Nerissa laughed softly and went to join Diamond as she lifted the lid of an old steamer trunk. Her dilemma was momentarily forgotten as she wondered about this stranger from New York City.

Cecelia's eyes flashed. "She's your daughter. When are you going to start disciplining that child? She probably took off on another one of her silly little treks."

Jacqui eyed her mother dangerously. "Your type of discipline is enough for my child to handle and I'm warning you to stop. I've had enough and I'm darn well certain Nerissa has," she snapped. Forgetting her mother for the moment, she glanced at her watch. "She knows we eat at exactly four-thirty. Where is she? Have you seen her today, Christopher?" Jacqui eyed her husband hopefully.

"We had lunch together," Christopher replied, looking worried. "I haven't seen her since around one."

"As her mother, why haven't you seen your child at least once today?" Steven's eyes were dark and his voice was like ice as he stared at his sister.

"Don't you start with me, Steven," Jacqui warned heatedly. But her voice cracked as her eyes pleaded with her brother for help. "Not again. Has she run away this time?"

Steven eyes softened as he stared at his sister. She really was concerned and he hadn't heard her talk back to their mother like that since she was a teenager and had gotten slapped for her rebelliousness. He stood up. "She's around." He indicated Diamond's empty chair. "Did anyone think of them being together?" Everyone looked at him and then at each other as he walked to the living room and returned in seconds. "Diamond's car is here, so they must be in her room," he said easily. "I'll go check."

Jacqui made a relieved sound. "Why didn't I think of

that? Nerissa used to visit Elise . . ." She stopped as her brother stiffened. "Steven, I'm sorry . . ." But her brother was already walking from the room.

Steven stopped briefly on the landing. Why had he elected himself to go fetch? Any of the others could have gone as well. Did he really miss her that much all day? While riding today, his thoughts kept drifting to the day before and then to this morning when he'd seen her at the window. Yes, he finally admitted, the inevitable had happened. Diamond Drew had gotten under his skin. The question was how was he going to play the hand? He started up the stairs again and headed down the hall to her room, when he stopped. "Riss?" he muttered. His niece's laugh came from the attic.

"Riss?" Steven was standing in the doorway, looking from Nerissa to Diamond. Both were on their knees, pawing over things in his father's old trunk. Neither had heard him because of their intense chatter, one trying to talk over the other. He fell back against the wall in amazement. He'd never known his niece had such a head full of words. And laughing? When Diamond's laugh joined hers, the sound was like sleigh bells. Speechless, he watched, enjoying the rare sound in his house, but Diamond turned and saw him and the laugh died in her throat.

"Steven!" she said.

"Hi, Unc," Nerissa said.

"Diamond. Nerissa." Steven acknowledged them with a nod. "I'm the militia," he said solemnly.

Diamond glanced at her watch. It was almost five o'clock. "Oh my God," she exclaimed. "Dinner."

Steven stared at them, looking each one over with a skeptical eye.

"As hungry as everyone is, I think they can wait a few more minutes for you ladies to wash up," Steven said. His eyes twinkled. "I'll go tell them, but I wouldn't take more than ten minutes to come down. Tops."

They scrambled to their feet, and Steven turned and left, a wide grin splitting his face. Going down the stairs, he walked just as slowly, but only because the spring in his step might send him sprawling head over heels to the hard-wood floor below.

EIGHT

It was early Monday morning when Diamond heard the muted sound of the diving board and then the soft ker-plunk of a body piercing the water. She knew Steven was doing his laps but this time she stayed away from the window. *No need to get warm and sticky with lascivious thoughts just after she'd showered.* And she hoped that her body would behave at the breakfast table. She also hoped that Steven would find somewhere else to look with those sexy eyes. Last night it was all she could do to make intelligent conversation with the rest of the family. Like a magnet his eyes drew hers to his time and again until she wondered if anyone else noticed. Apparently finding his niece with her and *laughing* had done something to him, because Diamond caught him looking at her in a new light. Behind the ever-present desire for her body was something else. It was as though he had come to realize that he *liked* her. Before the meal ended, Diamond was more than ready to leave the table. As she and Nerissa excused themselves, she had hurried—no, escaped—from the room. She'd already explained to everyone that she would drive Nerissa to her friend's house since she was passing by Letty's, and had assured Jacqui that she would bring Nerissa back home.

Sounds from the backyard had stopped. Diamond finished making her bed, finger-combed her hair into the spiked peaks, and checked herself in the dresser mirror.

She'd chosen an undecorated sheath dress with capped sleeves and a round neckline. It was black, and she chose matching suede flats. Instead of her amethyst jewelry, she wore a plain gold chain and gold ball earrings. Satisfied that she would be presentable no matter where she wound up with Cecelia today, she left the bedroom.

Just as Diamond reached the foyer, she heard a car driving away and for some reason she knew it was Steven. Should she feel relief or deprivation? After three days of a constant sensual high, she decided that her body and brain would definitely experience deprivation. Entering the dining room, she realized that she was actually going to miss him and was already wishing the day away.

"Good morning, Diamond." Cecelia's critical eye roved over Diamond from head to toe, lingering on the unique hairdo. For the second time in the last few days she experienced the strangest longing to adopt a similar carefree hairstyle. But the moment passed quickly. What would she look like appearing in public with short peasy hair? And wherever had the notion come from?

"Good morning, Cecelia." Diamond sat down, surprised that no one else was at the table. "Where is everyone?" she asked. She turned as Tina came in carrying two plates. "Good morning. How was your weekend, Tina?"

"Mornin', Diamond. Just fine, thank you very much," Tina said with a big smile. "Here you go. Just let me know if you want seconds." After setting the plates before them, she left.

"To answer your question, Diamond," Cecelia said, as she began to eat, "Steven is at the hospital today and Nerissa has early make-up classes. Jacqui and Christopher are rarely seen this early."

At the last, Diamond frowned but kept her thoughts to herself.

"Something wrong with your food Diamond?" Cecelia buttered another hot roll and bit into it.

"No. But since you asked, I was wondering why breakfast is served in the dining room so formally when hardly anyone is here to enjoy it."

"Well, I dare think of myself as hardly anyone!" Cecelia answered in a huff.

"Oh, Cecelia, I think you know what I mean. It's just that the kitchen is so big, the table seats eight, and it's an absolutely gorgeous room!" She shrugged as she ate a spoonful of peaches. "And Tina won't have to carry back and forth."

"My God, girl, you do have a mouth, don't you?" Cecelia wasn't so sure she liked so much forthrightness so early in the morning. Especially when it wasn't coming from her son, and lately her daughter had been getting pretty verbal. *What's happening to these people?* she wondered.

Diamond said, "It's just a thought. You know, when people do things for so long for a reason and then when situations change, no one ever looks at why they're still doing the same things they do when there's really no longer any need?"

Taken aback, Cecelia looked at Diamond in surprise. She'd never thought about it, but there was a ring of truth to the girl's convoluted statement!

"Cyril loved that room."

"Cyril?" Diamond asked.

"My late husband." Remembering, Cecelia spoke as though to herself. "Cyril built that kitchen and he always loved it. Made it for his family. He said that dining rooms were for stuffy company who liked to brag they dined with the doctor." Cecelia wasn't aware that she was smiling and fondly rubbing her diamond wedding band. As if realizing she wasn't alone, she looked at Diamond, who was staring at her frankly. Cecelia poured more coffee, busying herself with the minor task. "When my mother came to live with us it was more convenient to use this room," she said, stiffly. "After her death, we never went back to using the kitchen." Absently, she added, "It really is beautiful, isn't it?"

Diamond believed if she had answered, Cecelia would not have heard, so she ate in silence. It was almost as if the woman had shown her persona of a time long past and when discovered, became embarrassed and cloaked herself again with the cold, unfeeling exterior. Why? Diamond wondered. Who would mind more glimpses of a gentler, kinder Cecelia? Was this Cecelia Rumford then a lie? Very curious, thought Diamond.

"Nerissa? What about her?" Diamond said, realizing that Cecelia had spoken.

"I said that you and the girl became pretty chummy in such a short time," Cecelia replied with a touch of asperity in her voice. "Last night, the child really could have walked three blocks, dear. There's no sense in spoiling her."

"I doubt that you'll have to worry about that very much, Cecelia. I haven't seen anything that remotely resembles that behavior since I've been here." *Hush your mouth, girl!* Diamond saw the older woman's eyes flash lightning bolts and then narrow to slits, and she knew her mouth had done it now. Cecelia Rumford attacks like a wildcat when someone so much as befriends her granddaughter. Why does she hate such a sweet girl? *Lord, here it comes!*

"You were hired to be *my* companion, Diamond Drew, and it will do you well to remember that! There are enough people in this house to see to my granddaughter's needs when necessary." Cecelia pushed away from the table, preparing to leave, but then fell back in the chair and briefly closed her eyes.

"Are you feeling all right?" Diamond asked, watching closely as Cecelia opened her little blue bag and started removing her medicine bottles.

"Yes, yes," Cecelia said impatiently. She began swallowing pills.

Every meal that Diamond had taken with her, Cecelia never failed to open the bag that always sat on the table close to her plate. Diamond watched.

"I have to take these every day for the rest of my life. Anti-rejection drugs." Her mouth twisted in a grimace. "My heart will love me for it."

Diamond almost shrank at the words but kept expression from her voice and face when she quietly said, "I think it already has."

Cecelia glanced over at Diamond, wondering at the curious remark. "What do you mean by that?" she asked, continuing to down her lifesaving pills. *She sounds as though the organ had a life of its own,* Cecelia thought.

"The very fact that you're alive is because someone cared enough to donate his or her organs. You received the most precious gift of all," Diamond said, giving Cecelia a direct look. Then, at the startled look on the older woman's face, Diamond softened her voice. "I meant that someone loved a stranger enough to give a part of himself." She shrugged. "That's all."

Cecelia closed her medicine bag and gave her outspoken companion a long look, wondering if she'd done the right thing in hiring this woman who wasn't about to bite her tongue for anyone—not even her employer.

Cecelia was wearing rimless glasses, and she dipped her head to stare over them at Diamond. "You sound like some members of my group," she said in disgust.

"Group?"

"You haven't forgotten my heart transplant support group?"

Diamond shook her head, curious at the sudden look of fright that had appeared in the woman's eyes, then disappeared. "I remember," she replied.

"Every time we meet now, someone has had some kind

of experience that they absolutely *must* share," Cecelia said. Her voice was tinged with annoyance. "I have no patience to listen to such nonsense. If you ask me, I think they intentionally dredge up these stories only to make a remarkable statement at our meetings. Apparently looking for attention. You'll see for yourself today."

"Today?" Diamond answered, surprised. She was certain that Cecelia had never mentioned her plans before now.

"Yes. Every April a week is given to National Organ and Tissue Donor Awareness. Consequently, there are several events planned in the city that speak to the subject." Cecelia paused. "I'm scheduled to appear at Roper Hospital in Low Country to speak to an audience about my transplantation experience. I wasn't going to attend, but I've changed my mind now that I'm feeling better."

"Speak?" Diamond raised a brow. Cecelia didn't appear to be the type of person to willingly share her private experiences, especially with strangers.

"I don't see why you're surprised, Diamond," Cecelia said, noting the young woman's look. "After all, Roper Hospital is one of the leading institutions in heart health care. I've spoken on several occasions to various groups about my experience." She sniffed. "You'd be awed at the number of skeptics and ignorant people who actually object to organ replacement!"

"Why ignorant?" Diamond bristled. "You fault others for their opinions and beliefs?"

"Surely, you're not serious!" Cecelia looked aghast. "I don't believe you said that. If it weren't for these informative seminars and lectures, how many people do you think would come to know of the desperate need for donors?"

Diamond looked away, suppressing the fit of melancholia that threatened to overwhelm her with thoughts of her mother. She remembered the invites to such meetings and had always refused them. Inevitably, she would be told about what went on and as usual, would close her ears and change the subject.

Cecelia's voice interrupted her thoughts. "I'm sorry?" Diamond said.

"Today's event begins at nine o'clock with breakfast," Cecelia repeated in agitation, wondering at Diamond's distraction. "I'm scheduled to speak at eleven-thirty, just before the lunch break. We'll leave here at ten-thirty which will give us plenty of time to get there and settle in before I have to speak." She paused. "Afterward, we'll have lunch at the Sonoma." Cecelia looked Diamond over. "You're dressed suitably for our activity today, although black is a rather dreary color. I do hope you don't plan to wear such dark colors all the time. And, please, not so formal. Unless I have an engagement, casual attire—your jeans and slacks—will do fine for work every day. As the weather warms, we'll be spending a good deal of time outdoors."

Diamond nodded and smiled as she thought about Steven's remark about her jeans. Won't he be surprised, she thought? It's almost as though Cecelia is experiencing a change of heart. Oddly, the thought made Diamond shiver.

Cecelia stood. "If you've finished breakfast, I want you to join me in the sitting room. Ferdie has rearranged an area for you. The PC is at your disposal."

"I'm ready," Diamond said as she followed Cecelia out of the dining room. Strangely, the words *jeans* and *coconut cake* were rolling around in her head, bringing a fit of discomfort. Shrugging off the feeling, Diamond listened to her employer give a rundown of her duties.

A half hour later, at nine o'clock, Diamond was left alone while Cecelia went to dress. Bored, Diamond stared at the work she was to start on tomorrow. She had briefly leafed through the letters that required a response, and while Cecelia was explaining what was what, Diamond could barely contain her yawns. *Is this all there is?* she thought. The woman is vain, selfish, and expects the world to wait at her feet. Why Steven agreed to add another salary to his accounts was a mystery, Diamond thought. Cecelia needed a paid companion as badly as she needed another grandchild to verbally abuse.

With thoughts of Nerissa, Diamond suddenly wondered how the young girl was doing. A worried frown wrinkled her forehead. Suppose B. J. would be waiting for her after school? Diamond couldn't help the small smile that parted her lips when she'd confronted the very surprised young man last night. He had been startled to see Diamond walking toward him and Nerissa.

While driving to Nerissa's tryst, Diamond had thought it best that Nerissa meet with B. J. alone and without any interference from Diamond. B. J. would be upset enough, anticipating one thing and getting nothing but deprivation and disappointment.

"There he is," Nerissa said as Diamond pulled up to the curb beside the deserted school playground.

It was dusky but Diamond could make out the surprised features of the young man, who watched them warily. "Just tell him how you feel, exactly the way you told me," Diamond said, softly.

Nerissa looked nervous. "He looks mad. Suppose . . ."

Diamond interrupted. *"Suppose* is not why you're doing this, Nerissa. Your body is yours to do with what you want, when you want, and having sex with B. J. is obviously not the move of the day!" She added softly, "Is it?"

"No," Nerissa answered with a firm shake of her head. She got out of the car and without looking back at Diamond, walked to meet B. J.

Diamond watched carefully. They were too far away for her to hear their conversation, but by the angry gesture B. J. made toward the car, Diamond could guess that he wasn't taking too kindly to what Nerissa was saying. She saw him fling Nerissa's hand away and then grab her wrist.

Diamond got out of the car, anger making her temples throb. When she reached the startled couple, she silently searched the ground until she found what she was looking for.

Holding the condom packets out to B. J., Diamond said, "I believe Nerissa gave these to you. It's her way of telling you that she doesn't intend to use them. Not now. Not with you. Not with anyone. Not in the near future. I'm certain she's made herself perfectly clear. And if you don't understand any of this, tell me now. I don't mind repeating myself, B. J." Her voice was ice cold and she was sure the frost was in her eyes as she stared at the young man's changing face. In place of the macho bravado was disbelief, as he must be wondering who this crazy stranger was. Diamond could almost tell when he decided that challenging a nutcase was more than he wanted to handle.

"Do you think he'll leave me alone, now?" Nerissa asked as they drove home.

"If you want him to, he will," Diamond answered. "There are too many other girls that he'll be able to get over on. Just stand your ground whenever he confronts you and don't back off. He'll get the message. If he doesn't, don't keep it to yourself. You have a family that loves you and will protect you any way they can. So don't suffer by yourself in your little hideaway." She smiled. "Besides, I'm not going anywhere. At least for now."

After a while, Nerissa said softly, "I'm glad."

Now Diamond wondered if B. J. had recovered enough to harass Nerissa. Although he attended school in Mount Pleasant, it obviously wasn't a problem for him to get his friend Ki to shuttle him back and forth over the Cooper River Bridge to Nerissa's school.

Wondering if she shouldn't have interfered, Diamond sighed. "Too late now," she said. She left the sitting room and walked upstairs to get her purse and jacket. Diamond was trying to figure out a way to stop and pick Nerissa up from school. But she knew that was out of the question unless she wanted to bump heads again with Cecelia.

Diamond looked on with grudging admiration as Cecelia fielded questions from the interested audience. The woman who held her in awe was not the same woman who employed her and who also made the lives of her family miserable. Cecelia Rumford, to these people, was a courageous human being who, if not for her heart transplant, would be dead. They admired the woman's forthrightness in explaining the agony she went through when it was thought that no donor would be found in time. Diamond listened as Cecelia wound up the Q and A period with one last plea.

"People, the very fact that you are in this audience tells me that you are concerned. Especially to sit through a half hour of listening to my voice. Maya Angelou's it's not."

The audience laughed and Diamond smiled. Cecelia started to speak but was suddenly interrupted. A man stood up in the row in front of Diamond's. She was taken aback by the anger in the man's voice. Although she could see only the side of his face, the rapidly throbbing temple needed no definition.

"Ms. Rumford," the man said, "my name is John Jeffers. I'm visiting from New York. Your talk was very powerful and encouraging, and I'm glad that you are alive to talk about your experiences."

Diamond looked from the man to Cecelia, curious at what the surprised woman would do at this unexpected interruption.

"I want to know how is it that you received a heart transplant so quickly? There are upwards of five thousand who die every year while on a waiting list for a heart, lung, kidney, livers, or pancreas. The number of people still on those lists probably has reached fifty thousand."

Cecelia's eyes darkened. *Who is this man and why is he questioning my right to life?* In as pleasant a voice as she could, she said, "May I remind you, Mr. Jeffers, I too was on that list."

"For thirteen months?" John Jeffers said. "My mother was waiting for a heart for almost three years until she could wait no longer. She died last June, the same month you received the gift of life."

Diamond froze as she empathized with Jeffers. She tried to put a face to the stranger who wanted to live but had died waiting in vain. Diamond was overcome with sorrow for her and her brokenhearted son. So different from a son whose mother had been saved. The words from Steven's letter flashed before her.

"What are you asking me, Mr. Jeffers?" Cecelia said. Her fingernails dug into the wood of the lectern.

"Is it because of who you are in the community— wealthy, not a poor black? I'm sure you are aware that African-Americans are the least likely to wind up the recipients of organ transplants, especially the heart. We're more likely to become victims of presumed consent, a term I'm sure you're well educated on. I didn't hear a soul address that issue today." He stopped and looked around. "Over half your audience is black, the very audience you people recruited to listen to this calculated whitewash. Donate your organs to save a life? Whose? Certainly not my black mother's, and definitely not half the people sitting in this room," Jeffers said, anger almost quieting his voice to a whisper.

Diamond felt all kinds of emotions oozing from her pores. Here was someone who also shared her doubts about the transplant allocation. The term Jeffers had mentioned was familiar to her because she'd discussed the issue with her mother and Peaches. It lent to her old fears about her former teacher dying so soon after registering as an organ donor. Diamond was startled by another voice from the back of the room. All heads turned, including Diamond's.

"Just what are you implying, Mr. Jeffers?" Steven said. His jaws slammed shut like a steel trap as he eyed the man who turned to face him.

"I'm not implying anything, but stating the facts," said Jeffers. He stared closely at his adversary. Then, raising a brow, he said, "Dr. Steven Rumford." He bowed his head in acknowledgment. "The well-known son of the well-known Dr. Cyril Rumford." He surveyed the stunned audience who turned from him to the obviously angry doctor. "Now you should wonder if poor black folks really do have the same chances Ms. Rumford spoke so gloriously about." Turning back to Steven, he said, "Am I wrong, Dr. Rumford?"

Steven stared hard at Jeffers. He fought to control his voice and when he spoke his tone was even. "Yes, you are, for allowing this audience to walk out of here with their heads filled with your distorted views." All eyes were on Steven as he continued. "First," he said, speaking to the audience as well as Jeffers, "transplant allocation is a heated debate between the federal government and a national transplant network. Some people think that the allocation system is unfair because the recipient is not always the sickest but because the donated organ is first offered locally. The policy stands even if a medical urgency awaits in another state." Steven stared at Jeffers. "I'm almost certain that since you are so well versed in the laws that govern transplants, you are aware that at the time of Mrs. Rumford's surgery, the local-first rule was still in effect."

John Jeffers stared hard at Steven. In acquiescing with a nod, he said, "I knew that," he replied, then shrugged. "But who plays monitor?"

All heads turned to the front of the room when another voice boomed over the microphone.

Diamond turned from Steven's angry face to listen to the man who'd spoken. He was a doctor and had been acting as the moderator for the program. Cecelia had sat down and was staring at the audience with a stricken look.

"Folks, please calm down," the moderator said. "This was not to be a session on the ethics of organ transplantation. That discussion will take place at another time in the near future. However, since this portion of the program has ended and you are all more than ready for lunch, let's give a hand and our thanks to our speakers today."

Diamond was confused. The first thing she wanted to do was to meet John Jeffers before he left the room. She ached to talk with him, to share his views. She also wanted to go to Cecelia, not only because she felt that it was her duty as an employee, but because for the first time since she had met the woman, Diamond wanted to comfort her! She looked so forlorn, as if the world had come crashing down around her feet and she had not the slightest clue as to what to do about it. Diamond also wanted to go to Steven. He was so angry she thought he would walk down the aisle and punch Jeffers's lights out!

Turning to the rear of the room, Diamond searched for Steven, but he was already walking down the aisle toward his mother, who was surrounded by the sympathetic audience. Trying to catch his eye, Diamond stopped in her tracks and sank back down in her seat. Hanging on to his arm was a gorgeous creature who matched his stride step by step and hip to hip. Tall, brunette, bronzed skin, and classic ebony beauty, she was the definitive man's woman, with her high cheekbones and full, sensual mouth. Her figure was hidden by a lightweight coat, but Diamond could sense the undulating curves as she glided alongside Steven. Neither looked her way as they headed straight for Cecelia.

A murmur arose from the group around Cecelia, and soon Diamond saw her being led from the room, walking limply and supported by the arms of her son and the moderator. The gorgeous creature was fast on Steven's heels. Cecelia must have fallen into a faint, Diamond surmised. Not knowing where they'd taken her, Diamond remained where she was, suspecting that Steven would come for her with instructions. Surely lunch at the café would be canceled.

Deep in thought, Diamond closed her eyes, trying to sort out all that had happened on what had started out to be a boring morning. Uppermost in her mind was the appearance of the beautiful stranger with Steven. Was he involved after all? Why come on to her so passionately? He wanted her. Diamond knew that as surely as she knew her own name.

"Hello."

Diamond opened her eyes to stare into the dark brown ones of John Jeffers.

"Hello," she answered, surprised that he was still there.

"I see you were also affected by my untimely statements. I'm sorry." A frown appeared and disappeared as swiftly. "I suppose there's always a time and a place to air one's views on different platforms. Guess this wasn't it."

When speaking normally, his voice was quite nice to listen to, Diamond thought. Not as deep as Steven's but rather even and mellow, as if he took life at a slower pace than others. Perturbed, she wondered when she had started to use Steven Rumford as a point of reference in assessing other men.

"No," Diamond answered, "but you set some minds to thinking." She liked his crooked smile. But it did nothing to her. Not like Steven's. Annoyed again, she lifted a shoulder as if to shrug away the image of Steven's face.

"I'm sorry for your loss," she said softly. "We have that in common. I lost my mother to an accident last June."

John's eyes saddened. "I'm sorry."

"Thanks." Diamond hesitated, then said, "Her organs were donated."

"With her consent?"

Diamond nodded. "Yes."

John looked at the pretty young woman with the expressive eyes. They were sad. "You didn't approve," he said softly.

Before Diamond could answer him, footsteps and then a whiff of *Allure* caught her attention. Turning her head, Diamond looked up to see Steven's creature watching her. She stood and so did John Jeffers.

"My name is Juliette Malvenaux," the woman said, staring at the couple. Dismissing John, she glanced at Diamond's hair. Then, looking down at the shorter woman, she said, "I was told I'd find you here. Your boss is waiting for you. Follow me, please." Without another look at either of them, she walked briskly to the door that Cecelia had been half carried through earlier.

"Pleasant, isn't she?" John said.

"Only to look at, I think." Diamond slid out of the row and started down the aisle. "Sorry, I have to go. But I enjoyed meeting you. Have a safe trip back home. Bye," she said as she hurried after the woman with the world's finest manners. A twinge of regret piqued her at the interruption. She would have liked to get his phone number. Besides listening to him talk about the subject that weighed so heavily on her mind, he was a fellow New Yorker and they could have shared stories.

Cecelia was in the hall, apparently completely recovered, from the way she was chatting away with obvious friends, all of whom hovered solicitously. Steven was missing from the group, and that bothered Diamond. She had a sudden yearning to see and talk to him. But why? she asked herself. If he was seeing this Juliette person, why be concerned with him? *Because you know you want that man, so stop being a child and admit it.*

"Here you are, Diamond," Cecelia said when she spotted her behind Juliette. "I can just imagine what you were thinking with that awful interruption from that horrible man." She waved a hand in the air. "Let's hope that's the last we'll see of him."

Diamond said, "Are you feeling better, Cecelia?"

"Of course, dear. Just needed to get some air, that was all. I'm perfectly all right and we're keeping our plan to have lunch in town. You've met Juliette already, so let me introduce you around. Ladies, this is Diamond Drew, who will be living with us for as long as she wants."

Diamond suffered through the introductions with a polite nod and smile for everyone. The four women were in the same over-fifty age bracket, except for Juliette, who appeared to be in her early thirties. They all wore the same plastic smiles, again with the exception of Juliette, who regarded her with bold curiosity. Diamond returned the stare until the other woman looked away. *Worried about your man, are you? Well, you have a right to!* Diamond flushed. Now where did that come from, she wondered?

"Diamond, Juliette will ride with us. The others will meet us there," Cecelia said.

Diamond drove silently to the Sonoma Café on the newly gentrified part of King Street. She'd stopped in the upscale, European-style restaurant on occasion when she first arrived in Charleston. It was quiet and pleasant. Cecelia and Juliette were talking animatedly about something, but Diamond had closed her ears to their chatter. It was obvious that Cecelia favored the company of the young woman and treated Juliette as an equal. Must be wealthy, Diamond thought maliciously. Just the perfect match for her son. Suddenly the car jerked. *So that's it!*

"Diamond, are you all right?" Cecelia asked, concerned.

"It's a Benz, Diamond. Aren't you used to driving one?"

"Haven't had one in years, Juliette," Diamond answered easily as she pulled up in front of the restaurant. "Not since I traded for a 1988 Bentley. Much easier to handle." She looked in the mirror at her rear-seat passengers. "I'll

go park and meet you inside in a few minutes, ladies."
Diamond was still smiling as her speechless lunch companions disembarked with backward glances, then hurried inside the café.

After Steven saw that his mother was fine, he left her in the hands of her friends, refusing their invitation to lunch, and returned to his office. He'd mentally kicked himself for losing his temper with that stranger, personalizing a public forum. There was no need to confront Jeffers for his highly inflammatory remarks about the Rumford family. But the words had struck a tender nerve. At the time his mother had surgery, the very same thoughts had been in the minds of some of the oldest friends of the Rumfords'. Even then he had had to put people in their place. His mother was alive because of the grace of God and the circumstances that allowed her to be in the right place at the right time. He couldn't hold his tongue after seeing how stricken his mother was, defenseless against the fact that she was alive. It was rare that she was ever in such a predicament and Steven couldn't help but go to her defense. She was his mother and he loved her but he still could not bring himself to forgive her for interfering in his life. Because of her, he'd lost the woman he'd loved.

Steven stirred from his desk, poured a mug of coffee, and sat down again, trying to concentrate on the patient history he was reading. But big dark eyes kept meddling, and giving in to his restless mood he closed the folder and pushed back from his desk.

When he'd entered the room at Roper Hospital his mother was already speaking. Though he'd heard her talk before, it never ceased to amaze him what a changed person she was, but the real reason that brought him to the building was a neat package of high energy in the form of Diamond Drew. He'd spotted her in the audience almost immediately. The short cap of dark hair with the thin peaks arranged in helter-skelter fashion was hard to miss. After she'd swum the other morning, she'd pushed her wet hair straight back. Steven had wanted to finger it, bringing back the short tufts. This morning he had wished she would join him and he'd looked up at the window, hoping to see her watching him. He'd felt lonely and didn't linger over his exercise.

What is going on? he asked himself. There was no doubt in his mind that he wanted to make love to her. The taste of those full lips, and the feel of her slender body straining into his, warmed his loins even now. At first Steven thought his male hormones were in overdrive. But the more he thought of her and the more he saw her interact with his family, the more something else was in play, and he knew he was fighting against it. Having something deeper with Diamond was out of the question. She wasn't right for his family and he would not subject her to his mother's wrath. His eyes darkened. With Elise, he had been unsuspecting. Never again would he put a woman in the path of Cecelia and her vicious ways.

Steven poured more coffee. No matter how smartly he reasoned himself out of making love to Diamond, the fact remained that she was a constant in his thoughts and he was helpless to do anything about the endless heat in his gut. A knock on the door interrupted him, and he looked up as his nurse entered.

"Someone is here, Ginger?" he asked in surprise. Steven saw patients only on an emergency basis on Mondays, and he hoped it wasn't anything too serious. An uncluttered mind was needed for his Tuesday surgeries.

Ginger looked at her boss, who appeared to be disturbed about something. Keeping her voice bland, she said, "Ms. Malvenaux called. I didn't want to disturb you but she's called back and is insistent."

Steven frowned. He'd already told Juliette that dinner tonight was off.

"Thanks, put her through. I'll take it." Before she left, he said, "And thanks, Ginger, for clearing this mess I left last week. I can put my hands on what I need, now. Appreciate it."

"Not a problem, Doctor," Ginger said crisply and left. Seconds later she heard him answer his call. She pursed her lips at the thought of Steven falling for the likes of Juliette Malvenaux, a two-time divorcée at thirty-four. Each divorce had given more wealth to the woman who'd been born rich. "Guess it's true what they say," Ginger sighed. "Money smells money."

"Yes, Juliette, what is it?" Steven asked tersely. Seeing her once today had been enough. Cloying women left him cold.

"Steven, I wish you would reconsider our dinner engagement tonight," Juliette said, ignoring his distant tone. She wouldn't be put off again. "This really is the only night we have to finalize plans for the dance on Saturday night," she pleaded sweetly.

"What plans, Juliette? I thought the rest of the committee was handling everything. For God's sake, whatever is left undone a week before the affair obviously isn't that important!"

"I really don't see how you can say that after what happened last year with the seating arrangements. Since you're the head of that committee this year I know you don't want to be associated with a similar fiasco." Juliette waited, hearing the annoyed sigh, but knew she was breaking through his resolve.

Steven silently berated himself for getting involved in the first place, but there was a certain amount of politics to be played in the neighborhood.

Resignedly, Steven said, "Okay, I understand. But let's make it early, say at five o'clock. Since we're both already in town, why don't you meet me at the restaurant? Same place." He frowned as he glanced at the clock on his desk. "Where are you? Weren't you having lunch with my mother?"

Juliette sighed. "At the bar. I had to excuse myself. Can't hear myself think, much less get a word in what with all the chatter those women are doing with the help. You'd think they'd never met anyone from New York before."

"The help?" Steven asked.

"Yes," Juliette answered in exasperation. "The child hasn't stopped talking since the moment we sat down and they're all mesmerized by her, including your mother. Really, Steven, whatever possessed you to hire such a person? She certainly thinks she belongs."

Diamond. Steven's eyes narrowed. "Possessed me, Juliette?" he asked softly.

Astute enough to heed the warning, Juliette backed off. She was suddenly flustered and the acidity disappeared. She said, "I merely meant that a stranger from New York living under your roof . . . one Cecelia knows nothing about . . ."

Steven's voice was smooth when he said, "My mother knew what she was doing in hiring Diamond. She's the perfect companion as you can see," he ended dryly. Tiring of the conversation, he ended it after verifying the time and the place of their dinner engagement.

Minutes after opening the case folder again, Steven closed it, unable to concentrate. As before his thoughts drifted to Diamond. A smile tugged at his mouth as he imagined the restaurant scene and Juliette's consternation at the slender New Yorker who'd never learned to button her lips. *The help!*

Steven laughed out loud and picked up the phone, suddenly wanting some company. Maybe he could catch Russ for a quick bite. As he dialed the number, another laugh burst through as he thought of Juliette's reference to the *child*. "You couldn't be more wrong," Steven said. He licked his lips, remembering the sweet taste of Diamond on his mouth.

NINE

A few hours after Diamond parked the Benz in the garage and then sat with Cecelia for a while before she went to her room, Diamond sat in the big chair in her bedroom, reflecting on her day. Her first day at work had left her unfulfilled and wondering what she was doing in this house. Raised by her adoptive mother in the old manner of the work ethic—that is, to do a day's work for a day's pay—idling away a day with the "ladies who lunch" was not Diamond's idea of work. "Mama if you could see me now, you'd scalp me," she said aloud.

Diamond missed her work as a therapist and she toyed with the idea of volunteering again, as she'd done back home. But fitting it in with her daily "duties" would be an impossible task. Although the evenings were her own, Diamond didn't see how she could handle a part-time night job. But the boredom would kill her, she thought. She had to find a way to occupy herself before she went crazy. Coming up to her room every night after five, going back down for dinner at six-thirty and back to her room for the balance of the night was unthinkable. Maybe she should think about joining some clubs; at least she'd have a meeting or two to attend once a month. *Or maybe she should just leave this house, period!* To go where? she asked herself.

Diamond loved Charleston, and she especially loved living in Old Village in Mount Pleasant. When she finally did leave, would she find affordable housing nearby? She didn't think so, because with the influx of whites who gobbled up the premium land, absolutely nothing was available . . . or affordable to the average middle income person. During her excursions, she'd liked the look and feel of residential North Charleston and had given some thought to buying a condominium there at one time. But now that she'd seen and lived—if only for a few days—in the Rumford home, she would find it hard to settle anyplace else: besides the fact that she would be out of the life of Steven Rumford.

Adjusting her position in the chair, Diamond realized that after today she had to give serious thought to her feelings about men and stop pretending that she was a female eunuch. One day she would have to make love to the man she fell in love with. But how would she know him? For years Diamond had kept her body to herself after her two disastrous love affairs. She had given of herself so lovingly and so freely; she'd thought that that was what love was all about. Giving her passionate all, holding nothing back. But to be humiliated because she'd done exactly that; to be told that she was nothing more than a nymphomaniac had destroyed her confidence in her sexuality and deprived her of the desire to want to give herself ever again. From then on, it was almost as if she'd literally turned off the female mechanisms in her body that were labeled "sexual response." When men looked at her in that way, she responded in a sisterly fashion, which she knew was a complete turnoff, but that was the way she had to function. All these years it had worked for her, allowing her to live peacefully celibate.

Today, all that changed when she met John Jeffers. Although the encounter was brief and he'd been polite, she'd seen the look he'd given her. He wanted to make a move, and had he not been interrupted, he would have. But Diamond was not at all moved by the desire in his eyes, or his handsome smile and good looks. All she'd wanted from him was to share viewpoints on transplantation.

Her unresponsiveness to him was the reason for her present self-reevaluation, because she was disturbed at what she now knew to be true: that the only man who affected her in a sexual way, breaking through her cold exterior, was Steven Rumford. After so many years! The minute she'd looked into his eyes, days before, it was as if she'd turned the key, unleashing her passionate self. Was he then the man that she would love? Was she really falling in love with someone who probably was already spoken for?

Diamond felt somewhat relieved after her soul-searching. Standing and stretching her limbs, she felt better by being truthful to herself. Unsure of what that would mean, she could only wait and see. And that meant waiting for Steven to come home. She would take her cue from him and then just let things happen. Who knows, she thought, maybe her body was just sending her false signals and Steven Rumford was only another man that she could ignore. But as Diamond changed into a blouse and slacks, she had to laugh at that thought, along with her hilarious alter ego.

Passing Nerissa's door, Diamond heard music. She'd learned from Cecelia that Jacqui had picked her daughter up to take her to the doctor. Relieved that there would be no encounter with B. J., Diamond didn't seek the young girl out, respecting Nerissa's right to be alone with her own thoughts. When the time came, the teenager knew where to find Diamond when she wanted to talk.

The house was quiet at four-thirty, and as she made her way down the stairs, good smells wafted past her nose. Almost immediately, Diamond yearned to cook. She hadn't prepared a meal in weeks and the sudden yen to do so was overwhelming. Unaware of how receptive the cook would be to a visitor in the middle of meal preparation, Diamond walked toward the kitchen. Tina was the one person in the household whom she'd not talked to at length. She seemed friendly enough, Diamond thought. *Well, we'll just have to see.*

"Hi, Diamond," Tina said, with a big smile. "Smells gotcha, huh?"

Immediately, Diamond relaxed at the friendly greeting. Always feeling at home in this room, she responded in kind to the woman who appeared to be only a few years her senior.

"Hi, Tina. You're right. What is that you're making? You've got one of my senses working overtime and I can't wait to satisfy at least one more. Do you give samples?" Diamond walked closer and sat down on one of the tall stools at the breakfast bar. Her eyes widened when she spied the coconut cake on the counter.

"That's just one of the things I cooked up this morning. Wanna taste?" Tina said. "Ferdie told me about what happened on Saturday with Cecelia, so I figured I'd make one for her today. Here, have a piece. Guaranteed you'll still have room for dinner."

Already experiencing the same feelings as she had on Saturday night, Diamond tried to shrug them away and, as she bit into the fluffy confection, she marveled at the firm consistency of the vanilla icing. Almost identical to her mother's recipe, Diamond thought. Tasting another forkful, she was impressed with the moist texture.

Tina watched. "Something's missing?" she said. "Not like yours, I guess," she added.

Diamond gave her a surprised look.

"Oh, Cecelia's mentioned that you liked to cook, especially sweets. Ever try coconut cake?" Tina grinned. "From the look on your face, it's not the same, huh?"

Diamond swallowed. "No," she answered, "but this is delicious. So close to mine, I'm suspicious that my recipe is traveling around in the south. We'll have to have a bake-off one of these days." She attempted a small smile, trying to overcome the queasy feeling in her stomach. "Although coconut cake is one of my favorites, sweet potato pie is my specialty." Diamond finished her small slice. "That was delicious," she said, then turned at the sound Tina made.

"Sweet potato pie?" Tina said, surprised. "Funny you should mention that. Before she left this morning, Cecelia spoke to me about making one." She frowned.

"She did?" Diamond's throat went dry. Afraid to ask why Tina was looking so perturbed, she said, "Is that so unusual?"

"It sure is," Tina answered. "Downright odd. The very first week I started here, four years ago, I made one and it was a disaster. No, not the pie," she said at Diamond's look, "Cecelia's reaction. She went a little crazy, I think."

"Why?"

Tina shrugged. "Couldn't stand the taste of it. When she was a kid, she gagged on it, said her mother didn't know how to make it right. But she remembers liking it at her friends' houses. Once, she brought home a recipe and asked her mother to try it and her mother gave her the devil. She's never eaten it since, she said."

"So, why now, after all these years?" Diamond asked, trying to keep the fear out of her voice. *Did she really want to know?*

"It's the wildest thing you've ever heard." Tina gave Diamond a skeptical look. "Said it was a dream."

"Dream?"

"You heard me right. Cecelia said for weeks she's been dreaming about food." Tina shook her head in amazement. "Course, I don't see anything odd in that. Since her operation, she hasn't had to watch her diet as strictly as before, which is why Steven hired me in the first place: to regulate her diet. Cecelia can eat anything she wants, since she's got that healthy heart."

Diamond's lashes fluttered, but she persisted, "What did she dream?"

"Said she dreamed that she would like sweet potato pie if grated orange rind were added to it." Tina cocked an eyebrow. "Now that's an old recipe that my grandmother used only for her potato pudding, not her pies." Tina looked curiously at Diamond. "You ever use that?" she asked.

"Yes." Diamond's voice was barely audible.

Tina lifted a shoulder. "Well, Cecelia said the rest of the dream was a little fuzzy. Said she couldn't remember what else the woman told her to add. But there was another ingredient she had to use to make it taste right." Tina paused. "Can't think of what that could be."

"What woman?" Diamond asked, her heart beginning to thump wildly.

"The woman in the dream. Always the same woman, same dream. Same fuzzy part where the other ingredient evades her."

Allspice. Always just a pinch, Diamond. You're not supposed to taste it! Diamond could hear her mother's voice so clearly she almost looked to see if she was bending over the oven. *Allspice and grated orange rind!* Her mother's recipe that had made her sweet potato pies famous.

Tina pointed to the large covered pot on the stove. "I boiled the potatoes but I never did anything with them. Instead, I decided to surprise Cecelia with the cake." With a sly smile she said, "Why don't you make us a couple of your specialty pies for dessert tonight. There's still plenty of time. This room is certainly big enough so we won't get in each other's hair."

Diamond heard Tina's voice from afar. All she wanted to do was to run to her room and close her eyes and ears to the madness that was going on inside her head. *This can't be happening,* she told herself. This stuff only happens in Stephen King movies. My mother is dead and so is her spirit! Diamond repeated the chant over and over to hold on to reality. She can't zone out like she did with Steven. She can't, she can't, she can't!

"So, what about it, Diamond?" asked Tina as she slid a tray of capons into the oven. "Bet you'll be a big hit."

Finally finding her voice, Diamond said, "Sure. Not a problem, Tina." Hopping off the stool, she walked to the door. "Let me wash up, I'll be back in a few minutes." Diamond rushed upstairs and into her bathroom where she doused her face with cold water. Her limbs were shaking so badly she had to sit down on the toilet seat where she held on to the sink until her body quieted. Almost afraid to think about it, she knew that if Cecelia described the woman in her dream, a picture of Phyllis Yarborough would emerge: a brown-skin woman with a short natural. Diamond just knew it.

Diamond left the bathroom, removed her wet shirt and bra, and put on dry clothes. Composed, with closed mind to Cecelia and her dream, she left her room and went to the kitchen with one objective: to make sweet potato pies for dessert.

Feeling unusually tired after arriving home from lunch, Cecelia ended her discussion with Diamond and went to her room, where she undressed and slid under the covers. Almost immediately, she could feel herself drifting to sleep.

Cecelia had quietly awakened over thirty minutes ago from a deep sleep and she knew that she'd dreamed her dream again. She lay looking at nothing in particular, remembering. For the first time since the dreams began, she didn't awake afraid and confused. Because she knew all about dreams! For months, when her support group members spoke about their experiences—how their organ donor had appeared to them—she had kept silent about her own dreams. It was silly and preposterous to believe in that hogwash. What would people think if she laid claim to such nonsense? She could just hear Cyril laughing at her foolishness.

But now, she thought, she had to admit the truth, if only to herself, and to Tina. Otherwise she was certain that she would go crazy. How long could she pretend before the strain of keeping her fears to herself showed? When she attended her meeting this week, would she have the courage to give testimony to what she'd been experiencing all this time? She'd scoffed at the others when they'd admitted to trying to find out the identity of their donor. By hook or crook, one woman had said, and she'd eventually found the family of her heart donor. The earth didn't open up and swallow them because they'd broken the rules, nor did the troops come and cart them off to jail. Both the recipient and the family had felt a sort of closure. After the one meeting, there had been no further contact.

Cecelia admitted now that she too had wondered about the person whose heart beat inside her chest. Always she'd thought how disgusting it would be to sit across from the family, who'd be staring at her, wishing that she had been the one to die, not their loved one! She closed her eyes briefly as the thousands of jumbled thoughts and odd feelings flashed across her mind. All the strange sensations and every foolish idea that she'd had now seemed to loom up like so many helium balloons released by a clown at a child's birthday party. Had it been a man or a woman who had committed so selfless an act? It must have been a man's heart, she'd always reasoned. She felt so robust, as if she could do anything, go anyplace, without ever tiring. The only reason she stopped her morning exercise was to get on to doing something else, not because she was tired.

Cecelia pushed away the covers and got out of bed. It was nearly time for dinner and she didn't want anyone to come knocking at her door. She was completely relaxed and fearless when she allowed the image of the woman in her dream to surface. The woman with the pleasant face and the natural hairdo. The woman who made sweet potato pie, with grated orange rind. Without a doubt, Cecelia knew that her heart donor was that woman. And she also knew that she was going to love eating that pie. Just like she did when she was a young girl.

Jacqui looked at her mother curiously. "Are you all right, Mother?" she asked.

Cecelia looked at her daughter. "Of course, I am, why wouldn't I be?"

Of course, she's all right, Jacqui thought. Why did I ever think something could be wrong? "Nothing. Forget I said anything. You look just fine, Mother."

Wondering, as she'd feared, if her earlier thoughts were producing signs of strain, Cecelia grew tense. *They can't know her feelings*. What would they think? They would laugh and think of her as silly. Then who would ever listen to her again in this house? Her control would be lost.

Cecelia threw her daughter a withering glance. "I must not be, if my looks prompted such an idiotic question. If I weren't okay, would I be sitting here with all of you?"

Diamond groaned inwardly. The meal thus far had been quiet and pleasant until Jacqui's question. Even Christopher was acting amiable although most of his conversation was directed to his daughter, who kept up a running dialogue with her father. The only person missing was Steven. She kept listening for his car and then the door, expecting him to fill the room with his huge presence. But when the meal was almost ended, it was quite apparent that the master of the house was not coming home, at least not for dinner.

Diamond sighed. *It's probably just as well*, she thought. One less night for him to settle arguments.

Ignoring her mother's argumentative question, Jacqui

turned her attention to Diamond. She'd seen the expectant look fade to one of disappointment that she tried to conceal, but with eyes that expressive, it was a feat, Jacqui could see. Knowing that she was looking for Steven, Jacqui said, "My brother doesn't usually come home for dinner on Mondays, Diamond." She threw a glance at her mother. "Too chaotic the night before he performs surgery."

Diamond looked from Cecelia to Jacqui. "Makes sense. So why bother to come home at all?" she asked, hoping that she was hiding her disappointment well.

"Steven keeps an apartment in town, Diamond," Cecelia answered. "We rarely see him on Mondays and sometimes not on Tuesdays, depending upon how his patients are doing." Her eyes narrowed at her daughter.

Christopher made a sound, then eyed Diamond. "So that leaves only five days for the manor house to be in an uproar."

Cecelia's eyes flashed a warning to her son-in-law. "Be careful, Christopher."

"Or?" Christopher said, insolently. "You'll ask me to leave? Well, don't bother, I've taken care of that for you."

"Christopher!" Jacqui stared at her husband. "I thought we had an agreement."

Nerissa looked at her father, understanding what he was saying. He was finally leaving them. She stared at her mother, who acted surprised, and Nerissa wondered why. She'd suspected all along that her father wouldn't stay long in this house, and her mother certainly should have known. And what agreement was her mother talking about?

"Yes, we did. The tests were negative. Nerissa's doctor said she's okay." He shrugged. "So . . ." He left his words hanging, giving his wife a look. He really didn't care to discuss his family business in front of Cecelia and Diamond or even his daughter, who had suddenly lost her animation.

Jacqui understood. She too followed her husband's glance to her daughter. Nodding at Christopher, she said, "We'll discuss it later."

Cecelia was alert to the dynamics between Jacqui and Christopher and wondered what they had planned without her knowledge.

"So, you're abandoning your family, finally. Is that it?" Cecelia's voice dripped with sarcasm. "Well, I'm certain it will be no great loss to them. When is the banner day?"

Christopher's mouth twisted in anger, but because of his daughter, he swallowed the venomous words that were on his tongue. Very slowly, he answered, "You'll be the first to know, Cecelia."

"Mother," Jacqui said, "it's time you kept your nose out of our business. If it weren't for you, maybe our marriage could have had a chance and he wouldn't be leaving in the first place." Her voice shook with anger. "I was a fool to ask him to move back into this house because of you. You don't need anyone but yourself and you never did."

"Me?" Cecelia's eyes blazed. "I didn't have a thing to do with making him an irresponsible father and husband. If he were half the man your brother was he would have left years ago. And you could have left right along with him, so don't blame me for your failings as a wife."

Diamond's stomach knotted as her eyes flew to the dining room entrance. She was obviously the only one who saw Steven standing there, watching and listening. Her heart went out to him as she saw the pained look in his eyes. *Oh, Steven, why did you have to come home?* she cried silently. Almost as if he'd heard her, his eyes met hers. Briefly, something else replaced the anger and then he turned from her.

Steven walked into the room, stopped at his niece's chair, and bent to whisper in her ear. "Riss, are you all right?" When she nodded, he said, "Okay," and kissed her forehead.

"Evening, folks." Steven surveyed the table as he sat down. "Good, I see you've eaten already. I haven't had dessert either," he said amiably. "But I will have some coffee." He prepared a cup while his family watched him in silence.

"I thought you were having dinner with Juliette," Cecelia said. "What happened?"

"I did have dinner with Juliette, mother," Steven answered in an even tone. "I just didn't stay for dessert."

Diamond's heart sank. *He is involved!*

"But it's Monday," Cecelia threw at him.

"So it is." Steven looked up as Tina walked in burdened with a cake and a pie.

Tina set the plates on the table and smiled at everyone. "The coconut's mine and the potato is Diamond's doing." She winked. "Don't blame me for any stomach upsets. The recipe is all hers," she said and left the room.

Cecelia, ignoring the sweets, said to her son, "Why are you here?"

Steven tore his eyes from Diamond's to answer his mother. "Juliette's idea of discussing business over dinner is apparently not mine," he said dryly. "She doesn't need me to tie up any loose ends." He helped himself to a slice of cake and a slice of pie.

"That still doesn't explain why you're here on Monday night," Cecelia persisted.

"Dinner was interrupted by a summons from the hospital. My patient developed a fever so there's no operation tomorrow. That's why I'm here," he said, turning from his mother and staring at Diamond. When she flushed at his direct look, he smiled and bit into the pie.

Diamond could hardly sit still under Steven's bold look. He as much as told everyone at the table that he was home because of her and he didn't care who thought squat about it. So what about Juliette? Thoroughly confused, she found her voice, keeping it light.

"So, what do you think?" Diamond asked. She included the rest of the family in her inquiry since they all selected the pie first. She didn't look at Steven.

"This is great," Nerissa said. "You *do* know things." Her face was bright with a smile.

Diamond winked at her. "I told you so."

Steven raised a brow at the exchange between his niece and Diamond. Somehow the thought that they were becoming friends gave him good feelings.

"I'd give you the blue ribbon if I had one." Christopher took another slice and helped himself to the cake also.

"Diamond, this is delicious," Jacqui said. "You've got the touch. Haven't tasted anything like this in years. And never in this house!" She gave Diamond a curious look. "Family recipe?"

"You could say that," Diamond answered, guardedly, hoping that this wasn't going to become a twenty-question episode about her family. She didn't know how she'd be able to handle it.

"Don't you think you're being selfish not to share?" Steven regarded her discomfort with amusement. "It's the best I've eaten."

"Share?"

"With Tina. After you've left us, we'd be deprived." His look was innocent as he finished the pie and drank more coffee. Steven ignored the stares of the other adults.

Nerissa stared at Diamond with widened eyes. "You're leaving?"

"Of course not, Riss," Diamond said, with a smile at the young girl, wondering why she sounded so scared.

"Nerissa, Diamond! Nerissa." Cecelia's voice cracked across the table like a clash of thunder. "Nerissa is her name!"

All eyes turned on the older woman, staring at her as if she'd gone mad.

Christopher was the first to speak. "Why in God's name

can't you leave my daughter alone?" He stood up, pushing back his chair, and walked around the table to Nerissa. He took her hand. "Come. Let's get out of here. Jacqui, we need to talk. Now." Without another word, he marched out of the room with his daughter, who gave her grandmother a backward look that was filled with fear.

Jacqui pushed away from the table. "I hope you live to regret what you've done to my family." She hurried after her daughter and husband.

Steven stared at his mother in disgust and then turned to Diamond. "Why am I not surprised?" Without a word to Cecelia, he strode from the room.

Cecelia glared at Diamond. "There's no need for you to remain. You're off duty, you know."

Diamond stood, giving the angry woman look for look. "Well, since you put it that way, I guess I will follow the leader. Not a lot of sense in staying to play whipping boy," she said with an innocent smile. She left, still bewildered by the caustic attitude of the woman. Was this really the same woman she'd wanted to comfort earlier this morning?

Steven was in the softly lit sitting room, twirling a tumbler of scotch and water between his hands. He passed a hand over his forehead as if to erase the last fifteen minutes of chaos from his mind. When, if ever, would there be peace under this roof?

There was no excuse for his mother's cruelty toward her son-in-law or her granddaughter. But he had to look at Christopher in a new light after the man's rare emotional display of anger toward Cecelia. Steven had silently applauded him—and Jacqui. Maybe the two could plan to make things better between them. But deep down, he knew that it was too late. His mother's venom had been spewed for too long. Steven was deep in thought and he didn't hear the door open.

* * *

Diamond complimented Tina on a fine meal and spoke briefly with her and Ferdie, who was having her dinner, then left the kitchen. Restless, instead of heading upstairs, she walked to the sitting room. Maybe a glass of wine in the quiet room would settle her down and force her to come to a decision. After tonight, she must give serious thought to leaving. She'd seen enough. What more was there to discover about the recipient of her mother's heart? Diamond was afraid to learn more.

When she opened the door to the sitting room, Diamond was startled to see Steven, who was unaware of her presence. He was facing the glass doors and was lost in thought. Unwilling to disturb him, she turned to go.

Steven turned his head to see Diamond reach for the doorknob. Surprised but happy to see her, he spoke quietly. "Don't go, Diamond."

"I didn't want to interrupt," Diamond answered. "Are you sure you won't mind?"

Mind? Steven choked back the word. He couldn't get her *off* his mind.

Standing, he said, "Can I fix you a drink?"

"White wine, thanks," Diamond answered. She sat on the sofa and watched him, filling her eyes with the look of his strong muscular body and marveling at the strength in his hands that were so gentle. She remembered that his touch on her neck in the restaurant had been as tender as a lover's caress.

Steven handed the stem to Diamond and sat down beside her. He'd replenished his own drink, and after taking a sip, held the glass in both hands as he relaxed.

After a while he said, "That wasn't very pleasant in there." Then he added thoughtfully, "Since you've been here, it's been one uproar after another, hasn't it?"

Unable to deny it and not knowing how to answer, Diamond splayed her hand in a helpless gesture.

Steven's face grew grim. "Nothing you can say about my family's behavior can embarrass me, Diamond." Disgustedly, he said, "Maybe I should have stayed in town."

"Yes, it probably would have been best," Diamond replied in a soft voice.

"Really?" Steven gave her a bold look. He shook his head. "I don't think so. Not for you or for me."

"What do you mean?" Diamond's breath came rapidly.

"I think you were as happy to see me as I was to see you. That gave me a lift because you were the reason I did come home." Steven smiled at the startled look in her dark eyes. "I know everyone else guessed too." Trying to coax a smile from her, he said, "C'mon, admit it." He persisted, a twinkle in his eyes, "You don't usually hold back when you want me to know what's on your mind."

Diamond nodded. "I was." That was all she could manage, afraid of what she'd blurt out. She couldn't possibly tell him that she'd wanted to leap into his arms when she'd spotted him in the doorway.

"There, that wasn't so hard, was it?" When he was rewarded with a smile, he reached out and took her hand. The warmth that shot through him was no longer a surprise and he welcomed it like a familiar friend. She didn't resist his touch, and Steven was encouraged to do what he'd yearned to do since two days ago. Freeing both their hands of glasses, Steven pulled himself close to her and caught her in his arms.

Cradling her head on his shoulder, he just held on to her like she was his lifeline. Steven buried his nose in her hair, inhaling the clean, sunshinelike smell, then brushed his lips against the softness of her neck. "Diamond," he rasped. "Put your arms around me." The soft command was obeyed, and he breathed deeply. She lay soft and pliant against his chest, and the swell of her breasts sharpened the groan that burst through his lips. His tongue darted out to taste the delicate skin of her neck and lingered in the hollow of her throat. Her moans thrilled him down to his toes and he sucked the soft skin, not getting enough of the salty deliciousness.

"Steven," Diamond breathed, straining into him, wanting more of his touch, forgetting about the little warning signals in her brain. This is what her body craved since she'd first laid eyes on him. *Shut up and go away,* she cried to her disapproving conscience.

Steven found the buttons of her blouse and unbuttoned them, slipping his hand inside and fondling her satin-covered breast. "God, Diamond, you feel so good. Don't let go," he commanded, as he felt her move away, then realized she was only adjusting herself to him. He pushed away the fabric. Then quickly shifting his body, he bent his head to take her breast into his mouth. "Jesus," he breathed. "Jesus."

Diamond gasped as the warm moistness of his mouth embraced her and the touch of his teeth brushing her hardened nipples made her dizzy with pleasure. Releasing her other breast, he twirled his tongue around the nipple until it was a taut peak in his mouth.

Steven groaned and suddenly stood, pulling Diamond up with him, catching her close. "I want to feel all of you," he whispered. "Diamond, I want you." He crushed her against him, sliding his hands down to her buttocks and holding her to him. Capturing her lips in a hungering kiss, Steven shivered at the unexpected touch of her tongue seeking his. *She does want me!* The realization emboldened him to ravish her sweet mouth with searing kisses. When she rotated her hips against his swollen sex, he nearly screamed out from deprivation.

Diamond returned Steven's kisses with a hunger that was released from the depths of her soul. Unleashed was the passion she had bridled so long ago. Hidden only until it could be given unashamedly to the one she truly loved. And she knew that she was in the arms of that man.

"Diamond, can I love you?" Steven whispered against her mouth.

"Yes, God, yes," Diamond breathed. Her body and her mind seemed to suddenly dance in such a fit of rejoicing that she had to suppress a giddy giggle.

Her response sent Steven into a tailspin. Although he felt sure of her feelings, if he'd been denied, he would have gone a little crazy. He wanted to possess her where they stood, but he knew that would be a disastrous mistake. Her tiny whimpers sent more shivers down his spine, as he loosened her hands from around his waist. Catching her by the shoulders, he looked into her eyes.

"Diamond," he murmured, stealing one more kiss from her swollen lips. "Not here," he said huskily. He fixed her bra and pulled her blouse closed, buttoning it slowly, all the time, nuzzling her neck and pecking her face with tiny kisses. When his lips touched her eyes, he was surprised. Her lashes were wet with tears. Frowning he said, "What's wrong?" How had he hurt her? he wondered. Surely, she could understand that anyone could burst in on them. "Diamond, what's wrong?" he repeated softly.

Catching her breath, and smoothing her clothes, Diamond sat and pulled Steven down with her. She held his hand tightly as she sought to regain her composure. He had been right to stop them because she had been perfectly willing to have him take her right here on the sofa. Her body ached to release the love that was still pent up inside her. Her tongue darted out to taste him on her swollen lips. Feeling his worried gaze, Diamond brushed a hand on his cheek.

Steven watched her inner struggle. He caught her hand and kissed the slender fingers, then waited.

"Steven. I do want to make love with you, but it . . . it wouldn't be right."

"Right?" Steven frowned. "It certainly feels right to me," he said huskily, wondering what was coming.

"To me too," Diamond whispered. "Lord knows it does. But you would hate me and I'd hate myself to let something happen between us and then, just leave." She hesitated. "I'm . . . I'm glad you stopped us." Her voice was filled with misery.

"Leave?" Steven looked in stupefaction.

TEN

"Steven, I can't stay here any longer. I . . . I should never have come here." Diamond swallowed, and after taking a deep breath, continued. "After tonight . . . well, I can't work for your mother. She's a hateful woman and I can't stand by watching and biting my tongue when she verbally abuses her granddaughter the way she does." Steven squeezed her hand and she saw his lashes flicker. "A few times I couldn't help myself and I smart-mouthed her."

"She likes the confrontation," Steven said. "That's why she hired you. But strangely, my mother doesn't like the fresh remarks coming from any of us."

"I've noticed that." Diamond looked baffled. "But why?"

Steven shrugged. "I don't know. It's a mystery to all of us." He looked away as if remembering. "She wasn't like that when we were kids. She used to laugh and smile with us, and joke with my father. She had a rich laugh, like yours," Steven said as he turned back to Diamond. "After my father died suddenly, it was as if she went through some kind of metamorphosis. Her personality gradually changed into how you see her now."

"Your father wasn't ill?" Diamond asked.

"No. He had a stroke and he died instantly in his office. My mother went into shock when she heard."

"How awful!"

"Yes, it was. Soon after that, she became so impersonal toward us."

Diamond remembered something and she asked, "You used to call her 'Mam.' "

Steven looked surprised. "Yes."

"I heard you call her that, once."

"Jacqui and I used that pet name when we were younger."

He didn't have to add why they stopped, Diamond thought.

"I don't mean to pry into your business, Steven, but why does she verbally abuse her granddaughter the way that she does?"

A pained look crossed Steven's face. "You'll find this house full of mysteries," Steven said, trying to make light of a heavy situation.

They still held hands and his tightened over Diamond's.

"For whatever reason, when Nerissa was born, my mother never showed the joy a grandmother would normally exhibit. She definitely didn't carry a brag book in her purse and her visits were rare when Jacqui and Christopher lived in their own home."

"I wonder why," Diamond said almost to herself.

"Her dislike of Riss," Steven continued, "was starkly noticeable when Jacqui moved back home." Steven lifted a shoulder. "I was so busy back then and away from home a lot. It wasn't until a few years ago I actually noticed how unhappy and withdrawn Riss had gotten. Her parents were useless in defending her so I did."

"She's crazy about you. Her eyes sparkle when you're around," Diamond said, giving him a smile.

"She laughs when you're around," Steven said, returning the smile. "I couldn't believe my ears when I heard Riss laughing with you. That's a rare sound in this house. And tonight?" He cocked his head to one side. "Do you two have a secret?"

Diamond laughed. "It wouldn't be a secret then, now would it?" she said mysteriously.

"I guess not," Steven answered. His look turned somber and he suddenly stood and walked to the patio doors, staring into the darkness.

Diamond could see the stiffness in his back and knew that he'd gotten uptight. No wonder, she thought. Talking about his mother wasn't the same as taking an after-dinner aperitif to soothe the mind and soul. She waited until he sorted his thoughts. Soon he was beside her again.

"Diamond. I don't want you to go," Steven said quietly.

"Why?" Diamond asked in a breathless whisper.

"Because you can't promise me wild and wonderful things and then drop out of my life." Steven sat without touching her, but his eyes bored into hers.

"Am I in your life, Steven?" Diamond murmured. A whiff of Allure invaded her senses. She'll never use that scent again, she thought vaguely.

"I want you to be."

"Do you?" Diamond held her breath.

"Yes." he answered, thickly. Steven remained where he was, almost afraid to touch her. "What I'm feeling now is driving me crazy. I haven't held your naked body in my arms, yet I know that loving you will be an experience that I'm not likely to ever forget. Don't ask me why, because I can't explain."

Diamond shivered. "I feel the same," she whispered. "Since I first saw you. I wanted to run away that first day."

Steven moved to her and kissed her mouth tenderly. "I know. I wanted you to, because my body turned into a cauldron the moment you looked into my eyes." He groaned when she leaned into him. "You knew it, didn't you?"

"Yes, because you affected me the same way." She smiled. "Remember the drink?"

Steven did remember and he grinned. "I do believe the whole thing went over my mother's head."

"I'm glad it did, or else I wouldn't be here," Diamond said, then laughed softly.

"I'm not so sure she's so oblivious now," Steven murmured against her lips.

"As I'm certain everyone else isn't," answered Diamond, passionately returning his kiss. Catching herself before succumbing to his drugging kisses, she looked into his dark eyes. "I think we'd better stop or I . . ."

"Or I'll have you right here on the spot, and to hell with caution," Steven whispered in her ear.

"Then I'll really be drummed out of this house, branded a man-crazy hussy." Diamond missed his sweet mouth already.

"It'll never happen, not as long as I have anything to say about it," Steven answered. With great effort he pulled away, finding it misery keeping his hands to himself. He regarded her closely.

"Diamond?" Steven spoke quietly.

"Yes?"

"Have you changed your mind? You'll stay?" Steven held her eyes.

Diamond was slow in answering and she tore her eyes from his, before she drowned in them. How could she bring herself to stay here if in only three days she wanted to run away? The temptation to stay because of Steven was so great she feared that she'd make a fool of herself all over again. And to leave Nerissa? She'd already become attached to the teenager. However would she know what happened to the sad girl?

"Diamond?" Steven's voice held a sense of urgency. *She can't leave!*

Unsure of how she should say it, Diamond hesitated. "Steven." She forced herself to look at him. "I . . . I want to stay, but . . . because of you." She faltered, finding it difficult to convey her deepest feelings when she saw his body relax. But he remained impassive, waiting for her next words.

"There really is no work here for a companion. Your mother is perfectly capable of going anywhere or doing anything that her heart desires." *Oh, God, what an expression for her to use!* Flustered, Diamond continued. "I mean that she is finding busy work for me to do and I can't stand to be idle for five days a week. I need to work! It was a mistake for me to come here. I just can't play pretend secretary."

Steven's lashes flickered, but he said, "Am I not reason enough to stay and pretend?"

"That's just it," Diamond cried. "How can I do that? Slipping into your room at night, making passionate love with you and then looking at your mother the next day like an innocent!" Her eyes pleaded with him. "Can't you see that it won't be long before she and everyone else figures out that we're sleeping together?"

"All of them probably already know that if we haven't it won't be long before it happens." He gazed at her with desire. "I haven't tried to hide my feelings from anyone in this house."

Diamond felt miserable. "I know," she whispered.

Steven reached over and took her hands in his. "Diamond," he said in a steady voice. "I want to love you in the worst way, and it's killing me. There's no doubt that I desire you but apart from that, deeper feelings for you are attacking all my senses, constantly. What that means is a mystery because it's been years since my head has been in such turmoil over a woman."

He's thinking of Elise, Diamond thought. "Do you mean that you may not be just exercising your hormones?"

"You mean more than that!" Steven rasped. "You can't deny that you're aware of it!"

Diamond shook her head. "I can't deny it. I feel you too much," she murmured.

"Then stay." Steven held her hand tightly. "Sometimes I think that your moving into this house has saved my sanity." He stroked her cheek. "If you can make me feel that way in three short days, God, in time I'd feel like you'd given me the world!" He made a sound of disgust. "I promise to respect your wishes—for now," he growled. "With you right next door, I don't know how long I can play Superman. Steel, I'm not!"

Rarely was Diamond ever speechless, but Steven's words so filled her up that she could only return his tug on her hand. Apparently he understood her silence, because he did not speak, allowing her to regain her composure.

"I'll stay," she whispered. Then with a twinkle in her eyes, she added, "On one condition."

"Condition?" Steven looked at her warily, but noticing the sparkling dark eyes, relaxed his shoulders. "Okay, what is it?" he asked resignedly.

"That you give your mother a book on How to Utilize the Services of a Companion."

Steven laughed. "Don't worry about that," he said. "You haven't got your feet wet yet. Lunching with the ladies today was only the beginning."

Diamond looked skeptical. "I'm not so sure. Aside from answering a few letters tomorrow, there's nothing else in the date book."

Looking puzzled, Steven said, "She didn't mention the dance on Saturday?"

"No, I'm certain she didn't." Diamond was interested. "Is that the dance you and Juliette were making plans for?"

Steven grimaced. "Ridiculous nonsense," he scowled. "But yes, it's the culmination of this week's activities. It's an annual thing and the money raised is quite substantial." He looked thoughtful. "I wonder why my mother didn't mention it. As the cochair, she's certainly got a full plate and could use your assistance."

"Probably had other things on her mind," Diamond answered. "Maybe she'll mention it tomorrow." Looking at her watch, she said, "Since I still have a job, I'd better get some sleep. Don't want to be late."

Steven stood and pulled her up with him, holding her as close as he did before. "Thanks for not leaving, Diamond," he whispered in her ear. After a long moment, he held her at arm's length, then gave her a crooked grin. "I like the idea of being here on Tuesday morning for breakfast." He looked thoughtful. "Up for a race?"

"Swimming?" Diamond shook her head. "Thank you, no. We're barely going to have sixty degrees tomorrow! I can wait for a warmer day, thank you very much."

Steven laughed and hugged her again. "I'm going to love having my mother's companion around," he said. They walked to the door, and before Steven opened it, he said, "You go on up. No need to subject you to the stares you'll get if we run into someone." He whispered, "Can I come to you later?"

Diamond blushed at the hopeful tone. "Steven, I'll never get to sleep with what you just started," she protested, squirming from the sudden warmth in her loins.

"That was the idea," he said, warmly. He felt her body heat and he reluctantly released her.

"But . . ."

"Okay, just teasing. A guy can try, can't he? You've got a reprieve tonight, but that doesn't mean that I won't try again tomorrow night, Diamond Drew." He opened the door and gently pushed her through it. "Now hurry up those stairs before I renege on this foolish agreement."

Steven watched until she was out of sight, then closed the door. Emptying the glass of the drink he'd never finished he fixed a fresh one and then sat in the big chair.

Uncanny, how at peace that woman makes me feel, he

thought. Since the moment she had walked into the room he had felt the tension leave his body. What was it about this stranger from New York City who worked magic not only on him but on his niece and even his sister and brother-in-law? Nerissa laughed and talked freely and Jacqui and Christopher had found their tongues in defense of their daughter. How could Cecelia stand the changes? he wondered.

The scotch went down smoothly as Steven envisioned Diamond undressing, which led him to envision her naked, which brought on images of her coming to his bed. It wasn't the drink that burned his groin. He swallowed deeply, the amber liquid not so smooth all of a sudden. His words haunted him and he repeated, "Steel, I am not!"

Steven awakened to the sound of his pager, startled to find he was still in the sitting room at midnight. He realized he'd dozed off. "Russell?" Steven frowned at the number. Why the cell phone this time of night?

"Russ," Steven said when his friend answered the return call. "Why the page?"

"Obviously, you're not picking up your private phone, man," Russell answered. "Got a call to get over to the pediatric center. Quite a few kids were hurt. Thought I'd catch you before you left—see where you'll be working."

"What in God's name are you talking about?" Steven said, wide awake.

Russell was in his car driving over the Cooper River Bridge to Charleston. "Turn on the TV, get the news. Major fire downtown on Spring Street. Some kind of explosion set off fires in several buildings."

"What?" Steven had the news on in seconds, watching the chaotic scene of fire trucks and water hoses, ambulances pulling away. "Jesus! What're the casualties?"

"Bad. Surprised you weren't called. Heard it's hectic

downtown. People made it to the floor of a four-story and tossed their kids without waiting for the ladders." Russell swore. "They panicked. Only a few minutes more . . ." He swore again.

"Damn," Steven said, "I'd better . . ." He stopped. Checking his pager, he said, "That's MUSC. I'll beep you later." Steven hung up, racing up the stairs to call in and to change into some comfortable footgear. It was going to be a long morning until sunrise.

Diamond awoke to a sharp rap on her door. "What . . . who's there?" she said getting out of bed.

"Diamond, it's me, Nerissa. Can I come in?"

Diamond was at the door, flinging it open, panic rising in her throat. "Come in. What's happened? Your grandmother . . ."

Nerissa pushed past Diamond and turned on the TV. "Look. A fire, downtown."

Diamond joined the teenager on the bed and watched the scene in horror. The reporter, in an excited voice, told of the casualties from smoke inhalation and three deaths resulting so far from the fire that was out of control.

"It's after midnight; what were you doing up watching TV?" Diamond said, her eyes taking in the scene of bedlam.

"I wasn't. I heard Uncle Steven and then my mother and father race out of their rooms," answered Nerissa.

"Steven?" Diamond caught her breath. "God. Have you seen him?" She strained to catch a glimpse of the faces that were caught by the scanning cameras.

"No, but I saw Dr. Padget get into an ambulance. I'm pretty sure it was him."

"Who is he?" Diamond asked. She was anxiously listening to the reporter give updates as he got them while in between he interviewed some of the burned-out residents.

"Uncle Steven's best friend. He's a pediatrician," answered Nerissa.

Diamond remembered. "Why did your parents go?" Diamond asked, annoyed that the camera wasn't panning the ambulance crews. Maybe she'd see Steven.

"My mother's cosmetology shop is on Spring Street. In the same block as the explosion." Nerissa frowned. "She just finished fixing it up, too."

"How awful! Are you sure it caught fire? Maybe it was spared," Diamond said hopefully.

Nerissa shook her head. "I don't think so," she said, her voice full of doubt.

Diamond and Nerissa watched and listened in silence. Diamond prayed that no more lives would be lost and prayed for the safety of the firefighters. She didn't want to think of Steven somehow getting hurt in some bizarre fashion.

The news story ended with the station going to a commercial. Nerissa flipped the channels in hope of hearing more coverage, but all the stations were "paying some bills," as they called station breaks, or had gone to other stories.

"Maybe I'd better see if your grandmother is all right," Diamond said, slipping on her robe. She looked at the young girl, who rolled her eyes at the mention of Cecelia.

"Nothing bothers her," Nerissa muttered. "She probably never even came out of her room when she heard all the commotion. If it's not about her, she's not interested."

Diamond couldn't help but agree with the girl, but she couldn't in good conscience say so. "Come on, suppose you try and get a few hours of sleep before you have to get up for school." They walked to the door. "Once I see to your grandmother, I'm going to do the same." She paused. "If you hear them come in before I do, will you wake me again?"

Nerissa stared at Diamond's face. "You really like him, don't you? I mean, *really*."

Diamond blushed, but she wasn't going to treat her like a child. She answered, frankly. "If you mean your uncle, that's a yes."

Nerissa said somberly, "It shows a lot. I don't think anybody minds though, except grandmother. She wants Uncle Steven to marry Juliette."

Diamond stopped at Nerissa's door. "Now how would you know that?" *Not true. Not true.*

Nerissa shrugged. "People say things when I'm around as if I don't exist. And what I think is not so important."

"Nerissa, you're wrong about that. Which people think you're invisible?"

"Juliette. When she says hello it's always over the top of my head and she doesn't *see* me. Know what I mean?"

Diamond knew exactly what Nerissa meant. A perfunctory smile and false hello while dismissing the person in the same action. Diamond had run across such self-centered and rude individuals during her growing-up years. And many more as an adult. She guessed age didn't rule out bad manners.

Nerissa's comment about Juliette and Steven bothered her. Squashing the temptation to pump the teenager for more explicit information, she said, "Go on now, I'll see you at breakfast if not before." She hurried to the stairs, thoughts of her conversation with Steven buzzing in her head. *He wants me in his life*, he'd said.

Diamond's mouth was dry as she reached the door to Cecelia's bedroom, which was behind the stairs not far from the dining room entrance. All was quiet and Diamond stopped to listen, wondering if Cecelia was watching the news. If she was sleeping, there was no sense in awakening her. Morning would be time enough.

"Don't worry, she's asleep," Ferdie said in a whisper. She had come from the kitchen. "I looked in when I first heard the news. She's fine. No need to disturb her now."

"Hi, Ferdie, so you've been watching?"

"Yes, I was up when they all came flying down the stairs." Ferdie shook her head. "Come on in for a cup of tea. Settle your stomach."

Diamond joined the housekeeper in the kitchen, where the kettle was already boiling. Soon she was sipping the hot beverage. "Any late news?" she asked.

Ferdie snorted in disgust. "No, everything is in such a mess. Different stations were giving different information so I guess they said the heck with it until they get their stories straight." She shrugged. "Probably on the morning news we'll get a better picture of what really happened. Last time we had something happen like this we didn't see the doctor for days."

"When was that?"

Ferdie shrugged. "Can't remember the year, but it was a few years back when two eighteen-wheelers collided on Highway Seventeen South. Set off a chain reaction of collisions that you wouldn't believe."

"Yes, I would," Diamond shuddered. "I've been around for such disasters." She remembered doctors and nurses catching catnaps wherever they could, on duty constantly. She finished her tea and hopped off the stool. "Does Steven stay at the hospital?"

"Probably most of the time," Ferdie answered. "No telling when he has an emergency surgery. When he's just too tired to drive over the bridge, then he'll stay in his apartment on Huger Street."

"Well, I hope it's not as bad as it looked on TV," Diamond said. "Guess I'll try to get some sleep. Thanks, Ferdie, I'll see you in a few hours."

"Night, Diamond." Ferdie watched her go. "That's one worried woman," Ferdie muttered. She frowned as she hoped that Diamond wasn't setting herself up for a big hurt. There was no one who could replace Elise. Not even Juliette Malvenaux.

When Diamond awoke on Thursday morning, she knew instinctively that Steven was still gone. Ferdie had been right. Steven hadn't been home since he left three nights ago. He'd called briefly to let Cecelia know that he was fine. He'd performed a few operations and he was staying nearby in case he was needed. That had been late Tuesday night, and Diamond felt a little left out that he hadn't asked to speak to her; then she had chided herself. The man was dead tired with sick and injured people on his mind, she'd scolded. But she missed him.

Surprisingly, Tuesday and Wednesday had come and gone in a flurry of activity, and Diamond couldn't believe she'd complained about having nothing to keep her occupied. Each morning she accompanied Cecelia on a one-mile walk. After a mid-morning snack, they dressed and Diamond drove Cecelia to beauty appointments in preparation for Saturday. She sat with her in her doctor's office, and picked up her dress. Then, changing her mind about accessories, Cecelia led Diamond in and out of exclusive shops until she was satisfied. Before dinner, Cecelia took a few turns on her exercise bike while her exhausted companion headed upstairs for a few winks. Diamond was in excellent shape but by Wednesday night, she'd welcomed her bed.

She walked into the dining room and was surprised to find it empty. The table had not been set and there were no warming trays on the sideboard. Frowning, she headed for the kitchen. Granted, the room was too huge for just her and Cecelia, but she'd gotten used to that setup. Half the family was gone.

On Tuesday, after he'd returned from Charleston with his

wife, Christopher had spent the day packing and by evening had moved out. Jacqui had packed some clothes and left almost immediately. She'd taken a hotel room in town to be close to her burned-out business. Later, she'd sent for Nerissa to stay with her so she wouldn't have to shuttle her back and forth to school.

Now when Diamond entered the kitchen she was greeted with a grin from Tina.

"Morning. Breakfast is being served in here. I'm here early to get a head start on my dinner. I don't mind the company, though."

"Morning, Tina," Diamond said looking around. The table was set for one.

"Just you. Instead of walking, Cecelia did her bike thing, had some fruit and juice, and she and Ferdie just took off. Said you'd be delighted to eat in here."

"What?" Diamond looked at the clock. It was just five minutes past eight.

"Want waffles or pancakes?"

"Pancakes." Diamond looked baffled. "Have I been replaced?" she joked. Lord knows she'd done her best to keep up with the energetic Cecelia.

"Of course not," Tina answered, flipping the pancakes. "Cecelia said she wanted a different hairdo to match her dress."

Diamond looked incredulous. "But she spent hours getting those braids. Besides, it looks perfect!"

Tina shrugged. "That's what she wants and she knows it's going to take all day, so she took Ferdie. Didn't want to keep you from other things. She left a few instructions for you on the desk." She held up an egg. "One, scrambled. Right?"

Diamond nodded as she poured a cup of coffee, got up, and carried her utensils to the breakfast counter and sat on the tall chair. "I'll eat here, if you don't mind, Tina."

"Be comfortable. This is your home now. Here you go."

She set the generous plate of food on the counter. "Mind if I join you in a cup of coffee? I ate a while ago."

"Of course I don't mind. Love the company," Diamond answered.

"Yeah, I know what you mean. Pretty lonely around here this week. Steven away. Christopher gone for good. Jacqui and Nerissa in Charleston. Seems like the house is too big now."

"It does seem like that, doesn't it," Diamond answered as she ate. "But thank goodness it's only temporary."

"Well, I don't know about that," Tina said. She threw Diamond a curious look. "Guess you haven't heard." She paused. "Ferdie told me everything."

"What?" Suddenly she wondered if Steven was finally leaving his family. He'd be better off, Diamond thought. But how could she stay on here?

"Monday night, Jacqui came back downstairs to see her mother. They were in Cecelia's bedroom arguing. Ferdie couldn't help but overhear. Jacqui didn't mince her words. Anyway she said that she was taking her daughter and moving out of this house for good."

Diamond remembered what she was doing Monday night and she flushed. "To live in a hotel?" she managed to say.

Tina shook her head. "No. This was before anyone heard about the fire. She said something about a condominium in Myrtle Beach."

"Myrtle Beach? So far from her mother?"

Tina shrugged and didn't answer.

Both women knew the reason for the distant move and neither commented on the volatile family situation.

Diamond scraped her plate and put her dishes in the dishwasher. "Well, I guess I'd better go see what my duties for the day are," she said.

"Hold up. I got one of 'em right here." Tina opened

the refrigerator door and pulled out a wrapped package. Here you are. Careful with it."

"What is it?"

"Sweet potato pie."

"My pie?" Diamond was curious. "Exactly what am I supposed to do with this?"

"Carry it to the doctor."

"Steven?"

"That's the one," Tina smiled. "He called Ferdie last night. Seems he needs some laundry and other stuff and asked if she'd bring it to him. The last thing the doctor requested was a slice of your pie if there was any left. Since nobody is here to eat it, I'm sending the whole thing."

Diamond couldn't hide her pleasure. "He . . .did say that he liked it," she finally said.

"He'd be a crazy man if he didn't. Everybody loved it." Tina shook her head in amazement when she added, "I think Cecelia finished off the other one all by herself. And after staying away from it all her life. No telling about sudden cravings, is there?"

Diamond turned away. "No. I guess not," she said softly. Then, "I'd better go see what's what."

Tina stopped her. "Cecelia said that after you drop off Steven's things, take the rest of the day off, because she won't be back until late. She and Ferdie will be in North Charleston all day, so they'll eat dinner over there." She made a mock groan. "Wish I'd known that before getting here so early this morning. Oh, Ferdie said that you'll find Steven's things all laid out on his bed and ready to go. And don't forget to take the pie when you leave."

"His bed?"

"Sure. The door's not locked. Go right on in."

"Okay. See you later." Diamond walked out of the room. She wondered if Tina could hear her thumping heart.

ELEVEN

Diamond found the Huger Street address with no problem. It was only two blocks from Parkwood Avenue, where she'd lived when first arriving in Charleston. The Hampton Park neighborhood was one of quaint Victorian homes, many still boasting the original architecture. The bed-and-breakfast on Parkwood—only minutes' drive from The Citadel, a military college that in recent years had accepted its first female students—was a dream, and Diamond could have lived in that house indefinitely. The friendly hostess with the ebullient personality welcomed and treated everyone like an old friend. The furnishings, an eclectic mix of antique and contemporary, were delightful and invited a body to relax and feel at home. Old wide pine floors and the elegant curved staircase lent an air of old-fashioned grace and gentility to the house. When Diamond left Mount Pleasant, this is where she'd come until she bought a place of her own.

Diamond parked behind the black Lexus and took a deep breath before getting out of her car. She hadn't seen or spoken to Steven in three days, and all she remembered was how they'd spent that last night together. She couldn't remember a time when she'd been made love to without actually making love. Steven's kisses were sweet, heated, gentle, passionate . . . everything she'd want to feel with his naked body next to hers.

"Stop this foolishness," she muttered. That's all she'd

need was to let him see her desire. The man was probably bombed out of his head from fatigue and the last thing he'd have on his mind was an amorous romp in the afternoon with one of his employees! Would she never learn? Setting herself up in the perfect position for rejection. Then, whom could she blame? Only herself!

Diamond draped the suit bag over her arm while in her other hand, she carried a small duffel, holding what she supposed was a change of linen and shoes. The pie was balanced in her other hand. Ferdie had assembled the items and packed the bag, leaving everything on the bed as she'd said. The thought of going through his dresser drawers, handling his underwear, had given Diamond a rush when she was walking to his room. She'd been relieved when all she had to do was pick up the stuff and exit the room in a hurry.

Diamond walked around the side of the house as instructed and rang the doorbell. Steven's apartment was on the second floor. She waited, giving him time to come down the stairs. She rang again when she peered through the lace-covered glass and saw no sign of him. Frowning, she rang again. Seconds later, she saw him coming.

"Hi," Diamond said.

"Diamond?" Steven stepped back in amazement.

"That's me," Diamond answered, not sure of how to take his response to seeing her. Was he glad or sad? He was still speechless so Diamond said, "Your mother sent me instead of Ferdie." Her eyes shifted to his bags.

Steven reached for the bags and then grimaced. But he said, "Here, let me have those."

Diamond saw the restraint with which he moved and realized he was favoring his shoulder. *He's hurt,* she thought.

"Got a few minutes?" Steven asked, shifting the weight of the bags to his right arm. He didn't want her to leave. If he never had believed in magic he did now. For days his thoughts had been full of her and her sensuous kisses and sultry eyes, and here she appears on his doorstep. How could he let her leave? But would she want to be alone with him?

Diamond saw his discomfort and knew he was being courteous in inviting her in although she sensed that something was wrong. As much as she wanted to stay, she'd better go and let him get some rest. Days' growth of beard told her he'd used precious time for sleeping, not shaving.

"I really should go," she said. "There arc some things I need to take care of before the day slips away from me."

Disappointed, Steven kept his voice level when he said, "Thanks for these." He shifted the bags again. "Then, I guess I'll see you when I return to the house."

"I'll get the door," Diamond said, "you have your hands full."

"Right," Steven said and started up the stairs.

Reluctant to leave, Diamond stifled a sigh, turned and opened the door. She heard him suppress a grunt and she looked back in time to see him falter. Diamond closed the door, leaning against it.

"Steven." Her voice made him stop and he looked down at her, quickly hiding the pain in his eyes. "You're hurt."

"It's nothing," Steven said as he continued up the stairs. "I'll be fine."

Diamond followed him up the stairs and into the apartment, pushing the door shut. "Put those down," she said, taking the duffel bag from him and putting it on the floor. She took the suit bag and hung it on a doorknob to what she presumed was a closet.

"Now what's bothering you?" she demanded. "And don't say 'nothing' again. I can tell when something's bothering a man."

An amazed Steven said, "You can?" Mischief replaced the pain in his dark eyes.

Diamond blushed. "I mean professionally," she answered, flustered.

Steven looked crestfallen. "Is that all you see? A potential patient?" His voice lowered. "That's not how I see you." His eyes roamed over every inch of her body. "A patient is definitely not what *I'm* looking at," he said in a husky voice.

Diamond swallowed and almost gasped for air. Her skin was seared from his look and she wanted to escape. "Steven, you know very well what I mean. Now stop that and tell me what's wrong," she demanded.

Steven smiled at her frustration. "Okay, Doc. Professionally speaking, I wrenched my shoulder yesterday morning and its been giving me the devil ever since. Haven't had a chance to work it out and the hot, cold bit is slow in working." He sat down heavily on the sofa, wincing from the impact.

Sore muscle, Diamond thought. And painful! Sympathetic, she said, "Mind if I give a try?"

Steven looked at her skeptically. "If you can get this wing to working decently, the stars are yours."

"No moon?"

"That" you'll get when I'm a hundred percent," Steven said, his eyes raking her again.

Diamond grew warm all over as, husky-voiced, she replied, "Then get ready to deliver. I'm excellent at what I do."

Steven nearly melted from the heat in his loins. He had to stop this before he took her where she stood in the middle of his living room. He stood, retrieved his bags, and carried them into the bedroom, returning to her as she watched him with curious eyes.

Rubbing his beard, Steven said, "Let me get rid of this and shower up so that I can give you a presentable body to work on." He could almost feel the heat radiating from her body, at his words. Steven forced the groan to remain in his throat. "Make yourself comfortable. There's cold drinks in the fridge. I won't be long." He strode to the bathroom, wondering if he should have his head examined instead of his shoulder.

He just knew I needed a cold drink, now, didn't he? Diamond immediately poured a glass of grape juice and downed it, soothing her burning skin. Feeling relieved, she looked around the small apartment. From where she sat, she could see it was a one-bedroom with a living room, kitchen, and bath. Scanning the room she searched for a place to do the massage. Dissatisfied, she walked to the bedroom, glancing at the queen-size bed and the two dressers. Feeling the mattress, bouncing on it, Diamond left the room. "This will have to do," she said. The shower stopped and she heard Steven close the bedroom door. When he reappeared, he was dressed in gray sweat shorts and a black short-sleeve T-shirt. The beard was gone and he smelled heavenly, Diamond thought. *Get yourself together, girl. You're working now.*

Steven spread his hands, gesturing around the room. "Where do you want me?"

"On the floor," Diamond said thoughtfully. She wanted a harder surface than the bed provided.

With one brow cocked, Steven breathed, "Really?"

"Dr. Rumford, are you going to cooperate? I don't take my work lightly," Diamond said in a stern voice. "Now, if you would help me push this coffee table aside, we can use this whole area."

Steven complied, using his good arm, but Diamond had practically moved it by herself. He stood in the vacated space. "Let's do it." He was serious, and when she looked at him in exasperation, he realized how he'd sounded.

"I didn't mean anything by that, Diamond," Steven said simply. "I'm ready."

"Okay," Diamond breathed. "Just take your shirt off and lie on your stomach. No, wait," she said. She hurried to the bedroom, found what she wanted, and returned to the living room. "Take one end, please." When the comforter was folded into a pallet, Diamond stepped back. "Okay, lie down, please."

When Steven was in position, Diamond took off her sweater and knelt on her knees. Before she touched him, she willed herself to think of him as another patient who was in dire need of physical therapy.

Diamond didn't have to worry about a thing because she was in her professional mode, giving relief to tired, aching muscles. She'd spied a bottle of Lubriderm lotion in the bedroom and snatched it up along with the comforter, and now she poured a few drops, warming the smooth liquid in her cupped hands.

Starting with the firm, long strokes of the expert's relaxing or Swedish massage, Diamond was lost in her work. None of her touching even hinted at the possibility of a sensuous massage as her hands skirted the erogenous zones. Manipulating the back muscles with long, gliding strokes, she proceeded in an upward direction toward the heart. She kneaded, and pressed in small circular movements, eventually making circles down toward the spine, pressing with the palms of her hands. She moved to Steven's left arm where he had the pain, and using her thumbs and fingertips circled around the joints; then, using both hands, she made long gliding strokes up his arm. Without losing contact with his body, she moved to his back and with her fists began making short taps in rapid succession. Firmly placing her hands on his back and pressing and shaking in a rhythmic fashion, she vibrated the muscles, moving evenly and quickly all over the area. When she finished, she started the series of movements all over again.

Steven, from the first touch of her hands, knew that an expert was at work. Diamond's touch was nonthreatening, and in minutes his body and mind were relaxing under her deft ministrations, removing days of tension. He closed his eyes and gave himself up to the firm manipulations. Minutes into the massage he tried shrugging his shoulder and was amazed at the amount of soreness that had left his aching muscles. He'd nearly dozed off when he started at the feel of her hands on his thighs and legs.

"No sense in leaving you half done," Diamond said, sensing his curiosity at the full-body massage.

"No, none at all," Steven murmured, half drugged with sleep.

Diamond hardly heard, as she was intent on performing the same long, gliding strokes on his lower body. When she finished, she almost had to wake Steven as she asked him to turn on his back. When he did, she warmed more lotion in her hands and proceeded to perform the same firm strokes on his stomach and chest, once again working on the shoulders and arms.

Steven went limp as a newborn kitten and closed his eyes.

When Diamond finished, she sat back on her haunches, satisfied with her work. She'd felt the tension leave Steven's body as she worked and she knew that when he awoke he'd have mobility in his arm and shoulder. She smiled at his still form.

"Damn, I'm good," she murmured. Contemplating whether to let him sleep and have his muscles stiffen up again or wake him to get into bed, she finally decided to wake him. No sense in letting her expert efforts be for naught.

"Steven," she said in a low voice. He was sleeping soundly, and she hated to wake him. This was probably the most tension-free sleep he'd had in days.

"What?" Steven mumbled, opening his eyes. He saw Diamond through a sleepy haze.

Diamond put her hands around his upper arm and gently

tugged. "Here, help me get you up," she said. "To bed with you."

Steven moved druglike, following her instructions. "Sure," he said. Before he knew what was happening he felt himself sinking down on the bed. A fog covered his eyes and he knew nothing else.

Diamond covered Steven with the comforter, satisfied that he was sleeping peacefully, and closed the door. After she pushed the table back, she went to the bathroom and washed up. In the living room she did a few stretching exercises and then sat down feeling more relaxed than she'd felt in weeks. She realized more than ever that she missed working at her profession. Her mind full of jumbled thoughts, Diamond restlessly went to the fridge. It was already eleven-thirty and Steven would be starved when he awoke. She'd spied the remnants of his so-called breakfast: instant coffee and toast. Finding little more than a few eggs and a carton of half-and-half, she was convinced that there wasn't a thing she could do with that. She had to go to a market. Thinking about where she was, she made a face. The biggest market with a variety of foods was over the Ashley River Bridge and she didn't want to deal with that distance or the crowds. Then remembering a small, fresh fish and produce market on Moultrie Street a few blocks away, Diamond slipped on her sweater and got her purse. She left the latch off the door so she could get back in without waking Steven.

Almost two hours later, Diamond was taking corn muffins from the oven. She'd drained the fried catfish and placed them on a warm platter. The fried okra was hot and the potatoes in the microwave were nearly done. She whipped up some chive butter and set it on the table. Then she proceeded to set the rest of the table. Intent on her work, she didn't hear Steven open the door to his bedroom.

Steven watched Diamond move silently about the kitchen, his eyes wide in amazement as he saw what she'd prepared. His nose picked up the smell of catfish, which he suspected was in the towel-draped dish on the stove. With her back to him, Diamond struggled to reach the glasses on a cupboard shelf above her head.

"Here, let me get those," he said close to her ear. He easily lifted the glasses off the shelf and closed the door.

Diamond jumped at his voice and his nearness. She hadn't heard a sound.

"Steven!" she said. "You're awake." *Well of course he is!*

"You are a miracle worker, aren't you," Steven said, gazing down at her. "In more ways than one."

"What do you mean?" Diamond was uncomfortable under his scrutiny.

Steven gestured around the kitchen. "This," he said, and without breaking his stare, added, "and this." He moved his shoulder in a circular fashion. "The hurt's all gone. Thank you."

Diamond moved away, trying to catch her breath, wishing she'd had some warning of his approach.

"You're welcome." She added hurriedly, "Are you hungry?"

A long moment passed before Steven answered, his dark eyes hiding his thoughts. Then he said, "Funny you should ask. I'm starving."

"Good. Everything's ready." Diamond was relieved when the bell of the microwave sounded and she moved to take out the potatoes. She felt him walk away and soon she heard the water splashing and sounds of him brushing his teeth. When he returned, he was wearing the black T-shirt and had changed to long sweat pants. The food was on the table and she was sitting down, waiting.

"Please, help yourself. There's plenty of everything."

Steven inhaled sharply, then busied himself filling his plate and buttering a muffin. The fish flaked evenly when Steven touched it with his fork. After the first taste, he ate with relish, savoring everything. "Delicious," he said, giving her a pleased look.

Diamond ate just as heartily, realizing she'd worked up a big appetite. She was on her second helping of fish and refilled both their glasses with lemonade.

Sated, Steven was watching her, and when she pushed away her own plate, he said in a teasing tone, "A cook that enjoys her own cooking?"

Diamond grinned. "It shows that much? Didn't realize how hungry I was," she answered, studying the empty dishes. "Neither of us did bad," she noted.

"I overdid it," Steven said with a rueful smile. His gaze went to the counter and the covered sweet potato pie. "That will have to wait until dinnertime."

Diamond smiled.

"A cook and a baker too. When did you learn to do all of that plus handle your career?" He searched her face. "You excel in all three," he mused.

"My mother was ecstatic when I finally mastered her cooking skills," Diamond said happily. "But she was the master baker in the family."

"She taught you well," Steven answered. "I'm sure she's proud to have such a talented daughter." His tone was curious when he asked, "Did you leave her back in New York?"

"She . . . died some months ago," Diamond answered.

"I'm sorry." Steven saw the visible change and he sensed her discomfort. The loss was still raw, he thought. No wonder she'd wanted a change. They'd probably been very close. If his own mother had died last year—Steven stopped the morbid trend of thinking. A sudden thought hit him. If not for his mother, he would never have met Diamond. Would not be sitting across from her wishing that he were making mad love to her.

"Thanks," Diamond whispered. Painful memories invaded her mind and she got up, starting to clear the table, when Steven caught her hand. She stared at him.

"I'm sorry if I've caused you to remember," he said in a low voice.

"That's just it," Diamond answered. Her voice trembled. "I've never gotten her out of my mind. I can't forget."

Steven's heart lurched like a seesaw when he saw her eyes grow misty. He stood and was around the table in seconds, catching her in his arms. Poor kid, he thought. She never gave herself time to heal before escaping from the fond thoughts and memories that were probably driving her crazy.

"I don't think we're meant to forget the happy memories, Diamond." Holding her close, he breathed heavily to keep himself correct, but it was hard, especially when she wrapped her arms around his waist.

Diamond was surprised at her reaction, but talk of her mother was a surprise, especially with Steven. The last time she'd spoken about her was with Peaches, and that seemed like ages ago. Was she really feeling lonely and homesick for the only family she had left, and was just hiding it from herself? She hugged Steven basking in the needed attention. Finally, composed, Diamond straightened, pulling herself from his arms.

"Thanks," she breathed.

Steven stood back, letting her go without trying to grab her back into his arms. She felt so good lying against his chest. He couldn't help thinking that that was where he wanted her to stay. In silence, he helped her clear the table then wash and dry the dishes.

It was almost three-thirty when Steven and Diamond carried cold glasses of lemonade to the living room and sat down on the sofa.

"I'm afraid I've kept you from your other errands," Steven said when he noted the time. "Can you salvage the rest of the day?"

"Sure, but I'm really not in the mood for shopping."

"Now that's a switch for a woman, isn't it?" Steven smiled.

"Not really." Diamond sighed. "Your mother left instructions for me to shop for a fancy dress for the dance Saturday night." She threw an amused look at Steven. "She doesn't want me to 'look different' from everyone else with my New York style of dressing."

"What style is that?" asked Steven.

"You got me. That's what she wrote in her note." Diamond laughed.

"She did that?" *His incredible mother!*

Diamond laughed. "No problem," she said and stood, but looked down at him. "Are you sure you're feeling all right, now?" Diamond was really not ready for pushing a bunch of dresses around on a rack. She was quite contented where she was. And when she stared at him she was really not ready for the look of desire that burned in his eyes. She carried her glass to the kitchen and when she turned around, bumped into his broad chest.

"Thanks to you, I'm feeling fine, Diamond." Taking her hand, Steven rested it on his shoulder. He held it there until she felt the rippling muscles. "See, what you've done," he whispered. "Good as new."

Diamond didn't want to move her hand. She didn't want to move her body, except closer to him.

Steven felt her tiny movement and he grimaced. "Do you really want to go shopping, Diamond?" His eyes bored into hers.

Diamond's hand was still on his shoulder and now she slid it sensuously down his bare arm. They both breathed sharply at the touch of flesh against flesh.

"No." Her breath was soft against his neck. "No," Diamond repeated.

"Then stay here with me." With one finger under her chin, Steven tilted her head until their eyes met. "I want you, Diamond. Will you let me love you, now?" His deep voice shook with the intensity of his feelings. At this moment he knew that he never wanted her to leave him. Never! Waiting for her answer was like being suspended in space by his thumbs. Agony!

Diamond leaned into him, and on her toes, kissed his lips, murmuring, "Yes!"

Long anticipation and the fulfillment of whispered promises caused Steven to pull her into his arms, capturing her lips in a searing kiss.

Diamond accepted his plundering tongue into her mouth, hungering for his kisses. At last, her body screamed, as his hand snaked beneath her T-shirt to release her breasts. When he cupped them, she heard his grunt of anguish and suddenly, his kisses stopped.

"This won't do," Steven said in a guttural tone. He lifted the shirt over her head and swiftly unhooked her bra.

She braced herself against the refrigerator and slipped out of her shoes and slacks. In a blur, Steven moved and Diamond felt herself being drawn into his arms again. The sudden impact made her gasp as her body was thrust against his nakedness and his erection. The new and tactile feeling made her delirious with emotion. She felt Steven tug at her pants and they dropped around her ankles.

"God, Diamond, you're beautiful," Steven muttered. His absorbing gaze drank in every inch of her and his hand fingered the dark nipples that were brought to throbbing peaks under his touch. He slid his hand slowly down to her belly, then around her buttocks, his dark eyes capturing hers. When he touched her inner thighs, he watched her eyes moisten with passion and her tongue dart out to wet her lips. He immediately caught it between his teeth, gently nipping then sucking it into his mouth. Her gasp, when he touched her damp mound, sent shock waves through his body. When he probed with his fingers, then slid them deep inside of her, she stiffened and called his name.

"Steven," Diamond whispered, wiggling under the sweet agony. She fingered his sex and brought it to her female lips, but was stopped by his powerful hand grasping hers.

Steven nearly hit the roof at her touch. Feeling her need, he wanted to ravish her right there against the cold metal of the fridge, but stopped himself. He needed to protect her and there was nothing here in the kitchen. But God, he didn't want to stop her. Her mouth on his nipples drove him insane as she moved her hips against him, and he felt powerless against her onslaught of kisses down his chest while her hands massaged him.

Diamond whimpered as she felt him hold her back. She wanted him now, and couldn't understand why he waited. Never before had she felt such an insatiable desire to love a man and have him love her. She frightened herself with the fierceness of her assault on him, but she abandoned all cares, aching for his love. His pulsating sex was pressed hard against her belly, and once again she moved to draw him inside of her.

"Steven, please," she whispered. "You're torturing me. Love me, now."

Moaning and letting her guide him inside of her, Steven said, "Jesus, yes."

Seconds later, Steven cursed himself and withdrew, grabbing her hand and racing to the bedroom. "God, help me," he muttered. "Diamond. I'm sorry. Please forgive me."

Diamond was on the bed, almost dazed from loss of contact, but it was only momentary. He settled himself on top of her, kissing her lips, murmuring sweet apologies in her ear. She accepted him inside, locking her ankles around his, lifting her hips to meet his deep thrusts.

Steven was lost to the world when he plunged into her, assuaging the pent up yearning and desire for her that he'd had for days. He met her feverish movements and soon moved in perfect rhythm. He felt the moment when she sought to climb even higher than he could half expect, almost leaving him behind. Disbelieving of the incredible heights with which she took him, he followed. "Diamond," he rasped.

With an almost savage abandon, Diamond gave of herself, but also took, allowing the currents of deathly pleasure to wend through the deepest parts of her.

"Sweet Steven," Diamond whispered, unable to restrain the shudders that exploded within her. She whimpered because the joyous ride was coming to an end.

Steven absorbed the jolts from her body as he, too, felt the descent from their mutual high.

Diamond went limp, her arms releasing his middle and falling to her side. She was unable to untangle her feet from around his ankles. Her breathing was rapid and she had yet to open her eyes to look at him. She was afraid of what she might see in his eyes.

Steven lay breathing as hard as Diamond. Almost immobilized with the heavy emotions that sloshed through his body like a lazy waterfall, he moved from her, falling heavily beside her. His eyes were closed as he fought to regulate his breathing. By instinct he almost took his own pulse.

Finally, Steven opened his eyes and turned to look at her. She was so quiet. "Diamond," he whispered, "what's wrong?" She had her head turned. Raising up he said, "Look at me."

Diamond turned and caught his unreadable gaze. She didn't say anything but waited for him to speak.

Steven, wondering at her silence and his own inability to speak his mind, finally said in a low voice, "Diamond, the moon is yours."

Understanding penetrated her numb brain and Diamond smiled, her dark eyes holding his intense gaze. "Really?" she murmured. Suddenly her heart was full.

"That was the most incredible experience I've ever had,"

Steven spoke as if in awe. He planted a gentle kiss on her mouth. "That's the truth." He fell back against the pillow. *The God's honest truth*, Steven thought. Did he ever tell himself that he'd never know such passion again? Without his beloved Elise? His Elise who'd betrayed him?

Immediately, Diamond felt Steven's lightning withdrawal from her and suddenly her joyous feelings fled from her body as if they'd never been. *God, please don't let it happen to me again. Not with this man. Please!* Diamond knew that she'd fallen in love with Steven. Even before she came to this apartment today, she knew.

Diamond moved to get up, when Steven caught her.

"Where are you going?" he asked, almost brusquely. This slight but strong woman had a powerful hold on him—his heart. He wanted to love her again, yet was afraid. Could they experience the same emotions yet a second time? Could he?

Diamond responded lightly, pointing to his bedside clock. It was almost five o'clock. "I think that I should bring at least one package home after a day of shopping, don't you?" She twisted sprightly out of his grasp and left the room. Collecting her clothes from the kitchen floor, she hurried to the bathroom. In the shower, she tasted the salt from her tears as the spray of warm water pelted her face.

Steven wondered at Diamond's abrupt departure from his bed—and his arms. He knew that she'd experienced the same incredible feelings and sensed that she'd wanted to love him again. What had happened? It was as if she didn't believe his admission and couldn't wait to get away from him.

When he heard the bathroom door open, he was dressed in his sweats and T-shirt, sitting in the living room. He watched her closely.

Shrugging into her sweater, Diamond picked up her purse and walked to the door.

Incredulous that she could just leave this way, Steven strode to her, catching her, by the shoulders. "You'd leave without telling me what's wrong? Why won't you talk to me?" Then seeing the hurt in her eyes, he relaxed, dropping his hands.

"Diamond, have I hurt you in any way?" Steven said in a calmer voice. "You're walking out of here a changed woman." His dark eyes chilled. "It's as if I don't know you."

Diamond smiled as she raised up to kiss his mouth. "That's just it, Steven," she answered. "You've never really known me." She opened the door and hurried down the stairs.

Steven stared after her until she disappeared, her curious words boggling his mind. What did she mean? When he heard her car drive away, he felt, strangely, that she'd taken a part of him with her.

TWELVE

When Jacqui pulled up to her brother's apartment on Huger Street, she was in time to see the familiar blue car pull off in a hurry. Diamond? Arched brows showed her surprise. She parked behind the Lexus, wondering if now was a good time to talk to her brother. She had an hour to kill before she picked up Nerissa from dance class and she'd hoped that Steven was available. The fire had taken its toll on everyone, the medical community especially, and Steven must be exhausted.

Jacqui's cosmetology shop had been damaged beyond repair and she'd spent the last few days trying to salvage what she could and meeting with the claims adjuster.

Coming down with the blues, her whole life suddenly spinning out of control, Jacqui wished that she and Steven could bury their differences, and at least speak civilly to each other. She badly needed the advice of someone close to her, and who else should she turn to but her big brother? Talking to their mother was out of the question since Cecelia was part of the problem. All these years, since she and Christopher had moved back into the house, Steven and she had been at odds, a far cry from how they'd grown up, as friends.

Jacqui looked at the house, wondering if she should jump to conclusions. Diamond and Steven? Lovers? After a long, thoughtful moment, Jacqui decided against going inside. Whatever had happened between the two of them, it was obvious from Diamond's hasty departure that all was not well. Sorry for the missed opportunity, Jacqui pulled off. Now was not the time to make peace with her brother. How could he help her with his mind elsewhere?

It was past eight o'clock when Ferdie and Cecelia came home. The house was quiet and the two tired women went straight to their rooms.

Ferdie emerged from her bedroom and went to the kitchen to make a cup of tea, surprised to find Diamond sitting at the counter, apparently lost in thought. The young woman was startled.

"Hi. Long day, huh?" Diamond said.

Ferdie sighed. The water was already boiled and she prepared a cup of herb tea. Sitting beside Diamond, she answered, "Incredibly." She beamed. "But I think everyone will be quite taken with the results."

"Really?" Diamond was curious.

"Oh, no," Ferdie smiled mysteriously. "You'll have to wait and see." Looking at a note that was left by Tina, Ferdie cocked a brow. "No one showed for dinner? Not even you?"

"No. I called to say I was eating out. Running late with shopping."

"Boy, you must have gotten yourself a knockout of an outfit. Can I get a peek?"

"Sure, but how about tomorrow. I'm zonked out."

"Okay," Ferdie replied. Glancing at the note again, she wrinkled her forehead. "So, the doctor's still in town? He must be exhausted. And Jacqui and Nerissa, too? What a ghost house this has become." She tossed back her long braid and stood up, clearing the counter. "How'd the doctor look? Guess he was surprised to see you instead of me, I'll bet."

Diamond answered carefully. "He was. And he was looking a bit peaked. But a day's sleep will cure that."

"That's usually the case," Ferdie answered. "I'm glad he's okay. That man is a workhorse. Always on the go, never knowing when to say no to the next case." The mugs washed and put away, she said, "Well, better take advantage of this time while I can. Not too much to pick up around here with everybody gone." She gave Diamond a long look. "Sure you're feeling all right? Hope those are not circles I see around those beautiful eyes." Smiling, she said, "Better get rid of 'em quick. Can't let Saturday night catch you less than in the pink. Lots of eligible bachelors will be eyeing the beauty from New York City!"

Cecelia sat in front of her mirror, staring at the face made unfamiliar with the new hairdo. After months of thinking about it, she'd finally given in to the incredible urge. For the millionth time she raised her hand to her head and as usual was shocked as her fingers slid through the short strands. Her hair was gone! Even before she'd taken to wearing braids since her operation, her hair had been an abundant brunette mane. Never in her life had her hair been cut so short. After hours of removing the excessive amount of thin braids, her hair had been washed and conditioned, and it seemed like she'd fought for over an hour with that woman to cut her hair. The braider had steadfastly refused, and finally the shop owner gave Cecelia the style she wanted. The tapered sides were razor-cut and the back was shaped in a square, low on her neck. The top was tightly curled in tiny ringlets. All Cecelia had to do was brush and finger-style it.

"The woman in my dream," Cecelia whispered. She kept staring at her image in the mirror. Her hair was so like that woman's.

A shudder chilled her as she remembered a few nights

ago. Monday night, when she'd been abandoned by her family in the dining room! After they left, she ignored them all and ate her dessert. The taste of that pie had brought back memories of her childhood and she couldn't stop eating it. Diamond was an accomplished baker and she must commend her.

Later, while Cecelia was alone in her bedroom, the episodic dinner hour came to her in a rush. She tried in vain to rid her mind of the distasteful event. But when she got into bed, the look on her granddaughter's face when she left the room floated before her. Cecelia had tried to dismiss it but those big eyes, filled with fear, kept haunting her, and anger flared her nostrils. Why, only recently, did she care what people thought? She was the matriarch of this family even if her son was the male head of it. No one should question her wishes! Her eyes narrowed as she thought of Diamond and her smart remarks. If that young lady did not learn how to discipline that tongue of hers, she would not be in this house for very long. *But isn't that the reason she was hired? Diamond is a refreshing addition to this household. Admit it!*

Cecelia tried to shut the negative images out and prayed for sleep. It was then she dreamed. The brown-complexioned woman with the natural hairdo appeared again. This time she was not smiling gently but looked disapprovingly at Cecelia. She appeared to shake her head, and suddenly Diamond appeared beside the woman. They looked at each other and smiled and then stared with heavy frowns at Cecelia. They turned from her and then smiled at someone approaching in the distance. The face that appeared was Nerissa's. The two women raised their hands in greeting to the smiling teenager. Cecelia wondered why their hands were so white, and then realized that they were covered with flour. All three turned to Cecelia and their smiles faded. The older woman shook her head at Cecelia but never spoke. She looked sad. Soon they turned, and arm in arm, walked away.

Cecelia shook off the memory and got into bed. She heard voices coming from the kitchen but they soon stopped. She assumed it was Ferdie and Diamond, since she heard Ferdie's bedroom door close and then footsteps going up the stairs. Cecelia left the light on, unwilling to close her eyes.

Tuesday when she'd awakened, Cecelia had remembered her dream. She didn't think twice about it and had gone about her business with Diamond. That night the same dream occurred. Wednesday, Cecelia had gone about business as usual. And last night she had the same dream. This morning when she'd awakened she didn't want to spend the whole day in Diamond's company, so she'd taken Ferdie with her instead. Somehow the thought of spending another day with her companion after dreaming about her for three consecutive nights left her quite unsettled.

Picking up a magazine, Cecelia thought to read for a while, but she soon tossed it aside. With trepidation, she turned out the bedside lamp. She feared to dream.

On Friday morning, Steven was in his Ashley Street office, seeing patients. The day before, after Diamond left him, he'd instructed his nurse, Ginger, to call as many patients as she could and schedule them all for morning appointments because he would be spending the afternoon at the hospital. An elderly woman that he'd operated on wasn't responding to treatment. Before the fire she'd been bedridden with the flu and in trying to save herself from the flames, had jumped from her second-story window. She had three broken ribs and a broken ankle. He'd repaired the bones, but she'd developed pneumonia.

By ten-thirty, he'd seen his fifth patient. He was studying the chart of the sixth when Ginger walked in and shut the door and without a word took the folder from his hand and laid it on the desk. The bag she carried was placed in front of him. She proceeded to fix a mug of coffee. Steven gave her a scowling look.

Ginger saw, and threw him her own stern glance. "Eat. I had it delivered hot," she said and walked back to the door. "And don't wolf it down. You have three more patients and I explained that you've been going twenty-four-seven and then some, since Monday night. They saw the food delivery and they said take your time. They're not going anywhere!" She closed the door with a firm snap.

Steven's stomach growled at the good smells coming from the bag. Not a bit of it was good for him, he thought, but he opened it anyway. The last meal he'd eaten was yesterday. Only yesterday? Catfish and corn muffins seemed so long ago.

After the first taste of salmon patties, he ate heartily. "Ginger, you're irreplaceable." After his second mug of coffee, Steven felt rejuvenated and pushed a button.

Ginger appeared and briskly cleared his desk. She looked him over. "That did the trick. Now you won't keel over on one of your patients." Her eyes twinkled but her demeanor was strictly professional when she said, "Let me know when you're ready, Doctor."

"Ginger?" Steven threw her a grateful look. "Thanks."

"You're welcome." The door closed softly behind her.

After Steven left the hospital, he drove to Ann Street and parked. He'd phoned home to let Tina know that he'd be out again for dinner and had laughed when she joked that she was going to find a family that appreciated her cooking. After asking about his mother, he hung up. He didn't ask about anyone else.

The restaurant was a small seafood place that served excellent fresh fish. He and Russell liked it because it wasn't a tourist attraction, so there was always a table to have a quiet meal after a hectic day at the hospital.

Steven waved to his friend who had just walked in the door.

"Hi, guy," Russell said. He waved to a couple of colleagues and then sat down heavily, eyeing the scotch and water. "Beat me to it, I see." He caught the waiter's eye. "I'll have the same," Russell said, when the young man appeared.

Steven glanced at Russ. "I hear you. It's been a hell of a week." He took a sip of his drink then said, "I ordered for us. You're getting your usual."

Russell nodded. "Thanks," he said to the waiter, who set the drink on the table and left. "Ah." He drank and then relaxed against the cushioned booth, closing his eyes and throwing his head back. "I'm ready to sleep for a week, no doubt about it." Opening his eyes, he squinted at his friend. "You too, I see."

"I'm not so bad. I feel pretty good." Steven flexed his shoulders.

Russell stared. "Hey, you're not kidding. When'd you get the mobility back?"

"Yesterday." Busying himself with the dishes of food that were brought, he didn't bother to add any more information. Steven felt Russell's curious stare but ignored it.

Russell bit into a succulent morsel of lobster. "Don't want to talk about it?"

"What?" Steven pretended ignorance. His friend didn't miss the slightest nuance of change in a person!

All Russell did was raise an eyebrow but he continued to spear the tender fish. He shrugged. "That's okay," he finally said. "Your prerogative not to tell your best buddy what she's like. All he'd do is try to steal her anyway." He grinned. "No rings, no strings. Your motto, remember?"

Steven rolled his eyes. "You should have been a fool

detective instead of a baby doctor," he scowled. He speared a shrimp and clamped it between strong white teeth.

"Hey, man. Lighten up. It's already been killed for you." Russell laughed at the thunderous look on his friend's face. "Okay, okay. That's it for the funny stuff. Seriously, though. She must have come to you. I know you were too beat to go out and find one yourself."

Steven's heart thumped. "Who?" he growled.

Russell stopped eating. "Whoa, buddy." He threw Steven a curious look. "The masseuse. Or was it a masseur?" Then grinning, he took up his fork again. "Nah. It was a masseuse."

Steven gave his friend a menacing look. "Would you stop? We're here because I wanted a peaceful mealtime, for God's sake. I thought I could get it with you!"

Russell became contrite. "Yeah, I know. Sorry about that." He knew very well what Steven meant. That's why when he'd gotten the invite he agreed. The tension in that household was not to be believed and sometimes he wondered if it was only a matter of time before things came to a head.

"Okay. Forget it," Steven answered. He continued to eat in silence until Russell spoke, changing the subject.

"How were things at the hospital this afternoon," Russell said seriously. Steven had mentioned the sick woman. It didn't sound good and Russell knew how worried his friend was. Always wanting to go the extra distance for his patients.

"No change," answered Steven.

"That's a rough one," said Russell.

Both men enjoyed the rest of their meal in companionable conversation, pushing to the subconscious thoughts of the sick and injured. Both mentioned the need for more leisure activity and how it was and always had been a necessity, not a luxury.

Russell scoffed. "Am I hearing you right? Mr. Workaholic, himself? And when is this big event to take place?"

Steven gave his friend a wry smile. "Next month, Memorial Day weekend. I've been thinking about it since Mark Ellis called, and I'm planning to go."

"The Hawk from New York?" Russell grinned. "He hasn't missed Black Bike Weekend in years."

"Nope, sure hasn't. The last time we hooked up was when we were all together four years ago. He asked about you," Steven said. "Wants to know if you're coming with us." He prodded, "Why don't you? Take some of that good old-fashioned advice you're always dishing out."

Russell cocked his head, looking thoughtful. "You know, I think I can just swing that. What's the plan? Is he coming here or meeting you in Myrtle Beach?"

"Here. He'll trailer his bike down and park at my house. Then we'll hit the road. With good weather the ride should be great," Steven said. "But then you should know that. We've done it often enough."

"Yeah," agreed Russell, "but I'm a little stiff. Haven't ridden since I had the bike serviced over a month ago. What about you?" he asked. "The Ducati all you thought it to be?"

Steven grinned. "And then some. Actually, I took it out last week. Great show."

Russell laughed and shook his head. "Man, look at you. Such animation. Think you're talking about a woman!" Then, "What's Mark riding these days?"

"Same. The 996," answered Steven. "A slamming yellow, he said."

"The more you talk about it, man, the more I want to go." Russell shrugged. "Okay, you got me. I'm in."

Pleased, Steven said, "All right!" His eyes shone with excitement. Suddenly, he had an idea. "Why don't you work out some kinks with me tomorrow? Get in shape."

"Tomorrow?" Russell frowned. "The big shindig is tomorrow."

"Yeah," Steven said, bored with talk of the dance, wishing it was over. "But I'm taking the bike out early for a long ride. The thing doesn't start until eight in the evening so there's plenty of time." He eyed his friend. "Besides, you can use the wind-down time yourself."

Russell thought. "You're going alone?" Occasionally he and Steven joined up with the Low Country Motorcycle Club for daylong rides.

Steven's lashes flickered and then he answered, "Yeah." He saw Russell's inquiring stare. He waved a hand in exasperation. "You can stop your rotary brain. I was going to ask my mother's companion to take a ride."

"Oh?" Russell sat up in anticipation. "Well, don't stop there." Waving his hand in a circular motion, he said, "More, more."

"Diamond used to ride with a club in New York; had a spill, and she swore off. Hasn't been on a bike since." Steven glared at Russell's smile. "I only suggested she take a ride to help her get rid of her fear."

"Hmm, the hair of the dog kind of thing. I getcha." Russell nodded knowingly. But his eyes twinkled humorously. "Diamond, huh? Any chance that she looks like her name?"

Steven sucked in his breath. *Look like her name? She was her name*, he thought, suddenly uncomfortable under his friend's scrutiny.

Russell smiled and not going there said, "Okay, okay, you don't have to answer potentially incriminating questions." Instead, with a serious face, he asked, "So, are you gonna ask her?"

Relieved at Russell's astuteness, Steven replied, "No. May not be such a good idea after all. More than likely she'll spend the day getting all prettied up like the rest of the ladies. Mother insists that she attend to meet Charleston's society," he said dryly.

But Russell was thinking. "New York?" he asked.

"What?"

"You said she rode with a club from New York. Any possibility that Diamond and Mark are acquainted?"

Steven frowned. "New York City's a big place, Russ. Where'd that come from?"

"Yeah, but the world of black bikers probably isn't. You never know who knows who. And how could anyone forget a woman named Diamond? Especially if she is one!" Russell threw Steven a questioning look.

Steven swallowed the warning on his tongue. What in the world was the matter with him, getting hot with Russell? But every time his friend said her name, Steven felt a pang in his chest. As if her name on another man's lips meant violation of no trespassing. Diamond was not his possession!

Steven finished the last forkful of key lime pie and drained his coffee cup. "Your theory is far-fetched," he answered in a dry voice. He totally ignored Russell's reference to Diamond. "You about ready?"

"Sure. This was a great way to start the weekend," Russell answered. "You heading in tonight?"

Steven nodded. "I want to start up the bike tonight. Be ready for an early start." He eyed Russell. "Eight okay with you?"

"Fine enough," Russell answered. "We can breakfast on the road."

"Good." Steven felt great and was looking forward to tomorrow. He settled the bill and both men waved to acquaintances and walked from the restaurant.

Before going to his car, Russell said, "Do you think I'll get to meet her?"

"Who?"

"There's something to be said about instant memory loss, but I can't quite remember," Russell said facetiously.

Steven had to grin at the persistent man. "If not in the morning, there's always tomorrow night." He walked away. "Don't be late," he called back.

"Don't worry. I won't," muttered a preoccupied Russell. Was a woman named Diamond, a former biker from New York City, heaven-sent? It remained to be seen. Maybe now Steven could forgive Elise and allow her soul to rest in peace.

Jacqui was disappointed when she learned that her brother would not be home for dinner. She'd rushed through her errands, dropped Nerissa off at a friend's house, and then hurried home. But she soon got over it, realizing he'd needed some down time after his hectic week. She was lying on her bed, resting before dinner, taking in all that had happened in just a few days.

Only a week ago she'd planned to start her search for a home in Myrtle Beach. She'd never gotten there, what with her daughter getting sick. Nerissa's tests negated the possibility of an ulcer, and Jacqui had said a silent prayer. But Dr. Hamilton had warned of the continued stomach distress that could easily turn into a more serious condition.

"No need for the warning," she said aloud. Jacqui was taking her daughter out of this house. With Christopher gone, there was no need to stay and pretend to whomever that they still had a meaningful relationship. But first, she had to talk to Steven. With both of them leaving, what would the sudden change do to her mother's heart?

Friday morning Diamond awoke feeling out of touch with herself. She'd spent the night in bed wrestling with graphic images of her and Steven. The mad love that she'd made to him had burned her cheeks. The telegraphic pictures kept flashing before her until she nearly cried out with the intensity of her feelings.

Not in a mood for a walk, she reluctantly dressed in a warm-up, ready to exercise with Cecelia, and went downstairs. The house held the same quiet as it had all week with the absence of half the family, and she wondered if anyone else had returned home. The dining room was empty so she assumed that once again breakfast was being served in the kitchen. She found Tina just coming in from the backyard.

"Hey, Tina. What are you doing here so early again? Am I the only one up?"

"Hi, Diamond. Ferdie's out to the beauty parlor, so I came early, but that's not a problem. Jacqui's the only one upstairs."

"Oh." Diamond didn't know whether to feel relieved or sad that Steven had not come home. "Have you seen Cecelia?" she asked.

Tina poured a mug of coffee and then plopped down at the counter. "What in the world is going on in this house?" She raised astonished eyes to a startled Diamond. Tina gestured out back. "Cecelia is outside on her second cup of coffee."

"At seven-thirty?"

"That's right," Tina answered. "She was up at seven, did her bike thing, swam a few laps, and just finished breakfast. Said if you're up, come join her."

Diamond wondered too what in the world was going on. She looked out the back window but all she could see were Cecelia's sweats-clad legs in the high-back lounge chair.

"If you're not going to swim, I'll fix your breakfast now," Tina said.

"Is it warm enough out there?"

Tina nodded. "It's getting there. Almost sixty already."

"I'll pass," Diamond said.

"All right. Take a mug of coffee with you and I'll be right along with breakfast."

Diamond walked toward the pool, and when she reached Cecelia, she nearly dropped her mug. She stared dumfounded at the woman who looked up at her with a strange smile on her face. The light brown eyes glittered with an unreadable expression.

"Good morning, Diamond," said Cecelia. "Tina getting your breakfast?"

Diamond could only nod. "You . . . you look different!"

"Well, of course I do," Cecelia answered airily. "You've never seen me with short hair have you? *I* haven't seen me with such short hair, so of course I look different."

Diamond blinked. The look was different but the acerbic tongue was the same. She sat across from Cecelia, watching in fascination as the woman drew her fingers through the tight curls.

"It looks good," Diamond said, finally finding her voice. *Mama's hairdo!*

"Thank you. It took a bit of getting used to, but I think it's quite becoming. It feels so light." Cecelia stared at Diamond's head. "Now I can see the freedom you have with yours. Wash and go."

"Something like that," answered Diamond. She felt weak all of a sudden, and when Tina appeared with a breakfast tray, the smell of bacon made her gag.

"Thanks, Tina," Diamond managed. *The cake! The pie! Now the hair*! She had to get away from here before the people in this house drove her nuts, Diamond thought.

Cecelia kept up her pretense of nonchalance. She certainly didn't feel at ease. The faces in her dream swam before her the moment Diamond appeared. She tried in vain to reason it out, but nothing made any sense. Why all of a sudden was her paid companion floating around in her dreams at night? Cecelia fought to keep her composure but was finding it so difficult that she started to sputter on the pills she was swallowing at too fast a pace.

Diamond came back to reality at the choking sounds Cecelia was making.

Rushing to her, instantly realizing that it was not life-threatening, she patted Cecelia firmly on the back. Diamond was silent as she patted, waiting for the woman to slowly recover on her own. In a second, she could feel Cecelia breathing evenly. Diamond returned to her chair.

"Thanks for not asking stupidly whether I was all right. Can't understand why people ask that of a choking person." Cecelia's eyes were bright as she stared at Diamond. "Thank you," she said. "You are quite the professional, aren't you?"

"And a good one," Diamond replied. She was recovering from her own shock.

Cecelia slowly finished taking her medication and then said, "We really haven't seen much of each other this week. Did you find the perfect frock to wear?"

Diamond coughed. "Yes, I did." *After the most delicious delay!*

"Accessories? You know they make the outfit, after all."

"I really couldn't find the right shoes, so I'll wear something from my closet."

"Diamond." Cecelia sounded exasperated. "Wearing 'something' does not complete an ensemble. You really know better, I'm sure. What color is your dress?"

"Pink."

Cecelia clucked. "And I suppose you're wearing black shoes?" When Diamond nodded, Cecelia said, "I hope they're not patent leather!"

"They are." Diamond was suddenly amused. "Don't worry Cecelia, I'm not going to embarrass you. In fact, I'll be looking as fine as the rest of the guests."

"Not in black patent leather, my dear," Cecelia sniffed. She began to pack her bottles in the case. When she finished, she looked at Diamond. "There's nothing I need you for today. You have the rest of the day to find a pair of silk or satin shoes. Take your time. Believe me you'll be surprised at what a difference they'll make when you enter the ballroom."

"Mother?"

Both women turned at the sound of Jacqui's voice.

"Mother. You cut your hair?" Jacqui looked from Diamond to Cecelia and back at her mother in amazement. "What a difference it makes. You look . . . wonderful!"

Diamond laughed inside. *Only on the outside,* she thought. *Superficially, wonderful.*

After a few hours of waiting for a manicure, shampoo, and a trim, Diamond left the beauty salon and lazily walked around downtown Charleston. Her shopping completed for her must-have "silk" or "satin" shoes, Diamond headed for home. She reached the house at eight-thirty in the evening, contentedly exhausted and pleased with her purchases.

All day Diamond had refused to let her shock of this morning or the memories of yesterday haunt her. She made herself oblivious to serious thinking and decisions. Tomorrow was another day. When she locked the car door, she turned at the sound of a car and saw Steven pull up. She forced herself to breathe evenly.

Steven walked toward Diamond, surprised, yet happy to see her. His hands were loaded with bags and clothes draped over his arm. "Diamond," he said, nodding his head.

"Hello, Steven. I'll get it," she said, opening the door for them both. Diamond let him walk by her, locking the door after him.

Steven stared at her hoping to see something in her face that would give him a clue as to what she was thinking. Her polite expression told him nothing and he grew impatient. "Diamond, we have to talk."

They were already walking up the stairs together and Diamond turned her head and without stopping, said, "Okay." But at her bedroom door, added, "In the kitchen over a cup of tea, later?"

Steven glowered. He'd had a less public place in mind. "Fine." He watched her enter the room and close the door softly, still in the dark about what was on her mind. What was she feeling about him that made her leave him so abruptly yesterday?

"Steven?" Jacqui came out of her bedroom when she heard her brother's voice in the hall. She walked toward him as he opened the door to his bedroom. "Can I talk to you?"

A frown creased his forehead. "Is Nerissa all right?"

"She's okay. Doing much better."

Then what does she want to talk about? He wasn't in the mood for any family nonsense the minute he set foot into this house.

"Can't it wait until tomorrow?" he asked impatiently. "It's too late to argue, Jacqui." Steven sighed and walked into his room, ridding himself of his baggage. His sister appeared at the door.

"I don't want to fight with you, Steven," Jacqui said in a tone unlike her clear, assured voice.

Steven looked at her in surprise. It was years since he'd heard anything that remotely resembled a conversational tone from his sister. And she looked—confused.

"Come in." He cleared the chair of the bags, kicked off his shoes, and sat on the wide window seat, resting his back against the wood frame.

Jacqui smiled. They used to sit together on that seat as children, thinking up devilment. Now there was no room for her as Steven's broad body filled the whole space. "Thanks."

Steven watched her settle into the big chair, curious at her quiet mood. He'd always associated his sister with vibrant energy and lively eyes. Solemn didn't become her.

"Are *you* all right?" he inquired. Always it had been Nerissa who'd concerned him.

Again Jacqui smiled. Nodding, she answered, "There's nothing wrong with my health." Then, plunging right in, she said, "Steven, I'm moving out. I can't say when, because I haven't found a place yet. But I've been in contact with a realtor in Myrtle Beach and I doubt that I'll have a problem finding something suitable. I just haven't physically looked at anything yet." She hesitated. "You know that Christopher has finally left, so it'll be just Nerissa and me."

"I know." Steven's eyes darkened.

Before he could speak in anger about her estranged husband, Jacqui said, "He'll still see and support his child, Steven. He loves her."

"Hard to know," snapped Steven.

"Please," Jacqui said softly, "I don't want to go there with this conversation, not now."

Steven heard the plea and relaxed. "Okay," he breathed.

But then Jacqui reneged. "You two used to be friends. But since we moved back here it's almost as if you've hated him? Why? He wants nothing but to resume the relationship you once had, but you ignore him. The only reason he's lived under this roof this long was because I asked him to stay because of his daughter."

"And what about the other women, Jacqui? You can ignore that?"

"None of that is true!" she exclaimed. At her brother's look of disbelief, she said, "Okay, it was that one time. But . . . but, since then, he's stayed out because I . . . haven't really forgiven him." Jacqui lowered her eyes.

"You mean that you're not sleeping with him." He saw the answer when she looked up at him. "Christ! Do you think the man is made of iron? No wonder he hardly comes home! What'd you expect him to do?"

"I don't know," Jacqui said miserably. "I . . . I tried, but something just went out of the marriage. We finally agreed to a separation. He refuses to take Mam's guff anymore and he feels like the dirt under your feet when you look at him. He's a prideful man, Steven."

"Pride?" Steven snorted. "A talented luxury car mechanic and he throws it away to live off his wife's wealth? He was the best in the state, able to listen for a second to a Benz and analyze the problem. He was sought after, Jacqui. Yes, I lost my respect for him," he ended angrily.

"He finally told me Monday night what he's been doing . . . why he stayed away overnight sometimes." Jacqui gave Steven a defiant look. "He wasn't catting around as Mam says, he was freelancing."

"What?"

"You know Mam wouldn't agree to our marriage because of his position at Luxury Automobiles, Ltd. Said she couldn't abide having a grease monkey for a son-in-law. Wasn't fitting. So he quit."

"I remember." Steven knew very well what his mother thought was fitting. "Freelancing at what?" he asked.

"Mechanic. He gets referrals and he travels wherever the car is. He's extremely well paid for his work and I haven't had to ask him for a dime. It's his money that's keeping your niece in that private school, not yours or mine."

"You mean that all this time, I thought . . ." Steven grew angry. "Why didn't you say something?"

"Because he told me not to," answered Jacqui. "Said if you had questions you should confront him like a man."

"Damn."

After a short silence, Jacqui said, "Maybe one day you two can be friends again."

Steven was bewildered. "All the unnecessary bitterness and bad words. For what?" He shook his head. "Maybe." Catching her eye he said in a low voice. "Christopher isn't really the reason you're here though. What is it?"

"When I leave," started Jacqui, "how long before you leave too? Besides Tina and Ferdie, will she still have Diamond? And . . . if we both leave at the same time, what reaction will it have on her heart?" Jacqui touched her chest. "I don't want to feel guilty about leaving her if suddenly she starts rejecting her heart." Her voice grew firm. "If something like that did happen, I wouldn't want my daughter growing up with guilt feelings that she helped kill her grandmother."

Steven was understanding. "Forget that line of thinking. Our mother's new heart is strong and healthy. As long as she continues to take her anti-rejection medication and exercise like she does, there are no foreseeable problems." He lifted a shoulder. "But none of us is God. I speak to her doctor frequently, and he gives high marks on her recovery. There's no limit placed on reasonable activity."

Jacqui's sigh was audible. "I was worried, believe it or not." Then she grinned. "Mother does make it hard to like and worry about her, doesn't she?"

Steven had to smile in agreement. "Go on, Jacqui. Make your plans." He was hesitant. "I . . . I won't be leaving yet. At least not for another few months. If I accept the position in Connecticut, it'll take a while to clear up things here and get things started there."

"Connecticut?" So far away, Jacqui thought.

"Yes," Steven admitted. "I like the offer I was made." He rubbed his legs, then walked to the bed and sat down.

"Nerissa will miss you." She added. "So will I."

"I'll miss her too," said Steven. "You just take care of her and don't keep her in the dark about what you think are only adult matters. She's not a child, you know, and she feels left out of your life."

Jacqui looked serious. "She could always talk to you, couldn't she?" When her brother nodded, she added, "Thanks for being her friend. God knows she needed that in this house. I wasn't always there for her like a mother should be." A pained look crossed her face. "What is it about my daughter that our mother can't stand the sight of her? It's so unnatural!"

Steven looked angry. "Don't even try to figure it out. I believe that's something we'll never know." He looked at his sister. "I'm going to miss you too, Jacqui." Then he added, "About Mother's companion, Diamond, I don't really know how long she will stay. She expressed her dissatisfaction about her duties to me."

Jacqui guessed that she knew when that conversation had taken place but didn't comment on it, saying instead, "But if she leaves, will that change your plans?"

"No. Mother will be okay. I'm sure she'll just miss the rush she gets from hearing all the bickering. She'll get over it," Steven said.

Jacqui stood up. "You like her, don't you?"

"Our mother?" Steven looked innocent.

"Diamond," Jacqui answered, suddenly smiling at her brother, and liking the new feelings of friendliness between them.

Steven tossed his sister an amused glance. "As if you and the whole house doesn't know it," he said easily. "Frankly, I do, and you can't accuse me of hiding it."

Jacqui laughed. "No, we can't." Her eyes twinkled. "What does she say about you?"

"Now you're getting into my business," Steven said with an answering grin. "But if you must know, I'm on my way to find out. She's probably downstairs by now, wondering where I am." Before Jacqui left his room, Steven said, "I'm glad you trusted me enough to want to confide in me. Thanks." After a slight hesitation he asked, "Can we keep this up?"

"Sure can," Jacqui answered, swallowing hard. "I like her too, Steven. Says what she feels. I'm glad Nerissa's taken to her."

"My niece is pretty astute."

Jacqui smiled. "Oh," she exclaimed. "Have you seen our mother since you've been back?"

"No, why?" Steven asked, wondering at the devilish gleam in her eyes.

"You'll find out!" Jacqui laughed softly and closed the door.

Wondering at her strange remark, Steven shrugged. "What a homecoming," he muttered. More surprises with Cecelia? Grimacing, he dismissed thoughts of his mother. After washing, he went in search of Diamond.

Steven wasn't laughing as he went down the stairs. He wasn't amused at Diamond's remark. *You've never really known me!* Of course he'd known her. The passion that burned inside her matched his own heated desire. He'd always known that. It was almost as if she'd been sent to him to quench the burning need in his gut, to fill the emptiness in his soul and, God help him, to recapture the intense passion he'd known with Elise.

But from the moment that he'd been seized and engulfed by the love Diamond gave, he'd been lost—a willing victim to her fiery lovemaking. Steven believed he knew, when he'd fallen by her side, spent, and his thoughts reeling with what had occurred, that it wasn't just sex that they'd shared. She'd loved him! What he'd felt was her loving him with her whole being! But what had happened? He could feel her one minute, and the next she'd gone from him. Why? She had to believe that he didn't lie to her about his feelings. He'd never been to the places she'd taken him!

Later, after she'd gone, he'd asked himself over and over

what had gone wrong. What had he said or done to turn her passion so cold? The moment Steven realized that they weren't just two people giving in to sexual desire, that he wasn't looking to satisfy his own appetite, he knew that she was special and was not meant to pass through his life.

All day today he'd had the feeling that she'd changed her mind, that she would leave after all. What could he say to her to make her stay? That he loved her? Love. A shadow crossed his face. He'd had that once, he thought.

Steven walked into the kitchen to find it empty. He felt deflated, hoping that she hadn't gone to bed. Suddenly realizing his urgent need to see her, to hear her voice, he went in search of her, knowing he couldn't let her leave. He promised himself that if she let him he would come to know every inch of her, body and soul, before he'd let her walk out of his life.

You don't know me. Steven never wanted to hear those words again.

THIRTEEN

Diamond wondered what she was doing down here, waiting for another rejection. She'd finished her cup of tea a half hour ago. Unwilling to wait for Steven any longer, she stood, rinsed her cup, and left the kitchen, deciding to relax in the sitting room before she went up to bed.

Maybe Steven and his sister were discussing some serious stuff. She'd heard Jacqui approach him in the hall. When it didn't turn into a shouting match, Diamond felt happy that at last they could engage in some dialogue without going for each other's throats.

Desiring something stronger than tea now, she fixed a vodka and cranberry juice and carried it across the room. She opened the door to the patio to catch a little of the night breeze but didn't venture outside. Leaning against the door, she breathed in the sweet scent of the flowering bushes and listened carefully to the soft sounds, unable to identify a single night creature. So much for not growing up a southern girl, she mused. But she wouldn't change her life with her mother's for anything in the world. A soft laugh escaped when she remembered how her mother had defused the mysteries of the night by telling pleasant after-dark stories. She turned at the sound of Steven's voice.

"I thought you'd given up on me." Steven was beside her and he peered into the dark, wondering what had amused her. Her tiny laugh sounded happy.

"I did," Diamond said, lazily. "I came in here to settle down before going to sleep."

Steven looked her over. "You have," he said thoughtfully. "The nocturnal creatures and their sounds have relaxed you. You sounded happy a second ago when you laughed." His voice dropped. "I wish I was responsible. Instead of making you sad like I did yesterday."

Diamond looked away from his penetrating stare. What could she say? Agree that he did take the sparkle from her voice and her eyes? That would only lead to harsh words so she said nothing. He moved from her side and soon she heard the tinkle of ice against crystal.

"Diamond?"

"Yes?" She turned to see him sitting on the sofa.

"Sit with me?"

Diamond settled herself at the far end of the sofa.

"So far from me?" Steven murmured.

"It's a safe place."

"Safe? That's an odd word to use. You don't feel safe with me?" Steven asked, his forehead in wrinkles. "What did I do to you yesterday to make you suddenly afraid of me?"

"It's for me," Diamond said softly. "I'm making it safe for me." She looked at him with pleading eyes. "Steven, please," she whispered. "I thought that I could talk to you as if nothing had happened between us, to forget yesterday, but I need more time."

"You're kidding me, aren't you?" Steven looked incredulous. "Forget yesterday?"

"I should never have allowed that to happen."

"Allowed? Sweetheart, what happened between us was inevitable. We both know that." Steven grimaced. "Neither of us are magicians."

Diamond gave him a wan smile. "Would that we were," she said. "Tricks would be mighty handy about now."

"Is that what you want? Deceit?" Bad memories surfaced, causing his eyes to flash in anger. "I've had enough deceit in my life from women. I don't need any more!"

Startled at his outburst, Diamond didn't need any magical powers to tell her that Elise was the reason for his sudden fury. Realizing she'd touched a raw nerve, Diamond now understood that somehow his fiancée had deceived him in some way. He was still bitter, she thought.

"No," Diamond finally answered him. "I'd never want that. Especially since . . ." she caught herself. How could she tell him what other men thought of her?

Steven's keen ear heard her omission. What wasn't she telling him? Steven finished his drink and set the glass on the table in front of him. Instead of looking at Diamond he closed his eyes and laid his head back, remembering his thoughts as he went in search of her. He wanted this woman, and if they were to be together, he wanted honesty between them. At least he had to let her know his feelings.

When Steven opened his eyes Diamond turned from him to stare outside the patio door. The breeze had picked up and she welcomed the cool air. It held at bay the warmth his nearness always caused. The glass she held was empty and she was twirling it around absently.

"Diamond, look at me." When she turned to him, putting the glass down, it was with reluctance. "I want to talk about us. Tell you about me." Steven had her attention. "Will you hear me out?"

No, she screamed inwardly. Diamond took a deep breath. "I don't think that would be such a good idea, Steven." She ignored the sudden darkening of his eyes. "There can't be anything between us. I realized that yesterday, after we . . . we were together," she said.

"Made love! Can't you say the words?" said Steven with an edge of impatience in his voice. "We made love!" His jaw tightened. "*You* made incredible love to me. Do you want to sit there and deny that?"

"I could never do that," Diamond whispered. "It was incredible."

"Then why in God's name can you say you want to forget it? I sure don't and can't if I tried." Steven threw his hands up. "I don't know why I'm sitting over here trying to act civilized when I want you in my arms, re-creating yesterday. I want to make mad love to you all over again." His nostrils flared. "And I know you want the same. I can feel you, Diamond."

At that, Diamond froze. *Was she so obvious?* Was it only a matter of time before he hurled those horrible words at her too? *Oversexed. Nympho. Not a bring-home-to-mama type of girl.*

Steven couldn't believe what he was thinking. She was frightened to death and if he thought he knew the reason why, he was bewildered. His words had chased her to that same place she'd gone yesterday, when she'd left him a changed woman.

Steven moved to her and caught her by the shoulders. "What is wrong with you?" he said. "You're afraid to hear that you are a sensual woman?" He dropped his hands. "I don't believe you."

Diamond stared at him, waiting.

"What happened to you? Who the devil filled your mind with dirty words?" Steven held up a hand. "No," he said in disgust. "I don't want to know." He got up and walked to the door and went outside. She would squelch her normal sensuality, her feminine desire, and her heated passion for him, for what? Unable to comprehend or come up with a reason, he sighed deeply. She'd been hurt badly. It was so ingrained that she would deny herself the pleasures of a woman who wanted to give of herself freely. But she'd already had, he thought. So why forget?

Diamond watched Steven wrestling with his thoughts. When he turned and came inside, shutting the door, she didn't know what to expect nor could she find any words.

Steven sat beside her. "I don't know what happened to you in the past, Diamond, and you never have to tell me if you don't want to," Steven spoke quietly. "All I ask is that there be honesty between us from now on." He watched her closely. "I do know that in a matter of days you've come to be in my thoughts, day and night. I don't take that lightly. If it seems that I'm going too fast, I probably am, but I don't want to lose you." He hesitated. "Every time the thought of you leaving enters my mind, I see a void in my life where I thought there was none before."

Diamond shifted, uncomfortable under his intense gaze. If he could only see inside her heart, he would have no doubts about losing her.

"I don't know what you're thinking right now, but I don't mind sharing my feelings with you." Steven took her hand and held on tightly as if it were a lifeline.

"I was in love once, a long time ago," Steven continued. "When my fiancée died, that emotion in me died with her." He held her gaze. "You've stirred some of those same feelings in me with just one look into your eyes. The way you look, the way you walk, the way you talk."

Diamond smiled. "Aren't you plagiarizing the words to a song?"

"And that too, your frankness and sense of humor," he said with an amused look.

Diamond returned the squeeze of his hand. "Can I ask you something, Steven?"

"I want you to," he said seriously.

"The woman you loved, Elise, did she deceive you?"

Steven caught his breath and for a moment an old hurt burned his throat. But it was long past time to throw that anger away.

"You're the woman I want in my life now," he said evenly, "so you should know."

But not the woman you love now. Diamond did not let

that thought intrude upon her face. She encouraged him to continue, with another squeeze to his hand.

"Elise killed our baby."

"Dear God, Steven!"

"I never knew she was pregnant. Elise kept it a secret from me and when she decided to abort, it was too late for a safe procedure." He couldn't check his anger.

Diamond could hardly believe him. "My God. What did she do?"

"She found an incompetent out of town to perform it for her. She bled to death." Diamond was stricken. That poor woman must have been so distressed.

"Didn't you want children, Steven?" Diamond said softly.

"Yes."

"Then why couldn't she come to you? Surely you would have been understanding."

"Apparently she didn't trust me enough to confide in me," Steven said bitterly. "But she feared my mother more than she loved me. So she killed my child—and herself."

"Your mother?" Diamond was flabbergasted.

"Elise was frightened of my mother's tongue," Steven answered. Seeing the disbelief in Diamond's eyes, he explained the whole sordid mess in detail, down to the last argument he'd had with his mother and the unforgiving feelings he harbored for her and his dead fiancée.

"Steven," Diamond murmured, "I'm so sorry." She touched his cheek. "What Elise must have suffered. She did it for you, believing that she would be the cause of ruining your chances at a successful career."

"Diamond, that's a lot of crap!" Steven snorted. "I'm already a success. I've been a respected doctor in this community for more years than I'd like to remember. Elise fed into my mother's stupid sense of phony class pride and plain old ignorance!"

Both were silent, each with different thoughts. Steven

fought to regain his temper and Diamond struggled with new insight into another aspect of Cecelia's personality.

"You've been angry for a long time," Diamond said in a low voice.

"I know that. I've been less than intelligent about dealing with it."

"You were hurting," Diamond said. "Maybe now you can hold on to only the good memories."

Steven's jaw tightened. "Hold on?"

Diamond waited until his moment of anger passed. "You're still hurt over being deceived," she said softly. "None of us is perfect. Retaining the good memories about loved ones we've lost is a lot healthier than keeping hate alive. Just let the bad feelings go, so that Elise can rest in peace."

Steven looked with interest at Diamond. "So you think Elise's soul has known no peace because of my dark feelings toward her?" A bemused look appeared on his face. "It sounds like you believe in reincarnation."

"I'm not sure that I do," replied Diamond quietly. *If she did then that meant she believed Phyllis Yarborough was sleeping only yards away!*

She met his inquiring stare directly. "Sounds like I'm straddling the fence, doesn't it?"

Steven nodded.

"I'm not. It's just that some events in life can't be explained as black or white." She shrugged. "Things happen."

"The old gray area again."

"That's life," Diamond smiled.

Steven breathed deeply. "You analyze doom and gloom and put it in its place, don't you?"

"Yes, on the back burner." Diamond laughed. "Life's too short." She touched his cheek again, letting her hand linger for a long moment. "Don't you agree?"

Steven caught her hand and returned it to his cheek,

holding it there while looking into her surprised eyes. His body seemed to have been enveloped by a quiet peacefulness as his shoulders visibly relaxed. He closed his eyes briefly, brought her hand to his lips and kissed the soft palm, inhaling the sweet smell of warm grasses and jasmine.

"I said that neither of us were magicians," Steven murmured against her palm. "I was wrong. *You* are." He leaned over and kissed her mouth. Her pouty lips were soft and he wanted more, but he resisted. "Yesterday you healed my sore body with these," he squeezed her hands, "and now, you seek to chase away the demons in me."

Diamond said with an impish smile, "I told you that I was excellent at what I do." She grew somber as Steven's face turned into a serious mask. "What is it?" she asked in a quiet voice.

"There's more to us than a strong sexual attraction," Steven said in a voice that matched his face. "I've known that since yesterday, after you left me. All day today, I've thought about it and I believe now, that you, as well as I, know it is true." His voice softened. "Don't you agree, Diamond?"

"It's the truth," Diamond murmured, unable to break his stare. *I love you,* her heart cried.

Steven's eyes glittered. "Then you know you can't leave now. Not unless you're in the business of breaking hearts."

"Leave? But I'm not," she answered.

Steven shook his head impatiently. "I know, not now. But the time will come when my mother feels she no longer needs a companion. You'll leave. Just vanish." The thought repulsed him, bringing a frown to his face. "Your wanderlust may take you to New Orleans, or San Francisco, or back home to New York." A small pained smile touched his lips. "You may even lock eyes with a stranger and think you've fallen in love," Steven said in a gruff voice.

"Think?" Diamond asked, pretending coyness. "Couldn't that be possible?"

"No," Steven said harshly. "We belong with each other."

"Then you wouldn't want me to leave Charleston? Ever?"

"Never," Steven muttered. "I want you to be mine, as you are right this minute."

"Am I, Steven?" she murmured.

"Yes. You are mine, as you were when our eyes first met." The familiar warmth traveled his body. "We were being two conventional people in denying it for so long."

"How silly two people can be," Diamond whispered, staring at his delectable lips.

Steven guessed her thought. "Yes," he murmured, as he leaned to her and kissed her mouth. "Ridiculous."

Diamond pressed into him, as he granted her wish. Had she been so obvious? But she didn't care as she suckled his tongue, drawing it into her mouth. She placed her hand on his chest and massaged the broad expanse, squeezing the nipples gently. Through his cotton shirt she felt them harden at her touch.

Steven groaned. "Diamond," he managed in a husky whisper. "We're not going to take a mad drive to Huger Street, are we?" He felt her shoulders shake.

"No, sweet Steven," Diamond whispered in his ear.

Steven shuddered from the warm breath snaking through him. "Then, let's get out of here," he growled. He pulled her up and kissed the tip of her nose, afraid to reclaim her lips. "You'll come to me?" he whispered against the hollow of her throat.

Diamond kissed his chin. "Yes." A surge of excitement rushed through her in anticipation of loving him again. She felt herself being propelled from the room and up the stairs. At her door, Steven gave her a peck on the cheek and nudged her inside.

"Don't be long, or I'll come for you," he whispered.

Diamond leaned against the closed door, breathing heavily. "What must I be thinking?" she said aloud. But she suddenly didn't care. She wanted the man she loved to make wild love to her. She undressed and hurried to freshen up. At the door she hesitated. What if someone was in the hall? What would they think? Her cheeks warmed and she almost lost her nerve, but she opened the door. Her soft knock went unanswered and afraid of being caught trying to get into Steven's room, she opened the door and slipped inside. Steven was not in bed, but she heard the sound of running water. He was in the shower. Diamond envisioned his dark brown body, wet and glistening. Swallowing, she licked her lips, unable to stop the fire in her belly from spreading to the valley between her thighs. She found herself at the bathroom door and opening it she slipped inside. Steven's back was to her and she watched like a voyeur, wishing he would take her right there.

Diamond started when he suddenly turned to see her watching him. Embarrassed, she could only stand there, drinking in all of him and reading the message in his eyes.

Steven speared her with a smoldering look as he felt his desire rising. He held out his hand to her. Both were wordless as she let the satin robe drop to the floor. She was naked. "Come to me," he whispered.

Diamond stepped inside the shower and when he caught her by the waist to steady her, she trembled at his touch. The spray of water pelted her as Steven caught her close gliding his wet hands over her body. When his warm, moist mouth closed over her slippery breasts and his hands pressed her buttocks into his erection, her senses reeled and she went limp. The spray ceased to cascade over them as Steven turned the faucets off.

"I want to look at you." He slowly let his gaze wander the length of her, his breathing coming in uneven gasps.

"You're beautiful," he said in a gravelly voice. "Like your name, you're my precious diamond."

Diamond quivered under his bold, heated stare as her emotions went into another tailspin. He was loving her with just a look. She steeled herself when she saw him reaching out. When his hand touched her belly, she let out a sigh, then squirmed when his fingers feathered the wet hair between her thighs. He cupped her, then pressed his hand against the throbbing mound, teasing her as he rubbed in a circular motion.

"Steven!" Diamond closed her eyes but opened them after he brushed her lids with his lips.

"No. Look at me," Steven murmured. "You're telling me what you like and I want to please you, love."

"Oh, you are, and it's sweet torture," Diamond gasped.

"Then let me see if this pleases you." Without taking his eyes from hers, Steven inserted one finger, exploring gently the delicate flesh inside her tender lips. He smiled at the wild look that entered her dark eyes. "Ah, it does, I see." Holding her gaze, he murmured, "Tell me more, my love." He probed until he found the tiny pleasure-giving bud that quivered under his touch. Diamond's eyes were on fire as she tightened her thighs, rotating her hips to heighten her pleasure. When Steven felt the soft dew, he emitted a painful growl against her throat. "You've told me enough, sweetheart."

"Steven, please," Diamond whimpered. Her body was on fire with need. She wanted him now. She had her back against the wall and she relished the feel of the cool tiles against her burning skin. Unable to withstand another moment of the exquisite pain, Diamond swiftly guided his erect manhood inside her, nearly screaming in joyous relief.

Steven had held himself to the breaking point, trying to give her pleasure. But when she touched him, an uncontrollable spasm shook him to the core and he was lost, caught up into the whirling vortex of their emotions. His powerful thrusts were met with passionate rhythmic movements of her hips as she rose up to meet him.

Diamond welcomed every explosive move until she surrendered to his all-consuming passion. Waves of delightful tremors shook her from head to toe. He called her name and Diamond felt the warmth of his love.

"Steven," she gasped in sweet agony.

"Yes, sweet Diamond," Steven murmured against her cheek. Struggling for breath, he rested his heaving chest against hers. The thumping of her heart matched his own.

When Diamond was finally breathing evenly, she lifted her eyes to his and smiled. "One word."

Steven feigned disappointment. "Only one?"

"Incredible." Diamond wrapped her arms around his waist.

"Plagiarist," he whispered. But he couldn't hide his pleasure when he smiled down at her. "That's my word." He kissed her mouth tenderly. "But it's okay for you to borrow it once in a while." He fondled her breasts. "You'll have to come up with one of your own next time."

Diamond tilted her head. "Hmm. Really?"

"Yes," he murmured, nibbling her ear.

"Well," Diamond answered thoughtfully, "I already have one."

"What, so soon? Tell me." Steven coaxed.

"Uh, uh. You said after the next time."

"Did I say that?" He kissed her budding nipples. "Well, from the looks of things, that won't be too long." Suddenly Steven yelped as the cold spray of water splashed down on them.

Diamond laughed as she mixed the water to a comfortable temperature then began to soap his body. Steven glared at her and followed suit, but only after he gave her one more crushing kiss. Satisfied, he winked at her, his eyes making promises.

It was not until they'd toweled themselves dry and he left Diamond drying her hair that Steven stopped midway in dressing. He stared at the closed bathroom door then back at his face in the mirror. "You're a fool," he muttered to his stricken image.

Steven, dressed in pajama bottoms, sat in the chair, staring at Diamond. She had donned her robe and was lying on his queen-size bed, propped against the pillows. They'd been speaking in soft voices for several minutes when finally, Steven, in disgust, closed his eyes and swore again.

"I still should have exercised control, Diamond. There's no excuse for what I did," he said, still angry with himself.

"Steven, don't!" Diamond looked at him. "I've told you it's all right. I should have never walked in on you like that, but I did, knowing what might happen. You can't take all the blame. We'll be fine."

Steven looked at her sharply. "Don't make excuses. I should have stopped like I did yesterday to protect you. I was totally senseless!"

Diamond didn't know what else she could say to assure him that he was not the only one at fault. She thought of many funny one-liners but knew that he'd only be angered at her humor. Helpless, she just held out her hand to him. "Come sit with me?"

Steven looked at her like she'd gone crazy. Her shapely legs stretched out on the bed, and her robe inched up showing a shapely thigh. And she was naked underneath.

"You're mad."

Diamond smiled at his reluctance, guessing what he was thinking. "Okay," she shrugged. "I'll come to you."

When she sank down on his lap, putting her arms around his neck, Steven uttered a grunt. He rested his head on her breast, inhaling her sweet, fresh-smelling skin. He held her tightly.

"Diamond, Diamond," he murmured. "What am I going to do with you?"

"Shh," she said. "Be still." Brushing his face gently, she closed his eyelids and then kissed them. "Let me hold you." Diamond closed her eyes too.

"What?" Diamond awoke with a start. The sound of revving motorcycles rent the air and soon faded away. She looked around to find that she was still in Steven's bed. Sitting up, she said, "No, I didn't!" She blushed as she remembered last night. Had they made love again, she wondered? The last thing that she did remember was closing her eyes while on Steven's lap. No, she'd have remembered something so unbearably sweet.

Diamond got up, wondering whom Steven went riding with at eight o'clock in the morning. The roar of two bike engines was unmistakable. Fleetingly, she wished that she were on the back of his bike, holding on to him while they cut the wind. What a heady thought! Holding her breath and listening for sounds of movement in the hall, Diamond cautiously opened the door and quickly rushed into her room.

While showering, Diamond couldn't help wondering if last night's scene had been played before, only with a different female lead. Had thoughts of his former love distracted Steven so that he'd forgotten to whom he was making love?

Although Diamond had felt his intense love she knew that it was more than sexual desire. He loved her. But yet he'd never told her. Why did he hold back? Was it because he'd promised himself never to utter those words to another woman?

Be fair Diamond. You never uttered the words either.

While dressing, Diamond looked around feeling more at peace than she ever had in this beautifully decorated room. At first her heart pounded furiously from fright and then the fear subsided when she realized what had happened.

She was gone. With Steven's forgiveness, Elise was finally at peace.

FOURTEEN

"You're not the only one," Russell said to his friend as he eyed the crowded dance floor. His eyes were on the beautiful woman who was a dream in pink.

Steven frowned. "What are you talking about?" he said, keeping his eyes straight ahead.

"Whose eyes are blinded by a real live diamond. Don't be coy with me friend," Russell said. "She's beautiful. And I think all the men in this room will agree with me, even if you're trying to look so blasé that she walked in on your arm."

Steven caught his breath but said, "She is gorgeous."

"So why is it that you've only claimed her for one dance? Could it be that Juliette doesn't approve?"

Steven cut his eyes at Russell. "That doesn't deserve a response," he said dryly.

"Okay," Russell replied. He let out a sigh. "But if I had the chance to get her holding on to me on a bike, I sure wouldn't miss the opportunity." Russell looked sideways at Steven. "Bet you didn't even ask her, did you? You neatly evaded answering me this morning."

Steven lifted a shoulder. "She was—sleeping, I guess. Too early to wake her."

"You guess?" Russell said, taking a sip of his drink.

"I don't think you want to continue with that thought, Doctor." Steven spoke softly.

"I think you're right, Doctor."

Diamond could feel Steven's eyes on her as she boogied with an older man who thought he was Gregory Hines. The next time he twirled her she was going to sail right off the dance floor and disappear. *Steven, help me,* she implored. Her silent plea must have been heard because he was by her side the minute the dance ended.

"Thank God," she breathed.

"It looked like you needed rescuing," Steven said as he caught her in his arms for a slow number. "Enjoying yourself?" he murmured in her ear.

"Now, I am," Diamond whispered, as she fit herself comfortably in his arms. His hand on her back seared through the soft fabric, heating up her skin. Reluctantly, she drew away to a respectable distance.

Steven looked down at her, curious. "What's wrong?" he asked.

"We're being stared at," she said. "Can't you feel it? It's hardly appropriate for the respected doctor and the help to be embracing in the name of dancing." Her eyes twinkled. "I don't think your mother and Juliette approve."

"Forget about Juliette. My mother would like her to become Mrs. Steven Rumford, but that will never happen. She never was and never will be in my life," Steven said smoothly. His arm tightened around her. "Does what my mother thinks bother you so much?"

Diamond heard the meaning behind his words. Another woman that he'd loved did care what Cecelia thought—to the point of losing her life.

"No, not really," she murmured.

"Good," Steven said. His voice turned husky when he said, "Then can you hold me like you're not going to vanish any moment?"

Diamond complied but she didn't miss the look that passed between Juliette and Cecelia.

"Cecelia, dear, your son looks absolutely divine as usual," piped one of the group of ladies sitting at their table. "He's still the most eligible bachelor around, along with Dr. Padget, of course. Those two certainly keep the ladies guessing, don't they?"

"I'm sure Steven will know when he's found the right woman, dear," answered Cecelia. She stared at Diamond and Steven.

Another woman chimed, "Well, we all thought that Juliette was the lucky woman," she said cattily. "But looking at your companion dear, I don't know. What do you think, Juliette?"

Juliette's look spewed daggers at the gossipy women. Ignoring them and turning to Cecelia she said in her throaty voice, "Cecelia, I'm shocked that you've allowed yourself to become so influenced by that stranger. You speak of her like she's some kind of sorceress, weaving her spell on your family. Did she recommend that new hairdo of yours? You look . . . well, it's really not you. My stylist could have recommended a perfect do for you once you tired of those braids." She clucked her disapproval.

Cecelia was still watching her son and companion with interest, barely paying attention to Juliette's droning voice. Earlier, Cecelia had been surprised when Diamond walked down the stairs to the door where she and her son waited for her. She didn't miss the look of approval on Steven's face. Cecelia had never seen him look like that, not even with Elise, and when she turned back to the young woman, Cecelia couldn't help admiring the dress Diamond had chosen. The deep pink peau de soie was a perfect complement to the tawny tan skin, and the sheath style fell inches above her knees, showing off the smooth, shapely legs. A taffeta skirt flared from both sides of her slender waist, covering her hips and falling just below her calves. The low square neck and bare arms showed a wealth of healthy, beautiful skin. She didn't appear to be skinny at all, with her full bust filling out the bodice of the dress in a most becoming way. Cecelia looked at the matching silk shoes and bag with approval. Diamond looked ravishing, and Cecelia knew that the male heads would be turned tonight.

As Cecelia watched them dancing, she didn't think that her son would be one of those adoring males. Had she missed something this whole week? she wondered. A frown marred her forehead. Juliette was Cecelia's choice for Steven's wife, possessing the right family background and wealth of her own. She was also a high school principal. A much better choice for a daughter-in-law than Elise Cantwell!

Cecelia was annoyed. Juliette's voice had become an irritant, and now Cecelia turned to her as if seeing her for the first time, surprised at her sudden uncomfortable feelings. *She sounds like me*, Cecelia thought. *She sounds ugly!* To cover her confused thoughts, Cecelia turned to the younger woman with a withering look.

"Juliette, I hardly think that at my age I need your advice on my choice of hairstyles." Cecelia stared pointedly at Juliette's head. The long brown hair flowed to her shoulders in a straight, even cut. It was combed back from her face to show her wide forehead. "You've worn that style for so long, any change now would be a shock to us all, making us think wrongly that you are a progressive. So please, dear, if you will, don't recommend your stylist to anyone."

The hush at the table was broken by Juliette's cry of dismay and humiliation, as, flushed, she looked from one to the other of the women, who stared at her with overt amusement.

"Cecelia . . ." Juliette started, but stopped when the older woman turned away to watch the dance floor. Juliette followed her gaze. Then hastily gathering her purse, she stumbled from the table and hurried from the ballroom.

Cecelia watched as Steven said something to Diamond

and she walked away from him. He turned and approached the table.

"Lost your dancing partner?" Cecelia said.

Steven was feeling too good to be goaded by anything his mother had to say. He grinned, showing his devilish smile. "Not hardly," he said.

"Well I must say, Steven, she certainly has caught the eyes of the men in the room. She's quite stunning." Cecelia saw Diamond enter the room again, only to be stopped by another admirer. Amused, her eyes suddenly narrowed. "It appears by the worst sort. What's he doing here? I thought that he was from out of town."

"Out of town?" Steven looked around. Unable to place the face of the stranger, he said with disinterest, "Who's that?"

"How could you forget the man who knows more about the Rumfords and my surgery than I do?" she said dryly.

"Jeffers?" Steven remembered the stranger who had challenged the legality of Cecelia's heart operation. He looked with interest at Diamond and the man, who were engrossed in what appeared to be a serious discussion. Neither was smiling, and he wondered what had prompted a dialogue that required such somber expressions.

"Yes, of course I remember you, Mr. Jeffers," Diamond said when the man stopped her. "But I thought you'd left town."

"John, please. May I call you Diamond?" At her surprised look, he said, "Every man in here knows your name. I only had to ask one of them." He said solemnly, "An appropriate name."

In the past, Diamond would have welcomed the compliment from the handsome stranger, but as before, when they'd talked briefly in the lecture room, there was no spark of interest on her part. The man of her dreams was sitting only yards away. But she did want to speak to this man about his mother.

"I was very interested in what you had to say the other day," Diamond said, letting him know by omission that she wasn't about amorous adventures. Satisfied with the disappearance of the gleam in his eyes, she continued. "But I really want to know your gut feelings about transplants. I wasn't sure whether you were for or against them."

John Jeffers looked at the forthright young woman and wondered why he thought that she might be available. Accepting that as his loss, he listened seriously to what she was saying.

"I never had a chance to answer your question," Diamond said. "I never approved of organ donations and it was a sore point between me and my mother."

John nodded. "I'm not surprised. There are a lot of people who feel as you do. It's a scary situation for many of us who don't understand every aspect of the procedure and the possibility of unequal and unethical practices."

"Like monitoring, as you suggested?"

"Yes." John shrugged. "I do believe in organ transplants. It's just that I also believe in a watchdog outfit to assure fairness in allocating the donated organs."

"You belong to such a group? Is that why you know so much about Mrs. Rumford?"

"When I was watching my mother die," John said, "I felt helpless that there was nothing that I could do. I remember that she was so sad toward the end. She knew she was going to die and she cried out her frustration." He spoke as if remembering. "She wished that more African-Americans were educated about organ donation. The need for close matchups between donor and recipient blood types and genetic makeup is crucial to any kind of transplantation." He gave a wry smile. "She joked that her would-be unregistered 'match' was probably living right in the Bronx, unaware that they could one day be a lifesaver."

Diamond's heart went out to him. "Is that when you chose?" she asked.

He nodded. "I completed the back of my driver license, giving permission to use my organs upon my death. Just as in your mother's case. It was her decision to make."

"I know," Diamond answered.

"You're still disapproving, aren't you?"

Diamond nodded. "I suppose I am," she replied hesitantly. "Maybe one day I'll rid myself of my unorthodox fears."

"Maybe," John said. "Well, it's been interesting talking to you, Diamond, but I think my cousin is looking for me. We've a little drive ahead of us and I'll be heading back to New York in the morning."

Diamond held out her hand. "Good-bye, John. Thanks for listening."

"My pleasure," John answered. Then he added, "You're probably well informed about the donation subject but it never hurts to get as many viewpoints as you can. There's a community education group that is very helpful. It's the National Minority Organ Tissue Transplant Education Program in the Washington, D. C., motor vehicle bureaus."

Diamond nodded. "Yes, I know about them, but thanks."

"No problem," John said. "Good-bye, Diamond." He walked away.

Diamond was thoughtful as she walked back to the table, politely refusing offers to dance. When she sat down at the nearly empty table, she took a drink of water and then looked around for Steven. She saw him dancing with one of Cecelia's friends. A fast-paced salsa had the older woman keeping in pretty good step with the smooth-dancing doctor. Diamond smiled and looked away, meeting the curious stare of Cecelia.

"Nice dance, Cecelia," Diamond said cautiously, wondering what was coming. The woman had been looking at her strangely since yesterday, and Diamond wondered if Cecelia had guessed about her son's new love affair.

"Yes, it usually is. A lot of money was raised tonight."

Her eyes glittered and an amused smile appeared on her lips. "I'm surprised that Mr. Jeffers contributed to our efforts," she said.

"He's not opposed to the effort," Diamond said with a direct look. "Just concerned." She said no more and didn't invite any further comment from Cecelia when she looked away.

Cecelia didn't press Diamond, but found herself wondering more and more about this young woman who continued to walk through Cecelia's dreams at night. She looked at her son, who appeared by Diamond's side.

"Mother, I have to leave. I've made arrangements for Russ to drive you and Diamond back home." Steven turned to Diamond and said, "Could I see you outside?"

Diamond excused herself and walked with Steven to a secluded spot outside the ballroom. "Steven, what is it?" Her eyes filled with concern.

"Just this," he said, and took her in his arms.

His kiss was tender yet demanding, and Diamond welcomed him, leaning into his taut body. She was just as hungry for his kisses.

With reluctance, Steven lifted his head. "I couldn't leave without that," he said huskily. "It'll hold me until I get back from the hospital tonight." His dark eyes held hers. "I can't ask you to wait up for me, but can I come to you?"

"Wake me," Diamond breathed.

"Count on it." Steven kissed her mouth again, then hurried away.

Diamond watched him go, missing him already but happy at the thought of what a wild and wonderful awakening she was going to have before morning.

In the weeks following, the May weather was more summer than springlike. Diamond welcomed the change because now she could enjoy the pool. Even after early morning swims, she would return with Cecelia, who swam almost daily. Frequently, they spent afternoons sunning themselves in the yard, enjoying the quiet beauty of the fragrant flower gardens.

Diamond had to laugh to herself when she remembered complaining about doing very little work. Apparently Cecelia had impressed someone with her talk the month before because the week after, calls and letters started coming in, requesting her as guest lecturer. Pleased, Cecelia accepted most of the speaking engagements, confident that she was doing her part in community education. Diamond drove to parts of Charleston she'd never been, traveled to Hilton Head, and even to Georgia, where they'd stayed a few nights. And tomorrow, they were flying to Miami, Florida.

When Diamond made the arrangements for that trip, she had been ecstatic. She would be able to see Peaches! Because they'd arrive on the Thursday before the start of the Memorial Day weekend, Peaches and her husband were planning a cookout in their honor on Sunday. Diamond had joked about that, asking Peaches to brace herself for a candid Cecelia.

Cecelia gathered her paraphernalia from the table and picked up her towel. "I'm going in to double-check my bags before dinner," she said. She peered closely at Diamond, who'd been strangely silent all day. "You're not coming down with a cold, are you?" Cecelia was always wary of germs, a fear from when infections from the common cold would weaken her system. Although she was healthy, she did her best to stay away from infected persons.

Diamond lifted her head. "No, Cecelia, I'm fine. Just thinking." She picked up her things and joined Cecelia on the walk to the house.

Relieved, Cecelia said, "Tina is preparing a special dinner tonight." At Diamond's inquiring look, she said, "In honor of the family eating together for the first time in weeks." A grim look crossed her face. "And I suppose, a sort of farewell dinner because it will be a long time before it happens again."

Diamond knew what she meant. Jacqui had found a condominium in Myrtle Beach and she and Nerissa would be leaving Mount Pleasant at the end of the school year. Christopher had moved to Hilton Head but missed his daughter and was coming tonight to visit her. And Steven would be home.

As if reading Diamond's last thought, Cecelia said, "Steven is finally coming to his senses. Moping around like he's the only doctor on earth who's lost a patient."

"Now you have an idea how he would have acted had he lost you, Cecelia." Diamond brushed past the insensitive woman and rushed to her room, not caring about her rude outburst.

Cecelia's eyes widened in surprise as she stared at the fleeing Diamond. Thoughtfully, she walked to her room, making a mental note to be a silent observer at the dinner table tonight.

Diamond showered, put on her robe, and lay down on the bed. There was a two- hour wait before dinner and she didn't want to spend the time in the company of the rest of the family. Her thoughts were on Steven. She'd barely seen him in these last weeks and she missed him terribly. The night of the dance he'd never come home. The patient that had taken a turn for the worse that night had hung on for two days before finally succumbing. The elderly woman, his fire victim, never regained enough strength to fight the debilitating pneumonia. When Steven called her, Diamond had wanted to go to him, but he refused, saying that he'd be home soon. But he never returned home except for a hot minute and then he went back to the hospital. He'd become hawklike over his surgery patients, staying in the hospital or at his apartment so that he would be only a minute away if needed.

Diamond sighed. If that weren't enough, he took on the patient load of a vacationing surgeon. One Sunday, while Cecelia and the rest of the family were in church, Diamond visited Steven at his apartment. Happy to finally have some private time with him, Diamond was overjoyed at being held in his arms. Almost immediately, she felt his fatigue. She fixed him a light meal and after he'd eaten, insisted he get into bed. She joined him and instead of making love, they fell asleep in each other's arms.

Diamond breathed a prayer of thanks that his long-planned vacation to Myrtle Beach with his friends had finally arrived, knowing that he was dead on his feet.

She felt her eyes closing and deciding to catch a catnap, she took off her robe and got under the covers, the sheets feeling deliciously cool against her naked body.

Steven frowned when he knocked again on Diamond's bedroom door. She wasn't anywhere downstairs, he knew. He knocked again. When there was no answer he swore and walked to his room.

"Hi, Uncle Steven," Nerissa said as she came out of her room. "Missed you around here." She looked at her uncle with sad eyes, thinking of when she would never see him at all, once she and her mother moved so far away.

Steven turned from his door. "Hi, Riss," he said, going to his niece and giving her a hug and a kiss. "Missed you too." He held her at arm's length and squinted. "Did you grow? Now I know I haven't been gone that long!" He stared hard. "You look so grown up."

Nerissa laughed. "I am grown up. I'll be fifteen soon."

Steven gave a mock frown. "Since when is six months considered 'soon?' "

"Well, almost," Nerissa conceded.

"You're wearing makeup!" Steven looked again. "That's what's different," he said in surprise. His eyes narrowed.

"Whatever happened to a little lipstick? What's with the eyeliner and rouge?"

Nerissa shrugged. "Everybody my age wears it, Uncle Steven. I'm just trying to catch up."

Steven didn't like the sound of that. "Does your mother approve?"

"She said yes if I don't overdo it."

"Has she seen you yet?"

"No."

"Then I think you've overdone it," Steven said. "Trust me." When Nerissa just looked at him, he said, "Don't touch a thing. Wait and get her opinion." He winked. "I'm old, but I think I still know what attracts me to a young lady, and all that gunk ain't it," he said, giving her a serious look.

Nerissa looked thoughtfully at her handsome uncle. "Are you attracted to Diamond?"

Where'd that come from? Steven thought. "Yes, I am."

"Do you love her?"

Steven was silent. *What else is it but love?* He was going crazy being away from her. To his niece he said, "A gentleman doesn't discuss a lady's business, especially without her permission." He kissed her forehead. "By the way, have you seen her?"

"No. She was in her room a while ago though," Nerissa answered. "I heard the water running." She turned to leave, but hesitated. "Uncle Steven, I'm glad you're here tonight." She turned to go, but was stopped by her uncle's voice.

"Hey, hey," Steven said. He tilted her head up to his. "Are those tears?" He tried to joke. "Now a young lady who wears eye makeup knows enough not to cry. Black streaks on the cheeks ain't pretty." When the tears really began to fall, Steven said, "I'm sorry, Riss, just a poor joke." He waited a second then said, "Want to talk about it?"

Nerissa sniffed and wiped her face, smearing the mascara. "I used to dream about moving away from grandmother," she said. "Now that I'm going, I know I'll never get to see you. Mama and Daddy have finally split up. I knew it was coming but now it's real. I—didn't think that he would move so far away from me." The tears fell harder. "And Diamond . . . she's my friend now and I'll miss her so much when she leaves." Her uncle looked at her in surprise. Nerissa nodded her head. "I caught her looking so sad a few times. Especially when she looks at Grandmother when she thinks no one is watching. I have the feeling that she doesn't like being here anymore and is going to quit." Nerissa slid down the wall and sat on the floor, hugging her face in her drawn-up knees. "Everything is changing so fast," she mumbled.

Steven didn't know what to think and had no idea his niece was hurting so much. He sank down beside her and crossed his ankles. He waited until she quieted. When her sobs stopped he said quietly. "Riss, it's hard for me to know what to tell you about your parents. You're very wise to have seen it coming, but now that their breakup is a reality you'll have to respect their decision and try to handle it in the most sensible way that you can. You know they both love you. Your father had no choice but to relocate to his new job."

Steven struggled for the right words. What could he say to the teenager whose world was tumbling down around her ears? "And I'll do my damnedest to see you as often as I can. Just remember that you can always call me. Understand?"

Nerissa raised her tear-stained face and nodded.

"Good," Steven said. He frowned. "Now what's this about Diamond leaving?"

Nerissa lifted a shoulder. "She never said that. It's just a feeling I have." Nerissa sniffled again. "I think she misses you too," she said, sliding against the wall and standing up.

Steven stood up. "I miss her too," he said, glancing solemnly at his niece. "You feeling better?"

"Yes, I think so."

"All right. Remember what I said. And give your parents a chance."

Nerissa nodded. "I'll try." She gave her uncle a smile. "I'm glad you're here."

"You already said that." Steven flashed her a grin. "Sign of old age. Maybe you are getting older by the second." Squinting, he looked at her out of one eye. "I think your makeup needs a little attention."

Nerissa laughed. "See ya later." She disappeared into her room.

Steven watched her go, relieved that she could smile. He turned to Diamond's door.

Recalling Nerissa's words, he thought that Diamond must be asleep. Steven remembered a shower scene that made him grow warm. He knocked on her door again, hoping.

Diamond thought she heard Steven's voice and she half opened her eyes, but she was in bed alone. "Steven?" she said. Only a dream she thought, and closed her eyes.

Hearing his name, Steven opened the door. "Diamond?" He saw her in bed. "Diamond?" he repeated. He closed the door and walked to the bed. She was half asleep.

"Steven?" Diamond said dreamily. "Where are you?"

"Right here, sweetheart," Steven murmured. He sat down on the bed and kissed her mouth. How good she tasted and he wondered how could he have stayed away from her for so long. God, he'd missed her. He kissed her again, and she responded almost dreamily, lifting her arms to him. The covers fell away exposing her bare breasts. He gasped and bent to kiss them, nibbling at the nipples that tautened inside his mouth.

"Steven?" Diamond opened her sleep-swollen eyes. "Oh," she moaned, closing her eyes briefly, then smiling. "You are here." She hugged him.

Steven groaned at the feel of her breasts pressed against his chest. He wanted to feel her so he unbuttoned his shirt. Flesh to flesh, they clung to each other.

"I'm here, Diamond. You feel so good." He buried his face in her hair, kissed her eyes, nibbled her ear and tasted the tender skin of her throat.

Diamond lay back and unabashedly feasted her eyes on him, happy that he was beside her. "Hello." Her smile grew devilish. "It took you a long time to come to me." She was caressing his chest, massaging his nipples until they ripened beneath her fingers.

Steven groaned and caught her hand. He was slowly catching on fire. "I did," he whispered. "I must be a fool."

"No, you aren't," Diamond said softly. "You were feeling bad and only working out your frustration and pain." She reached up and smoothed his brow. "You look much better since the last time I saw you."

Steven gave a wry laugh. "I *was* a fool," he said, remembering falling asleep in her arms when she'd come to him.

"Uh, uh, just exhausted. I understood that." Diamond studied his face. "You are keeping your plans to go away aren't you?" He still looked a little weary and she worried that one week wasn't nearly enough time for him to give over the care of his patients to his colleagues.

"Trying to get rid of me?" Steven's question was playful but he suddenly realized that deep down it wasn't a very humorous thought.

"No, Steven. You need the time away and I wish you'd take two weeks instead of one."

"Ha, I thought so! I can barely stand the thought of being away from you for the one and you're talking about two weeks?" Steven's eyes narrowed. "You do want me gone. Admit it."

Diamond moved uneasily, then hastily said, "Never. I know you need the rest. Now 'fess up," she teased. "Am I right or not?" She quickly rid herself of the restless feeling that threatened.

Nerissa was right. Steven saw the quick edge of sadness in Diamond's eyes that quickly disappeared. Something is wrong. Was his mother finally getting under her skin, he asked himself. If she chased Diamond out of this house while he was away—he couldn't finish the thought.

Steven shrugged out of his shirt and kicked off his shoes, then propped himself on the bed. He cradled Diamond's head on his shoulder and kissed her forehead. "Tell me what's wrong," he murmured. His hand was on her shoulder and he slid it down her arm and beneath the covers. He touched her belly and her thighs, warming over when he realized she wasn't wearing panties. *Oh no,* he groaned inwardly, pulling his hand away. He wanted to talk to her—first.

"What could be wrong?" Diamond asked, trying to sound lighthearted. "Only that I'm going to miss you like mad," she added. She squirmed, wanting his hand back on her body. She wanted him to love her but knew she'd beg him to forget about going anywhere.

"Is it my mother?" Steven asked. "I'm serious, Diamond. If anything is going on, I want to know about it now. Whatever it is, can be taken care of without causing you any problems. Look at me."

Diamond raised her eyes to his. "We're doing okay. Stop worrying. You're the one everyone is worried about."

He had his doubts about her reference to "everyone." Steven frowned. "You would tell me if anything was bothering you?" He was breathing unevenly.

Diamond stirred. He's remembering, she thought. Well, she wasn't Elise!

"Diamond?" Steven's mind raced as he inhaled sharply.

"Since when have I held my tongue with you?" Diamond said. "Of course, I would tell you."

Steven exhaled. He hugged her close, almost ashamed at the way his thoughts had spun out of control, thinking the worse. Where was his trust in her? "Of course, you would," he echoed.

Diamond moved restlessly and turned to look at the clock. "I think we're going to be hunted down if we don't get ready for dinner." She raised up and kissed his mouth. "You taste good. I'd forgotten how good," she murmured, and kissed him again. When he kissed her back, demanding her tongue, wanting to turn it into something more passionate, Diamond resisted and eased out of his embrace.

"I want you back here," Steven said, catching her before she slipped away. "I want you to remember for a long time what I taste like." He pushed the covers to the foot of the bed. He propped himself on one elbow and gazed at her nakedness. "I don't want you to ever forget me, Diamond," he said in a gruff voice.

Diamond wilted under his smoldering look and without his laying a hand on her, squirmed from the heat that began to warm the place between her thighs. She wanted to love him with all her being, as she'd already done and as she was only capable of doing. She could never give him less. Quivering with the touch of his lips on her breasts and straining to give him more of herself as he tasted, she thought of nothing else but to take the pleasure he was giving her. How could she not? Diamond thought. "Oh," she moaned, as his lips seared a path to her belly, while one hand massaged her swollen nipples. "Steven, you're setting me on fire," she whispered.

"That's my intent, sweetheart," Steven said softly, flicking his tongue on the softness of her inner thigh. "I want you to remember."

Remember? *Love, I could never forget you.* Her cry was

silent and as she sought to feel him, loosening his belt so he would remove his pants, he stopped her.

"No," Steven whispered against her cheek. "This is for you, sweetheart." But to prevent bruising her, he quickly discarded his pants and was bending over her once again.

Diamond was filled up with her love for him, until she thought that she would burst. His fingers on her were like tantalizing feathers and when he parted the soft lips to feel her inside, she shivered with delight. Almost immediately, she felt the warm moistness of his tongue and stifling her scream with her fist, she writhed uncontrollably, surrendering to the heady passion that made her senseless. All too soon, the turbulence ended and she sank, weak as a kitten, her skin still tingling from the gentle touch of his hands skimming over her body.

"Look at me." Steven's voice was low and smooth.

Diamond opened her eyes. He was leaning over, watching her intently.

A small smile touched her lips. He was waiting for an answer.

"No, Steven," she whispered. "I'll never forget you." She closed her eyes, lest he see the question in them. *But will you remember me?*

FIFTEEN

"Diamond, I'm sorry, but please make my excuses to your godmother," Cecelia said. "I can't attend another event." She lay on the bed in the hotel room where they'd been since arriving on Thursday morning. It was Sunday afternoon, and Peaches and her husband, Jimmy, were expecting them for dinner. But Cecelia begged off, pleading exhaustion to the worried-looking Diamond. "I've overextended myself, apparently, thinking I'm some kind of robot," she joked. Unaccustomed to comic verbiage, she sounded false to her own ears. But she didn't care what Diamond thought. Cecelia didn't want to see that woman again. "Since we have an early flight in the morning, I think I'll just spend the day sitting around the pool and then resting for the balance of the day."

"Are you sure, Cecelia?" Diamond didn't really want to leave her alone, especially if she was feeling bad. Cecelia usually had so much energy, to see her acting this way was disconcerting. Diamond didn't know whether to be alarmed that it might be her heart or if she really was experiencing plain old tiredness. After Cecelia's engagements on Friday and Saturday, she was certainly entitled to a lazy day.

"I'm fine. Please make my apologies and enjoy the time with your friends." Her tone was dismissive.

Diamond frowned. "Okay. I'll look in on you when I return." As they'd done before, whenever they'd stayed overnight, Cecelia had insisted upon connecting rooms so each could have some privacy. And she didn't want to feel that she had a baby-sitter. The arrangement had been fine until now. Suppose she needed assistance during the night?

"That won't be necessary," Cecelia said sharply. "I'll see you in the morning at breakfast."

Diamond drove her rental car to Peaches's house, deep in thought. She missed a step in her directions and got lost. Eventually finding her way, she arrived at the house feeling frustrated and frazzled. Since arriving in Miami, after Peaches met them at the airport and drove them to their hotel, they had only spoken by phone. Diamond was anxious to finally get a chance to talk with her old friend and the closest thing to a relative that she had. When she got out of the car, the two women greeted each other with big hugs and smiles.

Peaches stepped back, eyeing her goddaughter with a critical eye. "Let me look at you, girl," she said. "Hmm, didn't lose any weight but didn't gain any either." Suddenly she grinned, "I'm not surprised that your lady backed out. When she laid eyes on me at the airport, you'd think she'd seen a ghost. Just as well, anyway, now we can talk. Come on inside."

"I thought you were having other folks over," said Diamond curiously.

Peaches's smile was replaced by a sad look. "Jimmy's been feeling a little bad all weekend, so I canceled the party. So it'll be just you and me, talking over old times, and I want to hear all about this oddball family you're living with."

"What's wrong?" Diamond asked quietly.

Peaches smiled. "You never did miss a trick, did you? I'll tell you later, after you say hello to Jimmy. He wants to see you."

"What's wrong?" Diamond asked again. They were sitting outside under a huge shade tree. Peaches had outdone herself, cooking all of Diamond's favorites, and as they ate, they talked of their experiences in the months following Peaches's marriage.

"He's got an irregular heartbeat," Peaches said quietly. "Three of his valves aren't closing properly. He may need open heart surgery."

"Oh my God," Diamond gasped. Tears sprang to her eyes. "Peaches, I'm so sorry. Why didn't you say anything? How long have you known?"

"Since March."

"Before I moved? You never said a word." Diamond feared the worse. "How bad is it?"

Peaches shook her head and shrugged her shoulders. "It hasn't improved."

"It's gotten worse." *This can't be happening to them!*

"I didn't say that. We have to wait and see *if* the condition worsens." Peaches smiled. "Now don't go thinking so morosely just yet. We do what we can down here and let the man upstairs work from there."

Diamond felt dizzy. *Why them? They are so in love and happy.*

Peaches went to Diamond and gave her a kiss on the cheek. "Now stop that worrying. I know that look. We can't always have things our own way, Rough Cut."

"It's not fair," Diamond whispered.

Both women were silent for a moment, each with deep thoughts about the ultimate treatment for heart disease if it should come to that. *Transplantation!*

Diamond's insides knotted up like a pretzel. Her thoughts were like a whirligig. *Close to home. Close to home.* The words were running around in her mind like Pavlov's dogs. Only Diamond felt as if she were the one spinnng like a top.

"Come on, sweetie, let's have dessert with Jimmy. He'll enjoy eating sweet potato pie with you again. Like old times." Peaches threw off the melancholy mood and

squared her shoulders as she and Diamond walked arm in
arm into the house.

After Diamond left, Cecelia swam, sunned herself by
the pool, and took a nap. Later she had dinner in the hotel
restaurant and then went up to her room, packed her bags,
and sat in the chair watching television. She was restless
and couldn't shake the feeling of impending disaster. The
strange feeling had started with the recurring dream, which
was now almost inevitable when she fell asleep. It was
almost as if she welcomed it to see if the players had
changed. Or if they changed outfits. Or if they even smiled
at her. No, always that disapproving look. Sometimes Nerissa would be missing.

Thursday when Peaches Johnson had walked toward
them with a big pleasant smile, Cecelia had stared at the
tall, slender woman in disbelief. At first she thought it was
the woman from her dream but a closer look told her that
it wasn't so. But she had the same body build and the
same short hairstyle as the woman from her dream. That
night, as she slept, the dream recurred. This time Peaches
was in the dream giving the same disapproving look as
the woman and Diamond. Nerissa was missing. And the
newcomer had flour on her hands! All three women shook
their heads in disgust at her and then walked away.

For the first time since the dream started, Cecelia woke
up frightened. *What does it all mean?* she asked herself.
In the morning when she'd awakened, she made her excuses to Diamond, preferring to have breakfast in her
room. She couldn't bear looking at the young woman so
soon after her frightening experience. Friday and Saturday
as they went about their appointments, Cecelia found herself looking at Diamond with a curious stare. *What part
does she play in the dream? Does she know the other
women? They all seemed so happy with each other.* Be-

wildered, Cecelia combed her thoughts for what she knew of Diamond and nothing she came up with associated her with anything in the dream.

Since the night of the dance, Cecelia had come to look upon Diamond differently. She'd suspected that her son was enamored of the pretty woman, and she'd laughed it off. But the night before she and Diamond left for Florida, and everyone was home for dinner, Cecelia had no doubt in her mind that something was happening between Diamond and Steven. Her son made no secret of his feelings while Diamond acted more reserved but unashamed if anyone suspected. It was after dinner that Cecelia searched her soul and finally admitted to herself that she liked the young woman. She'd known it all along but her own hardheadedness had refused to let her even think about accepting the stranger from New York as an equal. The possibility of Steven making Diamond his wife was a mind opener.

Juliette had always been Cecelia's choice for a daughter-in-law, and when Steven had chosen Elise, Cecelia had been livid. But the night of the dance, she found Juliette to be carpy and unwholesome. Seeing herself in Juliette had made her cringe. She suddenly wondered what in the world had made her think that the two of them would get on living under the same roof?

Cecelia flipped from channel to channel, unable to lose herself in something interesting. But she kept the TV on hoping the aimless chatter would be a distraction from her troubling thoughts. Thoughts that made her shudder. *Finally it was happening to her!* The changes she'd heard taking place in the lives of her other organ recipient friends. She'd closed her ears to their strange stories. Food cravings; learning to play an instrument where before there had not been the slightest interest. And dreams.

As she stared at the tube, Cecelia wondered if she had the nerve to tell her story. Finally become a part of the group instead of looking at them with pity. What would she tell them this week at their meeting? That she knew that the woman in the dream was dead? And that Cecelia was the recipient of her heart?

It was dark when Diamond left Peaches and Jimmy, assuring them that she could find her way back to the hotel. By now Cecelia would be asleep, and Diamond was grateful for that. She didn't want to talk to anyone. She talked herself into believing that the woman was just tired, not feeling ill. Diamond was still in a tailspin about Jimmy's health and was finding it extremely hard to deal with. What more could happen in her life? Her mother's death. Peaches's happiness suddenly muddied. The man that Diamond had fallen in love with would soon come to hate her.

Diamond circled the parking lot, finally finding a spot in the rear of the building. Too lazy to walk to the lobby to catch the elevator up three flights, she decided to walk up the rear stairs. But on second thought, she muttered, "Better safe than sorry." She headed for the lobby in the front of the building. Lost in thought, she was about to open the door when she knew someone was behind her. She felt rather than heard the stealthy step. Before she could scream, the person grabbed her shoulder bag, but Diamond instinctively held on to it, not thinking of the consequences. Scared, then angry, she turned to look at her attacker. He yelled at her, "You shouldn't have looked, bitch," and while holding on to the bag, gave her a powerful punch to her stomach, knocking the wind out of her. Diamond fell, but angry, she scrambled to her feet and gave chase to the young man, who was already off the grounds and running down the street. Diamond ran, and when he turned the corner down a darkened street, she followed. She was yelling all along but no one stopped. The only thought she had was anger at being accosted.

What was hers was hers and no one had the right to take her property. He turned another corner and she was gaining on him when suddenly he jumped. Not realizing why, she kept on and too late she saw the slope that he'd leaped down. Unable to stop herself she tumbled down and landed on the cement below. She blacked out.

Cecelia had fallen asleep in front of the TV. When the phone rang it startled her and immediately her heart started thumping. She knew something was wrong.

"Yes, what is it?" she asked, trying to sound as if she was in charge of her emotions.

"Ms. Rumford, this is the hotel manager. I'm afraid Ms. Drew has had an accident." He hesitated. "She's been admitted to the hospital."

Woodenly, Cecelia replied, "Where?" The only thought that she had at the moment was her son, Steven. He would be a crazy man all over again if the woman he loved was hurt. Yes, she told herself, he was in love with Diamond Drew, even if he'd yet to admit it to himself. She collected her thoughts enough to get all the information and then called Peaches.

Peaches and Cecelia listened carefully to the doctor, and when he finished explaining the extent of Diamond's injuries, the most serious being massive body aches, he said they'd watch her overnight. After that she should be fine.

On Monday, Cecelia flew home alone. On the plane, she wondered if the doctor had told her everything. If there were no serious injuries why keep Diamond overnight for a few scrapes and bruises? When she'd visited, Diamond had told Cecelia not to miss her medical appointment on Tuesday, that she'd be back in Charleston in a few days. Cecelia left with the understanding that Peaches would see to Diamond's needs. Not bothering to have someone from the house meet her, Cecelia took a taxi from the airport, really tired now and wanting to close her eyes and rest. Her eyes widened in surprise when Steven met her at the front door. He looked past her then stared at her with a questioning look. What was he doing home? she wondered.

"Hello, Mother. How was your trip?" Steven took his mother's bags and carried them to her room. He found her in the kitchen preparing a cup of tea.

"Where's Diamond?" he asked quietly.

Cecelia sighed. "She's in Miami."

Steven's chest started to ache. "Why?"

"Diamond had an accident yesterday. She's in the hospital." Cecelia saw the fright in his eyes and knew that she was right in assessing his feelings for Diamond. "It's nothing. She's being observed overnight, the doctor said."

Steven looked at his mother like she'd gone mad. "Accident? Nothing?" His temples pounded. Keeping his voice level, he said, "Since when does a doctor tie up a bed, staff, and equipment for 'nothing,' Mother?" Just as calm, he said, "What happened?"

"Diamond didn't use her head. I thought she had more sense than to chase a mugger." Cecelia clucked her disapproval.

"Mother, I asked you what happened to Diamond?"

Cecelia was sitting down drinking her tea. After one look at her son's face, she told him what had happened after Diamond parked her car at the hotel.

Steven listened to his mother without interrupting, and the more he heard, the more he felt that something was missing from the story. His mother stopped talking and was watching him curiously.

"You left her there?" He held his anger.

"I have my stress test appointment tomorrow, Steven."

Steven's eyes flickered. She couldn't miss that. "I'm sorry," he said.

"Diamond insisted that she would be fine. She'll be staying with her godmother for a few days and she'll call to let me know when she'll be returning to Charleston."

A few days. Something is definitely wrong, Steven thought. He stared at his mother, who was speaking.

"I asked you why did you cut your vacation short? You weren't expected back until the end of the week," said Cecelia.

"Russ had an emergency and Mark and I decided to call it quits. Two days of that crowd was more than enough. We got in yesterday." Steven grimaced. When Diamond was attacked! He followed his mother from the kitchen to her bedroom. After getting the hospital information and the Johnson's number, he left and went upstairs to his room. A million scenes flashed through his mind when he imagined following Diamond from her car to the point when she knew she was in danger, to her mad and angry but foolish dash after an equally angry thief.

Steven sat down on the bed and exhaled. He'd been wound up tight the minute he saw his mother arrive home alone. The thought of Diamond leaving Charleston for good was in the back of his mind and he didn't know what to think, because she'd promised him. But the word *accident* stabbed him in his gut. It was all he could do to keep from shaking the words from his mother's mouth. Cold had gripped his chest when she'd finished. He couldn't lose another woman that he loved. Steven admitted that to himself weeks ago, but for whatever insane reason never told Diamond his deep feelings. In Myrtle Beach, he couldn't wait to get back home to tell her. There was going to be no more hedging on his part and he prayed that she would want to spend the rest of her life with him, because he intended to propose marriage.

Steven sat for a long moment, wondering what his first words to her would be when he called. How does one propose to a bedridden woman doped with painkillers and expect a coherent answer from her? And to hear the only one he'd accept.

Taking a deep breath, Steven dialed the hospital number.

After Cecelia and Peaches left, Diamond took a deep breath and closed her eyes in thanks. When she opened them her doctor entered the room. She looked at him gratefully.

"Thanks for not telling them about the baby, Doctor." She spoke softly and she couldn't prevent the tears from appearing again. She took a tissue and wiped them away. "I'm sorry," she said.

"No need for apologies," the doctor said. His eyes were full of sympathy. "It was your wish, Ms. Drew, not to tell your friends that you lost the baby. I only complied." After a pause, he said, "The blow you took was traumatic for the four-and-a-half-week-old fetus. The fall to the pavement and the shock to your body contributed." He asked, "This was your first pregnancy, I believe?"

"Yes."

The kindly man clucked. "Well, you're healthy in every other way, so I'm sure there's no reason not to try again in the future."

I didn't try this time, Diamond wanted to scream after the doctor's retreating back. The tears started again. *I wanted my baby!* She closed her eyes, wanting to sleep to chase away her grief. There was no one to share it with. She realized she wasn't dreaming when the phone rang insistently. She picked it up and answered drowsily.

"Hello?"

"Diamond, it's Steven."

"Steven?" Diamond opened her eyes. How did he find out? "Where are you?"

"Home. Mother told me what happened." She was asleep, Steven thought, but he was relieved at the strength he heard. "Are you feeling a little better? I wasn't told too much about your injuries, apparently because Mother didn't know too much. The doctor is certain nothing was broken?"

Only her heart, Diamond cried inside. "I'm okay, Steven. I ache a lot, but everything is intact. After I'm released tomorrow I'll be staying with my godmother for a few days."

"Why?" Steven resented that plan. "Why won't you come home?"

"Home?" Diamond was surprised. She'd never thought of the Rumford house in that respect. The only home she'd ever known had been filled with love and caring.

"Yes." Steven was losing his patience. What was wrong with her? "My home is where I want you, Diamond," said Steven. "Don't you want to come back?" He started to breathe unevenly. Was he wrong in thinking that she loved him as he loved her? Was now the time to tell her? Deep down, Steven sensed something had changed in their relationship. He was afraid to ask. Especially now.

Diamond forced herself to respond as her old self would have, not holding her tongue. "Steven, how would it look to have the help lying in bed being coddled? I *work* in your home. Can't you just see your mother now taking the elevator upstairs to see to *my* needs?"

"Help?" Steven croaked. After what they'd become to each other, she could think of herself in that way? "Stop that kind of talk, Diamond," he said. "I want you home, now."

Diamond managed a weak smile. "Is that an order, Doctor? I'm afraid my doctor here gave strict orders that I rest overnight."

Steven raked his hair. "God, Diamond, I didn't mean that the way it sounded." But he heard the light tone behind her words and he felt heartened enough to add, "But I miss you and I want to see you. And I promise that my

mother will be fine without you until your bruises heal."
She didn't answer him and he felt he'd lost his appeal.
"Would you at least think it over tomorrow?"

"I'll think about it, Steven," Diamond answered, a little sleepily.

"Okay, that's a start at least. You get some sleep now and I'll call again tomorrow before you leave."

After Diamond hung up Steven pondered the conversation trying to pinpoint her attitude. She was so reticent. He wondered if her condition was more serious than cuts and scrapes. Was she being released too soon? Worried about possible bleeding from internal injuries, Steven's mind raced with all the possibilities and the chance that something may have been inadvertently overlooked. To put his mind at ease, he dialed the hospital number again. This time he identified himself in his professional capacity and asked to speak to Diamond's doctor.

After introductions and polite talk, Steven voiced his concern about internal injuries. Upon a negative response, Steven said, "Are you certain, Doctor?"

"I understand your concern, Doctor, but as I told Ms. Drew, she can look forward to having other healthy pregnancies." The doctor paused, then said with confidence, "She's going to be just fine."

Steven didn't know how he'd ended the conversation. Unfeeling, he sat like a stone figure on the edge of the bed.

Diamond had been pregnant! And she'd never told him. Steven thought back to the lovemaking in his shower. He hadn't protected her and the anguish he'd felt then seized him until he nearly choked. Why didn't she tell him? There must have been a good reason. How long had she been carrying that secret? He grieved for the second baby he'd fathered. Suddenly a cold knot formed in the pit of his stomach, as an insidious thought seeped into his mind.

"My baby, my child?" Steven whispered. His eyes darkened with fear over his increasing brooding thoughts.

"Diamond, I think you're being foolish," Peaches said for the umpteenth time. "What would your mama think of this crazy plan of yours? You're insulting me."

"Peaches, now you know Mama would say I'm right," Diamond said as she carried one of her bags into her new hotel room. After they'd left the hospital, Diamond had told Peaches of her plan and her godmother had fussed from her house to the new hotel. Even Jimmy had voiced his displeasure. But Diamond was adamant and stuck to her decision.

"I knew your mama almost as well as you did and I don't agree with you." Peaches put the bag down and looked around. "Well at least it's roomy enough so you won't go stir-crazy in here," she sniffed. She was still angry.

Diamond sat down on the queen-size bed, shaking her head. "Peaches, you can be as difficult as I can be sometimes. And Mama would certainly agree with me on that, now wouldn't she?" Diamond winked and smiled at Peaches, who slowly relaxed the angry look on her face.

Begrudgingly, Peaches smiled. "Well, at least you sound stronger and are looking better every minute. You even sound like your old self again."

"Thank God for that. I think I was beginning to feel a little sorry for myself in that place. Now come on, admit it. With Jimmy feeling tired and you waitressing in the restaurant, you won't hardly have the stamina to look after me and worry about doing for your husband too. I'd only be in the way." Diamond grew serious. "Peaches, you know I love you and I'd like more than anything to visit with you, but as sore as I am, I'd be a bore, lying down all day. I can do that right here without disturbing a soul. And I promise to be more careful."

"No more foolish sprinting after crazy strangers?" Peaches looked sternly at her goddaughter. "You could have really been hurt, Diamond. Promise me you'll do nothing as bold as that again? I don't know what I'd do without you, girl." She caught her breath and looked away. "You know, I still looking forward to calling your babies my grands." At the sound of Diamond's gasp, Peaches turned to see the stricken look.

"What's wrong?" Believing that Diamond experienced a pain, Peaches became alarmed.

At the mention of "babies" Diamond had been overwhelmed.

"I guess I'm not so strong after all, Peaches."

"Are you hurting? Where?"

"Inside. I hurt inside," Diamond whispered. "I didn't want you to know."

"We're keeping secrets now?"

"I was pregnant. I lost the baby," Diamond murmured. "I had no care for the danger I put my baby's life in, trying to get that man." She raised her eyes to the startled woman's and gave a little ridiculing laugh. "I was more concerned with my own anger at being assaulted. How dare anyone do that to me?"

Peaches looked bewildered, surprised, and sad all at once. She went to Diamond and hugged her. "Oh, you poor baby," she said. "How could you keep that bottled up inside? And not to tell me? Shame on you!" She felt Diamond's slender body shake. Peaches rocked her until the trembles stopped. She got up and got a glass of water and handed it to Diamond. Sitting beside her, she said quietly, "Does the father know?" She already guessed the answer.

"No, he doesn't."

"Are you going to tell him?"

Diamond looked at Peaches. "What's the point? The baby's gone and there won't be any others."

Peaches gasped. "No more children? Oh, Diamond."

"No, I mean not with him. My reproductive system is fine and I can get pregnant again." She tried to hide the bitterness in her voice.

"You didn't love this man?" Peaches found that hard to believe.

"Yes, but he doesn't know that I did, and I'm not sure that he ever loved me." Her voice shook. "I think it's hard for him to fall in love again."

Peaches frowned. "Again?"

Diamond tried to sound intelligent and unemotional. "Yes. He was in love with a woman who deceived him and he was very unforgiving. I was being deceitful in not telling him when I first knew about the baby."

Peaches's face and voice softened. "Is it Dr. Rumford you're talking about?"

Diamond nodded. "How'd you guess?"

"The sound of your voice whenever you mentioned him although you tried to sound so disgusted." Peaches smiled knowingly.

Diamond returned the smile. "You're too smart."

"Are you going back to your job?"

"Yes, to get my clothes," Diamond answered. "I'll give Mrs. Rumford my notice. I was planning to do that anyway, once we got back from this trip. I wanted to leave before Steven found out about the pregnancy."

"But why, Diamond? Don't you think he loves you?"

"No." She hesitated. "I think he would've let me know by now," she said. "We were so . . ." She colored, and then continued, "Even if he did, once he learned that I was in his house under false pretenses, he'd never forgive such deceit." Diamond was saddened at the thought. "The idea that I'm living under his roof to spy on the person who received Mama's heart would be a bit repugnant to him, I think."

Peaches was thoughtful. "You'd walk away from the man you love?" She thought about the man she'd loved for years and now feared for his future.

Diamond guessed her thoughts and she too became sad. "Life is so strange, isn't it?" she murmured. "You know, Peaches, when I first learned that I was pregnant, I was so sad, then frightened, and then glad of that life inside of me. I thought about my own biological mother. She was on my mind a lot those first days until I became used to the idea that I was going to become a mother. Nothing could have induced me to have an abortion. I wanted that baby so badly."

Peaches nodded, remembering the story that Phyllis had told her about Diamond's birth and how she'd adopted her practically from the hospital. "I know," she replied. "Lansella wanted you so badly she defied her mother in not having an abortion. Although she never knew you, she loved you so much."

Diamond recalled the stories her mother had told her about Lansella Drew. Now she understood a mother's fierce love for her unborn child. "She must have been so sad and unhappy."

"According to your mother, she was always an unhappy child. Her mother was unloving toward her. Joan Drew was a social climber and wanted Lansella to be welcomed in the right homes. But Lansella looked for friends on the outside, wanting to be accepted for who she was." Peaches, was saddened, thinking about the young confused girl.

"Yes, that's when she became promiscuous, Mama said, looking for someone, anyone to love her." Diamond looked troubled. "That's when I was conceived. She never knew who impregnated her."

"It is sad, Diamond," Peaches said. "But she knew that she wanted her unborn child to have a good mother and a good family, because her mother absolutely refused to let her bring the baby home from the hospital. Lansella was going to leave home and asked Phyllis to raise her baby." Peaches smiled. "She certainly gave you the right name."

"Oh, you think so now, do you?" Diamond's eyes twinkled. "You never let me know that all these years." But she too smiled. Lansella had wished for a girl, because she wanted to name her daughter Diamond after the beautiful brilliant stone. Everyone loved diamonds she'd told Phyllis.

Diamond looked at Peaches. "Such a heavy burden for a fourteen-year-old. And to die so young." She thought of Joan Drew's death too. Suffering a heart attack after burying her daughter.

Peaches patted her hand. "She died giving you life. Your mother said that was her greatest wish: to have you. That's why Phyllis gave you Lansella's last name. So that you would remember her love for her unborn child."

"I've never forgotten," Diamond said in a low voice. "I remember, more so now. I intended to raise my baby the way Mama raised me. The way Lansella knew she would." Diamond was thoughtful. *Suppose the older Joan Drew had never become friends with her younger neighbor? Suppose Lansella and Phyllis had never formed a bond? Such love the twenty-three-year-old Phyllis must have had in her heart to adopt an unwanted baby!*

Diamond was silent and Peaches looked at her unhappy face. *She's still in love with Steven Rumford,* Peaches thought. *Is she going to be stubborn and deny it?* she wondered. Peaches sighed and stood, then bent to kiss her goddaughter's cheek.

"Diamond, if you both love each other, you'll find a way to be together. In time all the hurt will be forgotten and soon you'll marry and have more babies. You can't deny me a grandchild," Peaches ended, giving Diamond a smile. "I have to get on home now, but I'll check in with you tomorrow, okay?"

Diamond walked to the door with Peaches. "Okay, I'm not going anywhere." She hugged the older woman. "Thanks," she murmured.

Peaches hugged her back. Without saying anything, she opened the door and left. The tears that were glistening in her eyes were beginning to fall.

SIXTEEN

On Wednesday at noon, Steven was sitting in the living room in the home of Diamond's godmother. They'd talked pleasantly for a few minutes, eyeing each other until both eventually relaxed. Expecting to find Diamond, he'd been surprised at her absence. Steven hadn't called her at the hospital yesterday morning, as he'd promised, afraid the wrong words would come out of his mouth. After a day of brooding on Tuesday and unable to stand his dark thoughts, he flew to Miami, arriving late last night. His tone turned serious.

"Where is she, Mrs. Johnson?" Steven asked. "I have to know that she is all right."

Peaches looked steadily at the doctor and suddenly knew in her heart that he loved her goddaughter. But what would he say to Diamond when he found out her secret?

Steven could see the woman's hesitation and knew that she was being protective of her goddaughter. "I need to see her." Speaking quietly, Steven gave her a direct look. "I don't intend to force myself on her. If she refuses to see me, then I'll leave her alone."

After pondering his words, Peaches said, "I believe you." Before giving him the name of the hotel and room number, Peaches thought of what she was doing. Was she interfering in Diamond's life, which she'd never done, except to discipline her when she needed it as a youngster and later as a rambunctious teenager?

Steven waited patiently. Peaches Johnson must really love Diamond, he thought, and he respected her caution. When he saw her writing down the information, he breathed easy. Standing and taking the slip of paper, he said, "Thank you, Mrs. Johnson."

Peaches walked with him outside. He'd parked his rental car in the driveway. "Are you flying back today?"

"Yes, ma'am."

"Are you going to take her back with you?" Peaches saw his hesitation.

"I don't know," Steven answered slowly. "That would be up to her, I think."

"You'll let me know?"

"Of course, ma'am."

"Doctor?" Steven stopped and looked at her. "Diamond's feeling pretty tender right now. Watch out for her, will you?"

"Don't worry, Mrs. Johnson." He got in the car and shut the door. "Diamond will be fine. I'll call if I have to. Good-bye and thanks."

"Good-bye, Doctor." Peaches watched him back out of the driveway. When he disappeared down the street, she couldn't help feeling that Diamond wouldn't be in Miami for very long. Steven Rumford appeared to be a very determined man.

Steven found the hotel with little problem, and when he parked and took the elevator up to the fourth floor, he erased all emotion from his face and tried to do the same with the ones inside. He knew that when he looked at her, all the old passion would fill him up. Disturbing questions had filtered through his mind and he required truthful answers from Diamond. He almost dreaded confronting her because he knew if her response was negative it would change their relationship. What Steven finally realized, af-

ter searching his soul through the night, was that no matter
what she told him he could never change the way he felt.
He was still deeply in love with her. But he could never
ask Diamond to be his wife.

Diamond was a little stiff when she woke up this
Wednesday morning, but determined not to lie around feeling sorry for herself, she dressed and went to the roof atri-
um to exercise. After stretching, she took a few turns
around the track, starting with a slow walk, then increasing
it to just short of a jog. She groaned a few times and then
grinned at herself. "So this is what my patients feel when
I put them through their paces," she muttered. After thirty
minutes she left, showered, and went down to the lobby
restaurant for an early breakfast. She had a hefty appetite
and ordered accordingly. While waiting for her deluxe meal
of a three-egg, cheese, and bacon omelet and hash browns,
she finished a small glass of tomato juice and then started
on a cup of rich-roast coffee. When her food arrived she
ate heartily.

Diamond sat reading the newspaper and enjoying a second cup of coffee. She felt better than she had in days
and she contemplated her next move. She already knew
that she was moving from the Rumfords'. It was only fair
to give Cecelia at least two weeks' notice. She was going
to need someone to travel with her for the balance of her
speaking engagements, which ran into late June. Suddenly
anxious to get it over with, Diamond decided that since
she was feeling okay, why not return to Charleston immediately? Deep down she knew that she was avoiding
Steven. But she had to eventually so why put the inevitable
off? Then in two weeks she would be on her own once
more, hopefully relocating to Hampton Park until she
found more permanent quarters. Diamond hoped that her
old room was available. Once in her hotel room, she began

making calls trying to find a flight out today. After a half hour, she lucked out on a flight leaving at six in the evening. Relieved, Diamond started to pack her bags.

Later, after an early lunch, Diamond returned to her room for a quick nap. She couldn't believe how tired she'd gotten from doing nothing all day but eat and sit around. She was saddened to think that her body had really suffered an ordeal, and thoughts of the baby surfaced and melancholia attacked her once more. Instantly, she stopped the tears that began forming in the corner of her eyes. She had never been a crier and there was no need to start now, Diamond thought. But she smiled as she recalled her mother's words. "Diamond, it's okay to cry sometime in your life. You can't always be a tomboy. As a young woman you'll find it's a great stress reliever. Believe me!"

Diamond closed her eyes. "I guess that time is now, Mama," she whispered. Almost immediately, she heard the knock on the door. She waited, apprehensive about answering because no one said "housekeeping" or some such identifier. So soon after her ordeal she wasn't quick to be trusting. The knock sounded again and she went to the door and peered through the viewer. "Steven?" she said in surprise.

"Come in," Diamond said. He was standing there, filling the doorway. From the enigmatic expression on his face there was no telling what he was thinking.

Steven stared at her, studying her face. He closed the door. "Hello, Diamond."

"Hello, Steven," she answered. Diamond sat down in one of the two chairs by the window. Gesturing to the other, she said, "Have a seat."

Steven sat and continued to observe her closely. She was wearing a sleeveless top and drawstring shorts. The bruises covered both arms up to her elbows. Both legs were scraped but one thigh was especially bruised. All of them were darkened and were healing. There was one tiny black-

and-blue mark on her chin; otherwise her face was untouched. By reflex, he thought, she must have taken the full force of the fall with her hands, saving her head but banging up her chest and stomach.

"How are you feeling?" Steven asked quietly. There was no smile in his voice or in his eyes.

"Better," Diamond said expressionless. "Why did you come?" Peaches shouldn't have given him the address, she thought. Tonight would have been soon enough.

Steven's jaw muscles worked, as he said, "I didn't want to wait a few days."

"I wanted to heal a bit," she replied. "It wasn't necessary for you to come, Steven. I said that I was doing okay. I could have told you yesterday, had you called. Why didn't you?" Diamond was curious.

"Because I wanted to see your eyes when I asked you." Steven's eyes grew dark.

Diamond drew in a breath. He knows, she thought. "Ask me what, Steven?"

He saw the fear and his heart sank. Now he knew that she had never had the intention of telling him. Regardless of whether she lost the baby, he was never going to find out that she was pregnant. She was planning to leave the house.

"Why didn't you tell me about the baby?"

"How did you find out?" Diamond whispered. She couldn't stand the cold, impersonal stare on his face.

"Your doctor obviously thought I was your doctor, not your lover. He inadvertently let it slip out." Steven's stoic expression didn't change when he said, "Why, Diamond?"

"I couldn't let you know, Steven."

Steven's eyes blazed with hurt and fury. "Then I was right in thinking that you were planning to leave after promising to stay?" He fought to keep his temper. "Why? What are you running from? My mother? If you'd come to me we could have worked things out!"

Diamond said, "No, it's not your mother."

Steven lost the battle. He exploded. "Then why in God's name can't you explain why you were leaving me?" he lashed out at her. Her eyes widened at his tone. With a hardened voice, laced with sarcasm, Steven asked, "Was I the father, Diamond? Was the baby mine?" He wanted to hurt her. "Did you ask the doctor for a quickie abortion, so you wouldn't be saddled with a baby when you left?"

Diamond sat disbelieving. Her chest hurt as if he'd punched her and she felt that she was suffocating. Her temples pounded until she wanted to knock away the pain. How dare he humiliate her like this? He thought so little of her? *Abort my baby?* Anger filled her eyes and pulsated in her body when the realization hit. *He'd never loved her or he would never have uttered those words!*

Defiantly Diamond lifted her chin. She refused to cry. *Not now, Mama. He can't know how much he's hurt me!*

"No answer for me, Diamond?" Steven's voice was cutting.

"You were the father, Steven." Diamond looked into his eyes but didn't flinch from the uncertainty she saw. Speaking coolly, she asked, "Did you ever ask my doctor how old the fetus was?" *No, not fetus, my baby!*

Steven's eyes flickered. He hadn't asked. "Would it have mattered?"

A bitter smile touched her lips. "I was only four-and-a-half-weeks pregnant. You're the doctor, figure it out."

Steven closed his eyes. *No, it can't be.* "The baby was mine."

Diamond stared at him, unfeeling except for her ice-cold anger.

"Then it makes no sense why you were leaving, Diamond." His voice was bewildered. "What is so terrible that you would want to deceive me; to keep my baby from me? What?"

Diamond's voice was as cold as the ice block surrounding her heart. "What difference would it make? You despise me now and you'd despise me more for my deception." She turned away from him. "Please go, Steven. I want to get ready for my flight."

"Where are you going?"

"To Charleston." She couldn't say "home." "I'm going to give notice to your mother. I'd thought to stay the two weeks until she replaced me, but under the circumstances, I can't do that."

Steven's voice was just as cold. "No, I suppose you couldn't."

Diamond lifted her eyes to his. "See? I told you that you never knew me."

That hurt, Steven thought. "I guess you're right about that too." He stared at her back as she walked to the bed and sat down, facing away from him. He heard the sigh as she sank down on the spread. She was still sore and it pained him to watch her move. She was always so full of energy. But he steeled himself against her. She'd been about to deceive him and he would never forgive her.

"Diamond, look at me," he said.

Turning toward that dead voice, Diamond, said, "Why? Is there something else you wanted to see in my eyes?"

"It doesn't matter now, but you asked me why I came here."

Diamond only shrugged, her dark eyes showing disinterest. She silently agreed with him. What did it matter now?

"I cut my vacation short because I missed you like hell. I couldn't wait to get home to see you." Steven held her eyes. "I'd realized that I had been a fool, not telling you how much you meant to me. When I saw my mother standing on that porch alone, my heart leaped out of my chest. I had the strangest feeling that I'd never see you again. When I heard that you were going to be okay, I knew I had another chance." He paused. "A chance to tell you that I had fallen in love with you . . . and to ask you to be my wife."

Diamond didn't know what she felt. But it wasn't love for him at this moment. She felt rather indifferent at his admission, and voiced her thought. "A case of lost love," she said. "It happens to the best."

"Drop the cynicism, Diamond," Steven said evenly. He stood up and walked to the door. "You're right about one thing. I never knew who you were."

After the door closed, Diamond locked it and sat back down on the bed, dazed from the last twenty minutes. How could one's life turn upside down in a hot New York minute? Her emotions had run the gamut in three short days. "Drop the cynicism, he says? How can I?" Diamond said. A bitter laugh escaped through her tight lips. Almost a week ago she left Charleston carrying a new life to nourish and eventually to raise and to cherish. Fathered by the man she loved. Now they were both gone.

"Hard not to become a cynic, Steven." Diamond undressed, preparing to ready herself for the trip to Charleston. She batted the tears from her eyes, refusing to cry.

Steven was sitting waiting for his flight to be announced. The last few hours his mind has been in a turmoil thinking about all that had transpired between him and Diamond. He rolled their relationship over and over, trying to pinpoint the time he'd noticed a change. After the first time they'd made love he'd noticed a difference in her demeanor. The second time they'd made love, he'd impregnated her. At that time she'd been her old self. The third time when he'd loved her, denying himself to pleasure her, she'd been different. Was it then that she suspected she was pregnant? She had seemed so distant. But it wasn't the baby that made her feel that she should leave him. It was something else; something so terrible that she couldn't tell him. As she'd told him a few hours ago, what difference would it make now? "All the difference in the world," he muttered.

While sitting in that room so close to her, with all the tension and animosity between them, he knew that he still had deep feelings for her. But exercising his iron will, he squelched them. Twice he'd been deceived and twice he'd lost a child he'd fathered. There wasn't going to be a third time. As long as she was in his house, he'd spend as little time there as possible. He picked up his bag and headed for the gate when he heard the announcement. His glance traveled around the room and he nearly stopped in his tracks. Diamond was standing in line, carrying a heavy bag in one hand and a shoulder bag, which she kept shifting. He saw her grimace.

Steven watched, realizing she was still sore. He wanted to go to her to help, but somehow knew that wouldn't be such a good idea. He saw her sway; before he went to her, she recovered. "She needs rest," he said aloud. Ignoring the woman who turned to look at him with a curious stare, he kept his eyes on Diamond. When the queue began to move slowly into the plane, he lost sight of her but saw her when he walked down the aisle to his seat. She was sitting by the window, eyes closed, and she was breathing hard. He continued down the aisle and stashed his bag overhead. Just as he buckled himself in, a man yelled from in front, "Hey, this lady's sick. Somebody help!"

Steven unbuckled his seatbelt and reached them the same second as the stewardess.

"I'm a doctor." He spoke quietly and with authority. "Let me look at her. Meantime get me some ice." The woman hurried away, and the man sitting next to Diamond made way for Steven.

Diamond was hyperventilating and couldn't catch her breath.

Steven sat down and took her pulse. It was racing away,

and he was concerned. "Diamond," he said softly, "Take a deep breath."

"Can't . . . breathe . . . hard to . . . breathe," she gasped.

"You have to," Steven said sternly. "Breathe deeply." The stewardess returned with a bowl of ice and a cloth. Steven rubbed the ice on her face and neck, opened her blouse, and did the same to her back and chest. "That's right, sweetheart," he murmured, "keep it up." He grimaced. With long sleeves and jeans, she was dressed for New York in May instead of ninety-degree Miami.

"It's just too darned hot in here," a woman's voice boomed in his ear. "There's no air. Maybe this will help until we take off and the air conditioner will come on."

Steven looked at the same woman who had given him the curious stare. She was holding one of those portable plastic fans that women pulled out of their purses at the appropriate time. "Private summers" they called them. He smiled his thanks and allowed her to hold the fan close to Diamond's face while he patted the back of her neck with the wet cloth. He felt Diamond's body begin to relax and her breathing stabilize. He took her pulse again and was satisfied. "Okay, sweetheart, you'll be fine," Steven whispered. His own heart went back to its normal beat when he straightened her blouse, leaving the neck open.

"How is she, Doctor?" The stewardess looked concerned. "Good," she replied when Steven said all was fine. "Please buckle her up; we'll be taking off as soon as I let the pilot know." She hurried away.

"Doctor, suppose we exchange seats."

Steven looked at the man who'd called for help. "Fine," he said. "Thank you." After retrieving his bag from the back, he sat down beside Diamond, who was watching him. She was drinking orange juice that the stewardess had apparently brought to her.

"Feeling better?" Steven asked, watching her closely.

"Steven," Diamond said, looking at him dazedly as if he'd appeared from another world. "I . . . I never saw you. Th—thanks." Why was he looking at her like that, she wondered? Feeling weak and sleepy, Diamond closed her eyes but opened them quickly, fighting sleep. "I'm sorry," she murmured.

Steven felt her pulse again. After a while he said, "You're tired. Don't fight it. Lie back and rest." Before he finished she'd closed her eyes. He felt her hand close over his. Steven's emotions were high. The scare he'd had when he thought something was terribly wrong was only now dissipating. If he'd had any doubts before, he knew that he was still in love with Diamond. But what good would that knowledge do either of them? he thought. They could never live together as husband and wife.

Diamond's head lolled toward him and he adjusted himself to cushion her head on his shoulder. He bent and kissed her forehead. "Sleep well, sweetheart," he whispered. After covering her with the blanket that the stewardess had brought, he stared broodingly out the window.

Diamond was in her bed at the Rumford home. She remembered Steven waking her up on the plane, remembered walking to the taxi and inside the house. She vaguely recalled everyone greeting her, solicitous of her health. Steven handed her over to Jacqui, who rode upstairs with her in the tiny elevator. Diamond remembered thinking giddily that she'd never been in the thing before and that no wonder it wasn't used much. It moved in slow motion. Finally she was under the covers. She knew nothing after that.

"Diamond, are you okay?" Nerissa looked at Diamond who lay so quiet.

Diamond turned her head at the sound of Nerissa's

voice. She was sitting very still in the big chair, looking very worried.

"I'm fine," said Diamond, smiling at the teenager. "How long have you been watching me?"

"About an hour. You've been sleeping all night. My mother asked me to look in on you in case when you woke up you were hungry. Are you?"

Diamond looked out the window then at the clock. It was after eleven o'clock. She pushed herself up against the pillows, then asked Nerissa, "Shouldn't you be asleep by now?"

Nerissa nodded. "I wanted to see that you were all right first."

Diamond felt warmed by that admission. She patted the bed. "Come here. I want to give you a hug. I've missed you these past few weeks." She hugged the girl who'd reverted to her shy ways. "Thanks for caring about me, Nerissa." She held the girl's hand when she pulled away. "No, sit with me for a while."

Nerissa stayed on the bed. "Okay," she said. "Do you want something to eat now?"

"You know, come to think of it I'm starving. If I remember correctly, I haven't eaten since noon." Diamond patted her stomach. Then she looked at Nerissa very closely. *She has that sad look in her eyes again,* Diamond thought.

"How is everything at school? You and Letty handling things okay?" Diamond saw the sudden discomfort as Nerissa fidgeted. *Something's happened.* "Is anything the matter?" she asked in a companionable voice.

Nerissa looked at Diamond and then down at her fingers. When she raised her eyes, she said, "Letty and I aren't that friendly anymore."

Diamond could almost guess the reason. "No?" she said in an even tone.

"No," Nerissa answered. "She and B. J. go together now. She . . . did it with him."

"After you wouldn't?" Diamond asked.

"Yes. I couldn't. I didn't want to. Letty said that B. J. loves her and he wasn't seeing anybody else but her. He promised her."

Diamond heard the hurt and bewilderment. "Do you believe that?" Diamond asked softly.

Nerissa almost laughed. "He's a liar. After he told her that, I saw him with another girl. He just looked at me and laughed. She did too, because she knew that I was Letty's friend."

"Are you sorry that you didn't do it?"

Nerissa did laugh now as she shook her head. "He's a fool and so is Letty for believing that junk he tells her. I'm glad that I didn't fall for that crap." She smiled at Diamond. "Thanks to you."

"Uh uh. You did that yourself. The decision was made by you. I only laid out some consequences and other possibilities for you to dissect. So give yourself credit for that, young lady."

Nerissa smiled at the compliment but quickly dropped her eyes.

"Is there something else bothering you?" Diamond saw the sudden look of discontent.

"I . . . I met someone else," Nerissa answered, feeling embarrassed.

Diamond didn't speculate. "Really? Who is he? A Mount Pleasant guy?"

"His school is not too far from mine. He started to talk to me one day while I was waiting for my mother to pick me up. He's very nice."

"You like him. What's his name?"

Nerissa hesitated. "Ulysses Watson. He's fifteen and lives here, over on Pitt Street."

"He's got a heavy name to live up to," Diamond said. She waited for Nerissa to finish.

Nerissa sighed. "Remember when I told you that I didn't have those feelings for B. J.? Well, I feel different when I'm with Uley. I . . . I want to do all those things with him that I didn't want to do with B. J." she said.

Oh, no! Diamond took a deep breath. "Has he pressured you like B. J.?"

"No, not even when we . . ." Nerissa blushed.

"Kiss and pet?" Diamond thought about her own teen-age years, which seemed like ancient history to her now. *Where do the years go?*

Nerissa looked up in surprise, then laughed. "Yeah, I know," she said. "You know things."

Diamond smiled. "What are you going to do?" she asked seriously.

"I don't know. This is so different. My head tells me one thing and my body says do another." She looked at her friend. "Did you ever feel like that?"

Diamond gulped. "Have I?" *Tell her the truth!* "When I was your age, yes. A lot."

"What did you do?"

"Well, I did like the guys do. Got away from there in a hurry and ran it off on the basketball court." Diamond threw out another question, sneakily evading more talk about herself. "Where do you find the time to do all these things?"

"At his house," Nerissa answered. "Uley is alone a lot. He's an only child. His mom works as a director of student programs at a college in Georgia and hardly comes home. His father works long hours in his computer parts company that he runs with his partner. When he comes home he's beat."

"Whew! You two do have a lot of time to get into anything you want, huh?"

Nerissa nodded solemnly. "That's why it's so hard to stop. No one will find out."

Diamond got out of bed and put on her robe. Sitting down next to Nerissa, she put her arm around her shoulders. "This a rough one, Riss. Before, you knew without asking me what you should do. You were listening to your head. Now," she paused, "the heart is another thing, messing with your mind. And forget about those mixed-up feelings! But I'll tell you something. This is going to be one of the hardest decisions you'll have to make before you come of age. You already know what's wrong and right. But will you have the courage and willpower to do what you know in your heart is the way to go? It's no longer a question of peer pressure because you've grown beyond that. You're a pretty fourteen-year-old wrestling with a woman's decision." She squeezed Nerissa's shoulders. "Can you understand where I'm coming from?"

Nerissa got up and walked around the room, touching things on the dresser, sniffing into bottles of perfume, and finally looking at herself in the mirror. "No one's ever called me pretty, before. Except my mother and my dad."

"They're the only ones who matter, Nerissa," Diamond said softly.

Nerissa thought about that and then walked to Diamond and kissed her on the cheek. "Thanks, Diamond. I hope you don't leave here before Mother and I move. With my dad gone, I couldn't stay here alone with my grandmother." She turned to go. "I'll let Mother know you're awake. She's in the kitchen watching TV with Ferdie. Before he left, Uncle Steven told her to fix you something light when you woke up. And you're to rest all day tomorrow. He had some cream delivered from the pharmacy for you."

"Wait," Diamond called. "Your uncle's not here?"

"No. He packed some things and said that he was staying in town for a while. But he'll call to find out how everybody's doing." Nerissa shrugged. "He's always so busy. Good night," she said. "See you tomorrow after I get home from school."

In the bathroom, Diamond dashed cold water on her face and ran a comb through her hair, flattening the tufts that usually stood in soft peaks. Steven left? She wondered if he'd told his family the reason: that he and Diamond were no longer lovers and couldn't stand the sight of each other. "Even though we love each other," she whispered aloud. She walked to the door and started down the stairs, a shadow covering her face. Even after all the hateful things they'd said to each other, Diamond remembered the look of fright on his face and the endearment. He'd called her "sweetheart." In her sleepy haze she had felt her hand clutching his as if she'd never let go. Diamond wondered if she ever could.

Jacqui looked up when Diamond entered the kitchen. "I was just about to come see about you." Her gaze traveled up and down. "You look a hundred percent. You feeling better?" She got up and opened the fridge. "I know you're starving but I was given orders to see that you eat light. So toast, tea, and scrambled eggs it is."

"Sounds like a feast. Thanks," Diamond said, sitting down. "Nerissa told me what her uncle said." She fixed a cup of tea while Jacqui prepared the eggs and toast. "What else did he say?" She tried keeping her voice impersonal.

Jacqui buttered the toast then set the plate in front of Diamond. "Oh, nothing except that you're to rest all day tomorrow." She pointed to a small white jar on the counter. "That's to rub yourself with." Lifting a shoulder, she said, "There wasn't anything else." Jacqui watched Diamond eat in silence.

"It's been quiet around here without you, Diamond. Glad to have you back."

Diamond looked up in surprise. "Really?"

"Really," Jacqui repeated. "You know when you first

came here, we didn't hit it off. But that's changed. We've been able to talk without the barbs, haven't we?"

Diamond smiled. "You can say that."

"I think if it weren't for you, Christopher and I would have lost our daughter by now. Don't look surprised. Nerissa is crazy about you. I think she'd like you for her aunt or cousin since she doesn't have any." Jacqui stared pointedly at Diamond. "I think she'd much prefer to call you aunt."

Diamond didn't answer but returned Jacqui's stare. Finally, she said, "How about just plain old friend?"

"Can I ask you something?" asked Jacqui.

"Ask." Diamond carried her dish to the sink and turned to the other woman, who didn't bat an eye.

"It would've been 'aunt' if you and my brother hadn't had a falling out. Wouldn't it, Diamond?" Jacqui's eyes softened when she saw Diamond's shoulders droop. "You were lovers, weren't you?"

"Is that what he told you?" Diamond asked.

"Don't be silly," Jacqui answered. "I know my brother. He's so straitlaced and I could never imagine a woman falling in love with him, much less the other way around. But he's changed overnight. I think it has something to do with you, especially since he's practically moved out."

Diamond didn't answer. What could she say to Jacqui?

"Okay," Jacqui sighed. "I suppose it isn't any of my business, Diamond. But I sure hope you two work it out." A sad look crossed her face. "I almost had a sister-in-law once. Now, I think I'd like it if it were you." She pointed to the jar. "Don't forget to use that. I don't want Steven jumping all over me, saying I forgot to give it to you." A devilish look entered her eyes. "An angry man in love can be so fierce." She left the room.

Diamond felt uneasy as she walked slowly up the stairs, fingering the small jar. Steven's concern for her touched her heart and she wondered how she would get on with her life once she left. Maybe she wouldn't stay in Charleston after all. The thought of knowing that he would always be so near, and untouchable, began to gnaw at her. Was she strong enough to withstand cold exchanges whenever they crossed paths? A half-smile touched her lips as she entered her room. Maybe now was the time to act like the nickname her mother had given her to match her namesake stone, Rough Cut. A hard surface was indeed what she required now. But her heart would be torn apart.

SEVENTEEN

Thursday morning, Cecelia awoke with a start. Her heart pounded in her chest as she sat straight up. It was barely dawn, thin slivers of light edging inside the shade. Pushing the blankets aside, she sat on the edge of the bed, quickly turning on the lamp and shedding light to dispel the sudden gloom of the room. Foolishly looking around, as if expecting to see the woman of her dream, Cecelia expelled the breath she'd been holding. This time the woman had appeared alone at first, and she'd seemed so alive! She didn't look at Cecelia but kept her face in profile but Cecelia knew that she was smiling. The woman was sitting on the floor, rocking back and forth, and swinging her arms as if cradling an infant. Cecelia could almost feel the happiness exuding from her. Suddenly Nerissa appeared. She was smiling and she stood over the woman and they laughed together when Nerissa lifted her arms, letting shiny things fall from her hands onto the bowed head. Cecelia could see that they were sparkling stones. In a flash the scene changed. The woman stopped rocking and threw her hands up in the air. Nerissa started crying and bent to hug her. The infant had disappeared. Then Nerissa disappeared. The woman turned to Cecelia with tears streaming down her face. She raised her outstretched arms and cried.

The dream was the same as Tuesday night. Cecelia had been so shaken by it she'd shared it at her group meeting on Wednesday afternoon. As she expected, everyone in the room agreed that Cecelia was in denial of dreaming about her heart donor. By bedtime, she'd been convinced. The woman in her dream had given Cecelia life.

Wednesday evening when Steven had returned with a shaken Diamond, Cecelia had been grateful for the young woman's immediate ascent to her room. All day she'd wondered how she would react to looking at Diamond again. Cecelia was actually frightened. Never in her life had she been so unnerved. She'd told herself a hundred times over that to be rattled by something that couldn't possibly be real was preposterous! Something had to be done, because she refused to awake upset each morning, with nothing to look forward to but trepidation when she went to bed at night. The dreams had been coming to her for almost two months now and she refused to stand any more of them.

Cecelia showered, and by sunrise she'd taken her laps in the pool and was back in her room before Ferdie appeared in the kitchen. Cecelia had wrestled with her inner self since her return from Miami. Now she was resolute in what she'd decided to do.

Diamond had awakened early, watching the sun come up, but she lay in bed resting. The cream she'd slathered over her bruises was a miracle balm that had eased the soreness. She wished her coloring would return to normal just as fast. She'd heard the splashing in the pool and guessed that Cecelia was exercising early. Diamond was relieved that she didn't have to face the woman so early. She was certain that the good doctor had issued his orders to Cecelia also, that Diamond was to rest today. But Diamond knew that before the day was over she would give her notice.

A sharp rap on the door startled Diamond. "Come in." She sat up.

Cecelia walked in, dressed in elegant daywear. The powder blue linen pantsuit fit her figure superbly. Her blouse and accessories were ivory and her face was made up meticulously. She arched an eyebrow at Diamond and her light brown eyes gleamed.

"Good morning, Diamond," Cecelia said. "My son said you're to rest in bed today. I see that you're following orders. How are you feeling?"

Diamond became wary. It was barely eight-thirty. "Good morning, Cecelia." The voice and the look were the same as the day she was interviewed. "Better."

"Good." She sat down on the edge of the chair. "I won't stay long. I want to say what I must and then I'll leave. I have a breakfast engagement and afterward I'll be visiting with friends for most of the day." Her lashes flickered and she cleared her throat.

"What is it Cecelia?" Diamond asked quietly.

Cecelia's laugh was pretentious. "Right to the point as usual, Diamond?"

"Why not? It's why you hired me, isn't it?"

Cecelia's eyes narrowed. "Then I won't waste any more of our time. As you can see, I've been able to keep up this hectic schedule without any problem. The next two weeks of engagements are local and I'm certain that I can manage on my own. Therefore, a constant companion, or my security blanket, is no longer necessary. I've put myself through the test and I survived and can go about my activities normally." She paused. "I'm releasing you of your duties, as of today." She stood and tugged on her jacket.

"But you can stay until you've found suitable quarters for yourself. If you require my assistance, I'll be glad to help you relocate. I have friends." Cecelia looked at the quiet young woman, who hadn't said a word. Nor did Diamond look surprised or annoyed. "Of course, you'll be well compensated for this short severance notice." She walked to the door. "I'll send Ferdie up with a breakfast tray, so you won't exert yourself at all today. Perhaps I'll see you at dinner." She pulled the door shut.

Cecelia shuddered as she bypassed the elevator and walked down the stairs. With Diamond gone, maybe the dreams would cease. Then Cecelia wouldn't have to look into those dark accusing eyes at night, or in the morning. The image of Diamond lying there, silent, caused another shudder. "It's almost as if she knew!"

Diamond wasn't surprised, yet was curious about the timing of her firing. For weeks—she couldn't pinpoint when—she'd noticed a change in Cecelia. It was very subtle, and because everyone usually stayed out of her way, probably never noticed anything different, except for the dramatic change of hairstyle. She'd caught Cecelia staring at her strangely, and when she would have enquired, the older woman always looked away, as if startled. When she heard the sound of Cecelia's car fade, Diamond got out of bed. She was hungry and she felt strong. The heavy weight was lifted from her chest, and she was relieved that the pretense was over. She'd come here falsely—which she'd felt justified in doing—and she'd found the answer to the gnawing questions that had burned her insides. Simple. No great mystery. Cecelia Rumford was not Phyllis Yarborough, nor would she ever be. Diamond had known that from day one. But for the fact that she'd fallen in love, she would have been long gone from Mount Pleasant.

Diamond pulled her luggage from the closet and began to pack enough essentials for a few days. Today was as good as any to start her new life, she thought.

It was just past noon when Diamond took her one piece of luggage and a jacket slung over her arm and left the house. Both Tina and Ferdie had tried to prolong the sad good-byes but Diamond had cut them short before she started to cry. She liked the two women, who managed to keep their sunny personalities in the gloomy house, and she'd especially liked the warm welcome she had received from both of them. Jacqui hadn't returned from taking Nerissa to school, and Diamond promised herself to call the woman who genuinely wanted to start a friendship. Her eyes clouded at the thought of not seeing Nerissa. She would miss the teenager, who was slowly beginning to think that she was a worthwhile person and that someone outside of her family could like her for who she was. Diamond said a silent prayer that Ulysses Watson would be the kind of person that Nerissa needed in her life right now.

Diamond drove over the bridge to Charleston, and it wasn't long before she checked into the Howard Johnson Hotel near Hampton Park. She dropped her bags and sat on the bed, looking around. The room was comfortable enough but she missed the coziness of her bed-and-breakfast accommodations. Earlier when she'd called, the proprietress had told her that all rooms were occupied but her old room would become available on Friday afternoon. Diamond booked it for the rest of the month.

Restless, she unpacked her toiletries and nightgown, deciding to live out of her suitcase until tomorrow. After that she sat down on the bed and picked up the phone. She needed to hear a friendly voice and she needed to let her godmother know where she was. Her face clouded at thoughts of Jimmy. Although Peaches would be at work, she would chat with him and leave her new address and phone number.

Startled at hearing the female voice, Diamond said, "Peaches, what's wrong?" Her temples began to throb.

Peaches tried to keep the alarm out of her voice because she heard the worry in Diamond's. "We just got back from the hospital. The doctor sent Jimmy for some more tests. They're deciding whether to go ahead and replace the valves now instead of waiting."

"Oh, Peaches," Diamond exclaimed. A dark cloud settled over her, bringing the worst thoughts to her mind. "When?"

"A matter of days. They'll call us." Peaches held back a sob. "Say a prayer for him, Diamond."

"I do that already," Diamond said softly. "And for you too," she added, wiping a tear from the corner of her eye.

"Thanks, sweetie. I have to go now. You take care of yourself up there now." Before she hung up, she said, "The doctor loves you, Diamond. Without him uttering a word about you, I know that in my heart. Don't walk all over a growing bud, Diamond. There's nothing more beautiful than to watch it blossom into a strong and magnificent bloom."

Diamond hung up after leaving her number. She was feeling more melancholy than ever, and spending the day inside watching the tube would drive her low spirits into the depths of a black hole. Diamond tried to smile as she got in her car, telling herself that she should be happy she woke up this morning. So many others hadn't.

"I didn't know that they were buried here," a woman beside Diamond exclaimed.

"I didn't either before my first visit," Diamond answered with a smile. They were on the top floor of the Avery Center on Bull Street, looking at the colorful floor. Diamond had learned when she first took the tour that the official name was The Avery Research Center for African-American History and Culture. It was a museum and archives that housed the history and culture of African-Americans in the Low Country. Formerly known as the Avery Normal School, it was started in 1885 to educate black children. When Diamond had first seen the cosmogram she'd been awed at the work. It was impossible to study and learn about its creation in one visit. The painting on the floor was called *The New Charleston* cosmogram. It was an intricate and complex work by several artists, a circular drawing in music and dance depicting the history of various religions and dances that connects cultures.

Diamond and the woman visitor had walked around the cordoned-off wooden circle together, pointing out familiar names and events of the past. The excited lady was talking about Morris Island, the burial site of the all black Fifty-fourth Massachusetts Regiment, headed by a white man, Colonel Robert Gould Shaw. The tour guide said that after years of hurricanes, most of the island was inaccessible. Diamond left the building feeling filled up with pride with all that her people had accomplished after the cruelty of enslavement and the dehumanizing auction block.

Instead of driving herself around the busy downtown area, Diamond had put her car into one of the many parking garages. Now with the afternoon heat, she wished for the air-conditioned vehicle. She'd walked far from the garage and was tired and hungry.

By the time Diamond arrived back at the hotel, she was fatigued. Thinking that she should call Nerissa, she found her eyelids drooping as she sat on the bed. "After I take a nap," she said drowsily. It was still light out when she fell asleep.

Cecelia finished her dinner, annoyed at the silence throughout the meal. Ignoring her daughter and granddaughter, she enjoyed the delicious lamb Tina had prepared. She didn't care how long they sulked about Diamond leaving; it had been her right to ask the woman to leave. She poured a cup of coffee.

"She could have at least had the decency to stay and say good-bye," Cecelia said with irritation. "I told her she could stay until she found a suitable place."

"Oh, Mother, would you cut the imperious crap! You've already messed up so stop trying to justify what you did," Jacqui said in disgust.

"I told you her services were no longer needed." Cecelia kept herself from cringing at the look of dislike on her daughter's face.

"They weren't needed in the first place," Jacqui said in a deadly quiet voice. If it were at all possible she hated her mother more now than she'd ever had in the past. "But you insisted and Steven placated you." She paused. "At least he still loves you, though I can't see why, the way you treat him." Her eyes narrowed. "You're a mean woman and I can't wait to get out of this house. To think I loved you enough to put up with you all these years after Daddy and Granny died. I thought you needed and wanted us. But you demeaned my husband for no other reason than he wasn't in your 'class.' God only knows why you hate my child so much and I pray for His forgiveness that I allowed you to verbally abuse her all these years." Jacqui looked at her daughter who still hadn't recovered from the news that Diamond was gone. "Look at her. Look at her face, Mother!"

Cecelia looked uneasy at her daughter's outburst. For the first time in her life she was afraid of her mild-mannered daughter. She glanced at her granddaughter.

Jacqui watched. "See the look you put back on her face? She smiled more in the last two months than she has in her life." Jacqui flung her hand in the air. "Wasn't the sound of laughter in this house pleasant and a change from the bickering Rumfords?"

Cecelia looked away from Nerissa's dark eyes that stared back at her with a hatred so fierce she nearly shuddered.

Jacqui flung her napkin down in disgust and pushed away from the table. "What's the use?" she said. "You're nothing but a coldhearted woman. You'll never change." She paused. To Nerissa she said, "Finish your dinner, sweetie, then come upstairs to my room. Okay?" She bent and kissed her daughter and without a look at her mother left the dining room.

Nerissa still stared at her grandmother. Why did she send her away, she asked herself again. *Diamond can't be gone. What will I do without her?*

Cecelia started to breathe heavily as she was mesmerized by the look on her granddaughter's face. *Like the dream!* Before she could speak, Nerissa stood up and walked over to her. Cecelia involuntarily flinched at the clenched fists.

Nerissa's voice was calm as she stared at her grandmother. "I hate you," she said. "Just like you hate me. Diamond liked me and you sent her away. She was my friend." Her voice rose as she stared at Cecelia. "I wish you'd died. I wish they'd never found that heart for you in time." Tears streaked her face as she backed away from her grandmother, who'd stood and was walking toward her.

Cecelia was livid and shaking. But she knew that it was from fright more than anything else. What venom, coming from this young girl. All she thought of was to clamp her hand over the girl's mouth to shut her up. How dare she say such things to her? Cecelia was almost speechless as she reached out for Nerissa. She stopped. *The dream!* That same look of hate and disapproval. Cecelia's heart was thumping. She clutched her chest and stumbled. When she slumped to the floor, Nerissa ran from the room, screaming.

"What the . . ." Jacqui ran from her room when she heard her daughter scream. She met Nerissa on the stairs. Trying to understand what she was yelling, she shook her shoulders. "Nerissa, stop screaming. What happened?" Jacqui's chest tightened. "What's wrong?"

"Grandmother. I . . . I killed her. She fell. I know I killed her. Let me g—go," she screamed, twisting out of her mother's arms.

"Jacqui? Jacqui," Ferdie yelled. "Come down here. It's your mother."

"Oh my God," whispered Jacqui, letting Nerissa go. She ran down the stairs to the dining room. Her eyes widened with fright as she saw her mother on the floor. "Mother!" she screamed.

Steven slammed the front door of his house after he and Jacqui walked inside. He'd been too furious at the hospital to even mention what'd sent their mother there. When Jacqui had phoned him, hysterical, he'd quickly made arrangements for an ambulance. Cecelia was taken to Roper Hospital North in North Charleston, where the facility specialized in heart emergencies. His mother had fainted and suffered stress. She was all right but advised to stay overnight for observation.

"What the hell happened here?" Steven yelled. They walked to the sitting room, where Steven fixed them both a bourbon and water. "I can't leave this house without you all going bananas. We may as well burn the damn thing down to the ground. Nobody'll ever miss it, with what goes on under this roof! You can't even refer to it as a loving home!" He flopped down wearily in a chair and covered his eyes. Taking a deep breath, he looked over at his sister, who was sitting on the couch, scared and speechless. She had stopped crying. Steven softened his tone. "I'm sorry, Jacqui." He smiled. "We've gone beyond this, haven't we?"

Jacqui nodded. Returning the smile, she said, "Yes, and it feels good to be back in that place. Let's not spoil it?"

"Right." He sipped his drink. "Start from the beginning." He already knew that Diamond's leaving had precipitated the argument.

Jacqui sighed and shrugged her shoulders. "Mother was cruel and so nonchalant the way she told everyone that she'd fired Diamond. As if she were just another second on the clock and insignificant in our lives. It was bad enough that Diamond didn't stay to say good-bye, especially to Nerissa, but at dinner Mother was acting like *she* was the wronged party because Diamond left so soon."

Steven kept his emotions in check but his blood was boiling. Diamond was gone. The possibility of never seeing her again wouldn't sit right in his mind. He listened as his sister related the events at the dinner table and the horrible things that were said.

"When I left Nerissa with Mother, she was eating, not making a sound," Jacqui continued. "She must have finally lost it after all these years." Her eyes clouded. "I wish she had done it years ago. Then maybe she wouldn't be plagued with a stomach disorder."

Steven frowned. "I thought that was cleared up."

"It was," Jacqui answered. "But any upset can bring it on again. You know that."

"Yes, I do." He gestured to her to continue.

"She was terrified, thinking she'd killed Mother." Jacqui fixed another drink. "The whole thing's just about made me crazy, Steven."

"Is Nerissa still up in her room?"

Jacqui nodded. "She probably cried herself to sleep."

Steven looked at his watch. It was after eleven. "Well, I'll look in on her. She shouldn't go to sleep with that burden. An adult would find that guilt hard to handle." He stared at Jacqui. "No one knows where Diamond went?"

"No. She only told Tina and Ferdie that she'd return for the rest of her things over the weekend. The bags are packed, so she'll be in and out in a hurry."

Steven stood. "You'd better get some rest yourself. I'll see you in the morning." He walked to the door.

"Steven?" Jacqui looked at him curiously. Knowing she might get her head bitten off, she said, "I was thinking

for a while that Diamond might become my sister-in-law."
He looked unblinking. "Were you thinking that way?"

"Was," Steven answered bluntly and left the room.

Jacqui turned when Steven entered the room again. She
nearly dropped her glass at his look. "Nerissa's not there."

"No. Her bed is rumpled but not slept in."

"Did you check the storage room?" Jacqui was hopeful
as horrible thoughts crossed her mind. *This can't be happening again,* she thought.

Steven nodded and frowned. "She must have left long
ago."

"Dear God," Jacqui whispered.

"I want you to go upstairs and see what's missing,"
Steven said. He had to keep her mind occupied for a little
while. He remembered the last time she'd gone to pieces.

An hour later, Steven and Jacqui sat in the kitchen, frustrated. After several calls they hadn't a clue as to where
Nerissa had gone.

"This is getting us nowhere," Steven said. "We'll have
to do our own search of the neighborhood haunts."

"Nerissa doesn't hang out, Steven," Jacqui reminded her
brother.

"A kid in trouble hangs, Jacqui." Annoyed, he said,
"Let's go."

At their cars, Steven said, "What did Christopher say?
Is he coming down?"

"I'll call and let him know the results of our search.
He was wild." Jacqui frowned. "If he does come, I think
it would be a good idea if he stayed at a hotel. He and
Mother should stay away from each other."

Steven nodded. "Good idea." After mapping their different routes they agreed to meet back at the house after
a certain time. Then they would decide the next step.

Friday morning, Nerissa hadn't returned home. After reporting her missing, they waited. Steven sent Jacqui to bed,
and getting an idea, he went to his mother's room and

searched her desk. Finding what he wanted he called the number of Diamond's former residence. He'd found the two of them together once before; maybe, he silently prayed, he'd find them together again.

When Steven pulled into the parking lot of the Howard Johnson Hotel, he circled it. Spotting Diamond's car, he sighed with relief. The proprietress of the bed-and-breakfast said she expected Diamond at noon. Diamond had told her where she was staying just in case there was a change in arrangements. Walking to the car, he felt numb. Steven didn't know whether he was feeling relief that his niece would be there or the excitement of being so close to the woman he still loved.

Diamond was dressed and packed. She had an hour left before checking out, but she decided to leave early, have something to eat, and arrive at the bed-and-breakfast on time. She couldn't wait to go home. A smile parted her lips. For the first time since she'd arrived in Charleston, that was the only place she referred to in that manner. The last hectic days had forced her to try and put out of her mind the whole Rumford clan. Including Steven. She fervently hoped that when she went back for her things he wouldn't be there. There was a knock at the door, and cautious as ever, she went to answer it.

"Diamond, it's Steven."

"What?" Flabbergasted, Diamond opened the door.

God, help him. The silent cry burned his throat as he stared at her. Fighting to keep his desire for her out of this meeting, he said, "May I come in?"

Diamond stepped back, putting distance between them as he locked the door.

One look around told Steven that his niece was not in the room. Hope disappeared. What now, he asked himself.

Diamond recovered from her surprise. Moments ago she'd thought of him and he materialized almost as if she'd willed him to appear. Why she lied to herself that she didn't want to lay eyes on this man she would never understand. He would always be a part of her and she would always mourn the precious life they began.

Steven sat in a chair by the window. Diamond was sitting on the bed, staring at him. "You never did follow orders very well," he said with a wry smile. "I believe bed rest was the prescription." The old feelings of warmth heated his insides.

Diamond's eyes brightened. He looked so delicious it was all she could do to keep from ravishing his delectable mouth. They both felt the electricity passing between them and both were doing a commendable job of ignoring it.

"I was feeling pretty good," Diamond answered. "Why waste a gorgeous day in bed?" *Especially without you in it!* Diamond flushed at her thought.

Steven's thoughts drifted for a second, but he guessed what she'd been thinking. "I know what you mean," he said smoothly.

Twisting her hands in her lap, Diamond was finding it hard keeping her hips from squirming. Calmly, she said, "You must have gone through a lot to find me, Steven. Is anything wrong?"

Steven's gaze was riveting. "Besides the fact that I don't have you?"

"Steven," Diamond gasped, "don't . . ."

"Sorry, Diamond," Steven rasped. "Forget I said that." He cleared his throat. "Nerissa ran away. We thought that she may have found you."

"What? Oh no, what happened?" Then, indignant, she said, "You think that I would keep her without calling you?"

"I didn't mean that, Diamond."

He sounded so weary, Diamond thought. But Nerissa's disappearance turned her heart cold. "What happened? She was okay when we last talked."

"That's just it. When she was told you'd been fired, she lost it with Mother."

"Lost it?" Diamond imagined the worst. "Tell me," she said softly.

When Steven finished, Diamond was stupefied. "How insensitive!" she sputtered. Then chastened, she apologized. "I'm sorry about Cecelia. She must have really been stunned. But it was so unlike Nerissa to say those things to her."

"That's what scared Mother," Steven said. "She'd never seen such bald hatred in Nerissa. Yet Jacqui said that she was frightened out of her wits running up the stairs, hysterical. Maybe, just maybe she feels something for her grandmother after all." Steven's voice sounded hopeful.

Diamond was doubtful about that and hardly blamed Nerissa at all. How she had stood all that abuse since the age of four was mind-blowing. Instead of returning the verbal abuse and running wild in the streets, she'd retreated into a shy shell of a world, always playing the expected role of respectful child.

"You don't think so, do you?" Diamond's silence told Steven volumes.

"Let's just say I'd be surprised if she did." She gave Steven a direct look. "Adults have to earn love. It isn't their right."

Steven knew she spoke the truth. He shifted in the chair, his mind racing to other possibilities to eliminate: street accidents, unidentified victims in hospitals, detention centers.

Diamond saw the brooding look and wished she could help them. Jacqui and Christopher must be frantic. Then, clear as water, she knew where Nerissa went. Where else would one go to seek solace? To a friend.

"Diamond." There was a sense of urgency, tinged with hope in his voice. He had noticed the change of expression on her face. When she looked at him he took a deep breath. "Do you know where she may have gone? Her parents do love her. And so do I."

Diamond struggled with betraying a confidence and doing what was right.

Finally she answered, "I may."

Steven exhaled. "Thank God," he muttered.

"I may not be right, Steven. It's just a guess."

"That's okay. We're all at a loss." He gave her a grateful look.

"Mount Pleasant on Pitt Street. Do you know a Watson family?"

Steven's brow rose. "The Old Village doesn't boast of such magnitude. Most families know of one another if not distant cousins. The Watsons are in church occasionally." He was curious. "Why them?"

"Ulysses Watson is their son. He's Nerissa's friend."

Steven didn't know what to say to that, stunned as he was. "A boyfriend?"

Amused, she said, "I didn't say that. There's a difference sometimes, you know."

"Is there?" Steven's voice had a slight edge.

Diamond blushed. The underlying meaning was all too clear. He doesn't trust me, she thought, but he still wants me. *Love, like he'd expressed? Or plain old lust?*

She glanced at the time. "I have to check out now," she said, suddenly feeling hot. "Since you found me, you obviously know where I'll be staying."

Steven nodded, though his jaw tightened. "Yes."

"Then would you follow me over to Parkwood so I can check in? From there we can go over to Mount Pleasant." Diamond picked up her bag, relinquishing it immediately when Steven reached for it, and walked to the door.

Steven didn't like that idea. He wanted her beside him. Why he was inviting the torture was a mystery he hadn't bothered to figure out. "Suppose you leave your car on Parkwood and ride with me?" he said brusquely. "You can tell me more—that is, if you care to—about this young man, and later I'll drive you back h . . . uh, to your place." He refused to believe that she was establishing a home. And a life.

Guessing the real reason behind his request, Diamond was reminded of happier times between them. The warm glow inside was threatening to become uncontrollable, but she mastered her emotions. They both realized the inconvenience to him but she also wanted to use this opportunity to be close and to extend their time together. Diamond was confident that she had the strength to retain her dignity and resist the strong pull of his sexual magnetism. She agreed to Steven's plan.

EIGHTEEN

The atmosphere in the house since Nerissa returned home with Diamond and Steven was tension filled. More than usual, Steven thought, as he sat with Christopher and Jacqui in the sitting room. He was grateful that Cecelia's doctor had recommended another overnight stay in the hospital; otherwise, his brother-in-law's rage would have been hard to restrain at the sight of Cecelia. Ignoring his wife's advice to wait for information, Christopher had arrived an hour before Nerissa was found and was finally calm enough to stop speaking between clenched teeth. Steven empathized with the man, who was dealing with a busted marriage and the separation from his daughter. Steven had made peace with Christopher, weeks ago, after Jacqui had made her startling revelation. Steven had apologized for being so hardheaded and judgmental. Relieved that Christopher had accepted and the past was buried, the two had yet to reach their formal level of friendship, but strove toward it.

Christopher raised his eyes to the ceiling. "They've really bonded haven't they? I never realized how much." He was referring to Diamond and Nerissa, who were upstairs in Nerissa's room. They'd been there for an hour. After Nerissa tearfully hugged her parents, she asked if she could talk to Diamond first. He looked over at a solemn Jacqui. "You noticed, didn't you?"

Jacqui nodded. "Right from Diamond's first weekend here." She looked at her brother. "Steven did too."

"Yes. It wasn't hard to miss." Steven saw the parents flinch. "That's not to knock you two. The atmosphere back then wasn't too conducive to us observing the feelings of each other." His face was determined. "But that's going to change."

"How do you plan to accomplish that with Mother?" Jacqui asked. "The only thing I have to do is take my daughter away from here. There's only a few more weeks left to the school year. I hope to be gone soon after and then Mother won't have to even think about changing. There'll be no one here to change for." She spoke bitterly.

"That's the kind of talk that's got to change," Steven said. "Somehow, we have to clear the air. This family is too small to disintegrate because we don't respect each other's opinion. Living our lives apart is not the solution to what ails the Rumfords."

Christopher spoke directly. "Are you sure the problem is with all of us?"

Steven knew where Christopher was coming from. "We have to take some responsibility for allowing Mother's ridiculous behavior to goad us all these years."

"I won't deny that," Christopher replied. "What do you plan to do?"

"I'll let you know after I talk to Diamond."

Jacqui and Christopher stared at Steven and then at each other.

All eyes turned toward Diamond when she walked into the room.

Diamond stared back at the silent family. "Nerissa wants to see you both now," she said in a soft voice, as she looked at the confused parents.

When they left, Diamond sat down. She was feeling tired and all she wanted was to go home and sleep. She especially wanted to leave this sad house.

Steven noticed the tiredness around her eyes and realized she was emotionally drained. He poured a glass of pale dry Manzanilla sherry. "Drink this," he said.

Diamond sipped the wine, which had a salty tang. She took another sip before she set the glass on the table. "Thanks." She slouched down on the couch and closed her eyes briefly. "I'm ready for sleep," she murmured. But then she opened them to find Steven watching her closely, in a professional manner. "Nothing's wrong, Doctor," she said lightly, "other than I need some sleep."

"That comes from disobeying orders yesterday," Steven answered. The banter in her tone satisfied him that she was fine. His eyes roamed over her, this time, very much unlike a doctor. She flushed but he drank in the sight of her for what might be the last time, unless she agreed to his proposal.

Diamond kicked off her shoes and propped her legs up beneath her. "She's okay now, Steven. Just scared, relieved, angry all at once. I think most of all she's glad that she didn't cause her grandmother to have a heart attack."

Steven said, "Thanks, Diamond. You didn't have to let us know and betray Nerissa's confidence in you. That was taking a chance. She didn't hold it against you obviously." In the car on the way home from Pitt Street, Nerissa had been silent, sitting in the back seat with Diamond. Neither spoke but sat holding hands.

"That's what I was afraid of," Diamond replied with relief. "It's hard to regain face once you've lost it with teenagers. She's a pretty astute kid, and understands a lot, so I'm not the enemy." She gave Steven a serious look. "She needs affection right now, not chastising for her behavior."

Steven got the opening he wanted. *Thank you,* he breathed. "I know," he answered, in a low voice. "That's why I'm asking you if you would come back."

Diamond stiffened, wondering if she heard right. "Come back here?"

"Yes. As you just said, Nerissa needs affection, and a friend. She trusts you, and as vulnerable as she is, I'm afraid she's too close to acting out her distress in a rebellious manner. It's a crucial period of her life."

Diamond was stunned. "But what could I do that none of you have been able to? You're her family."

"Just be around here. Spend time with her like you started to do. Talk with her." He was exasperated. "With Jacqui trying to rebuild her business, she'll be away a lot. She wants to relocate and expand."

"I know. She told me," Diamond acknowledged. "Aren't you forgetting something? Your mother fired me."

A dangerous look appeared in his eyes. "Mother has nothing to say in this matter." His voice crackled. "You'll be working for me . . . as my niece's tutor, confidante. You give it any name you want." Steven watched Diamond, analyzing her reaction to his proposition.

Diamond shook her head in amazement. "You would want me here in that capacity? One who is capable of deceit? Hardly the best of role models, I'd think."

Steven's eyes narrowed. "Enough," he barked. "That issue is between you and me and has nothing to do with Nerissa."

Diamond wondered at the intensity with which he spoke. *He really loves his niece and wants so much to help her,* she thought. But could she stand to see him almost daily, continue to sleep only a few feet from him, and endure the cold distance she knew he'd put between them?

Steven's stare was unwavering, probing her face with a steady gaze. He waited in silence.

Diamond stood, and barefoot, walked around the room. She had to get away from those penetrating eyes, as if they could see to her very soul. But that was hardly possible, she thought giddily. Then he would be able to see her love for him. He would see the reason why she deceived him. He would hate her for tricking the whole family. And what would Nerissa think?

Steven waited patiently for Diamond to work through her confusion. He guessed that she was at war with her secret reason for deceiving him. His lips compressed into a thin smile. He would not let her use that as an excuse.

Diamond turned and sat down. "Okay. I'll do it."

Steven heard the conditions coming and he forced his face to remain serious.

"But," she frowned at Steven who was doing a good job not to smile, "I want to treat this like a job."

Steven bowed his head. "Thanks for not refusing." Curious, he asked, "How do you mean?"

"I don't want to move back in here," Diamond said firmly.

"Then how . . . ?" Steven looked confused.

"I want to keep my place. Since I'll have weekends off, I want to spend them there. I also want to spend some evenings there if Nerissa and I don't have anything planned. The nights she has a school event she'll be with her classmates and I won't be needed to watch her like a hawk. That isn't the idea of the job, is it?" Diamond stared at Steven, waiting for his objections.

"No, it isn't," Steven replied quietly. "Does that mean you're off duty at five? You won't be taking dinner with the family? It sounds like you'll be a part-time employee. I want you full-time."

Diamond thought about that. What would she be doing all day while Nerissa was in school? "You're right," she conceded. "Okay. I'll pick her up from school and follow her schedule. And make pleasant dinner conversation. But, when we're tired of each other's company, I want to go home." Diamond lifted her chin in defense of her demands.

Steven remained stoic at her choice of words. She could have called his house her home! "Fair enough," he finally said. "I accept your conditions. When can you start?"

"Monday." Diamond was surprised at his acceptance.

Steven considered that for a moment. "Would you mind staying tonight for dinner? We can have a proper discussion with everyone involved without any interruptions."

Diamond was grateful that the "interruption" was still in the hospital. She welcomed a mealtime that was not fraught with tension. It would be a pleasure to hear Nerissa laugh again and to see Steven's smile reach his eyes, which happened all too rarely. "I accept your invitation," she replied softly.

After dinner, Diamond went to the guest room to get her luggage. Nerissa and Steven were with her. Nerissa was happy while Steven had a scowl on his face.

"Is this really necessary?" he growled. He picked up two bags and had a sudden flashback to a time when he'd carried them into the room.

"I think so, Steven." Diamond answered. "I was coming back tomorrow anyway to get them. I've told you that since Cecelia will be coming home, I'd rather not be here on the first day. She needs time to adjust to your changes."

"But this is still your room and you'll need clothes, for God's sake!" Steven was finding it hard to accept that she was not going to be in the house around the clock.

Nerissa laughed. "Don't get so uptight, Unc. Diamond will bring some things back on Monday."

Steven glowered at his niece. "Ganging up on me, huh?" He was thankful to see the smile on her face and hear her laugh.

"Not really," Nerissa replied. "Just makes sense to bring back a few things rather than to unpack and start sorting through everything. Waste of time." She shrugged her slight shoulders. "Well, I'd better go and hit the books and catch up. Boy, wait'll I tell Uley that I have my own private companion." She grinned at Diamond and then practically glided from the room.

Diamond and Steven exchanged smiles.

"I told you she was pretty quick," Diamond said.

"Yeah, I remember," growled Steven. "Let's hope I haven't started something."

Diamond laughed. "You know you love seeing her like that," she teased.

"I won't deny that." They were walking down the stairs and passing Jacqui and Christopher, who were speaking in low tones. Diamond and Steven waved good night.

Diamond looked back at the house as Steven drove away. "Do you suppose they'll be okay? They seemed to be."

"I think so," Steven answered. "They're relieved that she's home. We can only hope for the best." A frown was on his face as he thought about the day's happenings. What a relief that it was finally coming to an end. Tomorrow would be the test of wills when he brought his mother home.

Diamond noticed. "You're everyone's Lion King, aren't you, Steven?" she murmured.

Steven didn't answer but concentrated on driving over the bridge. He'd better focus on something other than his thoughts of her, he told himself. The drive to Mount Pleasant had been bad enough when she settled in and he'd caught a whiff of the fragrance she wore. It was different from what he'd remembered. His passion heightened as he was reminded of something wild and spicy, yet contradictory—soft, tender mimosa blossoms. A glance now and then at her tanned bare legs, and a bit of thigh, hadn't helped his situation.

Diamond turned to Steven when she heard him suck in a breath. "What's the matter?" He really was dead tired, she thought, and felt guilty that he had to make the same trip back tonight.

"Nothing. I'm fine." Steven cleared the rasping sound from his throat.

When they reached Parkwood Avenue, Steven was quick to leave the car to get the bags. Minutes later they were in her second-floor room.

"Nice," he said, begrudgingly. He could see why she would want to return here. The room was very spacious and had the feel of a suite with the inviting-looking sofa in front of the windows.

"Thanks." Diamond looked at Steven with his hand on the doorknob. "Steven, you look beat. Sit down. You're imitating a teeter-totter. You can't be serious about driving back this minute are you? I'm sorry I can't offer you anything but there's a hot pot downstairs usually until midnight. I'm going to bring you some tea."

"Diamond, you don't have to do that. I'm fine."

"Yeah, I know. You said that already. I'll be right back." She disappeared.

Steven shrugged out of his windbreaker and tossed it on the sofa, then plopped down beside it. "God, this feels good," he muttered. He didn't realize how tired he was, up all night calling people who may have seen Nerissa. Searching for Diamond. He felt his body sag and he closed his eyes. *Diamond knows what she's talking about all the time. Just one of the things I love about her.* That was his last thought.

Diamond set the plastic tray down on the coffee table, careful not to wake Steven. His head lolled at an uncomfortable angle, sure to produce a humdinger of a neck ache. After pushing him down and settling his head on the arm pillow, she did the best she could in getting his legs straightened out, and then finally covered him with the spread off the bed.

Her eyes softened. *You look so vulnerable now, don't you?* she said to herself. *The Big Bad Wolf is dead to the world.* "And so you should be," she whispered.

Diamond bent and kissed his mouth. "Sleep well, love."

After slathering herself with the cream, Diamond climbed into bed. If she did have any romantic notions with the love of her life so near, the salve was a definite turnoff. Nothing like it to dim one's passion, she thought. Diamond went to sleep with a smile on her lips.

"Christ," Steven muttered. It was one o'clock in the morning and he was in Diamond's bathroom splashing cold water on his face. He opened the door into the darkened room where Diamond hadn't budged. He stared down at her, smiling at the way she liked to sleep with one arm flung above her head. He'd had to move it off his face once before. "So long ago," he muttered.

Diamond stirred, turning on her side. She mumbled something and turned again.

Steven swore for disturbing her sleep. But when she mumbled again, he moved closer, trying to catch her words. She quieted and fell back to sleep. He caught one word. "Mama."

Diamond's eyes flew open. "Who's there?" she called. *Someone was at her door.* "Who's there?" she yelled again. Fright filled her voice.

The light came on. "Diamond, Diamond, it's Steven." He put the chain back on the door and strode to the bed. He sat beside her.

"Steven?" Diamond clapped a hand to her forehead. "God, I forgot you were here. You scared me." She pushed herself up and peered at the clock. "You were leaving?"

"Yes. You heard the chain," Steven answered. "I'm sorry for scaring you like that. I didn't want to wake you after you went back to sleep. You'd had a bad dream."

"Bad dream?" Diamond got up and went into the bathroom. When she returned, refreshed, she got back into bed, frowning. "I never have bad dreams. Did I say anything?"

Steven hesitated. " 'Mama.' "

Diamond's frown, deepened. "My mama would never be the cause of a bad dream, Steven. Are you sure you didn't hear anything else?"

Steven shook his head. "I couldn't understand."

"I had Jimmy and Peaches on my mind earlier," explained Diamond. "That must have been the cause."

Steven saw the shadow cross her face. He touched her cheek. "That kind of surgery is quite common," he said softly. "I'm sure he'll sail through it. Probably give you a run for your money around the block a few times." Touching her had been a mistake. And when she caught his hand and held it there, it was like a torch being lit.

"Diamond," he rasped. He caught her by the shoulders and crushed her lips to his. He tasted her mouth and ravished her tongue as he sought to quench the fire in his belly.

Diamond leaned into him, hungrily wanting more of his punishing kisses. She'd longed for his touch. She yearned to love him, but sadly knew she could not, and with a soft whimper tried to pull out of his arms.

Lord, Lord, Lord! What was he doing? Steven felt her resistance and let her go, agonizing over the sweet loss of her mouth. Coming to his senses, he murmured, "I know, sweetheart. Forgive me."

Diamond's head was resting on his shoulder and she was kissing his neck tenderly.

Steven couldn't stand the sweet sensation, so he gently pulled her hands from around his waist and moved away. He kissed her palm, then stood up, looking down at her sadly.

Diamond said, "What does this mean?"

"That we still love each other," Steven said, solemnvoiced.

"I never told you that."

Steven smiled. "Yeah, you did," he said softly. "A hundred times." He tilted his head. "Didn't you?"

Diamond shivered at the smoldering desire in his eyes. "I love you, Steven."

"I know."

"What are we going to do?" Diamond whispered.

Steven's face was strained. His eyes sought hers. "God help me, Diamond, I don't want anyone else but you." His tone was oddly gentle, and the calm look in his eyes turned dark with determination. "That's up to you. If you want me, really want me, you know where I'll be." Steven's voice dropped to a low tremor. "Whenever you want to talk, I'll be waiting, ready to listen, sweetheart."

Diamond watched his broad back as he walked to the door. He turned to look at her.

"Will you still work for me?"

"Of course I will." Diamond sounded indignant.

For the first time, Steven grinned. "Then I'll see you soon. Come put the chain on, sweetheart." He closed the door.

Cecelia was sitting in her bedroom and her son was resting against her exercise bike, watching her reaction to what he'd just told her.

"Well, it's a good thing you let me get in familiar surroundings before hitting me with that," Cecelia said. "Weren't you afraid I'd have another fainting spell?" Her bright eyes flashed indignantly.

"No, Mother," Steven replied calmly. "That's a strong heart you have. What happened to you could have happened to any normal healthy person. So don't rely on that for an excuse." He was relaxed and sure of himself when he continued and wondered why he had balked at confronting her after so many years.

"I want to talk to you first, before we have a family

summit. Something we've never done in the past but will happen from now on if I'm to remain in Charleston."

Cecelia's eyes widened. *He was leaving!*

"No," Steven said guessing her thought. "I'm not going. I was offered a position in Connecticut and I turned it down, for now," he said with emphasis. "I realized I was running from you and my problems and that was not the solution. You and the rest of the family would still be on my mind hundreds of miles away. When I do leave, this family will be back on track, the way it was before Dad died."

Cecelia's eyes clouded. She'd missed her Cyril all these years. She raised sad eyes to her son. "Your father was a good, kind man. So hardworking. Never refusing anyone a thing." Her voice hardened. "For his reward, he died at his desk."

Steven's eyes softened. "And you've never forgiven him for leaving you."

Cecelia turned away without answering. Her son was right.

Steven sat on the foot of the bed. "I'm certain that's eaten away at you all these years and I'm sorry that I can't do anything about that. But I can do something about the way you treat your granddaughter. That's why I asked Diamond to return and she agreed." Watching her intently, he added, "No one in this house but you knows the reason why you treat that child like dirt under your feet, as if she was not the blood of your blood. It's almost as if you stopped demeaning her father and made Nerissa the substitute for your meanness and cruelty. Why the man put up with you was a mystery to me until I found out that he wanted to stay with his family. Since it was his wife's wish to remain with her mother to be of some help, he endured your nonsense." Steven paused. "I told him that he was a better man than me." He grimaced. "But no more. You've succeeded in busting that marriage up."

Cecelia puffed up. "He was a grown man and could have made his choice years ago."

Exasperated, Steven said, "His choice was to stay with his wife and daughter! Don't you hear anything but what you want to hear?" He calmed down immediately, refusing to allow this talk to turn into a battle royal of old.

Steven's voice was even "When Diamond comes on Monday, you will not have to feel that you must entertain her or keep her occupied. She is now your granddaughter's nanny if you will, as odd as that may sound. But she is here to be a friend to a young girl as much as she can be, owing to the disparity in their ages. Diamond will remain here until Jacqui's place is available in Myrtle Beach."

Cecelia eyed her son. "After that?"

Steven maintained his even tone. "I don't know," he answered. "She'll find another job, I suppose."

"You're not going to marry her?"

"What?"

Cecelia rolled her eyes. "Come on, Steven, you couldn't hide the truth if you wanted to. Never could. You love her, don't you?"

Steven studied the patterns in his mother's wool rug, before raising his eyes to hers. "Yes, I do," he answered.

"Then are you going to marry her?" Cecelia persisted. "No."

"Don't tell me you're going to live under this roof, flitting back and forth from bed to bed without benefit of marriage? What kind of example is that for my granddaughter?" Cecelia gave him a triumphant look of one-up-manship.

Steven gave his mother a warning look. "It won't be like that. Besides, what is going on between me and Diamond is a personal matter and not open to discussion." He added, "Is there anything else you want to say before I go riding? Jacqui and Christopher are in North Charleston taking care of some business, so we'll meet with them tomorrow after church. We'll all speak our minds in a civil manner."

Cecelia felt strange. The look in her eyes was full of respect and admiration for her son. He'd refused to give in to her or fall prey to her goading him into arguing with her. But she was uneasy and strangely embarrassed about sharing her feelings with her son. Her support group was different; they all walked the same path.

"No," Cecelia said. "I guess tomorrow will be soon enough."

Steven was almost positive she'd been about to tell him something. Disappointed, he stood. "Are you sure, Mother?"

"I'm sure."

"Okay," Steven said resignedly. "Ferdie is here if you need anything, and your doctor is sending the visiting nurse by later to check on you." He walked to the door. "I'll probably miss dinner, but I'll see you later on if you're still up." He waited for a response but got none. He left the room.

Cecelia felt lower than she had in days. She'd thought with Diamond gone, things would have changed, but she only felt worse. She needed to tell someone.

"Steven?"

Steven was halfway up the stairs when he stopped at the sound of his mother's voice. He was at her door, immediately. "What's wrong?" For the first time, he saw her as being old. The look on her face worried him.

"Come back. There's something I want to tell you." Cecelia closed the door behind him. "No, no, sit in the chair. I'm going to sit here." She positioned the bed pillows behind her back and rested her head. She closed then opened her eyes and sighed deeply. "I know you don't believe in transference, because we've discussed it. But I want you to hear me out without interrupting. Understand?"

Steven was attuned to her voice, manner, and words. He'd never seen his mother like this. "Yes," he agreed.

"I've been having dreams almost every night for the last two months. Since Diamond came to live here." Cecelia closed her eyes.

Steven frowned and waited.

"I believe that Diamond Drew is the daughter of my heart donor."

Stunned, Steven could only stare at the woman on the bed as if she were a stranger speaking in a foreign tongue. "What are you talking about?" His voice was barely audible. *The donor's family name was Yarborough!*

"I know," Cecelia said. Her eyes were still closed. "It's a strange story but you promised to listen."

Steven listened as his mother began to speak. Her voice took on a storybook tone that reminded him of "Once upon a time" stories that she told to them eons ago.

Cecelia's eyelids fluttered as she looked at the ceiling, then closed her eyes again. "I made some calls after I returned from Florida. I had to. Otherwise go crazy. Peaches Johnson was the catalyst." Cecelia heard Steven make a sound. "I'll explain that part later. But let me start with the first dream . . . when only one person appeared." Cecelia related the dreams to Steven, from the first to the last, the one that kept recurring. The one with Nerissa, showering glittering stones, and eventually disappearing with the infant. She told him of her fears of how she guessed who the woman was and the support group's theory that she was in denial of it all. When she finished, Cecelia opened her eyes to find her son watching her with an incredulous look.

Cecelia gave a short laugh that was without much mirth. "I know," she said. "You're a man of science and such things are just not possible." Her eyes narrowed. "Everything I've said is the truth as it happened."

Steven found his voice. "What led you to linking Diamond with the woman in your dream?" He'd never told his mother about writing the letter to the donor family.

"The flour on the hands started it," Cecelia answered impatiently. "There had to be a reason for the flour. They weren't white gloves, for heaven's sake!"

"I still don't make the connection," Steven replied. "What's flour got to do with it?"

"Diamond is a baker."

"What? Where did you get that information?" Steven was shocked. "You know yourself that she's a physical therapist."

Cecelia sighed. "I told you I did some checking. I went to the agency that sent her and asked some questions. I demanded to see the application she filled out."

"What did that prove?"

"The occupations were listed in chronological order starting with the last or most current. The first one listed was baker-owner and the address was in Brooklyn, New York. The second one listed was physical therapist at a place I don't remember. I think it was in Manhattan."

Steven controlled his breathing. "Do you remember the name of the place she owned?"

"Yes. It was a different name. Yarborough's Bakery or some such name like that." Cecelia erased the frown from trying to remember. "Anyway, the name doesn't matter," she said.

Steven felt cemented to his chair but his mind was racing. So many questions that needed answers. Yarborough was hardly common enough to pop up in Diamond's background. But it was written in ink on an innocent application filed at an agency miles away from New York City.

Cecelia fluffed up the pillows. "I see you're in denial yourself," she said to her son. "It's not all in my imagination. Fables were never my thing, as you well know," she said dryly. Annoyance edged her voice, making Steven attentive to the sharpness. "What do you suppose made me almost burn the house down trying to bake a coconut cake? I hate coconut cake and now I can't get enough of it. And the sweet potato pie? You know I've never eaten it in this house in all the years since you were born!" She grinned. "Seems you and everybody else couldn't get enough of it either, if I recollect. That girl can bake a pie!"

Steven remembered all too vividly. The night in the restaurant when he'd spoken to Jacqui, that was when Diamond had had an anxiety attack. After she'd heard his mother tried to bake a cake. A coconut cake!

Cecelia looked at her son, who appeared to be still shocked, and wondered why he was taking her story so hard? *She* was the one who'd had the nightmares.

"Steven," Cecelia said, "would you send Ferdie in? I need a cup of tea and something to eat. Afterward, I'll rest until the nurse gets here. I'm feeling tired."

Steven looked at his mother, who'd closed her eyes. "Sure."

NINETEEN

Instead of taking out the Ducati, Steven went to his room. He had to think. His mind was racing over the events of the last two months and their significance in relation to Diamond Drew. He believed his mother, simply because of the person she was. If Diamond was the daughter of his mother's heart donor, then why was she here in Charleston? Was that Diamond's secret? She'd come to spy on the recipient of her mother's heart?

Steven was walking slowly from one end of his room to the other. He finally lay down on the bed, head resting on folded arms, as he tried to come up with a reason for Diamond's actions. First, he had to find something else to back his mother's findings. But what? Diamond had no friends here, other than the few she'd made since arriving in the city. Steven thought about calling Peaches Johnson, the other woman in Cecelia's dreams. He made a face. *She'd probably call me crazy if I started asking off-the-wall questions.* Calling Diamond was the last thing he wanted to do. He wanted to be able to talk sensibly when he saw her, and sense is not what he had right now, not with his confused mind. After several minutes, Steven got an idea, a wild and crazy long shot of one, but right now he was at ground zero. He sat up and retrieved his phone book.

By the time he was finished, the whole world would think he was nuts.

* * *

Diamond couldn't believe that two weeks had passed since she'd returned to the Rumfords'. She was in the pool drifting on a plastic raft, her head thrown back and her hands and feet trolling the delightfully cool water. The weather for the last week had been brutal, and every chance she got she headed for this pool. She raised her head to see if Cecelia was still lying on the shaded chaise. She looked like she'd fallen asleep.

Diamond was "off" this afternoon. Nerissa was on an all-day field trip and would return with the parents of one of her classmates. Later, after dinner, they would go to the mall to try again to find a suitable costume for the year-end school party. The committee had decided on period dress, and Diamond and Nerissa were still at a loss. The thrift shops they'd scoured resulted in zilch. Last night, Nerissa had had an idea. She wondered if any of her great-grandmother's old dresses would be suitable. Diamond said it would probably be too late to find something and have it tailored and cleaned in time. The dance was on Friday, only three days away.

Diamond decided to take one last dip before going inside. She'd much rather be here than in a musty attic. As she slid off the raft, she noticed Cecelia looking at her. After two laps, she climbed out, pushing back her wet hair.

"Hi," Diamond said. "Sleep well?"

"Too well," Cecelia answered. "My snores woke me up."

Diamond laughed. "It must have been something else or I would have heard them. It's quiet as a tomb out here."

Cecelia looked up at the vibrant young woman. It seemed that she couldn't help but stare at her and she had to catch herself many times. Since Diamond had returned, Cecelia had not had one dream. It was almost spooky and she didn't want to question the reason why. Cecelia had agreed to comply with her son's wishes that she say nothing to Diamond about their conversation and Cecelia's suspicions.

Diamond sat and dried her hair. "That felt good. You should take another dip before you come inside." She ignored Cecelia's stare. She'd gotten used to it ever since she returned to the house. The woman almost looked embarrassed when she was caught, so Diamond never questioned her. She slipped into her clogs. "I'm supposed to be working," she said, with a grin. "Maybe we'll see you at dinner. If Nerissa gets back too late, we'll eat out. See you later, Cecelia."

"All right, Diamond," answered Cecelia. She watched her disappear with that slow, long stride. As usual her head was filled with questions about the young woman. But Steven said that when the time came, he wanted to be the one to confront Diamond. She wondered when that time would come because Steven had not been back to the house since Diamond had started her new duties. Cecelia took off her top and flexed her shoulders. Another dip sounded like an excellent idea.

Diamond was dressed in shorts and halter, as naked as she could get and still be decent, while she sifted through the musty old trunks. She tied a scarf around her throat just in case she needed to muffle her nose and mouth. When she opened the door and climbed the few steps she remembered the last time she'd been in here: when Steven had found her and Nerissa giggling and laughing. Diamond turned on the light and chased away the thought of Steven. She hadn't seen him since that night in her apartment on Parkwood Avenue. The Monday she started with Nerissa, he'd called her at the house from his apartment and asked if she'd settled in all right and if she needed anything. After that, he never called her again, although she knew he'd spoken to Cecelia. He'd sounded preoccupied, as if he had a lot on his mind. She believed he was concerned about his scheduled surgeries the next day.

Diamond supposed that he figured this was the best way to handle their odd situation. Even Cecelia appeared different sometimes. Diamond found out why from Ferdie, who didn't miss much in the household. She'd told her about the family meeting, but she hadn't heard any of the conversation. She'd been out all day and returned late to find the family in the sitting room. Even Nerissa was there.

It wasn't long before Diamond noticed a calm settling over the house. The atmosphere wasn't constantly electrified. The most noticeable change was that Nerissa talked and laughed. One night she told a joke, and Diamond nearly broke her jaw gaping at Cecelia's smile. It was tiny and held little warmth, but it was there. After that, Diamond gave up trying to figure out what had happened and welcomed the good karma.

"Ugh," Diamond said as she lifted the lid of a dusty trunk. "Should have worn gloves too," she said in disgust. She wiped her hands on her shorts and covered her mouth and nose. The garments were men's clothing and shoes. "Not musty enough," Diamond said. "Too modern. Must have belonged to Cecelia's husband." Diamond didn't mind the sound of her voice in the quiet room. She couldn't hear a sound coming from anywhere in the house. She closed the trunk and opened another larger one. A little girl's clothes. How lovely they were, Diamond thought, as she picked up a dark green velvet dress with long sleeves and yards of lace at the hem and collar. These were definitely not old. They must be Nerissa's. "What a waste," Diamond clucked. "Some little girl would have loved wearing such finery."

Sitting back on her haunches, Diamond looked around. There had to be a plan here, she thought. There were so many trunks. And boxes too. What had happened to tags on these things? Steven's father and grandfather had lived in this house. There was years of stuff in here. Her gaze fell on an old suitcase. Something like that could have belonged to Cecelia's mother. She was about eighty when she died, so her clothes would be perfect. Diamond scooted over to it and then laughed about getting splinters in her behind. "Not good, Diamond," she muttered.

The brown suitcase was worn from age rather than wear and tear from use in its heyday, Diamond thought. "Whoa, what's this?" A grin split her face when she pushed away tissue paper from a gorgeous old gown. It was an ecru lace-and-satin confection that shimmered in Diamond's hands. The short sleeves were all lace and the V-neck front that went down to *there* was lace covered. "Nerissa, my dear, this is absolutely scandalous!" Gleefully, Diamond put the dress aside. "There must be accessories," she muttered. She frowned. There were more modern clothes beneath the dress that were definitely not from the same period. Curious, she lifted the dresses out. There were shoes and purses but no more gowns similar to the ecru. A satin pouch that looked like a jewelry roll caught her eye. Expecting to find jewelry to match the gown, Diamond unwrapped it and yellowed papers and photographs slipped out. The delicate newspaper clippings were disintegrating in her hand so she carefully laid them on the floor. Grateful for the daylight that helped the dim light, Diamond was able to read. She picked up some of the photographs first and was surprised to see Cecelia. The man who was hugging her was not Dr. Cyril Rumford. Their wedding picture was on Cecelia's dresser and looks don't change that much! "What?" Diamond gaped. The man that Cecelia was smiling up at was Christopher Craven! She stared hard, then carried the pictures and clippings to the window where the light filtered through. No, it wasn't Christopher but his twin. The man in the picture was dark-complexioned while Christopher's skin was lighter. They had the same high forehead and strong white teeth. And the same good looks. Diamond turned the picture over and her suspicions were confirmed. Cecelia had written on the back. "Me and Chris." There was no date. Christopher's father? There could be no other explanation.

Diamond knew she was looking at Nerissa's paternal grandfather. Nerissa looked like her father and her grandfather. Her beautiful dark skin was the same color as that of the handsome man in the picture. Diamond looked at the other pictures. All of them were of a laughing Cecelia and the handsome Chris. They were a striking couple and were usually in poses showing them hugging or cheek to cheek, smiling happily into the camera. They had been lovers. Or would it have been courting, Diamond mused. Cecelia was close to sixty and she looked no more than seventeen or eighteen in these pictures. About forty years ago, Diamond figured. Doing a quick calculation, she assumed that Cecelia and Cyril Rumford married and had Steven not too long after these photographs were taken.

Diamond set the pictures down and carefully read a yellowed clipping. It was from a North Carolina newspaper. The picture was of a bride and groom. It was hard to see the woman's face because of the creases in the paper, but the man was the "Chris" in the photos. Diamond read the caption announcing the marriage of Miss Esther Albermarle of Rocky Mount, North Carolina, to Mr. Christopher Craven of Gastonia, North Carolina. The article gave the usual background of the bride's and groom's schooling and occupations and the same for their parents. Diamond looked at another article, which was obviously from a gossip column, and the reporter wasn't too kind, Diamond decided. Esther Albermarle was a society woman whose family was not exactly enthralled with her choice of mates. Chris Craven was the jobless son of an automobile garage owner. Known to flit from job to job and woman to woman like a bee drawn to honey, the handsome, carefree man claimed that he was in love for the first time in his life. He swore that he was more than capable of giving his wife the kind of life that she was accustomed to living.

"Well, I'll be," exclaimed Diamond. The next clipping she read was from a Charleston newspaper. It wasn't from a society column but in the same gossipy vein of a tattler rag. It showed a picture of Cecelia and Cyril Rumford at a reception given for them by her parents. Apparently they'd had a small wedding ceremony with only the family attending. The family of Cecelia Bocheron were pleased that the heiress to the wealthy Bocheron Clothiers fortune had met and fallen in love with the respectable Cyril Rumford, who was studying medicine. The article went on to say that Chris Craven, whom everyone thought was the heiress's true love, was recently seen in the company of Esther Albermarle of Rocky Mount., North Carolina.

"Whew!" Diamond said, letting the story sink in. "Who broke the romance off first?" she muttered. She looked at a happy Cecelia and Chris Craven in the photographs. "It certainly wasn't you two," Diamond said emphatically.

The last article she read was the birth announcement of Christopher Craven Jr., in Gastonia. The same year that Steven was born. "Very interesting," Diamond mused. Both women were impregnated the same year. "Hmm."

Diamond gathered the delicate papers and put them back in the satin pouch. She sat down in the oversize chair, Nerissa's favorite, and mulled over her findings.

Cecelia had hated her granddaughter all these years because she looked like the man she had never married! The man she really loved. Every time she looked into that child's pretty face she saw her former lover, Chris. Why didn't they marry? Did he cheat on her? Their children were born the same year. So many questions, Diamond thought. So many mysteries.

"So I'm not the only one in this house harboring a se-

cret," Diamond said aloud. "But mine never ruined the life
of a child," she added bitterly.

Diamond wrapped the beautiful gown in the tissue,
turned out the light, and carried the pouch and gown to
her bedroom. She refused to let this mystery stay a mystery
for another forty years. Not if it meant freeing Nerissa
from low self-esteem.

Steven would know what to do, she thought. He had to.

"You would think such a prestigious school would have
a decent bus," Cecelia said in disgust.

"The school secretary explained that it was a hired bus
service, Cecelia," Diamond replied. "They have no control
over a bus breaking down." It was past six-thirty and they
were having dinner by the pool, after worrying for more
than two hours at Nerissa's late return. When the call came
in, Diamond had taken the message for Jacqui, who hadn't
come home yet.

Cecelia rolled her eyes and speared a cold spinach leaf.
"Humph," was all she said.

Diamond had finished the salad and was eating the delicious cold lemon salmon. The scorching heat had not let
up and everyone had been concerned about the busload of
students stranded on the road in over ninety-degree tem-
peratures.

"Well, they'd better come home unscathed from this in-
cident or they'll hear it from me," Cecelia said.

Diamond continued to eat without showing surprise at
the remark. In recent days, words used in subtle defense
of Nerissa came out of Cecelia's mouth at the least expected times. Always covert, Diamond mused in silence
that at least it was a start.

A car door slammed and soon Nerissa came in from
the kitchen back door. She walked toward them, showing

fatigue. "Hi," she said, plopping down on a padded chair. "I'm exhausted."

"Well, I shouldn't wonder. Sitting on a dirty road waiting for another bus is ridiculous in this weather." Cecelia waved a slender hand. "No matter what you say, Diamond, I'm still going to write the school board. They need to know the feelings of the parents."

"We were fine, Grandmother," Nerissa said. "Just hot as the devil. But we all found trees to sit under."

"Humph, the worst place! Suppose there was a thunderstorm? Then where would you be? Not sitting under a tree, I hope."

Diamond grimaced. "I don't think so, Cecelia." She looked at Nerissa. "You do look exhausted. Still want to try the mall?"

Nerissa shook her head. "Can we go tomorrow night instead, Diamond? I want to stay in a cold shower for hours and then sleep forever!" She raised tired eyes. "No luck today, huh? Oh, well." Before waiting for a reply, she got up. "I'll get something to eat and then wash this sweat off me. See ya." She loped into the house, her long legs glistening like polished chestnuts beneath her shorts.

Diamond watched her go and nearly sighed with relief at the turn of events. Now she could call Steven. Finishing her meal, she cleared the table. "Need anything Cecelia? I'm going inside. Since Nerissa is so beat, I think I'll go home tonight."

"Nothing, Diamond," Cecelia said, giving the younger woman a curious stare. She'd been acting restless all afternoon and could hardly concentrate on a conversation. She watched Diamond disappear inside.

Ginger picked up the phone, wondering who would be calling and hoping that it would not be an emergency. After performing two operations this morning the doctor was beat, returning to the office only to get away from the hospital, but still be near. She was certain he was sleeping with one eye open on the couch.

"Are you a patient?" Ginger asked, frowning at the name.

"No, I'm not," said Diamond to the protective nurse. Steven must be exhausted. "I work for him," she added. She smiled at the surprise in the nurse's voice.

"Just a moment, please. I'll see if he can take this call." Instead of buzzing him, Ginger opened the door, wondering who that person was. Her lips pursed, she decided that if the doctor was sleeping she would refuse to wake him. Her hopes sank, as she knew deep down that this was a social call. She saw Steven turn toward the door, rubbing the stubble on his chin.

"Who called, Ginger?" he said sleepily. He sat up, stretching out his limbs. "An emergency?"

"A Ms. Diamond Drew. She says she works for you."

Steven's head snapped up. "Diamond? Did she say where she was calling from?" His voice was brisk and his eyes alert.

"She's holding on," Ginger said, keeping her tone level.

"I'll take it." Steven was at his desk.

"Diamond? What's wrong?" Steven steeled himself for what was to come.

"Steven, nothing happened. Everyone is okay." Diamond spoke calmly.

Steven's heart stopped racing. "You're sure? Where are you?"

"Yes, I'm sure and I'm home." Diamond took a deep breath. "Steven, I wonder if I could talk to you tonight? It's important."

Time suspended. "About us?"

Diamond could almost feel him go still. She suddenly felt a chill. "No," she answered. "I'm sorry."

Steven's eyes darkened as his breathing went back to

normal. *What could be more important?* "If it could wait, Diamond, I'd rather make it another night. Is tomorrow good for you?" His voice was cool and impersonal.

Diamond bristled at his cold tone. How dare he take that hurt attitude?

"No, Doctor, I'm all booked up, but thanks for taking my call." Diamond hung up the phone. Suddenly feeling miserable, she muttered, "Now, what am I going to do?"

The beautiful gown was spread on the bed. Diamond had inspected it carefully and found it to be in perfect condition, hardly ever worn, she guessed. As slender as Nerissa was, alterations would be minimal except for the hemming. A trip to the mall would take care of the shoes and jewelry. Diamond fingered her amethyst pendant. "This would be gorgeous!" The trick was, she thought, how to explain the dress to Cecelia without Steven's help. Diamond was afraid if she broached the woman, another anxiety attack would occur. Disappointed, Diamond began to wrap the dress, once more running her fingers over the cool satin. She wondered what it was doing in Cecelia's suitcase. Had her mother loaned it to her for a special occasion? With Chris? Diamond would love to know what had happened between the two lovers that forced them to marry others. Cecelia probably looked at Christopher Craven Jr. as being her firstborn. Then there would be no Steven? Diamond shook her head. "No way," she muttered.

Steven buzzed his nurse. "Ginger, why don't you call it a night? I'll stick around here for a while. I'll see you in the morning." He lay back down on the couch and stared up at the ceiling, brooding over hearing Diamond's voice. For days he'd thought about how he would react to seeing her again. He knew it was inevitable, given the circumstances, but he tried to prolong it as long as he could. Her call startled him, and hearing her voice reminded him of his true feelings for her, God help him. It was almost as if his mother's illness and eventual salvation were meant to exist only to lead him to the love of his life. The feeling was uncanny and he'd done all the questioning of himself that he'd needed to do to try and make sense of the incredibility of events. Finding the answers was not so simple. During his lifetime would he have met and fallen in love with someone else? He'd mourned and then hated Elise for killing herself and his baby. He'd finally been able to let her rest with his forgiveness, but would never be able to forgive his mother for interfering in his life. But after the incredible story she told him weeks ago, he felt sorry for her and in his heart he knew that he could forgive her meddling. He recalled how frightened and suddenly old she had appeared to him at revealing her strange suspicions.

Steven rubbed his forehead. He would never again scoff at anyone's dreams. Unlike some people, he was not of the belief that dreams were an extension of one's daily life. But in his mother's case, Steven believed.

After he'd left her he'd made his own calls and had actually seen Diamond's application on file at the agency. The calls made to New York confirmed his mother's fears. Apparently, Yarborough's Homemade Cakes and Pies in Brooklyn, New York, was as famous to Brooklynites as Sylvia's restaurant was to Harlemites.

The clincher came when Mark Ellis laughed over the phone and said, "Are you kidding? Heard of it? I used to freeze my buns off waiting in that line for my mother. And I'd better not go home without two coconut cakes and three sweet potato pies! There was a fine sister in there, who was too young for me at the time, and wouldn't give a second look to the brothers though she was friendly. It was a tragedy, what happened, though."

"What happened?" Steven asked, fearful of the answer.

"Mrs. Yarborough died after she was hit by a car last

year. It wasn't too long after that the shop was closed down and then eventually sold. Never be another place like it."

"Do you remember the name of the girl?"

"Nah. But Peaches was the one who broke everybody up with her humor. People were downright cold and evil having to stand outside for so long. She tried to warm everybody up with her jokes."

Steven had ended the call without telling his friend the real reason behind it. Now Steven sat up on the couch, rubbing his chin. How much more proof did he need before confronting Diamond about her deception? And why did she do it? It sounded like the workings of a devious mind, someone naturally evil. But Steven knew that wasn't true about the woman he'd fallen in love with. Only she could clear up the mystery. And now was the time. She'd presented the opportunity with her call and he should follow his mind and act on it.

Steven finished shaving and splashed a citrus aftershave over his face and neck. He met his eyes in the mirror and wondered if he could keep the desire out of them when he saw her, because there wasn't a thing in the world that he could do about what was going on inside his body. Even the thought of being in the same room with Diamond again sent a chain reaction of heated passion from his brain to his toes.

"Thanks, Doctor," Steven said and hung up the phone. Assuring himself that his patients were fine and resting for the night, Steven picked up the phone again, hoping that his inexcusable behavior would be forgiven.

"Hello?"

"Diamond, it's Steven."

"Yes?" Diamond said.

"That was uncalled for. Can you forget that ever happened?"

"What?" Diamond asked

"You're going to make this difficult?"

"I don't know what you're talking about, Doctor."

"Diamond I'm trying to apologize here," Steven growled.

"You are?"

"Yes."

"Apology accepted. Good night, Doctor."

"God, life with her would never be boring," Steven muttered as he dialed the number again. "Diamond," he said, when she picked up, "if you hang up again I'm coming over there, right now," he threatened.

"Really?" Diamond said sweetly. "I thought that was why I called you in the first place."

Steven rubbed his temples and shook his head. He couldn't help the small smile that appeared. "I suppose you've already eaten, but I haven't. Do you want to meet me? We'll talk and you can have dessert."

Diamond heard the smile and she relented. "We have to talk here. There's something you have to see. Suppose you eat first and then come over." She paused. "But I'll have pecan pie for dessert, thank you." She hung up.

Steven arrived at Diamond's at eight-thirty. He hurried up the stairs, his curiosity quotient over the top. She sounded mysterious and happy at the same time.

"Hi." Diamond stepped back to let him pass. The intake of her breath was audible, and she blushed when he turned and looked at her with a raised brow.

"Are you all right?" Steven asked putting his bags on the round table.

"Fine," Diamond breathed. "Thanks for coming." *He looked like the dessert,* Diamond thought. He was wearing a white short-sleeve shirt, khaki shorts, and brown sandals. The muscles rippled in his arms and legs, and Diamond had a hard time keeping her eyes on a safe place.

Steven was doing his own appraisal but was trying his

best to keep it professional as his eyes roamed over her bare thighs and legs. The bruises were nonexistent and her skin was back to its natural luscious color.

"I brought you some tea," Steven exhaled. "You'll need it to wash down all that sugar. Eating that goo should be outlawed."

"Please. There oughtta be some sinful treats in life that are free and innocent." Diamond tasted the caramelized sweet. "Delicious," she said. "You don't know what you're missing."

Steven swallowed, watching her lips close over the fork. "I wouldn't say that." He could barely get the words out and he wished he'd gotten himself a cold beer instead of hot coffee for himself.

Diamond raised her eyes in time to see the look of discomfort flit across his face. Oh, no, she thought, we can't go there. Not after the last time. Tonight was strictly business. She took a sip of the tea and covered the rest of the pie for later. She would discuss her findings with Steven and send him on his way. She had no intention of relinquishing control over her emotions.

Steven watched her curiously as a serious look settled over her face. Whatever it was she had to tell him was obviously weighing heavily on her mind.

"Want to talk about it now?" Steven's tone was conversational.

"It's hard to know where to begin and how you'll feel about it, but I couldn't say nothing at all about it." Diamond's eyes held a plea for him to understand.

"I'm listening, Diamond," Steven said quietly. "Take your time."

"I think I've discovered the reason why your mother hates Nerissa and Christopher so much."

Steven could only stare. What she'd said was the last thing he'd expected to hear. "Nerissa? And Christopher? You are quite the magician aren't you? That's a family mystery that no one's had a clue to." He gave a short, incredible laugh.

Diamond's heart sank. *He'll never believe his own eyes, even when he sees the evidence,* Diamond thought. Maybe she read into those things just what she wanted to. She stirred in her chair. "Maybe you're right," she sighed. "Probably wishful thinking on my part."

Steven heard the dejection. "Diamond, you must believe in whatever it is that you've found out. Tell me." *Then, maybe you can find it in your heart to cure what's wrong with us.* He watched her walk to the dresser and open a drawer. He was curious at the garment she held in her hands.

"Isn't this exquisite?" Diamond said softly. She dropped the tissue paper on the bed, along with the satin pouch and held the gown up for Steven to see, holding it against her slender form.

Steven studied the gown. "It's old but very pretty." He raised a brow.

"I found it in the attic, in a suitcase I believe belonged to your mother. This was in it too." Diamond carried the pouch to the table. "Careful, they're fragile."

Steven looked at the worn photographs of his mother and a man who could be his brother-in-law, but that was an impossibility. "Christopher?" He raised curious eyes to Diamond, and at her nod he studied them all. "Christ," he murmured. Steven read the newspaper clippings in the order that Diamond passed them to him.

Diamond was silent as Steven carefully read each one, surprise covering his face and exclamations of disbelief breaking the silence.

Steven laid the clippings down, spreading them all out, and stared from one to the other, shaking his head as if to clear the shroud of confusion. He raised his eyes to Diamond's.

"Nerissa had to suffer from the mistakes made by some adults over forty years ago?"

Diamond nodded. "I think so," she whispered.

"And Christopher?" Steven's jaw pulsed with anger. "Mother always told Jacqui that a grease monkey with no skills didn't belong in the family! He had no class." Steven rested his head against the chair and rubbed his forehead wearily. "My God," he muttered. "Christopher was made to feel less than a man simply because she couldn't stand looking at him. Every time my mother saw her son-in-law she was looking in the face of her former lover!"

Diamond's heart wrenched. How painful to think that one's mother could harbor such hatred for the innocent.

Steven pushed back the chair and began pacing the floor. "Damn!"

Diamond watched in silence, empathizing.

Steven stopped and eyed Diamond. "You came to me first?"

"Yes."

"Thank you." Steven sat down again and read some of the articles over. "Gossip rags have been around forever, haven't they?" he said in disgust. "This one implied that Chris Sr. had impregnated both girls at the same time." He looked at the quiet Diamond who hadn't said a word. "What do you suppose happened?"

Diamond cleared her throat. "I think your mother's parents interfered. And the Albermarles."

"So my mother slept with my father on the rebound and got pregnant. I was the result." Steven grimaced. "No wonder what should have been a high society wedding turned into a quiet ceremony and days later a reception at the Bocherons' house." He laughed. "Me and Jacqui always wondered about that."

"Steven, we're only speculating," Diamond said.

"So we are," he remarked, bitterly.

"You're thinking that you were an unwanted pregnancy."

Steven's smile was humorless. "What would you think?" His eyes darkened. "Seems I'm haunted by unwanted pregnancies!"

Diamond gasped. How could he say that? *She'd wanted their unborn child!* She said, "Excuse me," and hurried to the bathroom. Her tears were not for him to see and mock. When the door closed, the hot tears burned her eyes and she put a towel to her mouth to muffle her sobs.

Steven was startled by Diamond's flight and couldn't imagine the reason. He'd said nothing out of the ordinary. What was so wrong about sounding off about his family history? His brow puckered in confusion. What the devil did he say that would bother her so much? Then his jaw gaped. The talk about the pregnancies didn't upset her until he put himself in the picture, alluding to unwanted babies he didn't know he'd fathered! *Hers!*

With a sharp intake of breath, as if someone held ether under his nose, Steven awakened to the realization that should have jarred him weeks ago. His low murmur was filled with disgust for his stupidity. "She wasn't going to have an abortion. She wanted our baby!"

TWENTY

Diamond was on the bed in her favorite position, her arms hugging her knees. Steven was on the sofa with his eyes closed. Neither had spoken since she'd exited the bathroom almost ten minutes ago. When Steven opened his eyes, she just stared at him.

Steven returned her stare. "You wanted our baby."

Diamond's lashes flickered. "I did."

"Would that have been so hard to admit?"

"I had no right to bear your child."

"Why not, Diamond? You love me. I love you. We would have been married."

"Not when you found out about me," Diamond said. "You would have called me every despicable name there is. I not only deceived you but Cecelia and everyone else. I was in your employ under false pretenses."

Steven thought that he would burst from holding his breath. *She was going to tell him without his prying it from her.* "What should I know about you, Diamond?" Steven asked quietly.

Diamond tilted her chin. "I'm the daughter of your mother's heart donor." The words sounded strange in the room, and suddenly Diamond's body shook.

Steven said a silent prayer of thanks. Now there was nothing between them. He wanted to go to her, but he remained on the sofa. She was finally released from the burden she'd carried for months. When he looked at her again he said, "Are you okay?"

Diamond took another deep breath. "Finally," she breathed. Realizing he hadn't reacted to her confession, she studied his face. "You knew."

"I wondered why you never answered my letter."

Astonished, Diamond flushed. "How long have you known?"

"Since Florida."

"That long?" Diamond gasped. "No wonder you stayed away. You really must hate me! Why didn't you fire me?" Realization dawned and her eyes clouded. "Because of Nerissa."

"No." Steven was emphatic. "Because if I sent you away I'd never find you again. Even if it meant never having you I wanted to know where you were and what you were doing. I was unforgiving toward you, yet I loved you."

"Does Cecelia know?" Diamond murmured.

"Yes. I asked her not to say anything until you and I talked."

"No wonder she's been staring at me so strangely." Diamond had to ask. "How did you find out?"

"My mother's dreams," Steven replied. "Her belief that she experienced transference."

Diamond's eyes grew wide. "Transference?" she whispered.

Steven nodded. "As you believed when you heard about the coconut cake. And her sudden craving for sweet potato pie."

Diamond shivered. "It's true. After all this time." She whispered, "Mama, it's true." This time she didn't run away but let the tears of relief fall as she buried her head on her knees.

Steven went to her and took her in his arms. He let her cry, holding her against his shoulder. He smoothed her hair and kissed her forehead. "Let it out, sweetheart," he whispered. When her shoulders stopped shaking, he just held her, rocking back and forth.

Diamond wriggled out of his arms and reached for a tissue to blow her nose. "You're drenched," she said tearfully. She kissed his cheek and then threw herself back on the bed. "I feel so relieved. Whew! All these weeks of hiding."

Steven kicked off his sandals, and lying beside her, he propped himself on one elbow and looked down at her. He could see the change in her whole body.

"Why did you feel you needed to hide the truth, sweetheart?" Steven smoothed her hair.

"Oh, Steven, you should have known my mother," Diamond whispered. "That was another thing you didn't know about me. Phyllis Yarborough adopted me. I never knew my parents and my real mother never knew who impregnated her. Your mother would really have a fit with that kind of background!"

Steven frowned. "Forget Cecelia Rumford." He kissed her mouth. "Tell me about your mother."

Diamond caught Steven's hand and kissed the palm. "She was the kindest, gentlest woman I've ever known. It was so hard to accept that she was gone. It wasn't fair that she was taken from me, and I resented the whole world for months afterward."

Steven lay back, and let her talk. Their hands were entwined.

Diamond continued. "I just had to know that her heart had been given to a deserving person, someone sweet and unselfish." She shuddered. "It became like a fever burning up my insides. I couldn't stand it any longer. I told myself that once I knew, I could rest and get on with my life."

Steven felt her hand tighten. "Then you met my mother." After a pause, he said, "That's why you wanted to leave that first week."

"Yes," Diamond murmured.

"You stayed because of me."

"Yes."

"I'm glad, sweetheart." His voice was low and husky. "Tell me more about your mother."

Diamond talked for what seemed like hours while Steven listened. Sometimes he asked a question or laughed but never interrupted with angry remarks about her deception. She explained her feelings about organ donation and the disagreements she'd had with her mother and Peaches.

When Diamond finished, the breath she expelled seemed to come from her soul. Her body was weightless and her eyelids drooped. She felt like sleeping for eons. Steven was so quiet, and her cheek resting on his chest hardly rose and fell with his still breathing. Diamond feared that her confession had stunned him right out of love with her and she was almost afraid to look into his eyes.

"Do you still feel the same?" Steven asked.

Diamond thought before answering. It was important that she be honest with herself. If there was going to be anything between them it wouldn't be filled with deception.

"I don't know," Diamond answered. "These past months, traveling with Cecelia, listening to all the different views and opinions from other lecturers and recipients, has been an eye-opener for me. But I guess so many years of thinking one way just can't change overnight. I still have that incredible and suspicious fear."

Steven understood. "You're not alone. You've a right to your opinion and have to follow the dictates of your own mind." He squeezed her shoulder. "That's why we'll continue these seminars to educate people and address their concerns and eliminate fears at the same time. Most people hardly ever think about organ donation until it hits close to home, usually starting with a kidney." He heard the soft sigh against his chest.

Diamond closed her eyes against the last look she'd had of Jimmy. "That's so true," she said wearily. "Peaches would gladly give her kidney to her husband if only that were the case."

Steven felt her arm slide limply down past his waist. He raised his head and tilted her chin to see her half-closed eyes. "Diamond?"

"Hmm?"

Steven had to smile. No, life with her would definitely not be boring, he told himself again. But the surprises? He would be on his toes. Steven gently laid her down.

"What, Steven?" Diamond mumbled as she curled into a fetal position.

Steven grinned. "Nothing, love. Go to sleep. I'll ask you in the morning." He'd never propose to a woman who was falling asleep in his arms.

Diamond woke when she felt the bed shaking. She saw Steven putting on his shoes. "Six o'clock?" she murmured. "I slept all night?"

Steven turned and looked at her with a critical eye. "You can say that again," he said, looking annoyed as he walked around the bed to sit beside her. "I guess I know how you feel about me, now. Fell asleep in the middle of my question."

"I didn't!" Diamond was embarrassed. "I'm sorry. Guess it was the heat," she said sheepishly.

Steven's eyes glittered with mirth. "Obviously. Used to be a time when a different kind of heat would keep you wide awake." His voice dropped.

Diamond studied his face after that sexy voice singed her ears. She realized he was cracking up inside. She caressed his biceps. "I'm awake now," she murmured.

Steven caught her hand, and still holding the serious look on his face, said, "Oh no, too late now. Some of us have to keep early morning hours." Unable to hold in his laughter, Steven bent and kissed her. "Good morning, love," he murmured. "Sleep well?"

Diamond reached up and hugged him around the neck. "You're a big tease. I'll get you for that," she whispered in his ear.

"God, don't do that," Steven growled. He untangled her arms and laid her back down on the pillows.

Diamond smiled. "Why not?"

"Because I have to leave," he muttered.

"Leave? Right now?"

"Yes," Steven said and moved off the bed. At a safer distance, he said, "I'm going to shower and change and then I have to go to the hospital. I'll be back for you at noon. Be ready."

"But Steven," Diamond said, "what about the . . ." Her glance fell on the items on the table.

Steven was at the door. "That's what we're going to take care of. My mother will be waiting. Oh, and you're not working today. I called Jacqui and she will be chauffeuring Nerissa."

"Steven? You never said what you were asking me when I rudely fell asleep."

Steven's eyes roamed over her. He'd removed her shorts and top while she slept leaving her dressed in bra and panties. The slow rise and fall of her breasts was tantalizing and titillated his sensory impulses. He ought to have his head examined for leaving her right now! He took a deep breath before answering.

"Nothing that important," Steven said with a great deal of nonchalance. "I wanted to know if you would marry me." He opened the door. "I guess you can let me know when I get back?" He closed the door then grinned at the sound of Diamond's outraged cry. Steven hurried down the stairs.

"Not important? Steven Rumford!"

* * *

Diamond was waiting impatiently for Steven. It was almost twelve-thirty and she hoped that his patients hadn't taken a turn for the worse. The dress was hanging neatly in a garment bag and the pouch held its yellowed contents. Aside from being anxious to confront Cecelia, Diamond had a very important answer to a very important question.

When Steven appeared on the second floor, the door was open. Diamond was standing there watching him, looking as delectable as she had when he left her earlier. The short, sleeveless white dress hugged her lithe body, the bodice doing justice to her ample breasts. Her tanned legs were bare and she wore white sandals. Her amethyst jewels glittered against her skin. She was dressed for a very important date.

"You're beautiful," Steven said.

Diamond drank in the sight of him and she wondered if he could hear her heart beating from where he stood. He was dressed casually in tailored beige slacks and short-sleeve yellow shirt. "Can you come over here?" she murmured. "I have something to tell you." She backed into the room.

Steven looked at his watch and frowned. "I don't think we have much time, Diamond. Mother's waiting. Can you make it quick?" He followed her into the room and closed the door. He leaned against it and still serious, looked at her. "Yes?" he queried.

Diamond shook her head and grinned. "That was my line, Doctor."

"Line?" Steven's eyes shone with the smile that he kept from his lips.

She groaned. "Heaven help this man who is learning how to joke after thirty-eight years," Diamond said as she walked closer to him. She looked up into his eyes and said, "Yes, Steven."

Steven held out his arms and she walked into them.
"Yes, what, love?"

"Yes, I'll marry you," Diamond murmured.

"I knew that." He enfolded her almost gently and held
her, kissing her softly on her forehead, her cheeks, her
eyes.

"You did?" Diamond whispered, answering his kisses
with tender ones of her own.

"Yes, because you were meant for me. It was written,"
Steven answered. "I love you, Diamond," he whispered in
her ear. Then he kissed her, really kissed her.

Diamond and Steven found Cecelia in the big formal
living room that was hardly ever used. Steven closed the
door.

"Hello, Mother," he said, watching her closely. He
squeezed Diamond's hand when he felt her shake a little.

"Hello, Cecelia," Diamond said, looking directly into
the woman's eyes. How strange this is, she thought. There
were no more secrets, and she looked upon the woman as
not the enemy but a tired, selfish woman who chose to
spend her life being mean and hateful to the very family
who would have loved her. If only she'd allowed them.

Cecelia's gaze was intense, as she looked her son and
Diamond over carefully, skimming over the bag in Diamond's hand. From the tone of Steven's voice when he'd
called her, she knew whatever he was going to tell her
was serious. She'd steeled herself against it but she knew
from years before that when a person fell in love it was
a beautiful thing. She was looking at two happy people.
She sniffed and rolled her eyes.

"Well, sit down," Cecelia commanded, "you're not
strangers here."

Steven and Diamond sat on the loveseat. "Mother, I've
told Diamond everything." A look passed between Cecelia

and Diamond but both remained silent. Steven said, "Mother, I've asked Diamond to marry me, and she's said yes."

Cecelia grimaced. "I'm not blind, Steven, I had heart surgery." She looked at Diamond. "I saw it coming; that's why I asked you to leave." Her eyes brightened. "I didn't know how I could look at you every day and see you and your mother giving me dirty looks at night."

Diamond's voice was direct, as was her look. She'd never been intimidated by Cecelia so there was no reason to start now. "Do you still see her?"

"No. I don't see any of you. Nerissa either." Cecelia sounded more surprised than relieved. "The dreams stopped after you left. When you came back, I thought they would begin again, but they haven't." She raked her short hair and sighed heavily. "At last, it's over," she said.

"Is it, Mother?" Steven wasn't smiling and his voice was dead serious.

Cecelia looked sharply at her son. "What do you mean?"

Steven was calm. "I mean that in the future, I don't want you to look at my wife and suddenly decide that she's unsuitable to be a Rumford." His meaning was very clear.

Cecelia held his stare, and when she looked away a shadow crossed her face, as she remembered Elise. She looked at Steven. "I said it was over."

Steven nodded. For his mother, that was as close to an apology as she could give, he thought. "Good." Maybe the day would come when she could forgive herself.

Cecelia looked at Diamond. "There's a lot we have to say to each other. I can't say that I'm not curious and awed by all of this, but like so many other things, it will take time to sort out." She glanced quickly at Steven, then continued. "And that's how I'd like to treat it—one day at a time." A half-smile appeared. "Now that you'll be around town, I hope that you'll agree?"

Diamond shook her head in agreement. "I think that'll work." *Baby steps instead of giant steps can accomplish a whole lot,* she thought. Finally, she settled down. Steven must have felt her, because he caught her eye and winked.

Cecelia ignored the silent love talk and gestured at the garment bag draped over the seat. "I suppose that's something you two want to talk about also?"

Diamond looked at Steven and he nodded. She unzipped the bag and shook out the satin gown. "I found this in a suitcase in the attic, Cecelia. I was wondering if Nerissa can use it for the school costume party?"

Steven was watching his mother closely. "It looks like something Grandmother may have worn," he said. He waited quietly for her reaction.

Cecelia stared at the garment. "My God," she gasped. When she spied the pouch in Diamond's hand, she was stunned. "What are you doing?" Her voice came in short spurts.

Steven was by her side in a second, taking her pulse. After a moment he looked at Diamond, relieved. "Mother, you're okay. Try to relax. Would you like something?"

Cecelia waved her son away. "Leave me alone." Her voice was harsh, and she stared at the pouch as if she couldn't believe in its existence. "Why are you prying into something that doesn't concern you?" she gasped. Her head was in her hands, and she started to moan unintelligibly.

Diamond started to get up but Steven stopped her with a gesture. They both waited until the low cries stopped.

Chris. Chris. So many years! Cecelia wiped her eyes.

"Are you all right, Mother?"

Cecelia had nearly forgotten they were in the room with her. She smoothed the tight curls on her head and raised her eyes. She held out her hand and Diamond brought her the pouch. Cecelia opened it and looked at the things she'd hidden away so long ago.

"Why am I looking at these?" she murmured, stricken, at fingering the pictures. She touched the face of her old lover. "Why, Steven?" Her voice was a ragged whisper.

Steven spoke quietly. "I believe you already know why. We'd like you to tell us."

Cecelia raised her eyes to him and then stared at Diamond. Her eyes were cool. "Us?"

"Diamond is going to be my wife. She's family, Mother."

Cecelia sagged back in the chair. "Family," she murmured. She read the articles again and muttered, "Families can be such a bane. The Bocherons certainly were." Cecelia spoke in a wooden voice. "I met Chris at a fraternity party at Winston-Salem, when I was seventeen. We fell in love instantly." She laughed bitterly. "You can see that for yourselves." She looked at Steven. "When I was twenty, I married your father. You were born soon after."

"What happened?" Steven asked.

"Chris wanted to marry me as soon as I turned eighteen but my parents laughed at the ludicrous idea." Cecelia's eyes held a dazed look as she remembered the past. "I went off to college and Chris and I still saw each other. We were still very much in love and couldn't stand being separated. We decided to elope. It was all planned. I took one of my mother's gowns to use as my wedding dress."

Diamond fingered the satin and her eyes saddened. That's why it was with Cecelia's things.

Cecelia noticed. "Yes, that was to be my wedding dress."

"What happened?" Diamond asked.

"Well, as you can see, the marriage never took place." Cecelia's voice was bitter. "My mother and father showed up at the court clerk's office in Atlanta, Georgia, the same time Chris and I arrived. I went back home with them."

"Why?" Diamond sounded incredulous.

Cecelia shook her head. "Because my father threatened

to besmirch Chris's name and make it impossible for him to have any kind of decent career, regardless of what field he entered. Chris made me promise to wait, that he'd be back for me. Of course, that never happened. Chris stopped writing and my calls were never returned. I began to wonder if he really loved me at all, letting my father scare him with those threats. I told him that we could be happy anywhere as long as we were together." Cecelia's mouth turned into a grim slash. "I began to hate him after I heard the rumors of him and Esther being a couple so soon after our separation. I thought the world had ended for me because I realized his love was never as deep as mine was. It wasn't long afterward that they married." Cecelia looked at her son. "I married your father."

Steven's jaw tightened. "Did you love him?"

"No," Cecelia answered. Her eyes brightened. "I fell in love with your father during my pregnancy with you." Her voice softened. "Cyril was the happiest man in the world when he found out he was going to become a father. He used to pat my belly and talk to you. He played music to you, and my stomach would be moving like a five-piece band." She wiped her eyes. "You were the most precious little guy in the world and I knew that you wouldn't be you without Cyril being your father." Cecelia paused, then said, "Chris ceased to exist for me."

Steven said evenly, "Until Jacqui met Christopher Craven Jr. at Howard University and brought him home."

Cecelia was silent. Finally, she answered with a touch of remorse. "The first time Jacqui mentioned his name I nearly fainted. When she brought him home I was looking at his father. I hated that young man from the beginning. Jacqui knew. But she married him anyway, against my wishes."

"She never knew the real reason," Diamond said.

"Of course not," Cecelia answered impatiently. "I had buried that part of my past."

Steven said, "You really didn't. Your hatred was transferred from Christopher Jr. to his daughter, especially when you saw that she is the female replica of her grandfather."

Diamond and Steven watched Cecelia's face crumple, and after a while she raised her eyes to theirs.

Cecelia whispered. "I hated her for reminding me of my past." She closed her eyes and rested her head back on the chair.

Diamond became alarmed. Cecelia was so still. She glanced at Steven.

After checking his mother's pulse, Steven said in a low voice, "She'll be all right." He gestured at the articles still in Cecelia's hands. "Leave her. She has a lot of soul-searching to do today." Outside the room, he took Diamond's hand and led her outside to the backyard, where they sat beside the pool.

Diamond was holding Steven's hand. "Are you sure this won't be a setback to her health?"

Steven shook his head. "Besides having a healthy heart," he squeezed Diamond's hand, "my mother has a strong constitution and is a survivor. What she intends to do to mend the rift in her relationship with her son-in-law and granddaughter is entirely up to her. We can only hope that she doesn't allow her misplaced sense of pride to get in the way of making a change."

Steven watched his niece stand on her toes and whisper something into Diamond's ear before Nerissa smiled and walked elegantly to the waiting limousine. Ulysses Watson climbed in beside her and the car pulled off. Following, in Christopher's car, was Steven's mother and Jacqui, who waved. Christopher had arrived after Cecelia called him two days ago. They were going out to a private supper club, and Steven could only hope that the three of them could find a place to begin healing years of anger and hurt.

Diamond had tears in her eyes and she sighed inwardly at Nerissa's words.

"Don't worry about me, Diamond. Remember those feelings? They're somewhere in my body. I'll know the time when it's okay to let them out. That's when I'm as old as you are and a man looks at me like Uncle Steven looks at you."

Diamond laughed. "Gee, thanks a lot." She whispered back. "You're beautiful, Nerissa."

"I know," Nerissa said happily. "I looked in the mirror." She fingered the amethyst pendant, hugged Diamond, and walked down the steps.

Diamond felt Steven's arm snake around her waist. She grasped it. "What was that all about?" he whispered in her ear.

"Woman talk," Diamond smiled. "Your niece is all grown up, Doctor."

"Is that so?" Steven grumbled. "She did look gorgeous." He nibbled Diamond's ear. "For a teenager. I like my women a little older."

Diamond grimaced. "Is someone trying to tell me something here?" She twisted in his arms to look up at him. "Want to show me how much?" she said in her sexiest voice. "I'm afraid I need reassurance." She kissed his chin.

Steven kissed her mouth. "I think I can handle that with no problem," he murmured, seeking her tongue.

Diamond felt him rise and the heat passed from his body to hers, causing her to react like she always did—feverishly. She broke the kiss and said, "It will be a problem if we don't handle this in private."

"Not for me," Steven muttered, "but if you insist." He took her hand and growled, "Come with me; I know a place."

Steven opened the door to the guestroom and before entering, looked at Diamond with a question.

Diamond understood. When they'd made love it had been in Steven's bedroom. Only once he'd pleasured her in this room. She entered and looked around. Elise's restless spirit had been freed long ago. By loving her completely in this room, she knew that Steven was avowing his true love for her. It was here that he had loved another, but that was a part of his life that was gone forever.

Diamond looked at Steven. "I'd love to love you in this room," she murmured.

Steven's eyes smoldered with his love for her. Words were unnecessary to express his thoughts on the past. He pushed the door closed, then placed his hands on her cheeks. He kissed her forehead, then looked solemnly into her eyes. "Diamond, you're the only woman I'll ever want in my bed and that's where you'll be from now on, sweetheart." He bent his head and brushed her lips tenderly.

Diamond's heart ached with her love for him. Deepening the kiss, she devoured his mouth hungrily. Warmth sped through her body like a raging fire as it always did at his sensuous touch. His hands on her bare arms singed her skin and when they found her breasts, she moaned against his neck, "Steven, sweet love."

Steven unzipped her dress and let it fall to the floor with the silk chemise. She started to slip out of her satin bra and panties but he caught her hands. "Let me do that," he said huskily. "Months ago, when I first saw you like this, I wanted to race up here to you. My imagination didn't do you justice." He inhaled at the sight of her naked breasts. The tiny buds were almost rigid from their passionate kisses and Steven could feel his sex rising from the thought that she was so ready for him. He bent to take one of the peaks in his mouth and when he slipped his hand inside her panties, she moaned and leaned into him.

"Steven," Diamond whispered, "make love to me."

"I am, my love," Steven whispered. The scent of her hot skin reminded him of strawberries and he suckled each nipple, bringing them to turgid peaks.

"All of me," Diamond murmured. She was struggling with his belt and she looked up at him with pleading eyes. "Help me." The plea was barely audible.

"God," Steven rasped, roused by the passion in her voice. She didn't have to ask twice. Seconds after he released her he was undressed. The last of her garments were gone and she lay on the bed, hands over her head, looking at him with those expressive eyes.

"No, sweetheart," Steven said, "you don't ever have to ask me again." He eased himself atop her and was immediately stunned by the sensual touch of their bodies. He nearly yelled in exquisite agony as her fingers caressed him before he entered her.

Diamond's hips rose to meet Steven's masterful thrusts as she quivered beneath him. Her whole being was consumed by the erotic charges that shot through her. Losing herself in the spiraling magic of the moment, Diamond soared among the stars. She gasped from the sheer starkness of the pleasure that racked her body as their urgent passion burst into red-hot flames.

"Diamond," Steven's voice was thick with desire. "I love you."

Diamond felt the heat slowly ebb away. She sank limply against the pillows, her body weak and tingling. *How could she think that she'd ever been in love before?* "I love you," she whispered. Steven was lying beside her and she turned to him and kissed his mouth long and deeply. Then with mischief dancing in her eyes, she propped herself on her elbow and stared at him. "Do you know me, now, Doctor?" she whispered in a sexy voice. Diamond kissed his taut nipples and when he groaned, she kissed them again, then stared laughingly into his dark eyes.

"Diamond," Steven growled, squirming at her busy

hands and mouth. "You're going to make me want you again!" He suckled her soft throat.

Diamond smiled. Giving him a come-hither look, she whispered, "That's the idea. But don't evade my question."

Steven caressed her cheek with his fingers. "Yes, Diamond," he breathed, "I do know you now. I'll always know you." He caught the back of her neck and brought her lips to his, then kissed her passionately. When she sighed with satisfaction, he grinned, something that he had been doing a lot of late. He tweaked her nose. "Bet on it!"

Diamond laughed and looked curious when he got out of bed. He rummaged in his pants pocket and came up with a small wad of tissue.

Steven sat down on the bed. "I just couldn't find the right time to give you these."

Diamond unfolded the crumpled tissue. She looked dazed at the sparkling earrings. Speechless, she could only stare. Tears appeared in her eyes. *It's okay to cry sometimes,* she told herself, then smiled at the old thought. Tears of happiness were just fine!

Steven watched her, then touched a falling teardrop. "Do you like them? I thought the pink diamonds would match your amethysts."

"They're beautiful." Diamond murmured. "Steven, they're so gorgeous." The gems twinkled against the whiteness of the tissue. "I . . . I . . ." She lost her voice.

Steven felt her deep emotions and knew that she was thinking of the jewel that her mother had given her. "Don't say anything, sweetheart," he said huskily. "Just wear them for me." He kissed her damp eyelashes.

Diamond and Steven were caught up in the passion of the moment, whispering their love for each other. Just before they succumbed to their desires, Steven muttered, "I forgot to tell you something."

"What?" Diamond murmured against his chest.

"You're fired, sweetheart."

EPILOGUE

"I don't want to know, do you, love?"

Steven smiled, watching as his wife rubbed her belly. "No, sweetheart. I like surprises. The little guy giving you a hard time today?"

"Could be your daughter, you know," Diamond answered, grimacing. "Whoever it is doesn't like me very much."

"Hmm. That settles it," Steven said firmly. "We'll ship the little person off to Cousin Peaches in Florida until it learns to give its mommy some love."

Diamond smiled as she sat in the backyard of their new home in Mount Pleasant. The building of it had been hectic, yet a joy. It was in Old Village, built on property left to Steven by his grandfather. They were close but far enough away from Steven's old home where Cecelia still lived.

"You have to earn love, Steven. It's not a given even in families."

Steven took her hand. "I should know that," he said solemnly. "Besides, Peaches and Jimmy would probably throw our rotten child back to us in a hot minute."

Diamond laughed. "Who're you kidding? Not a chance." Then, "You were right, Steven. Jimmy can give me a run for my money. I'm glad he's okay."

"God's will and a skilled surgeon," Steven said. He

stood up. "I'm going to take another dip. Do you two want anything before I go?"

Diamond raised her chin. "Just a little kiss," she said.

Steven frowned. "Little?" He sat down on the edge of the chaise longue. "Scoot over, let's see what I can do." He pecked at Diamond's lips. "Little enough?"

Diamond groaned. "You big ham. I forgot you're still a jokester-in-training. C'mere." She pulled his face close and kissed his mouth, sighing when her husband took control of the situation, making her skin tingle with the familiar sensation that she hoped would never end. Coming up for air, she breathed, "I'll take a dip with you."

Steven grinned and pulled her up. "Uh, uh. Feet only, Mrs. Rumford. You can watch me." He patted her stomach. "Next year, you'll be in shape to race me."

Diamond swatted at him as he ducked and dived into the pool. And she did watch him, and remembered her life over the past year.

After marrying in a small wedding ceremony in August, Diamond and Steven rented a house in Harleston Village in Low Country until their own home was built. Cecelia stayed in the house with Tina and Ferdie. Instead of lamenting the scattering of her family, she learned to travel with friends and was frequently away. It took time for her to show warmth toward Christopher and Nerissa but she was doing her best. For Nerissa's fifteenth birthday, Cecelia took her and two of her friends to the Caribbean.

Steven and Cecelia were friends but Steven would never have the same warmth for his mother as he had when he was younger.

Jacqui and Christopher never reconciled, and their divorce would become final in a few months. Nerissa told Diamond that her parents' breakup was for the best because they weren't happy. Her father didn't look at her mother the way Steven looked at Diamond. Nerissa saw Steven and Diamond often, because Jacqui scrapped her plan to move so far away, since Cecelia was trying to have a relationship with her granddaughter. They lived in a condo not far from Steven and Diamond, and Jacqui was ecstatic about finally being able to do the sister act.

It wasn't long after Diamond started her new job as a physical therapist in Charleston that she was ultimately able to lay her fears to rest. She began carrying an organ donor card. When she did, she felt as if a burden had been lifted. Peaches had cried.

Diamond got up and made her way back to the much softer seat of the chaise longue. She patted her stomach and murmured, "One week to go, you little person, you." When Diamond hadn't conceived immediately, she'd been frightened that losing her first child might be the reason. Angry at her negative thinking, her husband had patiently helped her to overcome those thoughts. The day they received news of her pregnancy, neither knew which of them had been the happier.

Steven smiled as he climbed out of the pool. He saw Diamond talking to her stomach just as he did. When she caught his eye, she flashed him her beautiful smile that was almost as brilliant as the diamonds in her ears. On second thought, he wouldn't mind having a precious little diamond as beautiful as her mother. Steven covered the distance to the love of his life with long, purposeful strides.

Dear Reader,

You already know how I love to use gemstones in my stories. This time I used the amethyst, as well as naming the heroine after one of the most brilliant of jewels.

I hope you enjoyed Diamond's story and felt the very real fear and superstition she harbored about organ donation. When she was an impressionable youngster, the death of the teacher following so soon after the class lesson never left her. When she met Steven, she knew instantly that he would become the love of her life. Steven's feelings mirrored Diamond's, and both were immediately aware of their dilemma.

While resolving their inner conflicts, I aimed to keep the sexual tension high due to their living arrangements. I hope this was accomplished to your reading pleasure and satisfaction. As always, I welcome your comments and suggestions, so please continue to write and include a stamped envelope for a reply.

Thanks for sharing,
Doris Johnson
P.O. Box 130370
Springfield Gardens, NY 11413

e-mail: Bessdj@aol.com

ABOUT THE AUTHOR

Doris Johnson lives in Queens, New York, with her husband. She is a multi-published author who has written several books. She enjoys lazing on beaches, poking around in flea markets, and collecting gemstones.

Coming in April from Arabesque Books . . .

__SWEPT AWAY by Gwynne Forster
1-58314-098-0 $5.99US/$7.99CAN

As the head of a child placement agency, Veronica Overton never expected to be crucified in the press by fiery advocate Schyler Henderson. With her reputation shattered, Veronica searches to rebuild her life and unexpectedly discovers a sizzling attraction to Schyler that she is determined to resist . . .

__STAR CROSSED by Francine Craft
1-58314-099-9 $5.99US/$7.99CAN

Jaded Fairen Wilder is unsure if she can ever risk caring for anyone again. But now the one man who helped her survive her pain, Lance Carrington, is back, still a suspect in his wife's murder. The couple must face down a vicious enemy together . . . and learn to trust in their growing love.

__DESTINY by Shelby Lewis
1-58314-100-6 $5.99US/$7.99CAN

Recluse Josephine Brennon is shocked when the ruggedly handsome drifter Hannibal Ray is able to open her heart to love. But these two loners must fight the town's most influential citizens and open up to each other completely . . . if they are to claim the love that is their destiny.

__ALL THAT MATTERS by Courtni Wright
1-58314-101-4 $5.99US/$7.99CAN

Honey Tate has returned to New Orleans to restore her family's home and discover the truth about her father. Although her search puts her at odds with lawyer Stephen Turner, passions soon flare between the two and they must find their way through pain and secrets if they are to find true love.

Call toll free **1-888-345-BOOK** to order by phone or use this coupon to order by mail. *ALL BOOKS AVAILABLE APRIL 1, 2000.*

Name _____

Address _____

City _____ State _____ Zip _____

Please send me the books I have checked above.

I am enclosing $_____

Plus postage and handling* $_____

Sales tax (in NY, TN, and DC) $_____

Total amount enclosed $_____

*Add $2.50 for the first book and $.50 for each additional book.

Send check or money order (no cash or CODs) to: **Arabesque Books, Dept. C.O., 850 Third Avenue, 16th Floor, New York, NY 10022**

Prices and numbers subject to change without notice.

All orders subject to availability.

Visit out our web site at **www.arabesquebooks.com**.

THESE ARABESQUE ROMANCES
ARE NOW MOVIES FROM BET!

More Arabesque Romances by
Monica Jackson